WHEN THE WIND BLOWS

A sound was coming to her. Her mind began to drift ...

Usually it came to her at night, when the wind was blowing. But today it was bright and clear; the wind was still.

And yet the sound was there. A baby, crying out for its mother.

Instinctively Diana knelt next to Christie and took the child in her arms. 'It's all right,' she whispered. 'Everything's going to be all right.'

Perplexed, Christie looked into Diana's eyes. 'I *am* all right, Aunt Diana. Really I am,' Christie insisted.

'But you were crying. I heard you. Good girls never cry. Only bad children cry. They cry. And cry. And then they must be punished ...'

When The Wind Blows

John Saul

CORONET BOOKS
Hodder and Stoughton

Copyright © 1981 by John Saul

First published in the United States 1981
by Dell Publishing Co., Inc.

Coronet edition 1982

British Library C.I.P.

Saul, John
  When the wind blows.–(Coronet Books)
  I. Title
  813'.54[F]   PS3569.A/

ISBN 0 340 28107 3

Printed and bound in Great Britain for
Hodder and Stoughton Paperbacks, a
division of Hodder and Stoughton Ltd.,
Mill Road, Dunton Green, Sevenoaks,
Kent (Editorial Office: 47 Bedford
Square, London, WC1 3DP) by
Cox & Wyman Ltd., Reading

Prologue

The wind swept down out of the Rockies like a living thing, twisting its way through the evergreens and aspens, curling through the ravines before spilling out into the valley where, gathering a cargo of dust, it ground eastward, choking the villages and hamlets that dotted the area like prairie-dog colonies.

The people hadn't known about the wind when they built their towns, but they discovered it soon enough, and, as with all such things, they chose to live with it, ignoring it whenever possible, hiding from it when it got too bad, wryly commenting about it to each other and comparing it favourably to the tornadoes they had left behind when they had migrated westward.

The wind was just one more thing to be lived with, contended with.

And besides, the mines were worth it.

Even the coal mine at Amberton, which, though neither as rich nor as glamorous as the gold and silver mines that seemed to be everywhere but there, was worth the wind.

And so, on a bright spring morning in 1910, the miners made their way into the tunnels of the mine, ignoring the wind, intent only on getting through another day, bringing up the coal to feed the railroad, and returning home to rinse the black dust from their throats with endless shots of whisky washed down with beer.

Within the mine there was no evidence of either the wind or the spring morning. There was only the flickering yellow glow of the miners' helmets, the hot, musty, coal-choked air, and the constant undercurrent of fear. Something could go wrong.

In the mines, something always went wrong.

That morning, though, fear mingled with a feeling of optimism, for on that morning they were extending Shaft Number Four, which promised the largest deposit yet discovered in the Amberton mine.

The dynamite had been set the night before, and through the morning the miners worked, checking the fuses, laying the wire, hooking up the blasting machines. Then, finally, they were ready.

They gathered outside the mine, the wind lashing at them as they prepared for the final moment.

The plungers of the blasting machines were shoved downward, and then there was a low rumbling from the depths of the mine.

The miners listened, then grinned at each other.

It was over.

Hundreds of feet down, there was now a pile of rubble, ready to be loaded and hauled to the surface. Picking up their tools, they went back into the mine.

At first no one noticed the water as it seeped through the shattered coal face at the end of Number Four.

When the first miner felt the dampness through his boots, he was more annoyed than worried.

But then the water began rising, and soon the miners realised what had happened.

Somewhere in the depths of the earth, there was a pocket of water, and the blast had disturbed it.

They began hunting for the source of the leak. Someone went to the surface and brought back the shift supervisor and the owner of the mine. Lumber was brought down, and the walls of Number Four were quickly shored up. But even as they worked, the water began to rise, and soon the miners were wading.

'At the back,' someone cried. 'It's coming in from the back!'

The men surged towards the far reaches of the shaft. Then they saw it.

What had started as a trickle was now a raging torrent, spewing from a gap in the wall.

As they watched, great chunks of coal broke away to be replaced by ice-cold, crystal-clear water that was quickly stained inky black by the pulverised coal over which it flowed.

Suddenly the wall of Number Four caved in, and water rushed over the men, flattening some of them on the floor of the shaft, pinning others to the walls.

The lucky ones were crushed immediately by the crumbling wall of the mine.

The less fortunate drowned in the first few moments of the flood.

For the rest, it was an even more horrible death.

For them, the flood played tricks, picking them up and sweeping them along, then pressing them up near the roof of the mine, where pockets of air were trapped, allowing them to keep their heads above the tide while the icy water numbed their bodies, allowing them to hope for a way out where there was none.

The pressure of the inrushing water began compressing the pockets of air, and for the men trapped against the roof, a new agony began.

Their ears began to hurt, and they swallowed over and over again, trying to clear the pain from their heads. But as more and more water – tons of it – drained into the unnatural shaft that the men had created, the pressure grew; the pain increased.

Some of them plunged into the depths of the water, then fought back up, their fingers clawing instinctively at the roof of the tunnel, trying to find a way out, even while their lungs filled with water. Soon their struggles ceased.

For the few who grimly clung to life even when they knew it was over, the mine had saved one last torture.

The current stopped flowing, and there was suddenly quiet in the blackness.

Each of the men, unaware that he was not alone in his survival, began to listen in the sudden silence.

None of them knew what he was listening for.

Voices, perhaps.

The voices of friends, calling out for help.

Or the voices of others, rescuers, perhaps.

The sound, when it came, was low. A distant murmur at first that grew and swelled to a chorus of voices. The voices of children, crying in the darkness. Crying for their mothers. Crying a lonely dirge of abandonment.

One by one, the last of the miners began to die. Outside the mine, dusk fell. The wind ceased. Towards the end of the day, it was over.

In the end, all that was left in Number Four was the sound of the children's voices, still crying, though there was no one left to hear them.

Down the hill from the mine, in a large house that stood alone at the edge of the valley, a woman lay in her bed, pain racking her body.

She was dimly aware that something had happened, that there had been an accident at the mine. And even in the agony of her labour, she knew that her husband had died.

As her baby moved inside her, struggling to release itself into the world, the woman began to know the taste of hatred.

Her husband was dead, and her life was over.

She hadn't wanted a child, but her wishes hadn't mattered to her husband – he had insisted. She had been clever for a while and lied to him about the ways of her body, but it had only been a matter of time before she became pregnant.

And now, as she delivered the tiny gift that her husband would have loved, he had abandoned her, leaving to her only the baby and the mine that had killed him.

The doctor, too, had left her, insisting that he was needed at the mine. The Indian woman who only days before had delivered a baby of her own, was perfectly qualified to care for her, he said. But all the Indian had done was sit by her, muttering to herself in a guttural voice about the curse of this day and the children she thought she could hear crying in the wind.

The woman herself could hear nothing.

Outside, the wind was screaming through the aspens, tearing at the house, rattling windows and plucking at the shingles on the roof.

Inside, the woman screamed silently, refusing to let the Indian woman see the anger and hatred that were growing within her.

As the child came into the world and began crying softly, the Indian crossed herself in the tradition of her religion, while in the depths of her mind she invoked the ancient spirits of her people to protect the child who had the misfortune to be born of this day.

Late that night, as the people of the town gathered in front of the mine to mourn their dead, the woman mourned the birth of her child.

And all through the night, while the wind blew down from the mountains, the sounds of children crying filled the depths of the mine.

For half a century there was no one to hear them.

1

Esperanza Rodriguez, her dark eyes set deep in her lined face, watched silently as the body of Elliot Lyons was brought up from the depths of the mine. All her life she had been expecting something like this to happen. Over and over her mother had told her the story of what had happened when she was only a few days old, and the *gringos*, in their stupidity, had disturbed the cave of the lost children. They had died that day – many of them – and the mine had been closed. For fifty years it had remained undisturbed, its depths flooded with water, until a month ago, when Señor Lyons had come from Chicago and begun poking around. And now he, too, was dead. Dead like Amos Amber, who had owned the mine and died in the flood; dead like her own father, who had also been in the mine that day.

Esperanza had no memory of the flood, but in the half-century since, as she had grown up near the mine, her mother had been careful to warn her of what would happen if the mine were ever reopened. It was part of the sacred cave now, the cave of the lost children. Though the *gringos* claimed the cave was only a legend, what the *gringos* thought didn't matter to Esperanza, for she knew the cave was real, as did all her friends. It was real, and it had to be left alone.

Elliot Lyons had not left it alone, and now he was dead.

Esperanza waited until they'd taken the body away, nodded briefly when the doctor whispered in her ear, then wrapped her shawl around her shoulders, told her son to stay at home, and started walking towards town, where, before obeying the doctor's instructions, she would go to church and pray.

Amberton had never been much of a town – not like the other Mineral Belt settlements, which had boomed for years with gold and silver. Amberton had prospered only mildly, its coal providing a fortune only for the Ambers, who owned the mine and most of the land as well.

And then, in 1910, the mine had flooded, and the people of Amberton wondered what had happened.

Esperanza Rodriguez knew what had happened.

As she paused in the little park at the centre of town, she looked up at the bronze statue of Amos Amber that kept watch over the village. Her own father, whom she had never known, had tried to warn Amos Amber of what could happen to the mine. But Amos had never been one to listen to the superstitious mumblings of a Mexican married to a Ute.

And because Amos Amber had not listened to Esperanza Rodriguez's father, Amberton had suffered.

It didn't show on the surface. The village was a pretty place, nestled in a valley low in the Rockies, its Victorian houses neatly painted in the bright colours that had been fashionable a century ago. Its streets, though never paved, were well-kept, and shaded by aspens that had long ago replaced the firs that once thrived there. It seemed, at a glance, to be prospering. Its shops were busy, selling memorabilia of days long gone when the town had been a centre of commerce, and its old railroad depot, restored and turned into a restaurant, was, during the summer months, constantly filled with tourists who paused on their way to Aspen or Denver, spent a few minutes absorbing the quaint atmosphere of the village, then moved on to the next stop on their Triple A tourist maps.

The tourists never went where Esperanza was going, for the tiny Catholic Church was near the edge of town, in the midst of the shacks that were occupied by Esperanza's friends, the few mixed-breed Indians whose Mexican,

14

Indian, and white blood left them fitting into no easily identifiable group. They existed in poverty, scratching out a living as best they could by doing the menial jobs that the shop owners tossed to them. Esperanza herself did not live in Shacktown – she still lived in the caretaker's cabin near the entrance to the mine, where she'd lived most of her life – but every week she came to the church to pray for the children who, though their graves were marked in the tiny churchyard, were buried somewhere else.

Today, she didn't stay long.

Today, she wasn't praying for the dead children.

Today, she was praying for the one who was still alive.

Christie Lyons stared straight ahead, her eyes unseeing, her tiny white hand lost in Esperanza Rodriguez's large brown one. Tears flowed down her cheeks, and her chin quivered as she struggled not to sob out loud.

She hadn't believed it at first. Her father was all she had, and she was sure that what was happening was all a bad dream, that any minute now her father would wake her up and tell her it was only a nightmare.

Dimly, she wondered if they were going to send her to an orphanage. She supposed they probably were. If you didn't have any family, where else could you go?

Though she was only nine years old, Christie knew exactly what had happened. Her father had gone to the mine by himself, and he'd fallen down the shaft. Many times, when she'd gone to mines with him, he'd told her what could happen if you weren't careful. Now it had happened to him.

And now she was alone and going somewhere with people she hardly knew at all.

She looked out the window of the car and realised they were driving towards the mine. Was she going to have to look at her father? Were they going to show him to her? She hoped not. Knowing he was dead was bad enough – she didn't want to have to look at him, too.

She stared up into the face of Esperanza Rodriguez, who

had held her in her lap while they told her her father was dead. Now Esperanza was smiling at her, the way her mother used to smile at her when she was very little.

Christie didn't remember her mother very well, but right now, with her father dead, she desperately wished that her mother would come back to her.

For some reason, she remembered how her mother used to wash her hair, making her blonde curls light and fluffy. Now they clung damply to her forehead, and she wished her mother were there to wash them for her. But that, too, would never happen again, for her mother had died five years ago.

She felt the man who was driving the car squeeze her leg and looked up at him. He was Dr. Henry, and even though she didn't know him very well, she knew he was a friend of her father's.

She touched his hand, and he squeezed her reassuringly before putting his hand back on the steering wheel of the car. Feeling hopeless, Christie Lyons stared out the window, not really seeing the house they were approaching.

At fifty-two, Bill Henry was still lean and ruggedly handsome. His brown hair was shot through with grey, and his skin, darkened by the Colorado sun, was the colour of saddle leather. He wished he knew how to comfort the little girl beside him, but she seemed to have drifted away somewhere, and he hadn't the least idea what to say to her. Unmarried, he had never really learned the trick of talking to children. And never had he had to deal with one who had just lost her only parent.

Rather than risk saying the wrong thing, Bill Henry kept his eyes on the road and, as he turned the car into the driveway of Edna Amber's mansion, examined the details of the house. The comforting of the child he would leave to Esperanza, or, in a few more minutes, to Diana Amber.

The house, the largest in Amberton, stood brooding on a rise that let it overlook the village like a sentinel. In contrast to the houses in the village, the Amber place had not been painted in years, and it had taken on the look of a derelict, its paint peeling, its shingles loosening. A few aspens and one or two firs dotted the scraggy lawn that surrounded the living quarters, and the outbuildings – a barn and a chicken coop, along with a carriage house that had been converted to a garage many years earlier – looked as forlorn as the house itself. Though Edna Amber still regarded the town as her personal fiefdom, she had never taken part in its restoration. Indeed, she had objected to the restoration every step of the way. Bill Henry supposed that, to her, turning Amberton into a tourist attraction meant admitting that the mine would never again produce – and that was one of the many things that Edna Amber would not admit.

'We're here,' Bill said. Christie, seeming to come out of her daze, gazed up at him.

'Where?' she asked.

'At the Ambers'. They're going to take care of you.'

'You mean they're going to adopt me?' Christie asked.

'Well, I don't know.' Bill wondered how to explain to the little girl that it was not at all certain how long she was going to be staying with the Ambers, and that almost surely she was not going to be adopted by them.

Christie fidgeted, her fingers twisting at the hem of her dress. She could only vaguely remember her father introducing her to the Ambers. Then she thought of the statue in the square.

'Isn't Mr. Amber the man in the park?'

'That's right. But the ones you're going to stay with are his wife and his daughter.'

Christie tried to make sense out of it all, but too much had happened. All she knew was that her father was dead and that she was going to live with strangers. She began to cry.

As Bill looked helplessly on, Esperanza gathered the child into her arms and cradled her against her ample bosom.

'*Pobrecita*,' she murmured. 'Is all right, baby.' She looked up at Bill Henry. 'I tell them,' she said suddenly. 'I tell them, but they don't listen to me.'

'Told them what?' Bill asked. He glanced at Esperanza, but the woman was staring into the distance, towards the mine.

'The children,' Esperanza said. 'I tell them not to bother the children, but they don't listen. See what happened.'

Dimly, Bill remembered a story he'd heard when he was a boy. He looked across Christie, then reached out to touch Esperanza. 'What are you talking about?' he asked. 'What children?'

She jerked away from his fingers as if she'd been burned. 'The lost children,' Esperanza replied, her voice low. 'You can hear them when the wind blows. When the wind blows, they cry. And it was blowing today.'

It didn't make any sense to Bill. So what if the wind had been blowing? In this part of the country it wasn't that unusual. On many days the wind came sweeping down out of the mountains, whispering among the aspens and caressing the tall grasses that grew on the floor of the valley.

'I don't understand, Esperanza,' he said. 'What children are you talking about?'

Esperanza looked at him pityingly. 'The ones who are waiting,' she said. 'The ones who are waiting to be born again.' Then she opened the car door and got out. Christie, who seemed not to have heard the conversation, slid reluctantly out after her.

She looked up at the house and wished she could go somewhere else. It was too big, and too frightening. She slipped her hand into Esperanza's. As though she had read her thoughts, Esperanza leaned down to whisper in Christie's ear.

'Is all right, little one. I will look out for you. You see? Up there?' She pointed off into the distance, where Christie could just make out the shape of a cabin crouching on the side of the mountain. 'I live there. You need me, you come up there. Okay?'

Christie nodded, then let go of Esperanza's hand and followed Bill as he led her up the steps towards the front door of the Amber house.

Diana Amber opened the door and, seeing who was there, immediately dropped to her knees. She took Christie in her arms and hugged her close.

At fifty, Diana wore the remnants of her prettiness well. Her blue eyes were soft, and there was a sadness in them that touched nearly everyone who had ever met her. As she gazed at Christie Lyons she smiled gently. Looking on, Bill realized that, in a way, Diana reminded him of a rabbit – warm and soft, easily startled. She held Christie for a moment, then stood up and led the little girl into the house. Bill Henry and Esperanza Rodriguez followed.

Diana took them to the parlour, where Edna Amber sat working on a piece of needlepoint. Unlike her daughter, Edna had bright hard eyes that sparkled with determination, and her body, though she was nearing eighty and getting stiff, was still strong. She didn't stand to greet her visitors; she was one of those women who expect others to rise while they remain seated.

Christie, unsure of what she was expected to do, stood quietly staring at the floor. Suddenly her nostrils filled with a strange odour and she sneezed.

'God bless you,' Diana said. 'Do you have a cold?'

Christie shook her head. 'I smelled something, and it made me sneeze.'

Diana sniffed at the air, then smiled. 'That's lavender,' she said. 'Don't you like it?'

'I don't know,' Christie said. 'What's it for?'

'It's just to make things smell good.'

Christie stared up at her. 'Why?'

'Why – why because –' Diana floundered, unable to find an answer for the little girl's question.

For the first time, Edna Amber spoke. 'It's to cover up sour smells,' she said. 'Like houses that haven't been properly cleaned, and old people, and children.' She got to

19

her feet and, leaning stiffly on her cane, walked out of the room. There was a long silence until she was gone, and then Christie, comprehending only that the old woman didn't like her, began to cry. Once again Diana gathered the little girl into her arms.

'It's all right,' she whispered. 'Everything's going to be fine. I'm going to be your mother now, and you'll be my little girl.'

The words struck a chord in Christie. Her crying abated, and she looked deep into Diana's eyes.

'My mama died a long time ago,' she said, her voice quivering.

'I know,' Diana told her. 'But now I'll be your mama.'

Christie's expression was uncertain as she searched Diana's face. 'Promise?' she said at last, her voice shaking.

'I promise,' Diana breathed.

Suddenly the little girl dissolved into tears once more, but this time she slid her arms around Diana's neck and clung to her. Lifting her up, Diana laid Christie gently on the sofa, then sat and cradled the child's head in her lap. As Diana and Bill talked Christie's sobbing eased until she lay still.

'Is she all right?' Diana asked. Christie seemed to have fallen asleep.

'She will be,' Bill assured her. 'She's still a little bit in shock, but I'd rather not give her anything – it seems as though every time something happens, we try to take something for it. But children are resilient.' He paused, then met Diana's eyes. 'Diana, are you sure this is wise?'

'What?'

'Taking her in. Obviously Miss Edna doesn't approve.'

'I'm a grown woman, Bill,' Diana said. 'Mother doesn't make all my decisions for me anymore.'

But even as she spoke Bill saw Diana's eyes flickering around the room as if she expected to see her mother somewhere, watching her, mocking her, contradicting her.

Controlling her.

He was well aware that Diana was all Edna Amber had left, and that she guarded her ageing daughter like a tigress with a cub, prowling around her, ever wary of any danger. Even Bill, after all the years he had known Edna Amber, still felt a certain awe of her. She carried about her an aura of power that no one in Amberton was immune to, even while they sometimes wondered if Miss Edna used her power to protect her daughter or only herself.

For Bill, Edna's protectiveness had an extra edge: there had been a time when he had wanted to marry Diana. It was because of Diana that he had come back to Amberton at the age of twenty-nine, finished with school, finished with his internship, ready to begin his practice. He had come back because he had been in love with Diana since they were children together.

But nothing had happened. Miss Edna, always polite to him, never raising her voice, had seen to that.

As far as Miss Edna was concerned, Bill Henry was just a town boy, trying to better himself by marrying above his station. Eventually she had convinced Diana of it, and now, more than twenty years later, his love had mellowed to a mixture of sympathy and pity.

'What's Miss Edna doing?' he asked now.

'She's upstairs, in her room,' Diana replied. 'If she needs anything, she'll let me know.' Diana's even features were momentarily warped by a strange grin that seemed to Bill to be based more on fear than on amusement. 'She pounds the floor with her cane.'

Charming, Bill thought, knowing he wouldn't be able to keep the sarcasm from his voice if he spoke the word aloud. Diana's grin faded to a wan smile.

'I've gotten used to it over the years.' A thought occurred to her: 'I hope it won't frighten Christie.'

Bill lit his pipe and waved away the cloud of smoke that rose from the bowl. 'She's likely to be afraid of everything for a while, Diana. Losing both parents at her age can damage a child, You might be letting yourself in for more than you can handle. She's probably going to have

21

nightmares, and she's likely to be demanding. She's going to need a lot of attention.'

'She'll get it,' Diana said. She paused for a moment, and when she spoke again, her voice had a strength in it that Bill had never heard before.

'I want to take care of her, Bill,' she said. 'I've been taken care of long enough. It's time I stopped being my mother's dutiful daughter and had a child of my own. And maybe I can talk mother into having Esperanza help out a little more.' She eased Christie's head off her lap and stood up, and Bill, realising that she wanted him to go, stood up, too.

'If you need me, call me,' he said.

Diana touched his arm and nodded. 'I will. But I don't think I'll need anything. I think I'll be just fine.'

As she walked Bill to the door, Esperanza appeared from the kitchen, nodded briefly to them, and moved on into the living room. Diana stood at the front door until Bill had driven away, then she, too, returned to the living room. Esperanza was kneeling in front of the couch, stroking Christie's forehead.

'What are you doing?' Diana asked. Esperanza looked up at her, her brown eyes sad.

'She is dying,' Esperanza saïd quietly.

Diana felt a surge of panic. 'Dying? What are you talking about?'

The Mexican woman shook her head sadly. 'Not now. But soon. The children will call her, and she will have to go.'

'Stop it, Esperanza,' Diana told her. 'Don't say another word.'

'But it is true, Miss Diana. You know it is true, no?'

As their eyes met, and Diana saw the great sadness in Esperanza's face, she felt a chill.

The same chill she had felt that morning when the wind began to blow.

2

From her front room on the second floor of the house, Edna Amber watched Bill Henry drive away. Her body rigid, she leaned on her cane, held firmly in both her hands, but as the doctor's old Rambler station wagon disappeared in a cloud of red dust, she let herself relax. Her ears, as sharp in old age as they had been when she was fifty years younger, listened to the sounds of the house. For the moment there was silence.

She liked the silence, for it meant that the wind was not blowing. The thing Edna Amber hated most about Amberton was the wind.

Amos Amber, twenty years older than she and used to the wind after his years in Amberton, had assured her that she would get used to it, that the only wind that was really bothersome was the chinook, the warm wind that came whistling out of the Rockies several times each winter, raising the temperature, melting the snow, and setting people's nerves on edge. She had not gotten used to it, not gotten used to it at all.

Instead, as the years had passed, she had learned to steel herself against the wind, learned to watch the sky and the mountains to the west, learned to watch for the signs that the wind was coming. Watchfulness had not been enough.

The day Diana was born, the wind had blown.

Ever since that day, she had hated the wind, always associating it with the death of her husband and the birth of her daughter.

She had considered leaving Amberton and going back to

Boston, but she had soon realised she could not. Despite the difference in their ages, she had loved Amos very much and had never wanted to leave him. Besides there was the ranch to run, and she had an instinctive feeling that if she left, the ranch would soon prove to be 'unprofitable,' and she would lose it. The prospect of being a young widow with no estate had not appealed to her.

And so Edna had stayed on, doing her best to maintain the life to which she felt entitled. The people of Amberton didn't blame her for the accident in the mine. She, after all, had lost as much as any of the rest of them. Over the years she had come to be called 'Miss Edna,' living apart from the town in her too-large house, tending to her affairs with a much stronger sense of business than she had ever expected to possess, and being very careful never to become close to any of the people she knew.

She had let herself become close to Amos Amber, and he had died. She had never made the same mistake again, nor had she let her daughter make it. Diana, she had decided on that day her husband died and her child was born, had only one purpose in life.

Someday, when all else was gone, Diana would take care of her.

All her life Edna had worked towards that plan.

Now, once again, it seemed as if the wind was reaching out to destroy her. It had reached out to destroy another child's father, and now that child was being thrust into her world.

She turned away from the window and left her room, pausing in the wide hallway that ran the length of the house on the second floor, to listen once more. From downstairs there was no sound.

Edna went to the back of the house and slowly climbed the narrow set of stairs. Once, this staircase had been used only by the servants, but in recent years it had barely been used at all. On the third floor a warren of tiny rooms were jammed beneath the rafters. Once they had been filled with the Mexican and Indian girls who had served the

Ambers as maids in better days – Esperanza Rodriguez had lived there with her mother when she was a baby – but now they were nothing more than storerooms filled with the castoffs of the years, a dusty breeding place for the rats that had slowly invaded the house.

All of them were storerooms, except one.

In the corner, facing the mountains there was a small room. Edna hadn't been inside it for thirty years, but this afternoon, as the sun began sinking behind the mountains, and the deep blue of the sky turned darker, she opened the door to the corner room and went in.

It was a nursery.

She and Amos had decorated it together, early in her pregnancy. She had known, somehow, that her baby was going to be a girl, so she had done the room in pink.

There was pink candy-striped paper on the walls, and the wood trim had been painted white. Over the two dormer windows she had hung white lace curtains, which she had stitched herself. All the furniture was still where she had placed it.

There was a rocking chair and an ornately carved cradle, which had been Diana's first bed. When she had grown bigger, she had been moved into the crib that stood in the northern dormer, and finally, when she outgrew even the crib, she had moved to a daybed just inside the door.

All the toys were still there – all the dolls and baby toys with which Amos had filled the room before Diana was born.

And years later when Diana had finally abandoned the nursery in favour of a room on the second floor, the nursery had never been opened again.

Not until today.

Edna sank into the rocking chair and stared at the room.

The wallpaper, once bright and pretty, had faded years ago. The pink and white stripes, barely visible now, were brittle and streaked with dust. The paper was peeling away from the walls, its seams curled back from the crumbling plaster behind it.

The curtains hung in shreds from their rods, greyish-brown remnants of the fresh, clean ruffles they had been fifty years before.

Cobwebs, heavy with dust, filled the corners of the room, and beneath the crib there was a pile of cotton batting mouldering on the floor. A rat had apparently robbed the mattress for its nest.

Edna sat in the nursery for a long time, letting her mind drift over her life. When finally she stood up, she had come to a decision.

The nursery was a child's room.

Now, for the moment at least, there was a child in the house once more.

Christie Lyons, she decided, would live in the nursery.

And, as when Diana had lived there, the nursery would remain as she had furnished it.

Her eyes, undimmed by age, saw what they wanted to see.

To her, the nursery was as bright and pretty as it had ever been.

Christie, she was sure, would love it as much as Diana had.

The dust swirled around Esperanza Rodriguez's sandals as she walked home that afternoon, leaving rusty stains on the hem of her long black skirt, but she didn't notice it. Instead she looked at the mountains, admiring the bands of colour that splashed across them as they rose from the floor of the valley. The aspens, bright green in their early summer foliage, glistened in the afternoon sun, garlanding the bases of the hills and shooting up the gulches that scarred the mountainsides, like guerrilla armies invading the dark green of the ancient firs that had conquered the Rockies centuries earlier. A few yards from the road Cleft Creek gurgled in its bed, its spring flood only recently abated, its water still icy cold. Soon she would take Juan fishing, and the two of them, she and her son, would be alone near the cave where *los niños* lived.

They would spend a day by themselves, away from the prying eyes of the world, away from the knowing looks of the *gringos* who watched them whenever they went to town, and then whispered to each other. Esperanza knew what they said, and there were times when she wondered if they were right and she had done wrong.

When Juan had been born, Theresa Whitefawn, the midwife from Shacktown, had told her to send Juan to live with the children in the cave, but Esperanza had refused. To her, Juan looked perfectly normal. His brown eyes had laughed at her, and his tiny arms had waved in the air. If he didn't grab her finger right away when she put it in his fist, it meant nothing. Only when he hadn't begun talking until he was four did she finally face the truth.

But still the doubts lingered. He was her son, and he had been alive when he was born, and she couldn't send him away. To send him away would have been a mortal sin.

Besides, she loved Juan.

He was nearly thirty now, and if he didn't talk very well and couldn't think very clearly, that was all right with Esperanza. She could take care of him, and he enjoyed helping her, as best as he could. And he was gentle, despite what other people said. It was just that he never realised that he was a grown man.

Esperanza, of course, never treated him like one. She understood, in her own way, that inside his head he was still seven or eight years old, and she saw no point in trying to make him be what he was not.

She bought him the comic books he loved and sat with him hour after hour as he turned the pages and tried to read the words. But Esperanza herself read only a little, and for her, English did not come easily. She preferred the Spanish of her childhood.

Living quietly together, Esperanza and her son earned a little money helping the Ambers. They were all that was left of the once-large staff of the ranch. Esperanza worked in the house two or three days a week, and Juan rode the land with Miss Diana, helping her mend the fence that kept the few head of cattle from wandering away. They lived in the old cabin by the mine, and Esperanza tried to keep an eye out for the children who loved to sneak up the mountain to play among the rusting mining machinery that, though long ago overgrown with weeds, was still strewn over the mountainside.

The stamp press was still there, a relic from the period when Amos Amber had briefly struck a vein of gold and had immediately invested in all the equipment he would need to develop it. The press, and the steam engine to run it, had barely been used before the vein had played out, and the miners had returned to their old duties of hauling load after load of coal out of the hillside.

Miraculously the mine had not collapsed during the 1910 flood – Amos Amber had always insisted that it be constantly reinforced with strong timbers, and although Amos had died, his timbers had held. Here and there, however, the honeycomb of shafts was weakening now, and there were tell-tale signs of the beginning of collapse where the constantly shifting temperatures, the freezing and melting of ice, and the workings of trees and animals had loosened the earth. Sinkholes were beginning to appear.

Esperanza, in her constant wanderings of the mountainside, was well aware of these places, and she watched them closely.

Only a week ago she had discovered one of the strange sinkholes not too far from the cave.

Los niños, she was sure, were stirring.

And now Señor Lyons had died in the mine.

Esperanza, with the wisdom of her ancestors, was sure that the children had killed him.

She went into the cabin and found Juan lying on the floor, his chin propped in his hands, looking at one of his comic books.

'Juan?'

He grinned up at his mother. 'Hi!'

Esperanza sat down on the floor beside Juan and gathered her skirt close to protect herself from the drafts

28

that flowed up through the loose boards. She gently took the comic book from Juan's hands and tipped his face up so his eyes met her own.

'Juan, were the children crying today?'

Juan's eyes took on a puzzled look, and he shook his head. 'No, Mama. I didn't see any children today.'

'Not the children you can see, Juan,' Esperanza said. 'The other ones. The ones you can't see.'

Juan frowned, then stood up. 'Should I go listen?' he asked.

Esperanza smiled at her son and reached for his hand. 'Both of us,' she said in Spanish. 'Both of us will listen.'

Together Esperanza and Juan went out into the evening, but that night the full moon cast a silvery glow over the valley, and only a soft breeze drifted out of the mountains to set the aspens to murmuring.

The children were silent.

Diana Amber let Christie sleep on the sofa until the sun had set completely. She wandered through the first-floor rooms, turning on lights until the whole house was illuminated. Only then did she return to the living room and ease herself onto her knees next to the sofa.

'Christie?' she said softly. The little girl's eyelids fluttered, then opened. At first Diana saw only blankness in the little girl's eyes, but then they slowly filled with a melancholy that tore at Diana's heart.

'Daddy,' Christie whispered. 'Please – I want my daddy.'

'He's gone,' Diana told her. 'Try not to think about it, sweetheart. All right?'

For a long time Christie lay still, her eyes fixed on Diana's face, and then a single tear filled her left eye, overflowed, and ran down her cheek. She made no move to wipe it away, and when Diana reached out to touch her face, she shrank away.

Diana's hand hovered in the air for a moment, and the softness in her eyes suddenly disappeared, to be replaced by a flash of anger. And then, checking herself, she dropped her hand to her side and smiled. 'Would you like something to eat?'

Christie shook her head warily, sat up, and looked around the room as if seeing it for the first time.

'Everything's old here,' she said, her voice filled with wonder. Her eyes went from the crystal chandelier suspended from the centre of the ceiling to the ornately carved rosewood mantel that dominated one of the walls. She ran a hand over the horsehair upholstery of the Victorian sofa. 'It feels funny.'

'When I was a little girl,' Diana said, 'I used to slide right off it. And I thought it was lumpy,' she added, dropping her voice to a conspiratorial level. Christie poked at the sofa, then nodded.

'It is.'

'Would you like to see the rest of the house?'

Christie hesitated, then nodded silently and stood up. Diana got to her feet, unsure where to begin. Finally she led Christie into the parlour, where there was another fireplace, two chairs, and an old-fashioned square piano.

'I never saw a piano like that,' Christie said. She reached out and pressed a key. A tinny note emerged from the antique instrument.

'It's a Bosendorfer,' Diana explained. 'One of my ancestors brought it out from Boston. Do you know how to play?'

'A little,' Christie replied. 'I took lessons before we came out here.'

'Well, maybe I can teach you more,' Diana said. 'Did you like your lessons?'

'They were fun. But I'm not very good.'

'Neither am I,' Diana admitted. 'Maybe we can practise together.'

'Who taught you?'

'My mother,' Diana said. She drifted into silence for a moment. 'But it wasn't much fun,' she added.

Christie looked at her curiously. 'Why not?'

Diana hesitated, then decided to change the subject. A

sudden vision had come to her in the parlour, a vision of herself as a little girl, sitting on the hard piano bench, her mother standing over her, pounding out the rhythm with the cane she had already begun carrying, demanding that Diana play the notes exactly, criticising the smallest mistakes, adding hours and hours to her daily practice sessions. She had hated the piano, and she hadn't played in thirty years. But now she might try again. In retrospect the discipline had been good for her and would be good for Christie, too. It might, indeed, be fun. But there was no reason to tell Christie what it had been like for her. No reason at all.

They wandered through the day rooms on the main floor, and for the first time in years Diana saw her home through the eyes of a child. She had always taken the books that lined the walls of the library for granted, but as Christie stared at them, then ran her fingers over the leather-bound volumes, Diana found herself wanting to touch them, too.

As a child, she had never been allowed in the library. It had been her father's, and even though she had never known her father, she had learned very early to respect his things. Even now, as Christie took one of the volumes from the shelves and opened it, she had an urge to take the book from the child's hand and put it back on the shelf. But it was, after all, only a book, and her father had been dead for half a century.

'Do you like to read?' she asked.

Christie nodded, turning the pages. It was a volume of bound copies of *St. Nicholas* magazine, filled with stories and drawings that appealed to her. 'Did you read these when you were little?'

'Oh, no,' Diana explained. 'I had my own books, up in my nursery.'

Christie cocked her head and looked up at Diana. 'You had a nursery?'

Again Diana's mind drifted towards the past. 'For years and years.'

'Can I see it?' Christie asked.

Diana felt her stomach tighten, and there was a ringing sensation in her ears. Why had she even mentioned the nursery? She hadn't been in it herself since – since when? She couldn't even remember, it had been so long ago. It had to be at least thirty years.

Yes, that was how long it had been.

She had been twenty, and she had been sick. She still vaguely remembered the illness. It had gone on for months, and for a while she had thought she was going to die. And then one morning she woke up, and she was no longer in the nursery.

Instead she was in a room on the second floor – the 'guest room,' though she couldn't remember there ever having been a guest. From then on, that room had been hers. In all the years since then, she had never gone back up to the nursery.

'I don't think so,' she said, coming out of her reverie. But Christie was no longer watching her. She stood perfectly still, the book in her hands, her eyes fixed on something behind Diana. Diana turned and saw her mother standing in the library doorway.

'What are you doing?' Edna asked, her voice crackling with anger. 'What is that child doing with one of your father's books?'

'Mama,' Diana breathed. 'I – I thought you were upstairs.'

'What has that to do with it?' Edna's icy blue eyes raked Diana, then went to Christie. 'Put that book down!' she demanded. Instantly Christie put the book on a table.

Diana moved close to Christie and slipped her arm protectively around the little girl's shoulders. 'Mama, she isn't going to damage it. She's just curious.'

Edna ignored her, her baleful gaze fixed on Christie. For the first time she analysed the odd resemblance between her daughter and the child. The soft blue eyes, the blonde hair, the pale complexion. She had to admit that Christie Lyons was a pretty little thing. But the way Diana had her

32

arm around the little girl bothered Edna.

Possessive.

It struck her that Diana was already being possessive about the child.

'Small for her age, isn't she?' Edna observed at last.

'Mama, she's only nine –' Diana began, but Edna cut her off.

'Most nine-year-olds are larger than that. Except you. You were always small for your age, too.' Abruptly, as if there were nothing more to be said about Christie, Edna changed the subject. 'Are you going to fix dinner?'

'Yes, Mama,' Diana said meekly. 'As soon as I take Christie upstairs and get her settled in my room.'

'No,' Edna said. Then, before Diana could ask what she meant, she explained herself. 'Until I decide what's to be done with her, she'll stay in the nursery.'

Edna turned and walked out of the library. At her side Diana could feel Christie trembling.

And, she realised, she was trembling, too. Her mother's words echoed in her mind: *Until I decide what's to be done with her*. Her mother was going to take Christie away from her.

She couldn't let that happen. No one would ever take Christie away from her.

Never.

3

The one problem with a restored house, Joyce Crowley decided as she wrestled with her wood-electric stove, was that you had to put up with a lot of inconveniences. The wood-electric itself had been something of a compromise. Her house, built in 1870, had certainly had no provisions for electricity. Or plumbing either, for that matter.

When she and Matt had bought the place ten years earlier, it had been a crumbling wreck. Its only saving grace had been its price. The restoration of Amberton had barely begun then, and no one, except Joyce Crowley, had been the least bit interested in taking over the two-storey hulk that sat across the street from the Methodist Church. The house itself was sturdy enough, though the roof had rotted badly. It was one of the few houses in town that had been built of sandstone blocks, but its featureless form was distinctly utilitarian. Two rows of four windows each faced the street, topped by an uninterestingly peaked roof. The front door was on one side, and the back door on the other, and at the rear of the house there was nothing. It was, basically, a square box with a lid on it, but at ten thousand dollars she had felt it was a deal they couldn't pass up. And now, after ten years of hard work, even Matt had to agree she was right. They had scraped away the layers of paint from both the exterior and the interior, reroofed, replumbed, and rewired it, then painted it white with what few features of interest it had – mostly fancy stonework at the corners and scallop work under the eaves – cheered up with reds and olives. Now, sitting only a couple of blocks from the centre of town, it was a landmark, and all summer long Joyce took a quiet pride in the number of tourists who stopped to stare at the house, read the plaque describing its history, which she had installed by the gate, then stepped across the street to photograph it. Only Jane Berkey's pink, white, lavender, and purple Easter egg of a Victorian attracted more attention, and Joyce took a certain not-quite-malicious satisfaction in the fact that while Mrs. Berkey had had professional help with her house, she and Matt had relied on no one but themselves for their own restoration.

Still, it would have been nice to have had a new stove instead of the wood-electric that had been rescued from the dump. But in Amberton it was a matter of pride to have your restoration as accurate as possible, excluding such details as outhouses, so Joyce cheerfully made do.

As she tested the meat pie her thoughts turned to her husband. Matt had been gone all afternoon.

She knew he was terribly upset over the accident – not only had he held Elliot Lyons in high regard, but Matt was one of those in town who hoped that the mine would be reopened and once again provide a flow of wealth into Amberton. To Joyce, the mine represented only a source of pain. Her grandfather had died in the 1910 accident, and her grandmother had never recovered from it. In Joyce's view, the mine had never been as good for Amberton as her husband liked to think. For years Amberton had been dependent on the mine, and when it had closed, the town had gone into shock and poverty that had lasted half a century. Only now was Amberton beginning to become hopeful again. And it had nothing to do with the mine.

Instead it had to do with the restoration. To Joyce's mind, the restoration was constructive – it was safe, and it didn't pollute the environment. She had silently dreaded the return of the mine and the black cloud that would hang over the valley – a cloud composed partly of coal dust and partly of fear that someday, any day, disaster would strike again. Though Joyce was sincerely sorry that Elliot Lyons had died, there was a part of her that felt relieved.

Now the mine operations would stop. At least no one else would die.

The back door opened, and Matt came in, his face streaked with sweat and black dust, his expression grim.

'Well, it's done,' he said. He opened the refrigerator, which had been built into the space once occupied by an icebox, with its antique façade retained, and pulled out a Coors. 'A damn shame, that's what it is.' He flipped the top off the bottle and pulled at it deeply as Jeff, ten years old and as darkly handsome as his father, slipped into the kitchen.

'What's a damn shame?' the little boy asked.

'What happened today,' Matt said. 'And don't say "damn."'

'You say it,' Jeff fretted.

'My father used to tell me to do what he said and not what he did. I'm telling you the same thing. Get it?' Behind his grim expression there was a gleam in his eye that let Jeff know he was in no serious trouble. He grinned at his father.

'The hell you say,' he said in perfect imitation of Matt.

'Jeff!' Joyce did her best to make her voice severe, but failed. She pointed to the drawer in which she kept the silverware. 'Set the table while your father drinks his beer, okay?'

'Aw . . .' Jeff complained, but not loudly enough so that his father would have to scold him. He scooped up some silver and began setting the table.

'I suppose they'll give up the mine now,' Joyce said carefully as she began mashing some potatoes.

Matt swished some beer around in his mouth, then swallowed it. 'Don't know. Don't know what happened to Elliot yet.'

'Maybe the water babies got him,' Jeff suggested.

Joyce stared at her son. 'Water babies?' she echoed. 'What on earth are you talking about?'

'You know,' Jeff said, his voice filled with the scorn children reserve only for the ignorance of their parents.

'They wait up in the mountains, and they eat people.' His face turned thoughtful and he frowned. 'But I guess it couldn't have been them, 'cause Eddie says they only eat children.'

'Eddie Whitefawn?' Joyce asked. 'Is that who told you?'

'Unh-hunh. And he knows, too. His grandmother told him. She told him when Indian kids die, they go up in the mountains and wait for other kids. Then the dead ones kill the live ones.'

Joyce shuddered, and Matt set his beer down. It was the same story he'd heard when he was a boy, with a few variations – the legend of a cave somewhere in the mountains where the Indians were supposed to have buried their stillborn. But how could he explain it? He decided not to try. Instead he reached out to take his son's arm. Jeff tried to pull away from him, but Matt's grip was like a gentle vice.

'Now, you listen to me, young man,' he said. 'There's no such thing as water babies, whatever they are. There's nothing in the mountains that eats people – nothing at all.'

Jeff looked at his father suspiciously, then zeroed in on the weakest point. 'If you don't know what they are,' he said, 'how do you know there's no such thing?'

Matt sighed and stood up. Children, he decided, were endlessly baffling. In the exuberance of youth he had thought it would be fun to have six, but Jeff, with his unending questions and constant mischief, was as good as six rolled into one. Now, as this tiny fraction of his intentions stared belligerently up at him, he shrugged helplessly.

'I'm gonna take a shower, honey,' he said. 'Think you can get me off the hook with our little genius here?' Without waiting for an answer, he left the kitchen. By the time he'd reached the foot of the stairs, he'd stripped off his shirt and was yanking at his belt. The strain of the day had exhausted him, and now, as he climbed to the second floor, he began laughing almost hysterically.

And yet there was nothing to laugh about. He could not

erase from his mind the sight of Elliot Lyons's body, barely recognisable at the bottom of the main shaft, a bloody pulp loosely encased in a sports shirt and khaki pants, lying in the muck on the floor of the mine. It was nearly incomprehensible to him that it had happened. Over and over as they had worked together, Elliot had insisted to him that under no circumstances should he ever work in the mine alone. Too many things could go wrong. And yet, today, Elliot had apparently gone to the mine by himself.

And something had happened.

Matt chuckled hollowly. Who knows, he thought. Maybe the water babies did get him.

In the kitchen Jeff listened patiently as his mother tried to explain to him that he mustn't take too seriously the endless bits of Indian lore that Eddie Whitefawn's grandmother was constantly dispensing.

'What she says isn't any closer to the truth than the fire and brimstone Reverend Jennings preaches,' Joyce said. In fact, she privately placed a lot more faith in Eddie's grandmother than she did in Jerome Jennings, but she realised that that might be due only to her liking for Eddie and her dislike of little Jay-Jay Jennings. Still, when it came to parental wisdom, she tried to do her best by Jeff, and fair was fair. 'You have to remember that the only things you can believe in are the things you can prove. Now, have you, or Eddie, or his grandmother ever seen one of these water babies?'

'No,' Jeff reluctantly admitted. He had a feeling his mother was working up to one of her lectures, so he decided to get her talking about something else. 'So if there aren't any water babies, what happened to Christie's dad?'

'I don't know,' Joyce told him. 'It was an accident.'

'But Dad says Mr. Lyons was real careful,' Jeff protested. 'He says Mr. Lyons was the carefulest man he ever met.'

'Most careful,' Joyce automatically corrected him. 'There's no such word as "carefulest." '

'Aw, Mom,' Jeff groaned. 'You know what I meant! I'm gonna go up and ask Dad.'

'You'll do no such thing! You'll stay right here and finish setting the table. And during dinner you won't mention one word about the mine, or Mr. Lyons, or anything else that might upset your father. Do you understand?'

Jeff nodded and decided he'd just have to wait. After dinner, he'd go out and find Steve Penrose and Eddie Whitefawn, and the three of them would figure out what had happened – even if they had to go up to the mine and look around.

Edna Amber sat in the small parlour, a fire blazing at her feet even though the evening was warm. An hour ago Dan Gurley, the Amberton marshal, had called to tell her that he and Dr. Henry were coming out to talk to her. And Diana. Ever since the call, she had been sitting there, her lips compressed into a tight line, her bright blue eyes reflecting the firelight. People were going to be coming into her house – people she didn't like – asking her questions, asking Diana questions, prying into their affairs.

Of course, it was all Diana's fault. It had been Diana who had insisted that Elliot Lyons be hired to supervise the revitalisation of the mine. Edna had known it was wrong, known from the start that they should have gotten someone from the East, someone who was competent. But she had given in and let Diana have her way. And now a man was dead.

She remained rigidly seated when the knock at the door finally came. If people wanted to see her, they would have to come to her; she wouldn't make so much as a move towards them. She was after all, an Amber. She continued to sit, waiting as Diana opened the door, then led the marshal and the doctor into the small parlour, where there were, conspicuously, not enough chairs for them to be seated.

'Good evening, Miss Edna,' Dan said. He stood uneasily in the doorway, wondering if he should suggest they move to the living room.

'Daniel,' Edna said. For the moment she ignored Dr. Henry.

Dan Gurley took a deep breath, then stepped into the room. Uninvited, he lowered his bulk into the empty chair beside Edna and gave her his warmest smile. Her stare remained icy.

'I'm afraid you're going to have to put up with a bit of inconvenience, ma'am,' he said. 'What with Mr. Lyons being dead.'

Edna's eyes glittered. 'If he fell down the mine shaft, he could hardly be alive,' she snapped. 'I know *what* happened, Daniel. You told me earlier, in case you've forgotten. What I want to know is *why* it happened.'

'Well, now, that's exactly why we're here,' Dan said, affecting a drawl he seldom used except for tourists. 'I'm afraid we don't rightly know what happened. In fact, we were hoping perhaps you and Miss Diana might be able to shed some light.'

'Us?' Diana asked. She leaned against the piano, and her fingers unconsciously played with the buttons that rose in a neat row up the front of her blouse nearly to her chin. 'What could we tell you?'

'We can't tell him anything, of course,' Edna said. She turned to Dan. 'Really, Daniel, I find this very annoying. What is the point?' She paused, then frowned. 'You aren't suggesting that what happened to Elliot Lyons was anything more than an accident, are you?'

'I'm not suggesting anything,' Dan said. 'All I'm trying to do is find out what happened. When I got up there today, the lights were on, and the elevator was running. It was at the top of the shaft, and there wasn't anything wrong with it. Given the –' He paused, wondering how to phrase it most delicately, then decided to ignore the Amber women's nerves. 'Given the length of the fall, there wasn't enough left of Lyons for Bill to examine. Now, all I want to know from you is if anyone else was up there this morning, besides Elliot Lyons.'

'At the mine?' Diana asked. 'Why would there be? You

mean you think someone might have pushed Elliot?'

'I don't know,' Dan answered.

'He means he doesn't know what happened,' Bill put in. 'It seems to both of us that Lyons wasn't the kind of man to stumble into a mine shaft. All Dan's doing is trying to figure it out.'

For the first time Edna Amber gazed directly at Bill, and her eyes held even less warmth in them for him than they'd had for Dan Gurley. 'And you,' she said. 'Why are you here?'

'I came to see Christie,' Bill said. 'I thought I ought to have a look at her, to see if she's all right. She's been through a lot today. Even you must realise that.'

Edna's knuckles tightened on the head of her cane. For a moment Bill thought she was going to rise to her feet, but she only nodded towards Diana.

'Bring Christie down,' she said. Diana started from the room, and Bill put a hand on her arm.

'It's all right,' he said quickly. 'I can go up. Is she in bed?'

Before Diana could answer, Edna's voice filled the room.

'Diana will bring the child down,' she insisted. Bill, his anger rising as he stared at the old woman, opened his mouth to speak, but before he could find the right words, Diana put a hand on his.

'It will be better, Bill,' she whispered. 'I won't be a minute.' Not giving him time to protest again, she hurried towards the stairs. A moment later she disappeared into the upper reaches of the house. While he waited for her to bring Christie down, Bill turned back to Edna.

'I suppose you're feeling a bit put out by all of this,' he said, his voice hard.

Edna's chin quivered with anger. 'I've never liked you, young man –' she began, but Bill cut her off.

'How you feel about me is of no consequence right now, Miss Edna. There is a little girl upstairs who has just lost her only parent. In fact, it was only luck that she wasn't

41

with him today. Now, there are some things that have to be done, and some questions that have to be answered. The mine is on your property, and Christie Lyons is staying in your house.'

Without saying a word, Edna Amber rose from her chair, her cane quivering in her grip, and left the room. Bill and Dan remained silent, listening to her mount the stairs, then start down the hall. The thumping of the cane stopped momentarily, then began again as she continued on to the back of the house. Only when they heard the sound of her bedroom door closing did either of them speak.

'Kind of hard on her, weren't you?' Dan asked mildly.

'You don't know her the way I do.' Bill's voice was bitter. 'I can't say I've ever liked her, and I think the way she treats Diana is inexcusable. Diana's so gentle, but Miss Edna only sees it as weakness. And do you know what happens when Diana shows any kind of emotion? Miss Edna starts talking about how she's "excitable," as if it were some kind of disease.'

'Oh, now, it isn't all that bad,' Dan put in, but Bill brushed his comment aside.

'Isn't it? Sometimes I think it's a lot worse. Sometimes I think that old woman is crazy.' Then, as he heard Diana coming down the stairs, he made himself calm down. He rose to his feet as Diana came into the little parlour, carrying Christie in her arms.

Christie, her eyes wide and fearful, stared at the two men and her arms tightened around Diana's neck.

'Christie?' Bill asked. 'Can't you walk?'

Christie glanced uncertainly at Diana, then shrugged. Bill reached out to take her from Diana's arms, and for a moment she seemed to resist. Then she let go of Diana and let him lower her to the floor. 'I'll take her into the living room, okay?' he asked.

Diana nodded, and smiled at Christie. 'Now, you remember what I told you, all right?'

Christie said nothing, but as Bill led her from the room,

42

her eyes never left Diana. When they were gone, Diana gave her attention to Dan Gurley.

'I can't believe it,' she said, sighing heavily. 'I-I feel like I killed him myself.'

She lowered herself into the chair that had only recently been occupied by her mother and stared into the flickering flames on the hearth.

'Do you know what it's like to be an Amber here, Dan?' she asked suddenly.

Dan Gurley was sixteen years younger than Diana, and had known her all his life, though only at a distance. To his knowledge, no one was close to the Ambers. Now he felt he was about to hear things that he was sure were none of his business and had nothing to do with Elliot Lyons at all.

'I'm sure it can't always be easy, Miss Diana,' he said quickly. Her eyes met his, and for the first time he saw the vulnerability that Bill Henry had told him was there.

'I don't have many friends,' Diana said softly. 'You know, in some ways, I think Elliot Lyons was about the only friend I had. I used to go up to the mine sometimes and talk to him. Just talk to him.'

'You have lots of friends ...' Dan protested.

'No, I don't, Dan,' Diana said, her voice suddenly free of the pathos that had been in it a moment before. 'I'm an Amber, and in Amberton the Ambers have no friends.' She stood up suddenly and smiled. 'Well, now maybe it will be different,' she said. 'You know, they say it's an ill wind that blows nobody good? Well, this may sound like a terrible thing to say, but even though what's happened is tragic, it may prove to be good for me.' Her voice dropped, and when she spoke again, Dan attributed what she was saying to the strain of the day. Surely she couldn't be serious. 'I've decided I want to adopt Christie. I've always wanted to have a child, and adopting her seems like the least I can do for Elliot. After all, it was my idea that he come here.'

'Your idea?' Dan asked. 'How did you know him?'

'I didn't. But when mother began making inquiries about hiring a mining engineer, I looked at all the material we were sent. Mother wanted to hire one of the men from Boston – she's one of those people who thinks civilisation begins and ends in Boston – but I liked what Elliot had to say.' Diana's fingers fluttered nervously at her throat. 'I suppose I wanted him because he was young. It seemed to me that if the mine were really going to be opened again, it should be by someone young, who knew all the most modern techniques. So I begged mother to hire Elliot, and she gave in. And now he's dead. I just can't help but feel responsible.'

Bill Henry had appeared at the door in time to hear the last. He crossed the room and placed his hand on Diana's shoulder. 'You didn't kill him, Diana. Whatever happened, it wasn't your fault. You weren't even there.'

Diana looked up at him, her eyes beseeching. 'Does that matter?' she asked. 'Does that really matter?'

Feeling suddenly uncomfortable, Dan Gurley stood up and cleared his throat. 'I-if you'll excuse me, I'd better get on up and talk to Esperanza and Juan. Bill ...?'

'Unless you need me, I'll stick around here for a while. Why don't you stop back after you've talked to them?'

'Sure,' Gurley replied. He put his hat on his head, then impulsively leaned over and kissed Diana Amber's cheek. 'I'm sorry, Miss Diana,' he murmured. 'I really am.'

Diana patted his hand and nodded. 'I know, Dan,' she replied. Then she smiled weakly. 'I'm sorry Mother was so awful to you.'

Dan shrugged and managed a faint grin. 'It's nothing unusual. As long as us peons stay in our place, she's not too bad.'

Diana laughed bitterly. 'Thanks for putting up with her. I know it isn't always easy.' Then: 'If anybody knows, I do.' She walked to the front door with Dan, then waited until he was gone before she closed the door and returned to the parlour. She sat down and for a moment studied the fire.

'Did you look at Christie?' she asked at last, though her mind seemed to be on something else.

'She's fine, all things considered,' Bill assured her.

Once more silence fell over them, and then Diana shifted in the chair and met Bill's eyes.

'I'm going to need some help,' she said.

'Anything. You know that.'

'Elliot Lyons had no family. His parents died years ago.'

'What about brothers and sisters?'

Diana shook her head. 'I don't think he or his wife had any. From what he said, I gathered he and Christie were alone.'

'Then what happens to Christie?' Bill asked.

'I'm thinking of adopting her.' She held up a hand to prevent Bill from saying anything, and plunged on. 'Bill, I've been thinking about it all afternoon, and it just seems to me like the right thing to do. I just –'

She broke off as she realised that Edna was standing at the parlour door. 'Mother. I didn't hear you come down.'

'No, I don't suppose you did,' Edna said. 'But I heard you. I heard you saying that you're going to adopt that child.'

'I-I'm just thinking about it, Mother,' Diana said nervously. 'I mean, she doesn't have any place to go ...'

'Is that any of our concern, Diana?' Edna asked. Diana's eyes widened in dismay.

'Mother, he was my friend. It's the least I can do to take his daughter in!'

'Is it?' Edna remarked. 'Well, we'll talk about it later, between ourselves.' She turned to Bill Henry. 'I suppose you have several things to attend to, don't you, Doctor.' It was a dismissal, and Bill decided not to challenge it. Diana had had enough for one day, without having to referee a battle between her mother and himself. He got hastily to his feet and picked up his bag.

'You know how to reach me,' he told Diana as she walked him to the door. 'If you need me, call. For anything.'

'I will,' Diana promised him. They were both on the porch, and at the same time both of them remembered. Bill had no car. 'Do you want to come back in?' Diana asked. Bill glanced back at the front door, then shook his head.

'It's a nice night, and I can use the walk,' he said. He gave Diana a quick kiss, then hurried down the steps and started along the driveway towards the road. Diana watched him go, then turned back to the house to face her mother.

Edna wasted no time in coming to the point.

'You will not adopt that child, Diana,' she said.

'I'll do what I have to do, Mother,' Diana replied, her tone as cold as Edna's.

Edna stood up, so her eyes were level with her daughter's. 'Are you defying me, Diana?' she asked.

Diana met the old woman's gaze steadily. 'Yes,' she said at last. 'For once I'm defying you.' Then she turned and walked from the room. Edna stood rigidly in front of the fire as Diana went to the living room, woke Christie up, then led her upstairs. A few minutes later when the old woman, her bones weary with age, climbed the stairs herself, Diana's door was closed.

Edna paused for a moment and considered knocking on her daughter's door. Then she changed her mind and went on to her own room.

As she carefully lowered herself into bed she thought of the nursery upstairs.

The nursery that had been empty so long.

She had made a mistake. It should have stayed empty.

4

It was almost eleven when Jeff Crowley slipped out of bed, pulled on his clothes, and opened the window of his room. He scrambled over the sill, suspended himself from the ledge for a second, then dropped to the ground. He waited, listening, then crept around to the side of the house, got his bicycle, and, pedalling as hard as he could, rode the halfmile out to Shacktown. Steve Penrose and Eddie Whitefawn were waiting for him.

'Where you been?' Steve asked him. Steve was a year older than Jeff, and it had been his idea to wait until their parents had gone to bed before sneaking out to the mine. That way, Steve explained, they weren't so likely to get caught. Now, not waiting for Jeff to answer his question, Steve mounted his bike, with Eddie riding double, and the three of them started out of town.

As they passed the Ambers' they looked up at the house and saw that one light was still glowing on the second floor.

'I bet it's Miss Edna,' Steve whispered in the darkness. 'Someone told me she never goes to sleep.'

They went on by, neither of the other boys questioning Steve's words, pedalling hard as they climbed the grade that led towards the mine.

'We better leave our bikes here,' Steve told them. The three boys dismounted and pushed the bicycles under a patch of scrub juniper, then began walking up the road. Soon they were at the foot of the mine tailings, and they left the road to scramble up the slag heap.

As they climbed, the wind began to blow.

Suddenly Jeff stopped.

'Do you hear something?' he asked. The other two boys listened intently. From above them a sound was barely audible, like faraway voices muttering softly.

'It's the water babies,' Eddie Whitefawn whispered. 'Let's get out of here.' He started to turn around but a movement at the foot of the tailings stopped him. 'There's something down there.' He pointed and Jeff and Steve peered into the darkness.

Below them, silhouetted in the moonlight, a shape was moving up the slag heap towards them.

Jeff's heart began to pound and he suddenly wished he'd stayed home. With the other two boys he shrank to the ground. 'What'll we do?' he asked, his voice quavering.

'Stay still,' Steve whispered. Though he was as frightened as the other two, he was determined not to show it.

The wind picked up, and the strange noises grew louder.

'They're coming,' Eddie whimpered. 'I want to go home.'

The dark shadow beneath them, coming steadily closer, advanced through the blackness.

'Let's run for it,' Steve said.

'Run where?'

Steve pointed off to the left. 'That way. Back to the road, then down to our bikes.'

They huddled together, wishing there was something else to do. But as the wind blew ever stronger the moaning noises seemed louder and the shadow, still moving towards them, seemed to grow.

'Let's go!' Steve yelled. The three of them bolted slipping and skidding across the loose rubble that made up the slag heap. The wind snatched at them, and down the slope they could see the shape veering off, moving parallel to them. Then they were on the road and pounding down the hill. They dashed by the hulking object just as it, too, reached the road.

An arm reached out, and a hand closed around Jeff Crowley's arm.

He squealed in fright and tried to wriggle loose, but couldn't. Then he heard a voice, close to his ear.

"You guys playing?"

Jeff stopped struggling and yelled to Steve and Eddie, who had paused a few yards down the road, unsure what to do.

'It's Juan,' Jeff called. 'It's only old Juan.'

Sheepishly Eddie and Steve came back up the road and stood staring at Juan Rodriguez. His face, smiling happily in the moonlight, beamed at them. 'You guys playing?' he repeated.

The three boys looked at each other, and it was finally Steve who spoke. 'We came out to look for the water babies,' he said. Juan nodded, though his expression didn't change. 'Now, you listen, Juan,' Steve went on. 'Don't you tell anyone you saw us, you understand?' Again Juan nodded, and Steve, followed by Jeff and Eddie, began backing away. 'Now, don't forget,' Steve said. 'Don't tell anybody!' He glanced at his friends, then back to Juan Rodriguez. 'If you do, we'll come back and kill you!' Then he turned and once more began running down the road, his friends at his heels.

As he watched them go Juan Rodriguez's smile faded from his face. He hated it when the other children teased him.

Hated it a lot.

Unhappily he turned and started back towards the cabin, listening to the voices of the children as he walked. Not the voices of the children he had just talked to, but the other children, the children his mother told him about.

The dead children. It was the sound of their voices that had lured him into the night while his mother slept.

The dead children, it seemed to Juan, liked him better than the live ones. The dead ones talked to him and never ran away from hm.

Sometimes he wished all the children were dead.

Diana Amber awoke and glanced at the clock by her

bedside. It was three in the morning, and she lay still for a moment, listening to the wind.

It had come up sometime while she slept, and now it moaned in the night air, its dry, tingling heat stifling her. Close by, Diana felt Christie Lyons stir in her sleep then roll over.

She slipped an arm around the child and drew her closer, cradling the child's head against her breast. She drew comfort from the presence of the little girl Christie's body, in contact with her own, somehow made her feel complete.

She closed her eyes and tried to go back to sleep, but the wind forbade it. And in the back of her mind, something was nagging at her.

Her mother.

Her mother wouldn't approve of Christie's sleeping with her. She had promised Edna that even tonight Christie would be in the nursery. She had made up the bed in the nursery that afternoon, but when she had led the sleepy child upstairs, she hadn't been able to leave her alone.

Not on her first night in the house.

Instead she had brought her to her own room and slipped the little girl into her own bed. But what if her mother awoke in the night, and began prowling through the house? Reluctantly Diana got out of bed, slipped into a robe, then leaned down to pick up the sleeping child.

As she was lifted from the bed Christie's arms curled instinctively around Diana's neck, and she murmured something into Diana's ear.

Mama? Had she called her *Mama*?

'I'm here, sweetheart,' Diana whispered. 'Mama's here.' She left her bedroom and silently moved down the hall to the back stairs, then up to the third floor. In the nursery, the bed, already turned back, lay bathed in moonlight, but to Diana it looked far too large for Christie. She hesitated, then carried Christie across the room and lowered her into the crib. Christie, only vaguely aware of what was happening, curled herself up within the confines of the small space. Then Diana went to the bed, stripped the top sheet from it, and tucked it around Christie's small form. She studied Christie's face for a time, envying the peace she saw in it, then left the nursery, quietly locking the door behind her.

In her own room Diana's bed suddenly seemed enormous to her, and lonely. She thought of Christie, sleeping alone on the floor above.

What if she woke up?

Wouldn't it be terrifying for her? But as the wind rattled the old house, Diana remembered when she had been a child, and how much she'd loved the nursery. Though its pink and white cheeriness had never brought her peace, she had liked the fact that it was high up, away from the rest of the house. Sometimes she had felt almost safe, tucked snugly up under the eaves.

But there had been other times, too.

She put the memories out of her head, turned over, and buried her face in her pillow.

She couldn't remember. She *wouldn't* remember. It was all so long ago, and the memories were dim, and she would leave them where they were, undisturbed, forgotten.

Except, she knew, they weren't really forgotten. Just put away to be taken out some other time. But not now.

In her own room Edna Amber also lay awake, listening to the wind and the creaking of the stairs. Diana, she knew, was trying to deceive her, but it wouldn't work.

Diana had always tried to deceive her, ever since she was a baby, but it had never worked. Tonight was no different from any other night.

An hour ago, unable to sleep, she'd gotten up and gone to the nursery. It had been empty, and she'd known immediately that Diana had taken the child to her own room. She'd crept to Diana's door and listened. Even through the heavy oak she'd been able to hear them breathing, Diana's breath rasping, that of the child smooth and even. As she'd listened, her heart had pounded, and fury had raged through her veins.

The child was going to take Diana away from her.

Already it was happening.

Diana, her Diana, was already pretending that the child was her own.

For tonight she had decided to do nothing about it.

But tomorrow she would think, and soon she would know what to do. Diana, of course, would have to be punished. All her life Diana had needed punishment. But what about the child?

Christie's aching body woke her the next morning. She tried to stretch, but the confines of the crib wouldn't allow it. Her eyes opened and for a moment she wasn't sure where she was.

Above her paint was flaking from the ceiling, and the sky was obscured by the dirt on the window a few inches from her face. She moved stiffly, sitting up.

What was she doing in a crib?

And where was she?

This wasn't her room. Her room was brightly painted and yellow and blue, and it was decorated with her collection of Pooh animals.

Slowly it all came back to her.

Yesterday.

Her father had died yesterday.

She was at the Ambers', in the nursery. She remembered it only dimly from the day before, and now, in the bright light of morning, she stared at its peeling paper and rotting curtains, the dust balls drifting across the floor. In the corner she thought something moved, but when she looked again there was nothing there – only a scurrying sound that seemed to come from inside the wall.

She looked around the room for a clock.

There was none.

She climbed out of the crib and went to the door.

It was locked.

Fear gripped her, and she started to call for her father, but then she remembered that her father couldn't come to her. Not now, not ever again. She began to cry, then sank down onto the bed just inside the door and let herself go. She sobbed loudly, her small body shaking, but still no one came. Finally, shivering in the chill of the morning, she pulled a blanket around herself and, curling up once more, lay still.

Her sobbing slowly subsided, and her body began to relax. She wanted to go back to sleep, but she knew she couldn't.

She got out of bed and went to the window. Up the hill, and off in the distance, she could see the mine. She looked down. Beyond the window ledge the roof sloped away, dropping off abruptly to the peak overhanging the kitchen. For some reason she thought that was sort of exciting. If she needed to, she could get out. Her fear began to abate, and she looked around the room more carefully. It looked like a baby's room. There was a cradle, and the crib, and some stuffed animals, and one of those things you used to change a baby. What did they call it? She couldn't think of the word.

Once more she rattled the door and tried to think why it would be locked. She listened carefully, hoping to hear Miss Diana moving around downstairs, but all was silent. She wished she could go down, but then decided it was just as well that she couldn't. If Diana – she remembered vaguely that she was supposed to call her Aunt Diana now – wasn't up yet, she might run into Miss Edna.

She didn't like Miss Edna, and even though Miss Edna had barely spoken to her, she knew that Miss Edna seemed to be mad at her, but Christie couldn't figure out why.

She sat down on the bed again and tried to decide what to do. The best thing, she guessed, was just to wait quietly and hope Aunt Diana came soon. She lay down again and tried to go back to sleep, but sleep wouldn't come. A terrible loneliness came over her and, once more, she began to cry.

She was still crying when Diana came into the room an hour later.

Diana touched the key gingerly. Who had locked the door? Her mother? Had Edna come upstairs during the night and locked Christie in, as she had locked Diana in so many years ago? Diana's flesh crawled as she remembered those nights when she had lain awake, terrified by the locked door but never daring to let herself cry.

She opened the door. Christie was sitting on the bed, looking at her fearfully, tears streaming down her face. The sight of the tears touched a nerve in Diana, and she was suddenly angry.

'What's wrong?' she demanded. 'Why aren't you in the crib? And why are you crying? Good little girls don't cry.'

Christie shrank away from her, and Diana suddenly reached down and grabbed her arm.

'Good girls don't cry!' she said once more. She whirled Christie around and swatted her across the buttocks. Christie, shocked and terrified, shrieked and tried to wriggle free, but Diana held her firmly by the arm. Then she sat down on the bed and stood Christie in front of her.

'Now listen to me,' she said. 'I know you're frightened, and I know you're upset. But you have to be a brave little girl and make me proud of you. And I can't be proud of a little girl who cries, can I?'

Christie numbly shook her head.

'Then you won't cry anymore, will you?'

Christie shook her head no.

Finally Diana smiled at her and kissed her gently on the cheek. 'Now, I want you to get back in your crib and wait there till I come for you. All right?'

Still too shocked by what had happened to do more than nod her head, Christie crossed the room and climbed back into the crib.

'Maybe you'd better stay there all day,' Diana said.

'But I'm not sick,' Christie protested.

'Of course not, baby,' Diana told her, her voice

reasonable but her tone relentless. 'But you're terribly tired. Let Mama take care of you today, and you'll be better tomorrow. All right?'

Christie frowned. If she wasn't sick, why did she have to stay in bed? And what was going on? Her real mother had never treated her like this. Or had she? Christie couldn't remember. It was all very confusing and frightening, and suddenly Christie didn't want to get up after all. All she wanted to do was go back to sleep . . .

Jeff Crowley woke up that morning with a sense of excitement. He was remembering the night before, when he and Eddie and Steve had gone up to the mine. He knew they shouldn't have. If his parents found out, his father might whip him. Or at least give him a long lecture – he couldn't remember the last time his father had actually hit him. Sometimes, in fact, he wished his father *would* hit him. Then at least he wouldn't have to feel so lousy about being a disappointment to him. He could just take his punishment and forget about it, like Steve Penrose did. The lectures, he decided, were worse. Still, maybe his parents hadn't discovered what he'd been up to last night.

Maybe Juan Rodriguez would believe Steve's threat. Of course, they wouldn't really kill him, but if he thought they would, maybe he wouldn't tell.

He got out of bed, pulled on his jeans and a T-shirt, and went into the kitchen. While he was eating his cereal Steve Penrose appeared at the back door.

Steve stood on the back steps, his hands shoved in his pockets, looking uncomfortable. For a moment Jeff was sure that something had gone wrong. He glanced over his shoulder nervously, waiting for his mother to move out of earshot.

'Did your mom find out what we did last night?' he asked when he was sure he wouldn't be overheard.

'Naw,' Steve replied. 'Juan won't tell. I scared him too good. I just gotta do somethin' this morning. You want to help?'

'What is it?' Jeff asked warily.

'My mom talked to Kim's mom and Mrs. Gillespie, and they say Kim and me and Susan have to go out to the Ambers'.'

'What for?'

'We're supposed to pick some flowers and take them to Christie Lyons. 'Cause her dad died. You wanna go?'

Jeff turned the matter over in his mind. He knew that when someone died, you were supposed to take flowers to their family, but he thought that was only at the funeral. Maybe when a kid's parents died, it was different.

'Okay,' he agreed. 'Let me tell my mom.' He disappeared into the house and reappeared a couple of minutes later, carrying a pair of tennis shoes. He sat down on the back steps and put them on. 'I don't see why I have to wear shoes,' he complained. 'Mom's always afraid I'll step on a snake or something.'

'I know,' Steve agreed. 'My mom's the same way.'

Janet Jennings, who had been known as Jay-Jay since the day she was born, was waiting with Kim Sandler and Susan Gillespie when the two boys met them in front of the drugstore, and Jeff groaned to himself. He didn't like Jay-Jay, mostly because she had a habit of always getting him into trouble, then blaming it on someone else. Besides, Jay-Jay was fat, and Jeff always thought she looked dirty.

'Why don't we just buy some flowers?' Jay-Jay suggested. 'Then we won't have to spend all day hunting for them.'

Kim, who didn't like Jay-Jay any better than Jeff did, shot her a scornful look. 'It won't take all day. The Ambers' field is full of them. All we have to do is pick them.'

The five children started out of town, Jeff and Steve kicking at rocks and cans, while the girls chattered among themselves.

'How come she's staying at the Ambers'?' Susan asked of nobody in particular.

'Because her father worked for them,' Kim replied. 'Where else would she stay?'

'Well, if you ask me,' Jay-Jay offered, 'anyplace would be better than out there. My mother says Miss Edna's crazy as a loon.'

'Then why'd she let you come with us?' Steve taunted.

'Who said she knows I came?' Jay-Jay shot back. 'The only reason I'm coming is that I want to see what that old house looks like inside. Mom says nobody's been inside it for years.'

'Well, your mom's full of it,' Jeff put in. 'Dr. Henry and Marshal Gurley were there yesterday, and Christie's dad used to go out there all the time.'

'What do you suppose is going to happen to her?' Steve asked.

'They'll prob'ly make her go live with her uncle,' Kim suggested. 'That's what happened to Billy Simons.'

'Mom says she doesn't have any uncles,' Jeff said. 'Mom and Dad think they'll have to adopt her out.'

'I thought they only adopted babies out.'

Now it was Jay-Jay's turn to be scornful. 'Anybody can be adopted out,' she told Kim. 'That is,' she added spitefully, 'if anybody wants them.'

They turned off the road and began picking columbine, daisies, and Queen Anne's lace, until each of them was holding a large bouquet. Then, cutting cross-country, they started towards the Amber house, looming in the distance.

'What if Miss Edna answers the door?' Susan, the shyest of the group, asked.

'She won't,' Jeff assured her. 'Dad says she never does anything but sit in the parlour and boss Miss Diana around. Anyway, she's just an old lady.'

'Well, she scares me,' Susan admitted. 'She always looks like she's mad about something, and the way she looks at you is weird. Like she wishes you were dead, or something.'

'Maybe she does,' Steve teased. 'Maybe she's just waiting

to catch you by yourself, then –' He sliced his finger across his neck and hung his tongue out. Susan glared at him.

'That's not funny, Steve Penrose,' she said, then retreated into silence as her friends all laughed.

Edna Amber stood at the parlour window, holding the lace curtains back so she could watch the children's progress across the field. They seemed to be coming towards the house. She called out to Diana, reaching up with her cane to punctuate her words by thumping the ceiling.

'Diana? Diana, I want you!' She waited a moment, and when she failed to hear Diana's footsteps hurrying along the upstairs corridor, thumped again. *'Diana!'*

A moment later Diana appeared at the door. 'I was in the kitchen, Mother.'

Edna glanced at the clock standing in the corner. 'It won't be lunchtime for at least an hour.'

'I was making some cookies for Christie,' Diana said hesitantly, sure of what was going to come with the admission. Her mother didn't disappoint her.

'I don't want you getting attached to that child,' Edna said. 'She won't be here but another day or so, and there's no sense you getting yourself all worked up.'

Diana sighed impatiently. 'Mother, it's only a batch of cookies. That's hardly what I'd call "getting myself worked up," whatever that means.'

Edna glared at her. 'Don't you sass your mother, young lady,' she snapped. Then she pointed towards the window with her cane. 'You'd better take care of *them,*' she said. 'I don't want them on the property.'

Diana went to the window and looked out. She recognised all five of the children coming through the gate. She knew Jeff Crowley best, though she had spoken to each of them at one time or another. But never before had any of them come to the house. She hurried to the door to meet them.

They stood close together on the porch, clutching their

58

bouquets. Jeff Crowley, his face serious, finally spoke.

'We came to see Christie, Miss Diana,' he explained.

Diana's hands, hidden in the pockets of her apron, clenched into fists, but she smiled at the children. 'Well isn't that nice,' she said.

'Is she here?' Kim asked. 'Can she come out?'

Diana's smile dissolved into a frown. 'She's upstairs, sleeping,' she explained. She hesitated, then spoke again. 'Perhaps you could come back another day. I'm afraid she's still terribly upset, and I don't think she wants to see anyone.'

The children glanced at one another and finally Steve Penrose offered Diana his bouquet. 'Would you give her these?' One by one the other children surrendered their flowers. Then there was an uncomfortable silence.

'I'll take them to her as soon as she wakes up,' Diana said at last. She smiled at the children once more, then quickly retreated inside the house. She leaned against the closed door for a moment, her heart pounding. Why had they come? They hadn't been invited. Did they really only want to visit Christie? Or was it something else? Maybe they had come to spy on her. She tried to dismiss the thought.

I'm just not used to children, she told herself as she went back into the kitchen, her arms full of the flowers the children had brought. She stood at the sink, her nose buried in the fragrant blossoms, then began hunting for a vase. But as she remembered that the flowers had been brought to Christie, she suddenly changed her mind. She slammed the cupboard shut and returned to the back porch. Her face set in bitterness, she dropped the flowers in the trash. Perhaps the children wouldn't come back again.

From her window on the third floor Christie watched her friends retreating into the distance.

She was sure they had come to visit her, but if they had, wouldn't Aunt Diana have called her? She decided she must have been wrong: they must have been bringing the flowers to Diana and Miss Edna.

But it was *her* father who had died. Why should the flowers have been brought to someone else? She sat on the bed and wondered what to do. Finally, in spite of what Diana had told her, she decided to go downstairs and find out what had happened.

She dressed quickly in the same jeans and shirt she had been wearing the day before. It occurred to her that maybe this afternoon Diana could take her home to get some of her clothes.

When she was dressed, she went down the back stairs and slipped into the kitchen. Working at the counter, stirring a bowl of batter, she found Diana.

'Aunt Diana?'

Startled, Diana whirled around and stared at Christie. 'I thought you were staying in your room.'

'I saw some kids,' Christie explained. 'Jeff, and some others. I – I thought maybe they were coming to see me.'

Again Diana felt her heart begin to race, but as she faced Christie she was careful not to let her nervousness show. 'Why would they want to do that?' she asked.

'They're my friends,' Christie said. 'Didn't they come to see me?'

Diana shook her head. 'They were picking flowers in our field, and they came to ask if it was all right.'

'But I saw them leaving, and they didn't have the flowers anymore,' Christie protested. 'Didn't they leave them?'

'Yes,' Diana replied. 'But I threw them away. Miss Edna's allergic to flowers.'

Christie stood still, trying to make sense of it all, but like so much that had happened since yesterday, it didn't make any sense.

Slowly she climbed back up to the third floor and went into the nursery.

She spent the rest of the day sleeping fitfully and wishing her father would come and get her.

But she was beginning to realise that no one was going to come for her ever again.

She was all alone in the world.

5

On the day of the funeral for Elliot Lyons, nearly the whole town turned out, gathering together on the small plot of land neatly enclosed by a black wrought-iron fence, where the dead of Amberton waited patiently for their resurrection.

It was a bright, clear morning that promised warmth in the afternoon, and the valley, spreading away from the village, was still a vivid green with not a hint yet of the dusty brown that would prevail as the summer wore on. Above Amberton the sky formed an immense dome that seemed to dwarf the village. It was the sort of day that made the citizens of Amberton glad to be alive, yet at the same time managed to remind them of their own mortality.

Now, as she stood in the shade of the willows that huddled over the graveyard like silent mourners, Diana Amber was glad she had not followed her impulse to leave her coat at home. But it was more than the morning air that was giving her a chill. She had never liked funerals, and it seemed to her that she had been to so many. Since she was a child her mother had insisted that it was the duty of the Ambers to attend every funeral, whether or not they had been close to those who had died. Though Edna insisted that the purpose was only to pay their respects to the dead, Diana had always silently suspected that it was also Edna's intent to display the flag – the Amber flag – lest anyone suggest that the Ambers had stayed away out of a sense of shame over the number of deaths their own wealth had cost.

Though the mine had been closed for nearly half a century, Edna had continued her tradition of never missing a funeral, and there were those in Amberton who joked among themselves that the only proof of Edna Amber's eventual death would be her failure to be among those present at her own funeral. Today was no exception. She stood next to her daughter, one hand grasping Diana's arm, while the other held the head of her ever-present cane. On the other side of Diana, Christie Lyons stood, her eyes fixed on the coffin resting on planks above the open grave.

Christie's face was placid, belying the turmoil that was inside her. More than anything right now, she wished she were in the coffin with her father, going wherever it was that he had gone. But that would mean she would be dead, and sad though she was, she wasn't quite sure she wanted to be dead. What she wanted, she guessed, was for her father not to be dead either. She wished she could close her eyes, pray very, very hard, and then open her eyes and see her father standing there, telling her that he wasn't dead after all and that everything was going to be all right. But that, she knew, wasn't going to happen. Still, maybe if she prayed hard enough ...

Unconsciously she squeezed Diana's hand, and when Diana drew her closer, Christie didn't resist. She never knew what to expect from Diana. Most of the time Diana seemed to love her, but sometimes, for reasons Christie could never quite understand, Diana seemed to be angry at her. She was starting to get used to it though, and had decided that once she learned what she was supposed to do, things would be all right. So far, today, they had been all right.

She pulled her eyes away from her father's coffin and looked at the crowd that was gathering in the cemetery. Most of them were strangers to her, but she waved shyly to her few friends.

Crowded close together were Jeff Crowley, Kim Sandler, Steve Penrose, and Jay-Jay Jennings. As Christie waved they smiled hesitantly at her and whispered among themselves.

The funeral began, and as Reverend Jennings talked about her father, Christie began to cry. It was, at last, real. Both her parents were gone now, and she would never see them again.

Diana Amber tried to listen to the minister's words, but as Jennings droned on in his steady monotone, her mind began to wander. Her eyes drifted to Bill Henry, standing with Dan Gurley, and for a moment their glances met. There was a warmth in Bill's eyes that told Diana that even after all the years that had passed since their long-ago courtship, he still cared for her; it wasn't the love she had once seen in his eyes, but something else – something that made her vaguely angry. She felt robbed of something, and she wanted it back. If it hadn't been for her illness, she would have married Bill, despite her mother. But now it was too late.

She thought about that for a while, trying to remember what had been wrong with her. It was gone; the memory of that illness locked away with the other memories. Sometimes, when the wind blew, she would feel the fringes of the memories, like faraway voices calling to her, but they never seemed to come close enough for her to really grasp them.

Her thoughts were interrupted by the tightening of her mother's grip on her arm, and as she shifted her attention from Bill to the woman beside her, Diana realised that it was as if Edna had known what she was thinking. Edna's blue eyes blazed, and her face was drawn into an admonitory scowl, but as soon as she had Diana's attention her expression cleared and her grip eased. Then both women were again listening to the words of Jerome Jennings as he eulogised the life of a man he had barely known.

Across from the Ambers, Dan Gurley nudged Bill Henry and spoke just loudly enough so only the doctor could hear.

'Still runs the whole show, doesn't she?'

Bill nodded, feeling oddly embarrassed by the know-ledge that the marshal had witnessed what had just

63

happened. Diana had lived her life submitting to her mother's domination, and it was no secret. Still, Bill wished she would find the strength to break away from her mother. Perhaps, he reflected, the child would do it. People would do practically anything for a child they cared about. And Diana certainly seemed to care about Christie.

'I'll bet Miss Edna's going to love having the reception this afternoon,' he heard Dan saying. 'The whole town tramping through her house? Huh!'

'What makes you think it's going to be in the house?' Bill whispered. Then, as Dan Gurley's expression shifted from amusement to puzzlement, Bill began edging his way through the crowd, intent on being at Diana's side when Reverend Jennings eventually came to the final prayer.

As the people of Amberton moved slowly past them, offering a few murmured words of sympathy to Christie and uncertain smiles to the Amber women, Diana again began to drift. A sound was coming to her, as though from within her mind. It was a sound she had lived with for many years now, though it usually came to her at night when the wind was blowing.

But today was bright and clear, and the wind was still. And yet the sound was there.

A baby, crying out for its mother.

Instinctively Diana knelt next to Christie and took the child in her arms.

'It's all right, baby,' she whispered. 'Everything's going to be all right.'

Christie, who had been standing silently through the service, looked into Diana's eyes, perplexed. It almost seemed as if the woman were talking to someone else.

'I'm all right, Aunt Diana,' she whispered.

'But you were crying,' Diana whispered back.

Christie shuddered, remembering what had happened when Diana had found her crying in the nursery. She had been careful not to cry since that morning. 'No, I wasn't,'she insisted, stiffening in Diana's arms.

'But you were,' Diana insisted. 'I heard you.'

And then, with her father's body being lowered into the ground, Christie did let herself cry. This time Diana only soothed her.

A few feet away, Bill Henry stood watching Diana comfort the child. Her love for Christie was apparent, and Bill wondered if perhaps her adopting the little girl might not be the best thing that could happen, not only for Diana, but for Christie, too.

Then his eyes locked on Miss Edna.

There she stood, both hands on her cane now, her face a study in anger as she watched her daughter hold the crying child. Whatever was to happen, Bill decided, was not going to be easy. Not for Diana, and not for Christie, either.

'It seems to me,' Edna said as Diana carefully manoeuvred their ancient Cadillac out of the cemetery, 'that if they want to have a reception, they should have it at the Crowleys'.'

Diana glanced across Christie to her mother, but Edna was staring straight ahead.

'We'll talk about it when we get home, Mother,' she replied.

'There really isn't any point in talking about it at all, is there? I mean, it's done, and everyone in town is going to be there, and no one really cares what I want, do they?' Edna began tapping the end of her cane against the floorboards of the car.

Instead of saying anything Diana merely gunned the engine, and the Cadillac lumbered forward, its transmission grinding at the strain.

'You're going to ruin a perfectly good car if you're not careful,' Edna snapped. The Cadillac, a 1934 touring car, was one of the few things Edna was willing to spend money to maintain, and it looked brand-new, its green paint shining in the sunlight, its top folded down, its fender-mounted spare tyres standing proudly on either side of its long hood. For Diana, though, the car – its upkeep, and her driving of it – was only one more source of criticism, and she wished she could convince her mother to trade it in for something more practical. It was, however, one more thing she knew she would never accomplish.

Let me get home, and let me get Christie out of the car and let people start arriving before I go crazy, Diana prayed. I won't respond. No matter what she says, I won't respond. And then everybody will be there, and for a while I'll have other people to talk to, and afterwards it will be over, and she can start on something else.

And what she'd start on would be Christie, Diana knew. For three days her mother had been insisting that it was wrong for them to have Christie in the house; that sooner or later Diana was going to have to face reality, and reality was that the child was going to become a ward of the state. Thus far she had not weakened in her opposition to Diana's wish to adopt the child. Over the years Edna had made it all too clear that she had no use for children, that she had done her duty in raising Diana, and that all she wanted in life was to be left alone with Diana to grow old in peace. But Diana still clung to the idea that somehow she would be allowed to keep Christie, to raise her as her own. To have Christie belong to her as she, Diana, had belonged to her mother.

Diana paused to let Edna out of the car, then drove around into the garage. Christie helped her pull the rickety sliding door closed, then followed her through the back door into the kitchen.

'Why doesn't Miss Edna want people to come out here?' Christie asked as Diana began helping Esperanza Rodriguez, who had been working in the kitchen all morning, pull a series of dishes out of the refrigerator. As she waited for an answer Christie stole a spoonful of potato salad and ate a devilled egg.

'Oh, she's just tired,' Diana replied. How could she explain her mother's attitudes to a nine-year-old? Should she say that her mother was a snob who thought she was better than anyone else, or should she try to explain that

Edna was just getting old? But Edna wasn't 'just getting old' – she'd *never* wanted anyone in the house, not, at least, anyone from Amberton. Even today she'd drawn the lines clearly. If Diana insisted on having a lunch here, Edna would allow it, but it would have to be outdoors. Even for a funeral Edna would not have her home invaded by the townspeople.

'She doesn't like me, does she?' Christie asked.

Diana stopped what she was doing and looked at Christie, who was staring up at her, her pale blue eyes large and frightened.

'It's not that she doesn't like you,' Diana said carefully, searching for the right words and wishing she knew more about how to talk to a child. 'It's just that she's not used to you. It's been a long time since I was a little girl, and she's forgotten what little girls are like.'

Christie shook her head. 'She scares me,' she said. 'She doesn't like me, and she scares me.'

Diana sat down at the table and pulled Christie onto her lap, while Esperanza, who was quietly listening to their conversation, kept working. 'How does she scare you?' she asked.

'I – I'm not sure,' Christie stammered. 'I guess it's the way she looks at me.'

'How does she look at you?' Diana pressed.

Christie thought for a moment. When she spoke, her voice was barely a whisper. 'Like she wishes I was dead.'

Diana's breath caught, and in the depths of her mind she again heard the haunting sound of a crying child. Out of the corner of her eye she saw Esperanza crossing herself.

'No!' she said sharply. 'She doesn't wish you were dead. She doesn't wish that at all. I know it!' She lifted Christie off her lap and stood up, as if trying to shake off the sudden fear the child's words had caused her. She glanced around the room, searching for something to do, something that would make her forget Christie's words. She could feel Esperanza's eyes on her, and that only made her even more nervous.

Suddenly there was a knock at the back door, and Diana turned in confusion, her fear of a moment ago turning into an odd sort of panic for which she knew there was no reason. Her hands went to her hair, smoothing it. I'm all right, she told herself. I've got to be all right.

'Come in,' she called. The door opened, and Joyce Crowley appeared, her arms filled with a cake box and a large brown bag.

'Hi! I thought you might need some help, and I brought along a few things, just in case.' She stepped inside, let the door slam shut behind her, and, never having been in the Amber house before, looked curiously around the big kitchen, with its enormous range, three ovens, and walk-in refrigerator. 'God, I wish I had something like this in my house.' She set her packages on the table, then faced Diana. Her cheerful grin faded and was replaced by a frown. 'Are you all right?' she asked. 'You look like you just saw a ghost.'

'I'm fine,' Diana said. 'Tired, I guess.'

Joyce nodded. 'That's why I'm here – I figured you could use some help. Where do you want all this stuff?'

'Outside,' Diana told her. As Joyce's frown deepened she felt compelled to make some explanation. 'It's such a pretty day, and mother thought –'

''Nuff said,' Joyce cut in, winking at Diana. 'Whatever Lola wants, as the old song says. Right?'

For the first time in three days the tension in Diana broke. Though they had known each other for years, they had never been friends, but suddenly she felt close to Joyce. 'I wish it could be different,' she said softly. 'I really do. But I guess you know how it is.'

'The whole town knows, Diana,' Joyce replied, her voice gentle. 'So we'll have the reception outside. Who knows? It could start a whole new tradition!' She turned to Christie, who was standing unobtrusively against the sink, and smiled.

'Would you like to help us out?'

Christie nodded automatically, though she was still

68

thinking about Miss Edna. There had been something in Diana's voice – she wasn't sure what – that had made her even more frightened of the old woman. But, try as she would, she couldn't think of what she might have done that would make Miss Edna hate her. Half-heartedly she began carrying out Joyce Crowley's instructions.

With Christie helping, the women began taking the plates of food out to the backyard, where a picnic table had stood for years, unused until today. And then the people came, and as Diana listened to them offer Christie their condolences, she began to wish that they had stayed away, that they had left her alone with the little girl she was already thinking of as her own. But she hid her feelings and made herself smile at each of them.

Esperanza Rodriguez moved adroitly through the crowd, listening to the *gringos* chatter among themselves, doing her best to clean up the mess as fast as the whites could make it. She spoke to no one, only nodding and smiling when she was occasionally spoken to. She knew what they were talking about – Señor Lyons, and how he had died. But none of them knew the truth, and even if they had asked her, Esperanza wouldn't have told them, for they would only have laughed at her again.

In the clump of aspens that flourished behind the Amber house, the children were sitting together, and Esperanza drifted over to listen to them. Children, she had decided years ago, had a lot more sense than their elders. they listened to the old stories and understood that things were not always as they seemed. One day, perhaps, she would tell them the story of the lost children, and then they would understand why they must not play near the mine.

But today was not the day, and Esperanza merely listened to the children talk.

'There's no such thing as water babies,' Jay-Jay

Jennings was saying. 'My father says that's just a legend the dirty Indians talk about.'

'They're no dirtier than you,' Steve Penrose told her. 'And they're sure not as fat!'

Jay-Jay leaped to her feet, her face red and her fists clenched. 'You take that back, Steve Penrose!'

'Make me,' Steve said, grinning up at her. Jay-Jay glared at him for a moment, then burst into tears and ran off to find her mother. 'She sure is a crybaby,' Steve commented when Jay-Jay was gone.

Kim Sandler shrugged. 'Who cares? I can't stand her.' Then she looked eagerly at Jeff. 'Did you really hear them?' she asked.

'Well, we heard *something*,' Jeff said slowly. For the fourth time he tried to describe the strange sounds he and Steve had heard a few nights before, but as Christie approached he fell silent.

'Hi,' Christie said. Her friends looked at each other nervously, and she wondered if they'd been talking about her. Then Kim smiled at her.

'Are you going to live here now?' she asked.

'I don't know,' Christie said uncertainly. She sat down and picked a blade of grass. 'I guess so.' Then: 'I wish I didn't have to, though.'

'Why not?' Susan Gillespie asked, her head cocked in a way that was habitual with her, as if she were never quite sure of what she was hearing. 'Don't you like it here?'

Christie wasn't quite sure what to say. Though she was frightened a lot, she didn't want to sound ungrateful towards Diana. Then she remembered the things she'd heard about Miss Edna before she had gone to live with the Ambers. 'Miss Edna scares me,' she finally admitted. 'It seems like she's mad all the time.'

'She's just cranky,' Jeff told her. 'Like Mrs Berkey.'

'Jay-Jay thinks she's crazy,' Susan put in.

'And I think Jay-Jay's crazy,' Steve said. 'Maybe we should sic the water babies on *her*.' All the children laughed except Christie, who looked puzzled.

'What are water babies?' she asked. The children, suddenly embarrassed, and wishing they hadn't talked about what might have happened to Christie's father, fell silent. Christie looked from one of them to the other.

'What are water babies?' she asked again, but before anyone could answer her, Esperanza Rodriguez stepped into their midst, leaned down, and took Christie's hand. Pulling the little girl to her feet, she looked severely at the other children.

'The babies are something children should not even talk about,' she said severely. Then she led Christie away. The rest of the children, left alone, stared at each other nervously. For the first time it occurred to each of them that maybe – just maybe – the water babies might be real.

Bill Henry was the last to leave, and when he offered to help Diana clean up, she told him it wasn't necessary.

'Because of Edna?' he asked.

Diana nodded. 'It was a nice day, and I'm glad everyone was here, but I'm sure you noticed Mother wasn't what you could call the life of the party.' She paused, remembering how Edna had sat silently in the shade of the willow, nodding curtly to anyone who spoke to her but making no effort to make the townspeople feel welcome. Instead her blue eyes had gazed stonily into the distance, and she seemed to be off somewhere in her own mind, as though she had shut out what was happening around her.

Diana shook her head as if to dislodge the memory, and when she spoke, her voice was bitter. 'Wouldn't you think she could have at least said hello to everyone? Would it really have been so hard for her?'

'She'll never change. But she's going to have to talk to me, at least for a few minutes. Or, anyway, she's going to have to listen to me.'

Diana met his eyes, then turned away to look across the yard to the chicken coop, where Christie was crouched in the dirt, watching a batch of newborn chicks scratching for gravel.

71

'It's about her, isn't it?' Diana asked, her voice dull.

'Yes.'

Diana turned back to Bill. Her voice was filled with the new determination that he was not used to. 'I won't let her become a ward of the state.'

'A ward of the state?' Bill repeated, puzzled.

'Mother says that's what she is, unless she has some relatives, which she hasn't. Elliot told me. That's one of the reasons we were friendly, I think – neither of us had any family. Except I have Mother, of course.' Her glance flickered towards the house, to the second floor, where Bill could feel Edna standing behind a window, watching them.

'Maybe we'd better go in and have a chat with her.'

'Shouldn't Christie be there?'

Bill hesitated. 'I think you and your mother ought to decide what you want to do, first.'

Diana shrugged. 'Mother already knows what she wants done. She wants Christie sent away. And I think Christie knows it – she as much as said so.'

'It might not be that easy for her,' Bill said. 'Not if you've got guts.'

Diana looked at him, her eyes suddenly eager. 'Bill, what are you saying? What's happened?'

'In his will, Elliot named you guardian.'

Diana's eyes widened and she stepped back slightly, her heart racing. 'My God,' she breathed. Involuntarily she turned to gaze at Christie once again. When she spoke, her eyes remained riveted to the child and her voice was low. 'Are you sure? There's no mistake?'

'I'm sure. I've read the will – it all seems very clear, and very legal.'

'But he never said anything to me. Never even mentioned it. And he hardly knew me.'

'Maybe he was afraid you'd refuse,' Bill said gently. 'It's a big responsibility. And as for not knowing you, maybe Elliot knew you better than you think.'

At last Diana's eyes left the child, and she faced Bill

Henry once more. 'Did you say it would be a responsibility?' she asked. For the first time in years Bill saw her face truly light up. 'Bill, having Christie for my own is the biggest joy of my life.' She turned away from him and began walking resolutely towards the house.

Edna Amber was waiting for them in the parlour. As Diana came in, followed by Bill, she looked coldly from one to the other.

'I saw you look up at my window,' she said. 'I know you've been talking, and I presume it has something to do with me.'

'Not directly, Mother,' Diana said.

'But indirectly?'

Diana chewed at her lower lip for a moment, then instinctively turned to Bill for help.

'It has to do with Christie Lyons,' he told Edna. He saw the old woman stiffen. 'Diana has been appointed her guardian.'

'Appointed? Appointed by whom?'

'Her father,' Diana said, her voice taking on a maliciously triumphant tone. 'Bill just told me. In his will, Elliot asked that I be named Christie's guardian if anything happened to him.'

'That's ridiculous,' Edna snapped. 'Why would he do that?'

Diana sagged into a chair like a punctured balloon. 'I – I guess he thought I was the best one to do it,' she said lamely.

'Well, he was wrong.' Edna stood up, went to her daughter, and placed her hand on Diana's shoulder, but when she spoke, it was to Bill Henry.

'Of course, you know the very idea is unthinkable.'

'To whom?' Bill asked, not bothering to conceal the anger he was feeling towards the old woman.

'To everyone,' Edna stated as if it should be obvious. 'Diana, with a child?' She snorted her contempt. 'Impossible!' Her hand fell away from Diana's shoulder and she went back to her couch, as if the matter were

73

closed. Silence hung over the room while Diana stared at her mother, her face reflecting the confusion of feelings that was churning inside her. But when she broke the silence, her voice was filled with renewed determination.

'I'm sorry, Mother, but I'm not going to refuse to do it.'

'Then I shall simply have to refuse for you.' Edna turned to Bill Henry. 'Diana cannot possibly accept the guardianship,' she said. 'I want you to notify the authorities and have them come and get Christie. Tomorrow would be best, I think.'

Bill glanced at Diana, who was now on her feet, her fists clenched, her face pale. Before she could speak, he went to her and put a gently restraining hand on her arm.

'I'm afraid it's not that simple, Miss Edna,' he said. 'The decision isn't yours to make. Lyons appointed Diana Christie's guardian, and unless she refuses, the courts will follow his instructions.'

'Against my wishes?' Edna's eyes glared dangerously.

Bill smiled, enjoying the old woman's discomfort. 'Unless you have a compelling reason why Diana shouldn't be made guardian, I don't think you have a say in the matter at all. It's up to Diana.'

'I see,' Edna said. 'Very well, Dr. Henry. You've told us what you had to tell us. Now, if you don't mind, I think we'd like to discuss this between ourselves.'

Diana stood up. Her voice, though shaking slightly, was still strong. 'There's nothing to discuss, Mother.' Then: 'Bill, will you come out with me while I tell Christie?'

'Wouldn't you rather do it yourself?'

Diana grinned at him crookedly. 'One thing Mother's right about – I don't know much about having a child. But I'll learn. For right now, though, I may need some help, and I could use your bedside manner. Okay?'

'Sure.' Suddenly he wanted to say something to Edna Amber, something to soften her defeat, but as he looked at her, he realised that if she were defeated, it didn't show in her face. For a second his eyes met those of the old woman, but he quickly broke away from her furious gaze. He followed Diana out of the room, pulling the door shut behind them. A moment later there was a crash as Edna Amber vented her rage on a crystal vase. As she heard the shatter of glass Diana's only reaction was a tightening in her jaws.

6

Edna Amber woke promptly at five o'clock in the morning, as she had every morning for fifty years. Ordinarily she would have propped herself up and spent the next hour reading, but this morning she left her bed immediately and laboriously climbed the stairs to the third floor.

She paused outside the nursery, listening, then unlocked the door and silently let herself into the room. On the daybed, Christie lay sleeping, her arms akimbo, her hair half hiding her face. Edna stood over the bed, looking down into the peaceful face. The past had come back to haunt her, and she was suddenly afraid.

It was hard for her to believe that this tiny child had the power to destroy her, yet she knew it was true. An impulse seized her, an impulse to lift her cane and smash it down into the sleeping face, to wipe away forever the soft blue eyes that reminded her so much of Diana when she had been the same age. But she wouldn't let herself do it. The child, after all, had done nothing. It was Diana who was to blame, Diana who was insisting that they bring the child into the little world that she had so carefully constructed for them. But in the end it was going to be the child who suffered. One way or another, she knew this child would leave her house.

Her lips tightening with determination, Edna turned away from the sleeping child and returned to her own room. An hour later, when Diana brought a pot of coffee up to her, Edna was propped up in her bed, a book open on her lap. She set the book aside and smiled at her daughter.

'I suppose I ought to apologise for the vase,' she said. Diana looked at her warily. 'Oh, don't worry – I'm not going to,' the old woman went on. 'I suppose I've forgotten how, if I ever knew. But I don't like fighting with you, Diana. I never have.'

'Then let's not fight,' Diana replied.

'You know as well as I,' Edna went on, as if Diana had not spoken, 'that I can't let that child stay here. Don't you?'

Diana suddenly felt tired. It was going to start again and go on all day. And the next day, and the next. How long? Until she gave in? But she had always given in to her mother. This time she wouldn't.

'You can't take her away from me, Mother. Elliot gave her to me, and she's mine.'

'If he'd known about you, he wouldn't have written that will. You know that.'

Diana felt panic rising in her. There was nothing wrong with her – nothing at all. Wouldn't her mother ever leave the past alone?

'That was years ago, Mother. It's done.'

'Nothing's ever done,' Edna replied. 'The past is all there is, Diana. No matter what you do, or what you pretend, the past is there. You can't ignore it.'

'*You* can't ignore it, you mean!' The words burst from her in a torrent. 'You won't let me forget, you won't let me live, you won't let me –'. She groped for the right words, then found them. Her voice, strident a moment before, was suddenly calm. 'You won't let me grow up, Mother. You want me to be your little girl, until the day you die. But that's the past, Mother – your precious past. I'm not a little girl anymore. I haven't been a little girl for forty years. I'm a woman, Mama, and there's nothing you can do about it. And now I'm going to be a mother, too. A mother – just like you.'

Diana's eyes, locked to her mother's, seemed to issue a challenge, then she turned and left the room. Edna, feeling suddenly drained, sagged back against the pillows.

77

In the kitchen, Diana began preparing breakfast for herself and Christie. This morning, when she had awakened, she had decided that today was the day her life was beginning again. The funeral was past. Christie was hers now. This morning, she would begin establishing a routine for the child and begin the long process of making Christie her own.

She began preparing breakfast for Christie, unconsciously duplicating the meals her own mother had fed her when she was a child. She set a single place for Christie at the table, and when the little girl appeared a few minutes later, there was a glass of orange juice sitting by itself in front of her chair. Christie stared at it mutely, then looked at Diana.

'Is that all there is?' she asked shyly.

'That's only the beginning,' Diana told her. 'But it's bad for you to mix your food when you eat it. Start with the orange juice, then you can have your eggs.'

Mystified, Christie drank the orange juice. At the bottom of the glass there was a shapeless, colourless mass of what seemed to be some kind of jelly. Christie stared at it in disgust.

'There's something in my glass,' she finally said.

'Vaseline,' Diana explained to her, smiling across the room. 'It's very good for you – it lubricates your stomach so you won't get indigestion.'

Christie felt her gorge rising as she realised she was expected to swallow the glutinous mass. She stared at it for a long time, wishing it would go away.

'Do I have to?'

Diana came to stand beside her. 'It's good for you,' she repeated. 'All the time I was growing up I had a tablespoon of Vaseline before every meal. It didn't hurt me, did it?'

Christie swallowed and reached into her glass with the spoon. 'My father never made me eat Vaseline,' she said.

'Maybe your father didn't love you as much as I do.'

Christie gazed up into Diana's face, but Diana was still

smiling at her. Yet there was something in the set of Diana's expression that told her it would be useless to argue. Shutting her eyes and taking a deep breath, Christie thrust the lump of Vaseline into her mouth.

It oozed between her teeth, a flavourless, shapeless bit of slime that she couldn't swallow no matter how hard she tried. Suddenly she began gagging and ran across the kitchen to throw up her orange juice into the sink.

When she returned to the table, Diana had another spoonful of the stuff waiting for her.

'Don't try to chew it,' Diana explained. 'Think of it as a pill.' Somehow Christie managed to swallow the second dose.

Diana began serving breakfast.

First the eggs, soft-boiled.

Then a piece of toast.

Finally a bowl of cereal.

After what seemed like an eternity, Christie got through the strange meal.

When she was finished, she washed the dishes as Diana watched her, and listened as Diana explained the daily chores that she would be responsible for.

Edna Amber watched from her window as Diana and Christie crossed the yard and let themselves into the chicken coop. The two of them, she reflected, looked for all the world like mother and daughter, much as she and Diana must have looked years ago. Except that Christie wasn't Diana's daughter. Edna turned away from the window and began to dress.

Half an hour later she took the car keys from their hook by the kitchen door and went to the garage. She tugged at the heavy sliding door and for a moment feared that it wasn't going to open. Then, with a protesting squeal, it began to move on its metal rollers. Edna pushed it wide, then manoeuvred herself into the old Cadillac. She stared at the dashboard, studying it. It had been years since she'd last driven the car, but she told herself it was like swimming: once you learned, you never forgot. She started the engine, pushed the gear shift into reverse, and slowly backed out into the driveway. Out of the corner of her eye she could see Diana, standing in the chicken yard, staring at her.

She ignored her daughter and kept the car steadily moving down the drive until Diana, blocked by the mass of the house, disappeared from her view. In front of the house, she turned the car around, then proceeded down the long driveway. For the first time in nearly twenty years Edna Amber was driving herself to town.

Ten minutes later she eased the car into the no-parking zone in front of the town hall, a narrow, two-storey clapboard building with a bell tower rising from its roof. The bell was still used to warn the town of fire and to call the volunteers to man the engine. She left the keys in the ignition and wondered exactly what she was going to say to Dan Gurley.

As Edna sat in the old Cadillac the marshal sat in his office, unsurprised that Edna Amber had come to town today. Indeed, when he had seen her drive up, he had smiled to himself, remembering his conversation with Bill Henry the night before. It was the little girl; Edna Amber, he was sure, wanted to talk to him about Christie Lyons.

He was on his feet waiting for her when the door to his office opened and she came in. He offered her his hand, but she ignored it. Instead she simply seated herself, and for a long moment stared at him.

'I find I need your advice, Daniel,' she began.

'Anything I can do, Miss Edna,' Gurley replied cordially, easing his large frame back into the chair behind his desk.

'It's not an easy thing,' Edna continued. 'It concerns Diana, and the little girl, Christine Lyons.'

Gurley raised his eyebrows. 'Is there a problem?'

'The problem, Daniel, is that I want Christie taken somewhere else.'

'I see.' Gurley swung his chair around and stared out

the window for a moment. Then, without turning back to face Edna, he spoke. 'Is it me you want to talk to, or a lawyer?'

'When it becomes necessary to talk to a lawyer, Daniel, I will,' the old woman said tartly. 'I came to you because I thought you could help me. I want to know how to have the child taken away from my daughter.'

Now Gurley swung around to face her again, his usually placid expression knotted into an angry frown. 'I thought Bill Henry already explained that to you: it's not up to you.'

'Dr. Henry told me that. What I need to know is under what circumstances it *would* be up to me. Can you tell me?'

Dan shrugged. 'I suppose if you wanted to try to prove that Diana wasn't competent to raise her, the courts might be inclined to set the will aside.'

'She's not competent,' Edna stated.

'Are you prepared to go to court to prove it?'

Edna sat silently for a long time, turning the question over in her mind. She had known he would ask it, but had put off deciding how she would answer. Now she could put it off no longer.

'I may be,' she said at last. 'I don't want to hurt my daughter, Daniel, but I feel I have to do what's right.'

Dan Gurley felt himself getting angry at the old woman. 'Right for whom? Diana? Christie Lyons? Yourself?'

Edna's eyes narrowed, and Dan could see her determination hardening. 'For all of us,' she said firmly. 'There are things you don't know, Daniel. Things nobody here knows. I hope they are things I can take to my grave with me. But if that child is allowed to stay in my house, I can't be responsible for what might happen.'

Gurley rose from his chair and came around the desk to stand in front of the old woman. He looked down at her and let his face settle into its most serious expression. 'I don't know what you're trying to say, Miss Edna, but to me it sounds almost like a threat. If it is, let me tell you that no

81

matter what happens now, I'll remember your words. As for any legal action you may be contemplating, I'd think twice, if I were you. You'd have to sue Diana, and I should think that any lawyer she retained would advise her to sue you right back. You're not a young woman, Miss Edna, and everybody in Amberton knows you're – what?' He paused for a moment, then flung the word in her face. 'Eccentric?'

Edna Amber rose out of her chair, her eyes blazing with fury.

'How dare you!' she demanded, but the marshal only met her gaze with a calm he had practised for years.

'You came to me for advice, Miss Edna,' he said. 'I'm giving it to you. I know you resent suddenly having a child in your home. You're used to having Diana's attention all to yourself, and now you won't have that anymore. As far as I'm concerned, you're welcome to try to convince Diana to give up the child. But I wouldn't try to take it to court, Miss Edna. Instead I'd try to get used to things the way they are. Life does not always go the way we want it to. Not even for you.'

With tension crackling between them, the marshal and the old woman silently challenged each other. In the end it was Dan Gurley who looked away, shifting his attention to the bright day outside.

'It's summer, Miss Edna,' he said conversationally, as if a moment before he hadn't been locked in wordless battle with her. 'It's going to be hot this year. Hot and dry. Folks are going to be edgy. Seems to me like the best thing we can all do is try to stay quiet, try to get by.'

'It's a summer like all others, Daniel,' Edna replied. 'And I intended to spend it like all others. At home, alone with my daughter. Perhaps I still shall.' She picked up her purse and left Dan Gurley's office. He heard the door close behind her, but remained by the window until he saw her move slowly down the steps of the building and climb into her car. Only when the Cadillac had pulled away from the kerb did he turn back to his empty office.

Diana led Christie into the shed above the root cellar. Lining the walls were sacks of food, and she carefully began explaining to the little girl what each of them was for, and how much of it was to be given to the chickens each day. But even as she talked, she wondered with half her mind where her mother had gone and why she had gone alone.

There had been a moment of panic when she saw the Cadillac leave the garage, but then, as Edna proceeded steadily along the road towards Amberton, the panic had lifted, leaving only a vague sense of unease.

She should have felt relieved. It had been years since her mother had gone anywhere alone, and Diana knew that she should be happy that her mother was at last doing something for herself. But deep inside, she also knew that the reason for Edna's trip had to do with herself. Herself and Christie.

'Do they really eat gravel?'

Christie's question interrupted her thoughts. 'It's for their gizzards,' she explained. 'They need the gravel to help them digest the seed they eat.'

'Yuck.' Christie's face creased in disgust. She looked at the various bags, sure she would never remember what all of it was. What if she fed the chickens the wrong food? Would Diana be angry with her? She'd have to be very careful not to make a mistake. But what if she did? The question nagged at her, worried her. Life was so different now. Everything was new, and there was so much she didn't understand. 'Can't we go see the horses now?' she begged. She understood horses and liked them a lot better than chickens.

Diana nodded and began securing the latch on the shed door. 'Always be sure this door is closed tight. Chickens are stupid, but they know where their food is, and if they get in here, they'll eat themselves to death.' Christie nodded solemnly, and they started across to the stable. 'Do you know how to ride?'

Christie bobbed her head eagerly. 'I took lessons in

83

Chicago, but it was with an English saddle.'

'Then we'll start you out with Hayburner until you get used to Western. He's big, but he's gentle. I think if you fell off him, he'd try to pick you up and put you back on.'

They went into the barn. In the second stall an immense dappled grey whinnied at them, his head hanging over the gate as he watched them move towards him.

'Is that him?'

'That's him. Do you want to pet him?'

Christie, happy to be back on familiar ground, let go of Diana's hand and approached the horse. 'Hi, Hayburner.' She reached up and scratched the horse's neck. 'My name's Christie. You're going to take me everywhere, and we're going to be best friends. How do you like that?'

Hayburner pawed the floor of his stall, and his tongue emerged from his mouth to investigate Christie's hand for a possible sugar cube. 'He likes me!' Christie cried. 'Aunt Diana, he likes me!'

Diana grinned. 'He likes everybody, sweetheart. I think he's some kind of a freak – he looks like a horse, but he acts like a dog.'

'He does not!' Christie protested. She opened the stall and went in. Hayburner backed up to make room for her, then began nuzzling her. Diana quickly moved forward.

'Be careful – he's not used to you yet.'

'Yes he is. See? He loves me! Can we put a saddle on him? Right now? Please?'

Diana hesitated, disturbed by the look of pure joy on Christie's face. She cast about in her mind for an excuse but found none. 'Why not?' she said. 'Come on – you might as well learn the tack room.'

They went to the back of the barn and began sorting through the various saddles.

'What about this one?' Christie asked. She pulled a piece of canvas off a saddle that stood on a rack in the corner. Though it was obviously old, it was polished brightly and smelled of saddle soap. Diana frowned slightly, then shrugged.

'All right – it was my saddle when I was a little girl – it'll be perfect.' They chose a blanket and a bridle, then Diana picked up the saddle. Returning to Hayburner's stall, they began saddling the horse, while the big grey continued snuffling at Christie. When they were done, Christie led him outside.

'Do you need a block?' Diana asked. She started towards the barn, but Christie was already scrambling into the saddle. 'Let me help you,' Diana cried, hurrying towards the struggling child.

'I can do it,' Christie protested. 'I'm not a baby, and my teacher in Chicago said you have to be able to get on a horse by yourself.'

The words stung Diana, and she watched helplessly as Christie put her left foot in the stirrup and swung herself up onto Hayburner's back. The horse craned his neck to peer up at her, then began walking slowly around the corral. Christie whispered to him, squeezed him with her knees, and he broke into a trot.

'How's it feel?' Diana called.

'It's neat! It's different than the saddle I used in Chicago. Wider.'

'Easier on the horse, harder on you.'

Diana climbed up onto the top rail of the corral and watched as Hayburner trotted around the corral once more. Christie, she realised, rode better than she had expected. In a way, Diana felt disappointed – she had hoped to be able to teach Christie riding, just as her mother had taught her. Then, as she watched the girl and the horse moving together so naturally, she began to wonder if she'd made a mistake. In her heart, she could feel the horse coming between herself and Christie.

'That's enough,' she suddenly called. Christie looked up, startled by the anger she heard in Diana's voice, and quickly reined Hayburner to a halt next to Diana.

'Can Hayburner be my horse, Aunt Diana?' she asked. 'Please? I love him, and I can tell he loves me, too.'

Diana was silent for a moment, her emotions in

upheaval. Finally, reluctantly, she nodded. 'All right,' she said slowly. 'He's yours. But I won't have you getting too attached to him, do you understand? He's old, and he could die.'

The happy smile faded from Christie's face. 'Why would he die?' she asked.

When she spoke again, Diana's voice was muted, and Christie had to strain to hear the words.

'Because that's what happens,' Diana said. 'You love things, and they get taken away from you. Or they die.'

As the words sank in, Christie's eyes brimmed with tears, and she patted the horse gently.

'You won't die, will you, Hayburner?' she whispered to him. The horse pawed at the ground nervously and tossed its head, then started towards the barn.

As she watched them go Diana remembered the words she had just uttered and wondered where they had come from. Surely not from herself. They were such cruel words, and she had seen the hurt they had caused Christie.

And yet she had said them.

She climbed slowly off the corral fence and started towards the house, still wondering what the words had meant.

They had come from somewhere deep within herself, from a part of her mind that she didn't like to think about.

The part where she buried things.

But somehow the things never stayed buried. Instead they kept coming back, demanding to be acted upon.

She went into the kitchen, letting the door slam behind her as she had slammed doors on so much of her past.

7

Kim Sandler and Susan Gillespie scuffed along the road, then veered into the field that lay between them and the Ambers' corral.

'Wow.' Kim's voice was awed, and Susan, who had stooped down to investigate a rock, looked up. Kim was pointing ahead. 'She's got a horse!'

Susan stood up and gazed across the field to see Christie leading Hayburner around the corral. 'Do you think she'll let us ride it?' Susan asked. They broke into a run, entranced by the possibilities of access to a horse. Arriving at the corral, they scrambled up the rails, and Christie brought Hayburner to a halt next to them. The big grey gazed placidly at the two newcomers. Kim put out a hand to pat him, and the horse snuffled affably.

'Is he yours?' Susan asked.

'I guess so,' Christie began uncertainly. 'His name's Hayburner, and Aunt Diana gave him to me this morning. Isn't he neat?'

'*Gave* him to you?' Kim demanded suspiciously. 'To keep? I mean, could you sell him if you wanted to?'

'Why would I want to?' Christie countered.

'I didn't mean you'd *want* to. I mean, is he really yours, or do you just get to ride him?'

Christie glanced at the house nervously, remembering Diana's strange words. 'He's mine,' she insisted. 'Anyway, that's what Aunt Diana said.' Then, as if to prove the horse was really hers, she turned to Susan. 'Want to ride him with me?'

Susan nodded eagerly, and after Christie had mounted, she scrambled from the corral fence onto the horse, her wiry body perched behind Christie. As Kim looked on enviously Hayburner obligingly trotted around the corral.

'Can he gallop?' Susan asked, her arms gripping Christie's waist. Christie nodded. 'Well, make him,' Susan begged.

'There isn't enough room in here,' Christie told her. She reined the horse to a halt, and Susan clambered back onto the fence. As Kim was about to take her place the three girls heard a voice calling from the house.

'Christie? Christie!'

All three of them turned towards the sound and saw Diana hurrying towards them. Instinctively Kim settled back onto the fence.

Approaching the corral, Diana ignored the two other girls, her attention focused on Christie. 'What are you doing?' she asked, her voice edged with annoyance.

'Just giving Susan and Kim a ride,' Christie replied, wondering what mistake she had made now.

'You barely know how to ride him yourself,' Diana protested. 'You could get hurt.'

'Hayburner wouldn't hurt anybody,' Christie said. 'He didn't mind. He likes us.'

'He really does, Miss Diana,' Susan added. For the first time Diana shifted her attention to the two other girls.

'What are you doing out here?' she demanded.

Susan and Kim exchanged a worried look, then Kim spoke for both of them. 'We just came to see Christie.'

'*To see Christie.*' The words echoed in Diana's ears and anger surged through her. Her first impulse was to order them off the property. And yet, even as she was gripped by the same surge of jealousy she'd felt earlier as she'd watched Christie ride, the voice of reason whispered to her. If she sent them away, what would they tell their parents? That she was crazy? That she wouldn't let anyone see Christie? She made herself calm down, and forced a smile. 'Would you like something to drink?' she offered. 'Some lemonade maybe?'

Again Kim and Susan exchanged a look. 'We were going for a hike,' Susan explained. 'We thought maybe Christie could come with us.'

'Can I?' Christie asked.

Again the strange anger swept through Diana, but this time she didn't try to overcome it. 'No,' she said. Then, feeling compelled to provide a reason for her refusal, she went on. 'Juan's coming, and we're going to ride fence with him.'

Christie slid off Hayburner and dug her toe into the ground. 'Do I have to?' she asked.

'I thought you'd want to.' Diana's voice was harsh, and Christie felt trapped.

'All right.' She gave in.

Diana's face cleared and she smiled. 'You can go for a hike another day. All right?'

Christie shrugged helplessly. 'I guess so.'

A few minutes later she watched her friends start off towards the hills. Wishing she were going with them, but knowing she couldn't, Christie obediently followed Diana back to the house.

Juan Rodriguez reined in his horse and waited for Diana Amber and the little girl to catch up with him. It had been that way all afternoon, like a game. He would ride ahead and try to find breaks in the fence, then see if he could fix them before Miss Diana and the little girl caught up with him. Mostly he had plenty of time to finish the work, because Miss Diana was talking to the girl, showing her things, and telling her how things used to be.

To Juan, it didn't matter how things used to be. The only thing that counted was the present, and he was having fun. His favourite days were the days he got to go riding with Miss Diana.

Now he paused and watched the two of them approach him. He wondered if it was always going to be like this, if the little girl was always going to go with them.

He'd been watching her for the last few days, wondering if she was going to be nice to him, or be like the others –

like those boys who had teased him the other night. From what he'd seen she looked like a nice little girl, and his mother had told him to keep an eye on her. He'd made it a game, hiding himself in the scrub juniper, watching her whenever she was outside but never letting her see him.

'Hi!' he called now as they drew up beside him. 'All fixed!' Diana dismounted and carefully inspected the splice that Juan had worked into the barbed wire. It had taken him years to master the simple task, and she always made a show of praising his work, while he happily nodded his head, eager to get on to the next break in the fence.

'Very good, Juan,' Diana told him. 'Think we should keep going?'

Juan looked towards the mountains, and his eyes squinted in the bright afternoon sun. Then he licked his finger and held it in the air.

'Wind coming,' he told Diana. She glanced westward and nodded.

'Looks like it. Why don't we do a few more miles, then call it a day?'

'You're da boss!' Juan dug his spurs into his mount, and the horse reared, pawed at the air for a moment, then broke into a gallop.

'I wish he wouldn't do that' Christie said as the Mexican disappeared in a cloud of reddish dust. 'All he has to do is squeeze him. He doesn't have to kick him.'

'It makes him feel like a cowboy,' Diana replied placidly. 'Besides, the spurs aren't sharp.'

'He still doesn't need to kick him,' Christie repeated stubbornly. She looked around at the rolling landscape, mostly grass, dotted with patches of aspens, some cottonwoods, and an occasional willow. Here and there outcroppings of red sandstone thrust upward towards the sky. 'How big is the ranch?'

'A township.' Then, as Christie looked blank, she explained. 'That's thirty-six square miles. Each square mile is called a section, and there are six hundred and forty acres in each section.'

'It's a whole town?' Christie breathed, and Diana laughed.

'Except that there isn't any town on it. It sounds like a lot, but it really isn't, not anymore. Most of it just sits here, waiting for a cow to come around.'

Again Christie looked around, this time searching for cattle. There were none to be seen.

'We haven't had many cattle for years. After the mine closed, mother tried to keep up the herd, but now we just lease grazing rights. We still have a few of our own just for fun.' Her voice dropped as she gazed across the valley. 'It must have been something,' she mused. 'Can't you just see it? Once, there were probably ten thousand head out there, and who knows how many men to run them.' With Christie beside her, Diana surveyed the land and wished that it were still the way it had once been, long before either of them was born.

'I'm glad I'm here.'

Diana heard the whispered words and turned to Christie. 'Are you? Are you really?'

Christie nodded, the beauty of the ranch overwhelming her. 'I wish my mother was here. I bet she would have loved it.'

'Do you remember her?'

'Only a little bit. But I miss her a lot.'

Diana glanced at the child, but her face was expressionless. The brief flash of jealousy she had just felt passed as quickly as it had come. 'Come on', she said.

The two of them shook their reins, and their horses started forward again, walking slowly along the fence. For a long time silence settled over them, but then, as the first breezes of the coming wind caressed them, Christie spoke once more, her voice shaking and choked with emotion.

'Aunt Diana?'

'Hmm?'

'Could – could you be my mother now?'

Diana pulled her horse next to Christie's and reached out to touch the girl's cheek. 'Is that what you want?' she whispered. The little girl nodded mutely. 'Then I'll be

91

your mother,' Diana promised. She straightened in her saddle and looked for Juan Rodriguez, but he was nowhere to be seen. She glanced up at the sun, which was lowering towards the mountaintops, and shivered slightly as the wind began to blow, then gently slapped her horse's neck with the reins. The horse moved placidly forward, with Hayburner keeping the pace. Ahead of them a grove of cottonwoods clustered around a small spring, and Diana guided her horse towards it. Juan was probably there, sleeping in the shade.

The snake, a five-foot diamondback, lay curled in the shelter of a rock, its eyes watchful, its tongue darting in and out as it searched the area for prey.

It moved restlessly as the vibrations of horses' hooves disturbed its environment, and its sinewy body slid further beneath the rock.

As the horses came into its territory a tremor went through its body, and the rattles at the tip of its tail whispered softly. It moved away from the rock and disappeared into a jumble of sandstone near the spring.

Christie pulled Hayburner to a stop and slid out of the saddle. She looped the reins around a low-slung branch of one of the cottonwoods and started towards the spring. 'Is it okay to drink the water?' she asked as Diana, too, tied her horse to its tree.

'Well, it hasn't killed me yet,' Diana replied. The wind was blowing stronger, and the cottonwoods began to creak. Diana, well aware of the way such trees tended to drop branches with no warning, decided to let the horses, too, have a drink from the bubbling spring. She untied their reins, and they ambled towards the water.

As Hayburner's hooves disturbed the sandstone rocks a small stone came loose and clattered into the pool. Immediately there was a flash of movement, and then the loud buzzing of the diamondback's rattle.

'What was that?' Christie asked. She looked towards Diana, totally unaware of the snake that was now coiled watchfully a yard from her feet.

92

'Don't move,' Diana whispered. 'Hold absolutely still.'

She stared at the rattler, its thick body coiled tightly, its tongue flicking the air as its triangular head bobbed in the sunlight. Its rattle, standing straight up from the centre of its coil, was vibrating angrily, and its eyes, black slits in the sides of its head, seemed to project hatred towards the little girl who had invaded its privacy.

Suddenly, as the wind gusted around her, one of the darkly closed doors of Diana's memory flew open and she saw herself, at the same age as Christie, playing near the back door of the house.

There had been a snake that day, too.

It had flashed out from under the back porch, its body writhing, and drawn itself into a coil close to her feet. As she had stood paralysed with fear she had heard her mother's voice drifting dimly from the kitchen as if from another world.

'It's come to punish you,' her mother had said. 'You're an evil child, and God has sent the snake to punish you.' And then there had been silence for what seemed to Diana to be an eternity.

Now, as her eyes fixed on the snake that threatened Christie, she heard her own voice.

'What have you done, Christie?'

Christie heard the words, and her mind churned. Wasn't Diana going to help her? What should she do?

For Diana, the moment was one of pure terror. She knew she had to move, to take some action. The snake's head was moving faster now, and she had a terrible feeling that at any second it would strike, its mouth agape, its fangs ready to sink deep into the soft flesh of Christie's leg. And yet she couldn't move. She stood frozen, her mother's voice echoing in her ears, asking her what she had done that had made God send a snake to punish her.

That day, it had been the cook who had saved her, bursting through the back door, a broom in her hands. The snake, whirling at the noise behind it, had been struck by the broom, and as Diana had fled across the backyard it had retreated under the porch.

Today, there was no one to save her. She had to do something. And then it happened.

She became another person. The rage that was bottled up in her subconscious, the fury that had lain festering within her since she was a child, burst to the surface and gave her the strength to do what had to be done.

And her body, the body that had been frozen in horror a moment ago, responded to the insistent will of the angry child within her.

She bent over and snatched up a rock.

With her newfound strength, she hurled the stone at the snake, and the serpent, distracted by the sudden movement, struck at it, its mouth wide, its fangs bared.

Christie, screaming, hurled herself towards Diana.

'It wasn't my fault,' she sobbed helplessly. 'I didn't do anything, Aunt Diana. It wasn't my fault!'

Diana stood still, her arms around the child, her mind whirling. The doors of her memory had slammed shut, and there was nothing left of the last few moments.

She tried to concentrate on what Christie was saying. Her fault? How could what had happened have been Christie's fault? It made no sense.

She didn't notice that the wind had slackened as quickly as it had come up.

Juan Rodriguez rode into the cottonwood grove and found Diana and Christie sitting on their horses.

'I found more holes,' he announced proudly, his face glowing with pleasure. 'That way!' He pointed off into the distance, but Diana ignored his gesture.

'Never mind, Juan,' she said, her voice shaking. 'We're going home. We ran into a snake, and Christie's upset.'

'Snake?' Juan asked. 'Where?'

'It was in the rocks,' Diana explained. Juan dismounted and started towards the spring. 'Juan!' Diana said sharply. 'It was a rattler. Leave it alone!'

His face reflecting his disappointment, Juan obediently climbed back on his horse. 'Can I go play now?' he asked.

'Don't you think you'd better go home?' Diana countered.

Juan shook his head.

Diana shrugged. 'Okay, but don't get lost! I don't want to have to send the marshal looking for you.'

'I won't,' Juan promised. 'I never get lost.' Then, waving good-bye, he spurred his horse and trotted out of the grove.

A moment later Diana and Christie left the grove, too, and as they started homeward Christie was silent for a while. Finally, however, she reached out and took Diana's hand. 'I didn't do anything,' she said softly. 'Really, I didn't, Aunt Diana.'

Diana squeezed the little girl's hand. 'Of course you didn't, sweetheart,' she said. 'I guess I was just as scared as you were.'

Assured of her forgiveness, Christie suddenly grinned and slapped Hayburner's neck with the reins. 'Come on,' she shouted. 'I'll race you back to the barn!'

Juan pulled his horse to a stop and looked down at the still water below him.

He'd discovered the pool when he was a boy. It was carved into the side of a hill, ringed by dense foliage, the waters that fed it springing clear and pure from the depths of the earth. Juan thought of it as his own, and it occupied a special place in his dreams. He liked to come here, strip off his clothes, and swim naked in the cold waters, then sprawl on a rock in the sun and look out over the plains, dreaming his dreams.

Juan dreamed that someday he would grow up and be like the other people his age. Then he would go to school and learn all the things that everybody else knew. Until then, though, he didn't mind living the way he did. He liked the ranch, liked helping Miss Diana with the fence, and he liked being outside, wandering around in his little world, exploring things.

Most of all, he liked this pool.

But today, it was spoiled for him.

Today, two little girls were swimming in his pool.

He watched them for a few minutes until they saw him. Then, as they ran screaming to hide in the foliage, Juan Rodriguez kicked his horse again and rode away. But he would be back; it was, after all, his pool.

The heat of the late afternoon was beginning to fade as Bill Henry urged his old Rambler up the Ambers' driveway. He saw Juan Rodriguez leading a horse into the barn, and tooted his horn, but if Juan noticed him, he gave no sign.

Bill parked his car in front of the house and took the steps onto the porch two at a time. He pressed the doorbell, then, hearing nothing from inside, knocked loudly. A moment later Edna Amber opened the door and stared at him.

'Yes?'

Bill smiled uneasily. 'Good afternoon, Miss Edna. I – I just thought I'd drop by and say hello.'

'To me?' The old woman made no move to invite him in.

'To you, and Diana and Christie.'

'I'll tell Diana you're here.' Adna Amber closed the door and left him standing on the porch. A minute went by, then another. The door reopened and Diana, looking preoccupied with something, nodded to him.

'Bill? What are you doing out here? And why didn't you come in?'

'I wasn't invited in,' Bill told her. 'What's going on around here? Your mother at least used to let me in the house, even if she made me feel like I should bow three times and back out of the room she was in.'

Diana led him towards the kitchen. 'She's making things difficult, that's all,' she said. 'She didn't even tell me who was at the door. Just "someone"? Oh, well, she'll get over it. Want some lemonade?'

'I'd rather have a gin and tonic. Does she allow that sort of think in the house?'

'Mother's a tyrant, not a prude.' They stepped into the kitchen, where Christie sat at the table, leafing through a catalogue. 'Christie, look who's here.' As Diana pulled a bottle of gin out of a cupboard, Christie looked up and grinned at Bill.

'Hi! Guess what happened to us today?' While Diana mixed Bill's drink the little girl excitedly told Bill about the snake.

Diana listened to the tale pour forth from Christie and realised that, from Christie's point of view, she had saved her life. And yet, try as she would, she could remember nothing except that she had been suddenly, helplessly angry. Then – nothing. A blank. And yet something had happened, something that had given her the courage to pick up a rock and throw it at the snake, something she would never have done under normal circumstances. Since she had been a child the sight of a snake had paralysed her with terror. But today something had happened. Something she had neither been aware of nor could control.

As she set Bill's drink in front of him, Diana was suddenly wary. What if he realised that she had no memory of what Christie was talking about? Would he think she was crazy? If he did, he, too, would try to take Christie away from her. Instead he was listening intently as Christie began telling him about her horse.

'Horse?' Bill replied, feigning disapproval. 'What horse? Kids your age don't have horses.'

'I do,' the little girl announced. 'Want to see him?'

Bill glanced questioningly at Diana.

'It's Hayburner,' Diana explained, relieved to have the subject of the snake left behind. 'Seems it was love at first sight, and since you can't live on a ranch without a horse, he is now Christie's. As you can see, she's currently shopping for cowboy clothes.'

Bill sipped at his drink. 'Why don't you just take her to Penrose's?'

'I'm going to, but not till tomorrow. And tomorrow, apparently, is a long way off.' She smiled. 'So far, I think she's spent about three hundred dollars.'

Christie looked up from the catalogue again, her face suddenly worried. 'I'm only looking,' she said.

'And looking doesn't cost a thing,' Bill told her. He turned his attention back to Diana. 'How's it going?'

Diana glanced quickly at Christie, then went to the sink and fixed herself a drink. 'As well as can be expected, I suppose.' Her voice dropped a little, and she tipped her head in Christie's direction. 'Why don't we go into the parlour?' she suggested.

They were silent until they'd seated themselves in the tiny front room, then Bill spoke.

'Your mother was in town this morning,' he said finally.

'I know,' Diana replied, her voice pensive. 'I saw her go.'

'Do you know why she went in?'

Diana nodded. 'She told me. She still doesn't want Christie here.' She paused, then changed the subject. 'Why don't you stay for dinner?'

'Here? With your mother?'

'It'll be all right,' Diana said, and Bill thought he heard a trace of desperation in her voice. When she went on, he was sure of it. I'll make it all right, Bill.'

The four of them sat stiffly at the dining room table, and for a while Bill thought that maybe Diana was going to be able to deliver on her promise.

But as Edna Amber sat at the head of the table, dressed for dinner in a severe black dress that was years out of fashion, a pearl choker around her neck, and her hair piled regally on top of her head, her cold silence threw a pall over the meal. It *should* have been all right, Bill reflected. A stranger would have seen nothing amiss in the scene: a middle-aged couple, their young daughter, and a grandmother gathered together for a meal. But it was a charade, and Bill wondered for a fleeting moment if Diana had planned it as a charade. Then, as he saw her misery in the situation, he realised she couldn't have. She had simply made a mistake and hadn't the techniques to rectify it.

Several times she tried. First she attempted to include Christie in the conversation.

'Why don't you tell Miss Edna about the snake?' she suggested. Christie looked eagerly towards Edna, but Edna only glared at Diana.

'Talk of snakes at the dinner table?' she asked. 'Really, Diana, I thought I raised you to have a certain amount of taste.'

A few moments later, as the silence had threatened to become embarrassing, Diana asked Bill if anything interesting had been going on in town. From the head of the table, Edna's imperious voice instantly came to life.

'There has been nothing of interest in Amberton in sixty years,' she said. 'And I hardly think things have changed since I was there this morning.'

As Diana's face reddened the silence gathered once more. Christie, feeling the tension at the table, only nibbled at her food and soon pushed her plate away.

'May I be excused?' she asked, her voice barely audible and her eyes large.

'Of course, dear,' Diana told her. She watched sadly as the child scurried from the room, and wished she had been able to save the evening. Determined to try once more, she turned to Bill and smiled brightly. But before she could speak Edna rose from the table. Bill scrambled to his feet, but Edna ignored him, speaking only to her daughter.

'I don't know what you're trying to accomplish with this, Diana, but I trust that even you can see that you're making a fool of yourself. Please come to my room before you go to bed tonight.'

Without so much as a word to Bill Henry, she, too, left the room.

When they were alone together, Diana gazed bleakly at Bill.

'I'm sorry. I – I hoped . . . oh, I don't know what I hoped.' She was on the verge of tears.

'It's all right.' Bill moved to the end of the table and took her hand in his own. 'What did you expect? She stayed right in character. She always does.'

Diana sighed heavily, dabbed at her eyes with her handkerchief, then regained her control.

'I know. I guess I thought maybe if you were here, she'd at least not say anything too horrible to Christie. Well, that part of it worked. But I'm not sure this wasn't even worse.'

'Well, look at it like this. No matter what happens now, things can't get any worse.'

Diana gazed into his eyes.

'Can't they?' she asked. 'I wish I could believe that.'

She began clearing the table, and Bill Henry wandered into the library, where Christie was sitting in a large wing chair, a book open in her lap.

'Hi,' Bill said. 'Okay if I come in?'

Christie glanced up from her book, and there was something in her eyes as she looked at him that struck Bill as odd. Christie seemed frightened, as if she were afraid she was doing something wrong. 'Are you all right?'

Christie nodded and closed the book. 'I – sometimes I'm not supposed to look at the books,' she stammered.

'Sometimes?' Bill repeated. 'What does that mean?'

Christie wriggled in the chair. 'Nothing,' she whispered, not sure how to explain to the doctor that she never knew when she was going to find herself in trouble.

Bill lit his pipe and settled into an easy chair. 'It must mean something,' he commented. He gazed critically at Christie. 'Do you like living here?'

Christie hesitated, then nodded.

'But it's different from the way it was at home, right?'

Again Christie nodded. 'Sometimes it's scary,' she said.

'Scary? How?'

Christie's eyes moved over the room once more, and it struck Bill that she was trying to see if anyone might be listening. Finally she started to speak.

'Sometimes I think everything's fine, but then other times –' She broke off, her eyes fixed on the door. When

Bill followed her gaze, he saw Diana, smiling uncertainly.

'Are you two having a private chat, or may I join in?'

'Nothing private,' Bill responded.

Diana came into the room and glanced at the clock. 'I think it's time you were in bed,' she said to Christie. The little girl hesitated, then got up to leave the room, pausing to peck Diana on the cheek. Then she was gone.

Diana moved to the wing chair Christie had recently occupied, and sat down. 'What were you talking about?' she asked.

'We weren't, really. We'd just started. She said that sometimes it's scary, living here.'

Diana's expression turned grim, and she hesitated before she spoke. 'It's Mother,' she said finally. 'She's not used to Christie yet, and sometimes she scares her. That's all.'

'But everything's all right between you and Christie?' Bill pressed.

'Of course it is,' Diana replied. 'Why wouldn't it be?'

'No reason,' Bill said quickly. 'I was just wondering.'

'Everything's fine,' Diana assured him. Then she stood up, glancing once more at the clock. 'It's late, isn't it?'

Taking the hint, Bill Henry got to his feet, and a few minutes later, feeling disturbed by the whole evening, he was on his way back to town.

And in the house, Diana Amber was even more disturbed.

8

Christie lay in bed, listening to the sounds of the night. She wished she were downstairs. There were lots of rooms on the second floor – why couldn't she have one of them? Why did she have to stay up here?

A wave of loneliness swept over Christie. She got out of bed and went to the window. The night was clear, and she could see the mountains glowing in the moonlight. Below her, in the chicken coop, the hens were clucking softly in their sleep, the sound clearly audible in the still night air.

She turned away from the window and looked around the nursery. She hated it. It smelled sour, and always there were noises in the walls – scufflings and scratchings that she was sure were rats. She dreamed about them sometimes, seeing their yellow eyes glowing in the darkness, brown teeth dripping saliva. Just thinking about them made her snatch up one of the stuffed animals and scurry back to bed. The toy was no comfort to her; it was musty and felt dead, and what she wanted was something alive.

The chicks.

Maybe she could sneak one of the chicks up to her room.

She put on her bathrobe and a pair of sneakers. She paused at the door, trying to remember if Diana had locked it that night. Finally she reached out and touched it.

It was locked.

She went back to the window and slowly raised it, then slipped out onto the ledge. Slowly she crept down the slope of the roof until she was over the kitchen. She eased her body over the edge until at last her legs touched the ridge of the kitchen roof. Moving downward once again, she paused at the edge of the eave and looked down. Should she risk the jump? What if the doors were locked? How would she get back in?

She thought about it for a few seconds, then made up her mind. If the doors were locked, she'd find another way. If she could get out of the house, surely she could get back in. Holding her breath, she jumped from the roof. A moment later she was scurrying across the yard.

As she approached the chicken coop the hens stirred, then, sensing no danger, tucked their heads back under their wings and went back to sleep.

Christie listened carefully. The faint sound of the peeping chicks reached her. She tried to locate the sound. Even in the dim light, she could see that one of the hens seemed to be fluffed up more than the others. Christie slipped a hand under the bird and found a chick. It wriggled frantically but calmed down as Christie gently stroked its head. When it was quiet, she stood up and started back to the house.

The kitchen door was unlocked, and Christie slipped inside, being careful not to let the screen door slam behind her. In the pantry she found an old shoe box full of spices. She emptied the box and gently put the chick inside. Keeping her tread as light as possible, she crept up the back stairs to the third floor and let herself back into the nursery.

But there was no way to relock the door. Well, maybe Diana would think she'd forgotten to lock it.

Safely back in the nursery, Christie sat in the rocking chair and opened the box. The chick was huddled down in one corner. It looked frightened to her. She reached down and touched it. The chick ducked its head and scuttled to the opposite corner of the box.

'It's all right, baby,' Christie whispered to it. 'I won't hurt you. I'm your friend.'

She captured the chick in her hand and held it until it

103

was once again calm. Then, putting the chick back into the box, and setting the box on the floor next to the cot, she took off her robe and curled up under the covers.

Somehow just knowing the chick was there made her feel better. Soon she drifted off to sleep.

Edna Amber waited until almost three before she left her room. She had been awake all night, but that was all right. As she got older she needed less sleep, and tonight there had been a reason to stay awake.

She had heard scuffling noises in the night and had gotten up from her bed to investigate them. She had watched as Christie lowered herself to the kitchen roof, then jumped to the ground.

She was puzzled when Christie went out to the hen house, and it wasn't until she saw the child returning to the house with something cupped in her hand that Edna realised what she was doing.

Bringing in a chick to keep her company.

It was when the wind began to blow that Edna began to formulate the idea.

Now, pulling on her robe, she climbed the stairs to the third floor and quietly let herself into the nursery. Christie was sound asleep, but on the floor beside the cot was the box.

Edna picked the box up, opened it, and smiled at the sleeping chick.

Then she wrung its neck.

She dropped the chick back into the box, replaced it on the floor, then, pausing as she straightened up, brushed Christie's cheek with her lips.

'I'm sorry,' she whispered. 'Really, I am.' Christie stirred in her sleep, but didn't wake up.

As the moon set and the glow of the night faded to blackness, Edna Amber returned to her bed.

Diana woke at seven and lay in bed, listening to the stillness of the morning. She had slept badly, worrying

104

about Bill Henry's reaction the night before. She knew that sometime during the night the wind had come down from the mountains, bringing with it the nightmares that had plagued her sleep. It had been that way since she was a little girl, and she had always looked forward to the beginning of summer when the winds would be over for another year and she could sleep peacefully.

Only twice had they come in summer, and Diana remembered those years very well.

The last time had been the year her mother had sent her to the hospital. It had been an awful year for Diana, and the summer winds had been too much for her. Everyone in Amberton had become edgy that summer, but Diana had fallen into depression. She had fought constantly with her mother that summer, but did not know why, really. Over the years, she had discovered that fighting with Edna was nearly useless.

She never won.

But that summer, she had tried. She remembered one day in particular.

The wind had been blowing that day, and the car had refused to start.

'What did you do to it?' Edna had asked.

'Nothing, Mother. It's just old.'

'Don't be silly, child. You must have done something.'

'I didn't, Mother. Cars just aren't built to be driven for twenty years.'

'If you taken care of them, they'll last.' Her mother's voice had taken on the querulous tone that Diana had learned to dread. 'But you don't take care of anything, do you? You never have.'

'Mother, that's not true!'

'Are you calling me a liar, Diana?' Edna had rasped.

'No –'

But it was already too late. Edna's hand had flashed out and struck her cheek, as it had since she was a little girl, and Diana had fallen silent, knowing that to say anything more was to risk further punishment. Instead she had crumpled in the face of her mother's fury, until, after an hour, Edna had relented and gathered Diana into her arms.

It was that night, during dinner, that Diana had suddenly begun clawing at her face, and Edna eventually had had to call for an ambulance.

At the hospital, they called it agitated depression, and tried to explain to Diana that it stemmed from her relationship with her mother. If she were ever to get over it, she would have to learn to stand up to the old woman.

After a few days she had come home, and for a while she had tried. But as time wore on she had come to realise that peace in the house was better than the constant fights that occurred whenever she disagreed with her mother.

There hadn't really been anything she thought worth fighting for, until recently.

Until Christie.

Now, for the first time in her memory, she was standing up to her mother, and Edna was giving in.

And this morning, the wind had stopped. Diana was getting out of bed when the scream ripped through the morning quiet.

It came from upstairs.

She grabbed her robe and ran out of her room. A few feet away, her mother was standing at the door of her own room, staring at the ceiling.

'What's that child screaming about?' she demanded as Diana dashed by. Diana ignored her.

She took the stairs two at a time, then burst into the nursery.

Kneeling on the floor, her face ashen and tears running down her cheeks, was Christie.

In the shoe box, the chick lay dead, its tiny eyes popping from their sockets.

Diana gently took the box from Christie and stared at the dead bird. 'Christie, what happened?' she breathed.

Christie tried to speak, but couldn't. Instead she began sobbing and threw herself face down on the bed.

'Stop crying,' Diana ordered. Her sympathy for the child's misery was turning into annoyance. 'Just tell me what happened.'

Christie rolled over on the bed, her eyes red and her cheeks stained with tears.

'I – I woke up, and – and I was going to pet my chick.'

'But where did it come from?' Diana asked.

Christie sniffled. 'I brought it in last night. I was lonely, Aunt Diana. I just did it so I'd have some company.'

'I see,' Diana said, her voice suddenly cold. 'And how did you get out of the nursery?'

There was a moment's hesitation while the little girl looked at her warily. 'It wasn't locked,' Christie finally said, her voice unsteady. 'I – I guess you must have forgotten to lock it last night.' She began crying.

As she watched Christie's face crumple a strange anger welled up in Diana. She shouldn't cry. *Little girls should never cry.* When little girls cried, they had to be punished.

'I didn't leave the door unlocked,' Diana said. 'And I won't have you wandering around at night.'

Christie shrank away from her, suddenly afraid of what was coming.

'Take off your pyjamas.'

'No,' Christie wailed. 'Please – no!'

But she knew there was no escape. She had done something wrong, and she would have to pay for it. She dropped her pyjama bottoms and leaned over. Slowly, deliberately, Diana began to spank her.

Her hand moved like a metronome, lashing the little girl's backside until it was red and sore. Only when Christie finally stopped crying did Diana stop.

'There,' she said at last. 'Now, go to bed, and don't get up for at least an hour.'

Christie stared up at her, her eyes filled with confusion. 'I'm sorry,' she said at last. 'I didn't mean to kill the chick.'

Diana ignored her. She stood up, picked up the box, then left the nursery. On the second floor she found her mother waiting for her. As she started to pass the old woman Edna suddenly lifted her cane and knocked the box from Diana's hands. It fell open, and the chick rolled out onto the carpet. Edna stared at it.

'I don't believe it,' she said. 'What in God's name has that child done?'

'It's only a chick,' Diana replied, struggling to keep her voice steady. 'Will you just go downstairs while I get rid of it? Christie's in her room, crying. Please don't ask me what happened.'

Edna looked at her appraisingly, and Diana felt a sudden chill of fear. 'When you're done, I think we'd better have a talk,' the old woman said. Diana nodded mutely.

She waited until her mother was gone, then took the box downstairs. Opening the back door, she dropped it into the trash barrel. She stared at the box a moment, then replaced the barrel's lid and returned to the nursery.

Christie was lying on the bed. She had stopped crying and was staring at the ceiling. When Diana came into the room, Christie didn't look at her.

'I thought you were a good girl,' Diana said, her voice cold. 'Perhaps I was wrong.'

Christie's eyes, wide as a fawn's, suddenly met Diana's.

'I didn't do it, Aunt Diana,' she whispered. 'Really, I didn't.'

'I'm not talking about the chick,' Diana said. 'I'm talking about your disobedience. I don't want you leaving this room at night. Do you understand?'

Christie nodded mutely.

'As for the chick,' Diana went on, 'I suppose it must have suffocated.' Inside, Diana felt something. A twinge, almost like a memory, but somehow different. She tried to grasp it, but it was gone. 'Or maybe it didn't,' she said suddenly. 'Maybe you did kill it. You loved it, and people always hurt the things they love.' She stared balefully at Christie for a moment, then turned and left the nursery.

When she was gone, Christie lay still. The world closed in on her, and suddenly she wished she were still a baby. Nothing bad, she thought, ever happens to babies.

Her thumb disappeared into her mouth.

Soon she drifted into a fitful sleep.

Edna was waiting in the kitchen but said nothing until Diana had poured herself a cup of coffee and joined her at the table. When at last she spoke, her voice was quivering with rage.

'And just how do you explain this?' she asked.

'For heaven's sake, Mother,' Diana replied, her voice reflecting the anger she was still feeling, but suddenly wanting to protect Christie from her mother's wrath. 'It was only a chick. Besides, she says she didn't do it.'

'Does she, indeed.' Edna responded sarcastically. 'And whom does she think *did* do it?'

Diana sighed heavily. 'Mama, I didn't even ask her. She doesn't know its neck was broken. I told her it must have suffocated.'

'Did you?' Edna remarked. Her sharp eyes bored into Diana. 'Now, what would make you say a thing like that?'

Again Diana had the strange sense of something half remembered, and she stared at her mother. 'What are you talking about?' she asked.

'I'm talking about you, Diana,' Edna said quietly. 'Have you forgotten what happened when you were the same age as Christie is now?'

'Mama –'

'It was a kitten, that time. Esperanza's kitten. Don't you remember? It wandered into the nursery one night. I found it the next morning. Its neck had been wrung, Diana.'

Diana's cup clattered against the saucer as she set it down, coffee slopping over the rim.

'Are you saying I killed that chick, Mother?' she asked.

'Did you?' Edna countered.

'Mama! Of course I didn't!'

Edna sat across from her. When she spoke, there was a sadness in her voice.

'You were always a bad little girl, Diana. I'd hoped that age would change you. It hasn't, has it?'

The room seemed to tilt, and Diana felt a dizziness overcoming her. What was her mother doing? She had the feeling she was going to come apart and her insides were going to fall out.

'Mama, please –'

But Edna was relentless.

'Diana,' she asked, her voice suddenly reasonable. 'If Christie didn't kill the chick, who did? There's no one here but the three of us.'

Diana reluctantly met her mother's eyes, and when she spoke, her tone belied her words. 'I – I don't understand.'

Edna smiled triumphantly. 'Did you know the wind was blowing last night, Diana?'

Diana nodded and chewed at her lower lip. 'It kept me awake.'

'It always keeps you awake, doesn't it?' Edna's tone had become almost hypnotic, but Diana shook her head emphatically. 'Not always,' she replied, her voice shaking. 'Not anymore. It used to, but it doesn't anymore.'

Edna went on. 'And you used to do strange things when it blew, didn't you, Diana?'

Panic welled in Diana, but she forced it down. 'I won't listen to you, Mother!'

Edna stared into the depths of her coffee cup, then smiled at Diana. 'Maybe Christie didn't kill the chick, Diana,' she said softly. 'Maybe she isn't lying at all. And if she isn't, it's even more important that she leave here, isn't it?'

Then, as Diana sat shivering at the table, Edna rose and left the kitchen.

There was a knot of fear in her stomach, and no matter how she tried to will it away, it remained there, gnawing at her.

Could her mother be right?

Could she have killed the chick herself and not remembered it?

Dimly the incident with Esperanza's kitten came back to her. She had put it out of her memory years ago, but now it

110

was back, and she knew that it had happened the way her mother had recounted it. Though she had no memory of having choked the kitten, she knew she must have done it.

The fear began to close in on her.

What if her mother was right? What if she had killed the chick and didn't remember? But it couldn't be true – she wouldn't let it be true. If it was, then she was crazy, and they could take Christie away from her. And that couldn't happen. She wouldn't let it happen.

She knew she was going to cry but couldn't help herself. Slowly at first, and then faster, the tears began to fall.

9

A week later the children came back.

This time there were three of them. Jay-Jay Jennings, Kim Sandler, and Susan Gillespie. Diana saw them coming across the field, and as they neared the back door she spoke to Christie, her voice cold.

'Why don't they use the driveway?'

Christie looked at Diana warily, wondering what to say. She was discovering that she couldn't predict her guardian's moods, so when she spoke, she was careful of her words.

'It's a shortcut,' she explained. 'We know all kinds of them. Like, to get from our house to the Crowleys', it's fastest to go through the Gillespies' backyard and over Mrs. Berkey's fence.'

'But the Crowleys live on this side of town,' Diana objected.

Christie's smile faded: she had made a mistake. 'I didn't mean this house,' she whispered. 'I meant our house – my house.'

Diana felt a flash of anger. *This* was Christie's house now. The other house – the house she had lived in with her father – was in the past. Almost of its own volition her hand rose to slap Christie's face, but a soft tapping at the back door stopped her. Christie quickly slid off her chair to let her friends into the kitchen as Miss Edna appeared at the dining-room door. Seeing the old woman, the children's greetings died on their lips, and Diana glanced

112

nervously from her mother to the children.

'Mother, wouldn't you like your coffee in the parlour?' she asked.

'When you have time.' Though she spoke to Diana, her eyes remained fixed on the children. Now Diana, too, shifted her attention to the youngsters.

'You're all out early.' She made her smile welcoming, though she could feel the familiar anger building inside her.

'We're going swimming,' Kim explained. 'Can Christie go with us?'

Diana searched her mind for an excuse. 'Well, I thought –'

But Christie, sensing the refusal to come, pled her case.

'Please can't I go, Aunt Diana? We won't go far.' She looked to her friends for support. 'It's not far, is it?'

The children shook their heads, and Kim Sandler explained: 'It's just a little ways past the mine.'

'You mean the old gravel quarry?' Diana asked.

'All the kids swim up there,' Christie assured her.

Diana searched her face, wondering if what Christie was saying was the truth. In the back of her mind she was beginning to have a suspicion that often they told you what they thought you wanted to hear. Finally she shook her head. 'I don't think so. I thought we'd go over to –' She hesitated, then decided to turn Christie's own words against her. '– to your house today. We have to get the rest of your things.'

As Christie's face reflected her disappointment, Edna Amber suddenly spoke. Though she hadn't moved from her position in the dining-room door, neither had she missed a word of what had been said.

'Oh, for Heaven's sake, Diana, let the child go! You and I can go get her things – there can't be all that many of them, can there? Besides, it would be nice to be by ourselves for a while, wouldn't it?'

Diana glared at her mother. Edna appeared not to notice. And yet, though Edna's face was placid, Diana's resistance crumbled. 'All right. But be careful, and be sure you're back by noon.'

Christie ran upstairs to get her bathing suit and a towel. Silence hung over the kitchen while she was gone. The children, sensing the tension, edged out the door, leaving the two women alone. Only when Christie reappeared, promised once more to be careful, and left, did Diana speak.

'Why did you do that, Mother?' she asked. 'That quarry's dangerous, and you know it.'

'You used to swim up there when you were a child,' Edna countered. 'You're still alive, aren't you?'

'We don't even know if Christie can swim!'

'Well, if she can't, she'll learn today,' Edna said coldly. 'Either that, or she won't come back.'

As Diana stared at her Edna Amber began sipping her coffee.

'How far is it?' Christie asked.

They'd been walking for half an hour, and, though they'd passed the mine ten minutes ago, there was nothing around that looked to Christie like a quarry, or that seemed to hint of water. The brush and juniper of the valley floor had given way to a stand of aspen, and the road, since they'd passed the mine, had been replaced by a steep trail.

Jay-Jay looked at her scornfully. 'I thought you said you were there before.'

'Well, I've heard you guys talk about it,' Christie said defensively. 'Besides, all I said was that the kids swim there all the time. I didn't say *I* ever had. Have you?'

Jay-Jay nodded. 'Me and Linda Malone were up there last week. It's really neat.' She carefully avoided mentioning how frightened they'd been when Juan Rodriguez had suddenly appeared above them. That, in fact, was why Linda had refused to come today.

They paused in the aspen grove, and Kim, the tomboy of the group, began passing around the canteen that was slung from her belt. Christie sucked at it thirstily.

'I wish I had one of these.'

'Maybe Miss Diana will buy one for you,' Kim suggested.

'I don't like to ask for things . . .' Christie replied. For a moment she was tempted to tell her friends how frightened she was most of the time. Ever since the chick had died, and Diana had made her feel like it was her fault, she had tried to be extra careful, and yet every day she seemed to make some kind of mistake.

Then, as if she'd read her thoughts, Susan Gillespie flopped down on the ground next to her and asked her a question: 'What's it like, living there?'

Christie shrugged. 'It's okay, I guess,' she said, wanting neither to admit that she was frightened most of the time, nor to say anything bad about the Ambers. Besides, she wasn't exactly sure what Susan wanted to know.

'I heard Miss Edna's a witch,' Susan said, cocking her head in the odd way of hers that always made people wonder if she was asking a question or stating a fact. Christie stared at her.

'A witch?'

Susan nodded. 'I even heard she eats raw meat. Yuck!'

'Well, she doesn't,' Christie said. 'She eats the same thing everybody else does.'

'My mother says she's crazy,' Kim put in. 'Not crazy like the people at the loony bin. Just . . . strange.'

Christie looked at her curiously. 'Strange how?'

'Well . . .' Kim began, but then hesitated.

'Well, what?' Jay-Jay demanded, her voice petulant. 'If you weren't going to tell, you shouldn't have started to!'

Kim looked uncertainly from face to face, wishing she hadn't begun. All her friends except Christie seemed to be challenging her. 'Well,' she said again, then took the plunge. 'Mom says Miss Edna used to lock Miss Diana up.'

Suddenly the attention of the group was riveted on Kim.

'Lock her up?' Susan breathed. 'Where?'

'In the attic,' Kim said.

Christie felt a sudden pang of fear. Each night, when Diana took her upstairs, the last thing she heard was the key turning in the lock. Was that why Diana locked her in? Because she'd been locked in, too? 'Why would she do that?' Christie asked.

'How should I know?' Kim shrugged. 'But Mom said when Miss Diana was a little girl, Miss Edna used to lock her in her room, and she even had to send her to the hospital once, but that was when she was already grown-up.'

'You mean Dr. Henry's?' Jay-Jay asked doubtfully. She was sure Kim was making the whole thing up, but Kim shook her head vehemently.

'That's not a hospital. That's just an office. Miss Edna made them take Miss Diana to the loony bin. But Mom said they should have locked Miss Edna up. She said if Miss Diana was crazy, it was Miss Edna's fault.'

'What was wrong with Miss Diana?' Susan asked. 'I think she's nice.'

Kim shrugged. 'I don't know. Maybe Miss Edna beat her up.'

Christie frowned, remembering the spanking she'd received from Diana. 'Why would she do that?'

'Search me,' Kim said. She looked at her friends and rolled her eyes. 'Mom said I was too young to understand.'

The rest of the kids groaned sympathetically. 'My dad always tells me that,' Jay-Jay said. Then she giggled. 'Especially when I ask him about sex. Then he turns red and says it.'

Agreeing that parents were strange people, the four girls continued on their way to the quarry. But although she walked along with the rest of them, Christie soon stopped listening to their chatter. Instead she was turning over in her mind the things they had said earlier.

'*Witch ... weird ... crazy ... lock her up.*' What did it all mean?

They eventually arrived at the quarry, and for a long moment Christie could only stare at it.

116

The pool was nearly round, and on the far side of it the hillside rose nearly straight upward. In the stillness of the morning the water made a perfect mirror, and the trees surrounding most of the pond were reflected on its quiet surface. Here and there a boulder protruded from the water.

'You can dive off the farthest one,' Kim told her. 'The others are only good for sunbathing. Come on.'

Kim led her to a clearing, where the other two girls were already putting on their bathing suits. 'Last one in the water's crazier than Miss Edna!' Jay-Jay whooped. She dashed out of the clearing, and a moment later there was a splash as she hurled her chubby body into the water. Susan followed her, leaving Christie and Kim alone in the clearing. Christie looked around uneasily.

'How do you know there isn't anybody around?' she asked. Kim was peeling off her clothes.

'Nobody's ever around here. Sometimes we don't even bother with our suits. Hurry up!'

Christie started changing into her bathing suit.

'Kim?'

'What?' Kim was fidgeting and glancing out to see what the other girls were doing.

'Do you think Miss Diana could be crazy?'

'How should I know?'

'I don't know. But sometimes she scares me.'

'How?'

Christie shrugged. 'I'm not sure. Sometimes she seems to love me, but sometimes she gets mad at me for no reason.'

'My parents are like that.' Kim said. 'That's the trouble with grown-ups. You never know what they want you to do, then they get mad at you when you don't do it. Are you coming?'

Still turning Kim's words over in her mind, Christie got into her suit and followed Kim onto the narrow strip of beach.

The water, bubbling up from an invisible spring below,

117

was clear and cold. Christie dipped her toes in, then jumped back.

'Chicken!' Jay-Jay taunted her from a rock a few yards from the shore. 'Come on!'

With the other girls already in the water, Christie took a deep breath and plunged in after them. She came up for air, sputtering and kicking.

'It's cold!'

'No, it's not,' Kim told her. 'In a minute you'll turn numb, and then you won't feel it!'

Christie struck out for the boulder on which Jay-Jay and Susan were lying and scrambled up onto the sun-baked granite. On the edge of freezing just a moment before, her feet were now suddenly burning.

'Get back in the water,' Jay-Jay told her, giving her a shove.

She went under, and when she came to the surface, Susan's face was grinning down at her. 'Splash the rock where you're going to lie. It cools it off.'

'Why didn't you tell me before I climbed out?'

'It's more fun to watch people burn themselves.' Jay-Jay giggled. Christie began splashing, making sure she covered not only her spot on the rock, but Susan and Jay-Jay as well. Suddenly Jay-Jay jumped in beside her and shoved her under the surface. Her feet hit the bottom, and Christie let her knees buckle until she was crouching below the surface. Then she pushed up and burst from the water, screaming at Jay-Jay. Jay-Jay screeched and paddled frantically away. Christie started to follow her, then changed her mind and climbed once more onto the boulder. She settled down next to Susan and felt the sun begin to take the chill of the water out of her body.

'This is neat,' she said.

'Yeah,' Susan agreed. 'I just hope we can keep on coming up here.'

Christie propped herself up on one elbow.

'Why shouldn't we?'

'Well, up till today, nobody knew we came here. At least

Miss Edna and Miss Diana didn't. What if they make us stop?'

'Why would they?'

'Miss Diana didn't want you to come with us,' Susan pointed out. 'What if she says it's too dangerous and tells us we can't swim here anymore?'

'Then I guess we'll have to stop,' Christie replied.

Jay-Jay, hauling her body out of the water, plopped down next to them. 'Or sneak up here anyway,' she said.

When Christie stared at her, she grinned maliciously. 'If we only did what our parents said we can do, we wouldn't do anything, would we?' Then, an idea suddenly striking her, she stared at Christie. 'Is Miss Diana your mother now?'

'What do you mean?'

'Is she going to adopt you?'

'I don't know.'

''Cause if she did,' Jay-Jay went on, 'someday you'd own all this. You'd own the whole ranch!'

Christie's expression turned sombre. 'But she'd have to die for that to happen,' she said. 'She and Miss Edna both.'

'So what?' Jay-Jay said blithely. 'Sooner or later everybody has to die.' She lay down once more and soon she fell asleep in the warmth of the sun.

But Christie did not sleep. Instead she wondered.

Did everybody really have to die?

It didn't seem fair ...

And yet her parents had died, and sometimes she had a strange feeling that she was going to, too.

'This house used to belong to the Traverses.'

Diana glanced at her mother as she parked the Cadillac in the driveway of the house that had, until two weeks ago, been occupied by Elliot and Christie Lyons. Two hours had passed since breakfast. Diana had been feeding the chickens when Edna had come out to the coop and insisted that they follow through with Diana's plan to collect the last of Christie's belongings. Most of them, however, had

119

been delivered by Dan Gurley several days ago and were already in the nursery. Diana had suggested that she finish the job with Christie some other day, but Edna had insisted.

'We'll do it today,' she had said, 'and we'll do it together.'

Now, instead of getting out of the car, Edna was staring at the house, her mind apparently lost in some dim memory.

'The Traverses?' Diana asked. 'I don't remember them. Who were they?'

Edna's sharp blue eyes appraised her daughter. 'There are a lot of things you don't remember, aren't there?' she asked, her voice not ungentle. When Diana made no reply, Edna opened the car door and eased herself out. 'Are you coming?'

They let themselves into the house, and Edna quickly scanned the living-room. 'Fakes,' she sniffed. 'Cheap copies of second-rate junk, every stick of it.'

'Elliot wasn't rich, Mother,' Diana reminded her.

'Nor did he have any taste, apparently. Which room was the child's?'

They explored the house, finally coming to the small room at the rear, which had obviously been Christie's. They found two suitcases in the master bedroom and began packing them. Christie's remaining clothes fitted easily into one, and her few toys into the other.

'She doesn't have much, does she?' Edna asked as Diana snapped the catches of the second suitcase.

Diana ignored the comment and carried the suitcases into the living room.

'I wonder if Christie will want any of this?' she said. On the coffee table she found a photo album and sat down on the couch to look at it. From cover to cover it was filled with pictures of Carole and Elliot Lyons and Christie. They looked to Diana like a happy family, and she found herself feeling resentful of their apparent contentment. Her hands trembled as she turned the offending pages. She

120

wanted to destroy the album, with its proof that Christie was not truly hers.

'Is something wrong?' Edna asked. She had sensed the tension in her daughter's hunched shoulders, the tight grasp with which she clutched the album.

Diana glanced at her mother and closed the album. 'No,' she said, her voice too sharp. 'Everything's fine. Why shouldn't it be?'

Wordlessly Edna took the album and began going through it. When she finished, she closed it, but she didn't give it back to Diana.

'What are you going to do with this?'

'Why, I – I hadn't really thought about it,' Diana stammered.

'Don't lie to me, Diana. I asked what you were going to do with it.'

'Keep it, I suppose. Keep it for Christie. When she grows up, she'll want it.'

Edna's hand flew up, and she struck Diana across the cheek. 'I told you not to lie to me,' she hissed. 'When your mother asks you a question, you answer her.'

Diana gasped and touched her face where Edna had hit her. 'I'm sorry,' she whispered. Then: 'I was going to burn it.'

'Burn it?'

Now Diana cowered miserably on the couch. 'I don't want her to have it, Mother. Can't you understand? All it will do is remind her of – of them. But she's mine now. She's my little girl now, and I want her to forget all this. Can't you understand that?'

Edna's lips tightened, and she reached out to touch Diana's hand. Instinctively Diana flinched. 'When we get home, perhaps I should put you to bed,' Edna said, her voice suddenly gentle.

The words struck Diana like another blow. When she'd been a child, her mother had sometimes put her to bed, locked in her room, for days at a time. She shrank further into the couch, her eyes beseeching.

'No.' Her voice quavered, and now she reached out to touch her mother. 'I don't need to go to bed,' she said desperately. 'I'll be fine, Mama. I've been all right for years now, haven't I? It's just that I'm not used to having her yet.' Her voice took on a childish quality. 'Give me a chance, Mama. I can be a mother, too – I know I can. Please don't make me go to bed.'

As her daughter began to cry Edna stood up and bent over her, her eyes suddenly blazing. 'Stop that,' she said. 'Stop that this instant, do you hear me? You know what happens when you cry!' On the couch, Diana shook.

Edna raised her hand, preparing to strike her daughter once more, then slowly made herself lower it. 'Don't, Diana,' she said, almost to herself. 'Don't let's start again.'

As Diana continued to cry Edna stood still, closing her mind to the sound. Finally Diana's sobs abated.

She stirred on the couch and sat up. Her mother was standing over her, looking at her oddly. 'Mother, what happened?' she asked.

'You started crying,' Edna told her.

'But why?' Diana asked. 'I was sitting here, looking at something.' Then alarm filled her face. 'You said something about putting me to bed.'

'You seemed tired, Diana.'

Now Diana frowned, puzzled. She tried to remember exactly what had happened. She had been looking at the old photo album and had felt angry. But *then* what had happened?

Diana didn't know. And the gap in her memory terrified her. Feeling numb, she followed as her mother led her from the house.

10

Esperanza Rodriguez finished cleaning Edna Amber's bedroom, then climbed to the third floor, where she let herself into the nursery.

She liked being alone in the house. When they were present, her sensitive spirit never failed to pick up the constant tension between Miss Diana and Miss Edna. If she'd had any other way of earning a living, Esperanza would long since have stopped working for the Ambers, but the ranch was her whole life, and she assumed that someday she would die there, as so many people had died there.

In the nursery she lowered her bulk into the rocking chair and waited for her breathing to return to normal. She remembered the nursery from when she was a little girl and had played there with Miss Diana, who was only two weeks younger than she was. It hadn't been often – even when she was very small, Esperanza had had chores to do, and sometimes Diana couldn't play.

Those were the days, Esperanza remembered, when her friend had bruises on her body, and her face was streaked from crying.

Esperanza remembered the nights, too, when she had lain on her cot in the little room – now filled with broken furniture and trunks – a few feet from the nursery. She had listened to the strange sounds, though she tried her best not to hear them.

It would happen on nights when the wind was blowing. Esperanza would lie in her bed, unable to sleep, and soon she would hear the creaking of the back stairs.

Then there would be footsteps, pausing outside her door, as if someone were listening. The footsteps would move on, and she would hear the door to the nursery open and close.

And then there would be the muffled sound of voices, and the sound of Diana screaming.

The next day Diana would stay in her room, but sooner or later Esperanza would find a reason to sneak into the nursery.

She would find her friend in bed, crying softly. When she asked Diana what was wrong, Diana would only look at her sadly and shake her head.

'I had a nightmare,' she would whisper. 'I dreamed I was a bad girl and I got punished.' Her eyes would grow wide as she remembered the dream. 'And when I got punished, I cried.' Once, after she had said that, there was a long silence, and then Diana had reached out and squeezed her hand. 'Don't cry, Esperanza,' she had said. 'Don't ever cry. Only bad children cry, and then they get punished.'

Esperanza never had cried, not even when her mother died. Instead she had done what most of the Shacktown girls her age did. Though she was only fourteen, she got married and moved out of the house into the cabin by the mine, where her husband was the caretaker. A few years later, soon after she became pregnant, Carlos went away, and she never saw him again. Even then Esperanza did not cry.

It wasn't until Juan was born, and the old Indian women told her she should take him to the cave to live with the other children, that Esperanza let herself shed tears. She remembered that day now as she sat in the nursery.

The women had come and looked at Juan, and had told her that she mustn't keep him. For a while Esperanza had believed them. But as she watched her baby, and let her tears flow, she had decided it was wrong. The cave, she knew, was only for dead babies – the tiny ones that never breathed when they were born but came into the world as if

124

they were little old men and women, their faces wizened and wrinkled, looking as though they had lived their lives before they were born.

Their little bodies would be taken to the cave, and prayers would be said over them, and then they would be left there, to await the day when they would be reborn. Esperanza knew it was true. Sometimes, when the wind blew, she could hear them crying, for her cabin was near the hidden entrance to the cave. Their voices, lonely and terrified, would drift down the mountain, crying out for the mothers that would someday come for them.

Having heard the stories, Esperanza could not send her son to live in the cave. So she had spent a day and a night letting her tears flow, and had come to her decision. Juan had not been born dead, so he must not be sent to the cave. Instead she must keep him.

And so the years had gone by, and Esperanza had begun to think that everything was going to be all right.

But now the lost children were stirring, and a man had died, and Esperanza was terrified, for she knew that one of the children in the cave was the child of Diana Amber.

She knew because she had been awake one night, not long after Juan had been born, and she had heard a strange sound outside her cabin.

She had heard a baby crying, and she had gone to her window and looked out.

There, moving through the night, she had seen a woman walking up the hill, carrying a baby in her arms.

The baby had been crying, and Esperanza had remembered Diana Amber's long-ago words.

'*Only bad children cry, and they get punished!*'

She had known that Diana Amber had been sick, and as she watched she realised what the sickness had been.

And in all the years since then, as she continued to work in the Amber house, no one had ever spoken of Diana Amber's child.

It was as if the baby had never existed, and it had not been Esperanza's place to ask questions.

But somehow, she knew, it was all tied together. The nightmares Diana had told her about, that Esperanza knew were not dreams at all, and the baby that had come from Diana's 'sickness' and been taken to the cave.

And now a child had come to live in the nursery once occupied by one of the lost children.

As she looked around the faded room Esperanza shivered.

Somehow *los niños* had been disturbed, and she was sure that as they awakened, people were going to die. For the first time since Juan had been born, Esperanza Rodriguez began to cry.

Diana Amber stared nervously out the living-room window.

She had come home two hours ago and found Esperanza in the nursery, crying, but had been unable to find out what was wrong. Finally she had sent the woman home, then spent the final hours of the morning unpacking and putting away the last of Christie's belongings. At noon, when Christie had not come back from her swim, Diana had gone to the window and begun her vigil.

The wind was picking up, and a dust cloud was forming, making everything indistinct. In the distance a figure was moving, but she couldn't see it clearly. As she watched, it disappeared; whoever it was, was going the other way.

By one o'clock Diana could stand it no longer.

'Something's happened,' she told her mother.

Edna scowled as she looked up from her needlework.

'What's happened is that you've gotten nervous. Sit down, Diana.'

'No, Mother. I've got to go find her.'

Edna rose to her feet, leaning on her cane. 'You can't go running off every time you get a feeling something's wrong with that child. What about me? What if you're gone and something happens to me?'

Diana's stomach tightened, but her resolve was strong.

'You'll be fine, Mother. You've never been sick in your life, and you're not now. But Christie's only a little girl – hardly more than a baby. I'm going to look for her.'

She turned and left the room before Edna could say anything more. When she was gone, the old woman stayed on her feet, moving to the window. She watched Diana go to the barn, then, a few minutes later, lead her horse out. Only when Diana had mounted the horse and started off towards the hills did Edna return to her needlepoint. As she worked she listened to the wind. It was growing stronger, moaning around the old house, causing its beams to creak. It was an evil wind, Edna thought. She wished Diana had not gone out in it. But ever since that child had come to live with them, Diana had changed. And the change, Edna knew, was not for the better.

The four girls sat on the strip of gravel that separated the quarry pond from the foliage that surrounded it. The sun was overhead, and in the protection of the hillside there was no breeze.

'I'm hungry,' Jay-Jay said.

Kim Sandler shrugged. 'I told you we should have brought some sandwiches.'

'Does anybody have a watch?' Christie asked. 'Aunt Diana told me to be back at noon.'

'Well, it's after noon now,' Kim told her. 'Look at the sun.'

'Christie squinted into the sky. The glare quickly blinded her, but her ears picked up a low moaning sound. 'What's that?' she asked, cocking her head in unconscious imitation of Susan Gillespie. The other three girls listened intently.

'The wind,' Jay-Jay said. 'It's starting to blow again.'

She and Susan scrambled to their feet. 'Let's go home,' Susan said. 'I hate it when the wind blows.'

'Then let's stay here till it dies down,' Kim suggested.

'That's dumb. It won't die down till tonight.' Jay-Jay followed Susan to the clearing where their clothes were piled, while Christie hesitated.

'I better go, too,' Christie said at last, afraid of what might happen if she were late. 'I promised Aunt Diana.'

'So go.' Kim's voice was petulant. 'I can stay here by myself. I like it better when I'm the only one.'

Christie went to the clearing, pulled her clothes on over her bathing suit, then went back to the little beach. Susan and Jay-Jay were waiting for her.

'We're gonna take a shortcut,' Jay-Jay announced. 'You want to come with us?'

'Does it go by my house?' Christie asked.

Jay-Jay shook her head. 'Nah. It starts by the mine, but you can take the road. We cut down the other side of the hill. Come on.' As if the matter were settled, Jay-Jay, with Susan following her, disappeared down the trail.

Christie hesitated, watching Kim, but Kim was studiously staring at the pond.

'Are you sure you don't want to come with us?' Christie asked her.

Kim shook her head. 'If you want to go, go. Nobody had to be back at noon except you.'

Still Christie hesitated, but when Kim continued to ignore her, she turned away. A few moments later she caught up with the others.

'Is Kim mad at us?' Susan asked.

Christie shrugged. 'I guess so.'

'Kim's weird that way. Everything's fine, and then all of a sudden she's mad about something. Just leave her alone – she'll change her mind and catch up with us.'

'But should we leave her out here all by herself?' It seemed to Christie that the quarry was lots of fun with the rest of the kids, but she didn't think she'd like to be there alone. The others, though, didn't seem to be worried.

'Kim likes to be by herself,' Jay-Jay said. 'Come on. I want to get home before it gets too bad.' Suddenly they were out of the dense vegetation of the hillside, and the heat and force of the wind struck them.

'Yuck!' Susan pulled a bandanna out of her pocket and

128

tied it around her face. 'Hey!' she yelled. 'I'm a bandit! Stick 'em up!' Falling happily into the game, the three girls quickly forgot about Kim Sandler.

Diana felt the hot wind in her face as she urged her horse along the trail that led up into the hills to the quarry. Dust, kicked up from the valley floor, was swirling around her, getting in her eyes and nose, choking her. She wished she had brought a kerchief but didn't consider going back for one; she was suddenly consumed with a need to find Christie.

As she wound into the hills she began to hear the voice.

A baby crying.

Like an echo from the past, it was calling to her, needing her, wanting her.

Crying for her.

A confusion of emotions tumbled through Diana's mind. Part of her wanted to go to the baby, to comfort it.

But another part of her, a part she couldn't control, wanted to stifle it, as her own crying had been stifled when she was a child.

She spurred the horse on, and in her mind the crying grew louder, tormenting her.

Childish anger flooded her, and she lived again the times so long ago when her mother had made her cry, then forced her to stop. Her eyes glazed over as she rode through the howling wind.

The voice grew louder, and she felt she was getting closer to it.

If she could find it, and silence it, she might be free of the past.

The horse picked its way through the loose rock that littered the trail. Moving steadily, it wound up the flank of the hill, then paused at the top.

Diana could look down on the quarry from there.

It seemed deserted.

But in her ears the crying of the baby grew and built, torturing her, calling her. Why couldn't she find it? Where was it? Ahead of her? Around her? Inside of her? She couldn't be sure.

But the sound was driving her crazy.

Somehow she had to find the baby, for the door to her subconscious was wide open now, and the memory was clear. '*Crying babies must be punished.*'

Unaware of the world around her, heeding only the driving forces of her mind, she gave herself to the wind ...

Juan Rodriguez squatted in the mine entrance and watched the three girls go by. By the direction they had come from, he was sure they had been up at his pool. But they were gone now, and he could enjoy the water by himself. It would be good today – the heat was building, and the wind blew dust in his eyes.

As soon as the little girls were out of sight, Juan began the long walk up to the pool. He didn't hurry – Juan liked to look at things as he walked, and he stopped several times to examine wild flowers or watch the butterflies as they flitted around his head.

He veered off the trail as he drew closer to the quarry, and began climbing the hill so that he could do one of his favourite things: creep up to the edge of the bluff and peek down onto the pond, to see if anything was in it. Sometimes he could see a turtle or two, and once there had been some kind of an animal in the pond.

And last week, those children.

He dropped to all fours and crept through the aspens that covered the crest of the hill. Then he poked his head over the lip of the precipice and looked down.

Below him, the pool lay clear and still.

But then he realised that someone was there.

Even though three little girls had passed him on their way down the hill, there was still one in his pond.

Slowly Juan backed away from the ledge and got up. As quietly as he could he began to make his way down the hill. Today, since the little girl was all alone, he wouldn't go away. Instead he would surprise her.

After her friends had gone, Kim sat by the pond for a while. Maybe she should have gone with them after all. It was lonesome all by herself. Though the wind couldn't reach her, she could hear it all around her, whistling in the trees and scouring the hills.

She got up and stuck a foot in the water. Now that the day had grown hot, the water seemed even colder. Maybe she ought to dress and go after the others.

She heard something.

A rustling, coming from the aspen grove.

Something was in the woods, moving towards her.

'Hello?' To her own ears, her voice sounded small, and she realised she was frightened.

But it was the middle of the day. What could happen in the middle of the day?

Maybe her friends were playing a trick on her.

'Jay-Jay? Christie? Is that you?'

There was no response, and Kim decided to get dressed. She strippd off her bathing suit and picked up her underwear.

A few yards from her a twig cracked.

Kim froze.

'Susan? Who's there?'

There was no answer.

Kim had put on her underwear when the familiar figure stepped into the clearing. She felt the fear drain out of her.

'Hi,' she said. Then she realised that something was wrong. 'Are you all right?'

Suddenly her fear came rushing back to her, and she began backing away.

It was the eyes. There was something about the eyes that didn't look right.

'Are you mad at me?' she asked.

There was no answer, but the eyes remained glued to her, as if fascinated.

Instinctively Kim began pulling on her jeans, but then realised that she wouldn't be able to run if she were caught with her feet halfway into her pants. She dropped her

131

clothes and began backing towards the beach, the strange eyes still on her, never leaving her.

They made her skin crawl.

'Leave me alone,' she begged. What was wrong? She wasn't sure if the eyes could even see her now.

Screaming, she turned and fled.

Hands suddenly closed around her arms, and she was pulled to a stop.

This time the eyes were only inches from her own, and as they bored into her, her heart began to pound, and she had the sudden feeling that she was going to die.

She screamed again, and the hands suddenly whirled her around, then one of them left her arm and covered her mouth.

Though she could no longer see those strange eyes, she could hear the sound of heavy breathing close to her ear.

She was lifted from her feet and carried towards the water.

She struggled, but the arms held her fast. Then she was in the water.

She twisted and thrashed about, but succeeded only in turning over, so that she was looking up – up at the surface of the water and, beyond that, at the weirdly distorted face of her attacker, like a dark shadow against the brilliant blue of the sky.

She held her breath as long as she could, but finally the pain in her chest grew too great, and she exhaled, the air bubbling from her lips.

She began coughing and choking as the water flooded into her mouth, but still she couldn't get loose.

And then, as the water filled her lungs, a strange peace settled over Kim Sandler, and she stopped struggling.

The hands let her go, but she only drifted now, uncaring if she ever breathed the air again.

And then, for Kim Sandler, life turned grey, and the grey turned to black.

It was over.

Diana Amber backed away from the pool of water.

The crying of the baby faded away, and Diana paused.

Though the wind had eased, she felt oddly disoriented. Had she taken a wrong turn? She looked around.

No, she'd just come too far.

The quarry was behind her.

She clucked to her horse and turned him around. Suddenly she was no longer worried.

Somehow she knew that Christie was fine.

The child had simply lost track of time, that was all. But it was all right – there was really no reason for her to have been back by noon. Why not let her enjoy herself?

Feeling content, Diana started towards home. As she came near the mine she decided to stop at the cabin and see how Esperanza was. She tied up her horse and rapped at the door. A moment later Esperanza appeared, but the look on her face when she saw Diana was one of disappointment.

'Esperanza?' Diana asked. 'Are you all right?'

Esperanza nodded, then stepped out onto the porch of the cabin. Her eyes looked first towards the mine, then swept the hillside above it.

'Juan,' she said, her voice worried. 'Have you seen Juan?'

Diana frowned. 'Why, no,' she said. 'Is he missing?'

Esperanza hesitated for a moment, then shook her head emphatically.

'No. He's just ...' Her voice trailed off, and she shrugged, as if the matter were of no importance.

'He just wanders off sometimes,' Diana finished for her. Then she squeezed Esperanza's arm reassuringly. 'But don't worry. He knows what he's doing as long as he stays on the ranch.'

Esperanza knew Diana was telling her the truth, but still she was worried. Ever since she had been in the nursery that morning, she had had a feeling that something was very wrong, and Diana's words did not comfort her.

Dan Gurley was considering the possibility of taking the

rest of the day off to go fishing when Juan Rodriguez came into his office and sat down opposite him, his hat in his hands, his expression fearful.

'Juan? Is something wrong?' Dan made his voice as gentle as he could. Juan, he knew, lived in fear of men in uniform. It had been a man in a uniform who had found him, four years ago, exposing himself to two little girls in the back corner of Penrose's Dry Goods store. That man had been Dan himself. If it had been anyone but Juan, Dan would have wasted no time in charging the offender, but, knowing Juan as he did, he had called the state hospital at Pueblo and talked to one of the doctors about the case. Finally he had taken a day off and, on his own time, had driven Juan to Pueblo so that the doctor could interview him. After the interview, he had brought Juan home again. The doctor – his name was Hilbert, if Dan remembered right – had told him that Juan Rodriguez's exposing himself to the little girls was on about the same level as a five-year-old playing doctor. So Dan had explained the situation to the children's mothers, who had reluctantly agreed that there wasn't much point in pressing charges. Then he tried to impress upon Juan the importance of keeping his pants zipped up in public. Mostly, to his own sorrow, he had only succeeded in terrifying Juan. And now Juan sat before him, wringing his hat, his eyes filled with fear.

'What is it, Juan? Can't you tell me?'

'A – a little girl,' Juan stammered. 'Up at my pool.'

'What about her?' Dan felt a sudden pang of anxiety.

'She's – she's not wearing anything,' Juan went on, and Dan had a sinking feeling in the pit of his belly.

'And she's dead.' Juan swallowed and looked pleadingly at the marshal. 'I didn't do it, Mr. Gurley. Really, I didn't.'

Dan's stomach turned over, but he tried to keep his face calm. He stood up and went around to put a hand on Juan's shoulder. 'Are you sure she's dead, Juan?' he asked.

Juan's head bobbed. 'I know it. She was in the water,

and she wasn't moving. Are you going to put me in jail?'

Dan tried to sort out the confusion of thoughts that was churning in his brain. Surely Juan must be wrong. It had to be a mistake.

He came to a decision. 'Come on,' he said. 'Let's go up there and see exactly what you found. Then we'll decide what to do.'

He led Juan out of his office, and the two of them got into his Chrysler. Juan, though still frightened, looked eagerly at the switch that activated the siren. 'Can I turn it on?' he asked.

Dan ignored the question and started the engine. As he pulled away from the kerb a thought crossed his mind, the kind of incongruous thought that often intrudes in moments of stress.

'Where's your mother?' he asked. 'Didn't you tell her about the girl?'

Juan shook his head emphatically. 'Oh, no! If something's wrong, you have to tell the police.' He paused, then spoke again, his voice faraway, as if he were talking to himself. 'Why was she up there? It's my pool! She shouldn't have been there.'

Dan made no answer, but as he drove out of town he had the horrible feeling that this time Juan's involvement was not going to be as innocent as that of 'a five-year-old playing doctor'.

Juan reached out and flipped the siren on. Dan made no move to stop him. After all, Dan thought, he's really only a little boy.

But he wondered if the people of Amberton would remember that when Juan came to trial.

11

Edna Amber listened as the screaming siren drew closer to the house. She waited until it had faded away, apparently headed towards the mine, then reached up with her cane and pounded on the ceiling.

'Diana? *Diana*!' She waited, then pounded again.

When there was still no answer, she sighed heavily and started up the stairs. Ever since that child had come into the house, things hadn't been right. She shouldn't have to go looking for Diana – a daughter should pay attention to her mother.

She found Diana in the bathroom.

She was kneeling by the tub, washing Christie.

'What on earth do you think you're doing?' Edna demanded.

Diana glanced up at her. 'Giving Christie a bath,' she replied.

'She's nine years old,' Edna snapped. 'Surely she can bathe herself.'

'I can, Aunt Diana,' Christie said. 'Really, I can.'

Diana wrung out the washcloth. 'But I want to help you. All mothers help their babies bathe.'

'I'm not a baby,' Christie protested. 'Mom stopped giving me baths when I was four.'

'And you're not her mother,' Edna added. 'Come downstairs, Diana.'

Diana hesitated, and Edna struck the floor with her cane. 'Didn't you hear me, child? Come downstairs!'

Diana dropped the washcloth in the tub. 'I'm sorry,

sweetheart,' she told Christie. 'I'll be right back.' She got to her feet and followed her mother downstairs.

Christie fished around in the tub, found the wash-cloth and squeezed the water out of it, then pulled the plug. She got out of the tub.

Ever since she'd come home, things had been strange. She knew Aunt Diana had been over to her house – the rest of her clothes were up in her room, neatly folded. But what about her father's things? What about the album? Where was it? After lunch, she had asked about it, but all she had been told was that she could have it when she was older.

When Diana had then insisted on giving her a bath, she'd objected, saying she'd been swimming all morning, but it hadn't done any good. Finally she'd had to submit, and as she sat in the tub she felt like a baby. It occurred to her now, as she pulled on her clothes, that, in fact, Diana was treating her more and more like a baby. She didn't like it, but she didn't know what to do about it.

She remembered what her friends had said, about Miss Edna locking Diana in her room when she was a little girl. Why had she done that? And why was Diana locking her in every night? She wished she had someone to talk to about it, but there was no one. She was beginning to feel terribly frightened.

Fully dressed, Christie started downstairs, but in the living room she could hear Aunt Diana and Miss Edna arguing. It was about her – she was sure of it. She decided she didn't want to hear it. Instead she went through the kitchen and outside.

She wandered over to the chicken coop, and the chicks flocked around her, cheeping to be fed. She started to pick one of them up, then, remembering the tiny body in the box by her bed, hesitated. She glanced towards the house, wondering if anyone was watching. She couldn't be sure. her gaze swept the yard and stopped at the barn.

Hayburner.

She would visit Hayburner, and the horse would make her feel less lonely.

Edna waited until they were in the living room before she spoke. Then she turned to face her daughter and searched Diana's eyes. 'What are you doing?' she asked at last, her voice containing both anger and concern.

Diana's face reflected her puzzlement. What had she done now? Why should her mother be mad at her?

'I was just giving Christie a bath,' she began, but Edna cut her off.

'In the middle of the day? And giving a nine-year-old a bath? Diana, are you all right?'

'Of course I am, Mother. Why shouldn't I be?'

Edna paused. Then: 'Didn't you hear the siren just now?'

'Siren? What siren?'

Now Edna's face tightened, and she glared at her daughter. 'Not five minutes ago, Dan Gurley went by, with his siren on. You must have heard it,' she finished, her voice almost desperate.

'I didn't hear anything, Mother,' Diana said quietly.

'Well, I didn't imagine it,' Edna snapped.

Diana's expression turned to exasperation. 'Mother, if Dan Gurley went past here with his siren on, I would have heard it. There was no water running, and I'm not deaf.'

'Aren't you?' Edna asked. Again she searched her daughter's face. 'Diana, I don't think we can keep that child here any longer. She isn't good for you.'

Sudden fury flashed through Diana. She understood what her mother was up to. 'Not good for me, Mother? Or not good for you?' Her body quivering with anger, she turned, left the room, and hurried upstairs to finish giving Christie her bath.

The bathroom was empty. Diana went to the third floor and into the nursery. It, too, was empty.

'Christie? Christie, baby, where are you?'

There was no answer, and Diana was about to leave the nursery when something outside caught her eye. She went to the window and looked out.

Christie was coming out of the barn, her face smudged,

138

her clothing covered with bits of straw. Diana's eyes blazed as she stared at the little girl.

That was the trouble with children.

You gave them a bath, and they went right out and got dirty again.

Still, she temporised, it wasn't the baby's fault. Not really.

Babies have to be taken care of.

And living things – things like chicks and horses – attract them.

Shaking her head sadly, Diana left the nursery to go down and bring her naughty baby in from the yard.

Dan Gurley stared down into the clear waters of the pond and swore softly. Even from where he stood, he knew who the little girl in the water was. With that wiry body, and the long brown hair, it could be no one but Kim Sandler.

She was facedown, her hair spreading out like a halo, arms akimbo, as if she were practising a dead man's float.

Dan ran down the hill and made his way through the thicket to the gravel beach. He waded in, picked Kim up, and carried her ashore. Though he knew it was useless, he tried to revive her, first forcing the water from her lungs through artificial respiration, then trying mouth-to-mouth resuscitation.

Juan Rodriguez stood next to him, clucking sympathetically. Dan gave up at last and stood, his breath coming in panting gasps. He waited until his breathing was normal, then looked sharply at Juan.

'She was in the water when you found her?'

Juan nodded.

'I thought you said she was naked,' Dan said, eyeing the panties the girl was clad in.

Juan shrugged, but made no reply, so Dan tried another question. 'Why didn't you pull her out?'

'I was scared, Mr. Gurley. I don't like dead people.'

'But she might not have been dead yet, Juan.'

Juan looked at him, his brown eyes as clear and

139

innocent as a cocker spaniel's. 'But she didn't move. I watched her, and she didn't move.'

Dan sighed, knowing he would get nothing else out of the young man. 'All right, Juan. Come on – let's get her out of here.'

He picked Kim up and carried her back through the thicket. He paused there and stared at the clothing that was strewn around.

A bathing suit, crumpled in the dirt, and next to it a pile of clothes, neatly folded.

Except for the underwear, which Kim still wore.

His first thought was that it had probably been an accident. If Kim had been swimming alone, she could have had a sudden cramp and, with no one to help her, drowned.

Now he wasn't so sure.

It looked as if she had been getting dressed.

Had she suddenly decided on one last dip? But she would have put her bathing suit back on, or gone skinny-dipping, wouldn't she?

To Dan, it looked as if something had surprised her.

Something, or someone.

He spoke none of his thoughts to Juan, who was fidgeting nervously next to him.

'Should we take her clothes?'

'No. Leave them here – I'll come back for them.' With Juan following him, Dan carried Kim back to his car, which was parked near the mine entrance.

Standing by his car was Esperanza Rodriguez. As she saw the body of the little girl in Dan's arms, she crossed herself, then went to her son. She looked into his eyes, then, as if satisfied with something, whispered in his ear. Juan listened, nodded his head, then got into the marshal's car. As Dan started the engine Juan smiled at him and spoke.

'My mama says everything's okay,' he said. 'She says I didn't do nothing.'

Dan sighed and put the car in gear. He didn't bother to

turn the siren on as he drove back to Amberton – there seemed no point in it. As he passed the Ambers' he saw Diana in the yard, talking to Christie Lyons and leading her towards the house.

After he'd taken Kim's body to Bill Henry's office, he'd have to come back out here and talk to Diana and Miss Edna, and Christie, too. Two deaths on the ranch in nearly as many weeks.

It was like the stories he'd heard of the old days, when the mine was going. Except that now the mine was closed.

Bill Henry came out of his office and shrugged.

'I don't know. I haven't opened her up, but so far there isn't much. Some bruises on the surface, but there're no breaks in the skin.'

Dan scratched his nose and nodded. 'Did you check for a sexual assault?'

Bill nodded. 'Nothing. Hymen intact, and no traces of semen.' Bill paused and glanced out the window at the police car where Juan Rodriguez still sat placidly in the front seat. 'Were you thinking of Juan?'

'I'm not sure,' Dan said slowly. 'I guess I must have been, except the docs in Pueblo told me he was harmless. But you never know, I guess. What do you think?'

Again Bill shrugged. 'Unless you have some reason for thinking otherwise, I'd call it an accident. But I won't write that down – I want her opened up by someone who knows what to look for. Have you told her parents?'

'Not yet. I called Alice Sandler – she's on her way down here.'

'It's going to be rough. Kim's all they had.'

'I know. I think that's the worst part of this job, having to deliver the bad news. Then I'm going back up to the quarry. There's still some looking around to be done, and I've got to let the Ambers know what happened.'

The front door of the office burst open, and Alice Sandler stumbled in, her eyes wild.

'Where's Kim?' she demanded. 'What's happened?'

141

'You'd better sit down, Alice,' Bill said, the tone of his voice telegraphing to the distraught woman what had happened.

Alice sank to the sofa and listened numbly while Dan explained. When he was done, she looked at him steadily. 'It was no accident,' she said. 'Kim's a good swimmer. She's been swimming since she was four.' Then, as if for the first time realising the extent of the tragedy, she began to cry. 'I mean she *was* a good swimmer,' she added, her voice breaking.

She sat still for a moment, then glared at Dan Gurley. 'Juan killed Kim,' she said. 'He's a sex fiend, and he always has been. Why is he sitting out in your car?'

'There's no evidence that he had anything to do with it, Alice.'

Alice Sandler was suddenly screaming, her face an ashy white. 'Nobody else in town would do a thing like that,' she wailed.

Bill Henry sat beside her and took her hand. 'Alice, so far it looks like an accident. Dan can't arrest Juan simply because he found Kim.'

But Alice was unconvinced. 'He – he did it,' she said brokenly. 'He killed my baby.' Then, her grief overcoming her, she buried her face in her hands and gave in to her tears.

Dan Gurley pressed the Ambers' doorbell and waited uncomfortably on the front porch. Except for Kim's clothing, there had been nothing around the quarry. Finally he had given up his search, gathered the clothes together, put them in his car, and driven down to the Ambers'.

The door opened, and Edna Amber stared at him suspiciously.

'What's happened?' she demanded.

'May I come in?'

Edna reluctantly stood aside as Dan stepped into the foyer, then led him into the parlour.

142

'Is Diana here?' Dan asked.

'She's upstairs.'

'Could you call her?'

Edna hesitated, and for a moment Dan thought she was going to refuse. Then she went to the stairs, pounded the ceiling with her cane, and called to Diana. A few seconds later Diana hurried down the stairs. She came to an abrupt stop when she saw who was there.

'Dan. Mother said you went by earlier. Is something wrong?'

Briefly Dan explained what had happened.

'My God,' Diana breathed when he was finished. 'Christie was up there this morning, too.'

'Christie?'

'And some others. Jay-Jay Jennings and Susan Gillespie. They came by on their way up to the quarry, and Christie went with them.'

'Then maybe I'd better talk to Christie,' Dan suggested.

Diana's eyes flickered towards the stairs, and her fingers plucked at her skirt. 'Do you have to?' she asked finally.

Dan frowned. 'Is there some reason why I shouldn't?'

'She's – well, she's only a little girl,' Diana said lamely. Edna shot her a sharp look.

'I'm going to have to talk to all the girls who were with Kim,' Dan said. 'Could you have her come down?'

Diana chewed on her lip. 'Of course,' she said at last. 'But don't upset her – please?' Then she went upstairs to get Christie. When she was gone, Edna turned to Dan.

'I warned you,' she said.

Dan frowned, wondering what she was talking about. 'I beg your pardon, Miss Edna?'

'I told you something would happen.' The old woman's eyes glittered almost triumphantly. 'A ranch like this is no place for children. No place at all.'

'Diana was raised here,' Dan countered, still unsure of what she was getting at.

Edna's eyes narrowed. 'That was different. I'm her mother, and I had lots of help. Someone was always watching Diana. But there's nobody here now. I can't have children wandering all over the ranch wherever they please.'

'They've been doing it for years, Miss Edna,' Dan informed her.

'If they have,' Edna muttered angrily, 'this is the first I've heard of it.'

Dan was sure the old woman was telling him the truth. He was aware that the children had, until recently, steered well clear of the house. And if Christie Lyons were not living there, they would undoubtedly still be avoiding the place. But none of that had any bearing on Kim Sandler's death, and he was about to say so when Diana returned to the parlour with Christie next to her.

The little girl looked at him worriedly. Was she in trouble with the marshal now, as well as with Diana? 'Is something wrong?' she asked.

Dan knelt by her and took her hand gently in his own. 'Well, something happened today, and I need to talk to you about it.'

Christie regarded him warily. 'Am I in trouble?'

'No. At least I don't think so.' Dan smiled at her reassuringly. 'Did you do something you shouldn't have?'

Christie shook her head.

'Then you can't be in trouble, can you?'

Memories of the last week whirled in her head. 'What happened?' she asked.

Dan ignored the question and asked one of his own instead.

'Were you up at the quarry today?'

'Unh-hunh. I was swimming with Kim and Jay-Jay and Susan.'

'You all went up together?'

'Unh-hunh.'

'And you all left together?'

Now Christie shook her head again. 'Kim didn't go with the rest of us. She stayed.'

'By herself?'

Christie nodded silently, and Dan went on.

'How come she didn't come back with the rest of you?'

Christie shrugged. 'I don't know. I guess she didn't want to.'

'Was she mad at you?'

Christie hesitated and glanced at Diana, hoping for support. There was none, and finally she turned back to the marshal. 'Sort of,' she admitted.

'And were you mad at her?'

Now Christie shook her head emphatically, her blue eyes reflecting the fear that was growing inside her. 'No,' she said. 'Did something happen to Kim?'

Reluctantly Dan nodded. 'She had an accident.'

Christie's eyes met his, and when she spoke, her voice was steady. 'Is she dead?'

Though Dan was sure the ingenuousness in her voice was sincere, he watched her carefully as he answered her question. 'Yes, she is. She drowned.'

Christie's hand tightened on Diana's, and Diana knelt beside her. 'It's all right, sweetheart. No one said you had anything to do with it.'

'But how could she drown?' Christie asked. 'She swims better than any of us.'

'We don't know,' Dan told her. 'That's what we're trying to find out. Now, I want you to think very carefully. Did you see anybody else up there? Anybody at all?'

A tear formed in Christie's right eye. She brushed it away, but when she spoke, her voice shook. 'No. The kids said nobody ever goes up there.'

'What about Juan? Did you see Juan up there?'

'No!' She pulled away from Dan Gurley and wrapped her arms around Diana. 'Please,' she asked, her voice tiny. 'Can't I go back upstairs now?'

'Of course you can, darling,' Diana murmured. 'I'll be up in just a few minutes.'

When Christie was gone, Diana faced Dan Gurley. 'What do you think happened?'

'I don't know. It looks like an accident, but there are a

couple of odd things. She was wearing only her underwear, and there seem to be a few bruises on her body. Nothing serious, but Bill wants them looked at by an expert.'

'I see,' Diana said pensively. Then she met Dan's eyes. 'Juan?'

Dan shrugged. 'I don't know. I hope not, but until I know exactly what did happen up there, I'll have to hold him. He's in jail right now.'

Diana shook her head sadly. 'Poor Juan. He seems so – well, he seems so harmless.'

'Maybe he is,' Dan said, trying to express more hope than he was feeling.

A few minutes later he was gone, and Diana was about to go back upstairs when Edna stopped her.

'Diana?'

'I have to go up to Christie, Mother.'

'In a minute. I want to talk to you.'

Diana sighed and sat down.

'Diana, didn't you go up to the quarry today?'

Diana looked at her mother blankly. 'I started to, but I didn't. I – I changed my mind.'

'But when you left here, you were so worrried.'

'I know –'

'What happened? What made you stop worrying?'

Diana thought about it. In truth, she didn't know. But she couldn't tell her mother that, nor could she explain to her mother what had happened up on the mountain that day – the wind screaming at her, the confusion, the minutes she had lost. It would only give Edna ammunition to use against her.

Besides, her mother always wanted answers. Simple answers. Suddenly she smiled.

'I just decided you were right, Mother. You told me I was being silly, didn't you?'

'But the wind was blowing when you left, Diana. I always worry about you when the wind blows.'

'That's in the past, Mother,' Diana replied. 'Can't we forget about all that? Please?'

As Diana left the room to go up to Christie, Edna sat very still. She wished she could forget about the past. But try as she would, she could not. The past was too much a part of the present, and it could destroy her.

Somehow Edna would have to find a way to use the past to *control* the present.

If it wasn't already too late.

12

Jeff Crowley wished he could go home.

He, along with his parents, was at the Sandlers'. All afternoon the word of Kim's death had rippled through Amberton, passing from one person to another among the shopkeepers and over the back fences, and late in the afternoon people had begun arriving to offer their sympathy to Alice and George, and to discuss what had happened.

Now, at nine o'clock, only the Jenningses and the Gillespies were still there, along with the Crowleys. While their parents sat talking in the living room, the children huddled in the kitchen, their ears pressed against the door, eagerly listening to every word.

'It could have happened to any of them,' Jerome Jennings was saying.

But it didn't, Alice Sandler thought bitterly to herself. It happened to Kim. Why Kim? Involuntarily she glared at Jennings. Why couldn't he take his prissy wife and his brat and go home? She chided herself for being uncharitable and tried to make herself believe that he was right – that it *could* have been any of the children. Deep in her heart, though, Alice was positive that what had happened to Kim was no accident.

'Juan Rodriguez should have been arrested years ago,' she said aloud.

The Reverend Jennings, who prided himself on being fair-minded, clucked sympathetically. 'Now, now. What he did then wasn't all that serious. Still, considering his background ...'

'And for that matter, it's the Ambers' fault, too,' Alice went on, ignoring Reverend Jennings. The rest of the people in the room were staring at her now. 'I warned them years ago,' Alice explained. 'I told Miss Diana that the quarry was dangerous and that it should have been fenced off. But did those high-and-mighty women do anything? Nothing! Nothing at all. Well, maybe if it had been one of their own who was dead –'

'Alice, that's not fair,' Joyce Crowley protested. 'I'm sure Diana and Miss Edna are as sorry as anyone else about what happened. And the quarry's not being fenced off doesn't make what happened their fault!'

Alice Sandler sighed heavily and shook her head. 'I don't know,' she said at last. 'It just seems to me that they're every bit as responsible as Juan.'

In the kitchen, Jay-Jay looked at her friends, her eyes glowing maliciously. 'Besides,' she whispered, 'maybe Juan didn't kill her at all. Maybe Christie did!'

The others stared at her, agog.

'That's dumb.' Jeff said.

'It is not,' Jay-Jay shot back. 'When me and Susan left, she stayed, didn't she?'

Susan nodded reluctantly. 'But it was only a couple of minutes,' she said, her voice revealing her uncertainty.

'It was *ten* minutes,' Jay-Jay insisted. 'I had my watch on, and I looked,' she added smugly.

'You did not,' Jeff countered. 'You're just trying to get Christie in trouble.'

'How do you know? You weren't there!'

'It doesn't matter. Everybody knows you're a liar!'

'You take that back, Jeff Crowley!' Jay-Jay shrieked.

'I won't! It's true!'

Joyce Crowley appeared at the door.

'All right, what's going on?'

'Jeff called me a liar,' Jay-Jay shouted, her face red with anger.

'Jeff!'

'Well, she is. She said Christie drowned Kim!'

'I did not,' Jay-Jay said sulkily. 'I said she *might* have.'

'Good Lord!' Joyce Crowley breathed. 'What would make you say a thing like that?'

Jay-Jay glanced at her friends, but Susan and Jeff were both avoiding her eyes. 'I was just kidding,' she hedged. Then her face set stubbornly. 'But she still might have.' She repeated her story to Jeff's mother, but when she was done Joyce shook her head doubtfully.

'Jay-Jay, why would Christie do something like that? Kim and Christie were friends.'

'Maybe they had a fight,' Jay-Jay suggested.

'And maybe you're letting your imagination run away with you. Now, all of you, settle down.'

'Can't we go home?' Jeff begged.

'In a few minutes,' Joyce promised. As she returned to the living room Matt looked at her questioningly.

'What was that all about?'

'Oh, nothing,' Joyce said. She saw no point in repeating Jay-Jay's story, since privately she agreed with her son that Jay-Jay was a liar. Minister's children, she thought. What makes them such little stinkers? Aloud, she tried to pass the incident off. 'I think they're getting tired, and I am, too.'

A few minutes later the group broke up, and as they drove home Joyce told Matt what had gone on in the kitchen.

'Oh, Lord,' Matt sighed when Joyce had finished. 'I hope Jay-Jay isn't going to start spreading that tale around. A thing like that can make a child an outcast. Hasn't Christie had enough trouble already?'

'But everybody likes Christie,' Jeff said.

'Everybody likes her a lot better than they like old Jay-Jay!'

'I only hope it stays that way,' Joyce said softly. 'But it's such a small town ...'

Diana lay in bed, listening to the sounds of the house. The day had exhausted her, but sleep wouldn't come. She tossed restlessly in her bed, willing herself to relax.

150

Finally she went downstairs, prowling the rooms like a restless cat. She had the feeling she was looking for something but had no idea what.

She went over the day carefully.

The blank spots were still there, and nothing she could do would fill in the blanks.

And then, after Dan Gurley had left, Christie had once more disobeyed her.

She'd told Christie to stay upstairs, but late in the afternoon, she'd gone upstairs. The nursery had been empty.

She'd found Christie in the barn.

The barn door was open, and when she'd stepped into its gloom, at first Diana thought it was empty, except for the horses.

And then she heard Christie's voice, coming from Hayburner's stall.

'Good boy,' the little girl's voice was crooning. 'Are you my good boy?'

Diana moved slowly through the barn until she could see into the stall. Christie was standing next to the horse, her arms around his neck, nuzzling him.

The horse stood still, his huge grey body looming over the tiny girl, his brown eyes placid. And then his head moved, and his eyes seemed to fix on Diana's face.

A strange sensation passed through Diana.

It was as if the horse were challenging her.

And then, as if to confirm the feeling, Hayburner suddenly whinnied and pawed at the ground.

Christie looked up and saw Diana at the gate. As Diana watched, Christie seemed to shrink back against Hayburner, and the horse, too, backed a few steps farther into the stall.

'What are you doing?' Diana asked. 'You're supposed to be in the nursery.'

'I – I got lonely,' Christie explained.

'Then why didn't you come to me?'

Christie's eyes darted around the stall like those of a

151

trapped animal. 'You – you were mad at me.' Her voice had dropped to a whisper. 'I wanted to be with Hayburner. He's my friend.'

'He's *not* your friend,' Diana snapped. 'He's only a horse, and he doesn't give a damn about you! If you want a friend, come to me.'

Christie cowered away from Diana's words, and suddenly, as if hearing herself for the first time, Diana realised how she must sound. Instantly she was sorry for what she'd said. 'Christie? Oh, Christie, I didn't mean that. Of course Hayburner's your friend. But I am, too. If you're lonely, you can always come to me.'

Christie seemed to relax a little, and Diana reached out to touch her. Once again Christie huddled against the horse.

'It's all right. I'm not going to hurt you,' Diana whispered. 'I wouldn't hurt you. I love you.'

A memory stirred in Christie. What had Diana told her a week ago, when her chick had died? *'People always hurt the things they love.'* And Diana had hit her that day, as if she'd done something wrong. But she hadn't done anything wrong, except sneak out of the nursery, and Diana hadn't known about that. Had she? Or had she spanked her that day because she loved her? It didn't make sense, any of it. She waited, clinging to the horse, as Diana came closer to her, then picked her up.

Was Diana going to hit her or kiss her? She didn't know.

Diana gathered Christie into her arms and lifted her off the floor. 'Come on, baby,' she whispered. 'I'll take you into the house, and we'll be together. Maybe I'll start teaching you the piano. Would you like that?'

Mutely Christie nodded her head, and Diana carried her out of the stall. But as she turned to close the gate Diana's eyes focused once more on the horse.

Christie belonged to her.

And yet the horse seemed almost to be claiming Christie.

Now, as she sat in the darkness of the house, and the wind began to blow, Diana remembered that moment.

And she remembered a time when she was a little girl and a stray dog had wandered up to the back door. She had made friends with the dog and begged her mother to let her keep it.

For a while the dog had been hers, sleeping in the nursery with her, romping in the yard with her, making up for all the friends she had never been allowed to have.

And then one day the dog had been gone.

Diana had never known what happened to the dog.

Not until tonight, when, with the wind rattling the old house, and the memory of Hayburner's eyes fixed on her own, it all came back to her.

She was in the barn, playing with her dog. She heard her mother's voice calling to her, but paid no attention to it. And then Edna was in the barn, glaring at her.

As Diana looked on, Edna had gone after the dog with an axe, and, his brown eyes fixed pitiously on his little mistress, the dog had died.

The memory crashed out of Diana's subconscious and flooded her being with hatred. She turned from the window and walked through the house to the back door.

She left the house and, with the wind buffeting her, started across the yard to the barn, where, so many years ago, her pet had died ...

Christie woke up the next morning and, as she was beginning to do every morning, hesitated to open her eyes. What was going to happen today? Was she going to do something wrong and make Diana mad at her? Miss Edna would be mad at her anyway, but she was getting used to that. With Miss Edna, at least she knew where she stood. But what about Diana? Last night everything had been all right, after that moment in the barn when she thought Diana was going to hit her. But then Diana had seemed to change, and the rest of the day had been okay. They'd sat at the piano together, and Diana had helped her start learning the notes. Then, after supper, they'd played checkers.

And last night, Christie was almost sure Diana hadn't even locked the nursery door.

She got out of bed and tried the door. It was unlocked.

Did that mean it would be all right to get dressed and go downstairs?

She listened for the sound of voices downstairs, but the house was silent. Then she went to the window and looked out. The sun was high in the sky, and she could hear the horses whinnying in their stalls.

She decided to surprise Diana by feeding all the animals before breakfast.

She pulled on her jeans and a shirt, slipped her feet into a pair of sneakers, then went down the back stairs as quietly as she could.

Outside, she decided to feed the chickens first, saving the horses for last.

The chickens flocked around her as she carried their feed into the coop, and began pecking madly as she poured the grain into the container. She changed their water, made sure the automatic valve was functioning properly, then started towards the barn.

She pulled the barn door open, and the horses, their heads hanging over the gates to their stalls, turned to peer at her and snuffle appreciatively.

All except Hayburner.

Christie frowned and started towards his stall.

'Hayburner?' she called softly. When there was no responding snort, she ran to the stall and pulled the gate open.

On the ground, his mouth foaming and his great brown eyes rolling in misery, lay Hayburner.

Christie froze, staring at the horse. He saw her and struggled to get to his feet but couldn't. Instead he rolled over onto his back, his hooves flailing at the air.

'Hayburner!' Christie screamed. 'What's wrong?' She moved into the stall and crouched by the horse, who seemed to calm down as she took his head and held it in her lap.

'Hayburner?' she said once more, her voice suddenly tiny as she realised the horse was dying. 'Hayburner? Please don't die.' Her mind whirled, and she tried to think what could be wrong. Only one answer came to her. 'I didn't mean to hurt you. I only wanted to love you. Please don't die. Please?'

But it was as if the horse had been making himself live only until she got there. His eyes rolled once more, his great tongue emerged from his mouth to lick Christie's hand, and then his breath rattled, and he gasped one last time and lay still.

Holding his lifeless head in her lap, Christie began to cry.

When Diana found Christie, she was sitting in Hayburner's stall, the dead horse's head still cradled in her arms. The little girl looked up at Diana, her eyes, usually so filled with life, drained and empty.

'He's dead,' she whispered. 'Aunt Diana, why is he dead?'

Diana pulled her eyes from Christie and looked quickly at the horse. A memory stirred within her, then was gone before she could grasp it. But it had to do with the barn and a dead animal.

An animal for whose death she was somehow responsible.

'What did you do to him?' she asked now.

Christie stared at her, her eyes brimming with tears.

'I didn't do anything to him,' she said. 'I was going to feed him, and I came out here, and he was sick. It was awful, Aunt Diana. He was lying here, and I could tell he was hurt. And I came in and tried to help him, but I couldn't. And then he died.'

She gave in to her grief and began sobbing, clutching the horse's lifeless head to her chest, burying her face in its mane. Diana watched the scene for a moment, then reached down and pulled Christie to her feet.

'I warned you,' she said softly. 'Didn't I warn you that

155

you hurt the things you love?'

As Christie shivered in the warmth of the morning, Diana held her close, loving her as she had never loved her before.

13

Joyce Crowley arrived at the Amber ranch in the middle of the morning, with Jeff sitting next to her on the hard seat of Matt's pickup truck. As she jounced to a stop and jumped out of the cab, she reflected that a car – a real car – had been at the top of her list of things to buy once the mine was running again and Matt was steadily employed. But now the car would have to wait. Joyce, however, was used to putting things off, and she reflected that as the tourist industry grew in Amberton something for Matt was bound to turn up. Meanwhile she made-do. After all, even the Ambers were making-do with their ancient Cadillac.

Ignoring the front door, Joyce and Jeff started around to the back of the house, then saw Diana coming out of the barn.

'Hi!' she called. Diana looked up, hesitated, then waved. But as she approached them Joyce could see in her face that something was wrong.

'It's Hayburner,' Diana explained. 'Christie's horse. He died this morning.'

'Oh, no,' Joyce groaned. 'What happened?'

'I'm not sure,' Diana said pensively. 'Christie found him in his stall this morning. He was still alive, but he couldn't get up. He died while she was trying to help him.'

'How horrible for her,' Joyce said. 'Where is she? Is she all right?'

'She's in the house.' Diana glanced uncertainly at Jeff. 'I – I'm not sure she wants to see anyone. She's terribly upset.' She started towards the house, with Joyce and Jeff walking with her. 'I've got to call the vet and have him come out here to see what happened. And take Hayburner away,' she added.

They went into the kitchen and found Edna sitting at the table, sipping a cup of coffee. She frowned when she saw the two Crowleys but spoke to neither of them. Instead she directed her attention to Diana. 'What's wrong with that child now?' she sked. 'She came through here crying about half an hour ago and wouldn't say a word.'

'It's Hayburner,' Diana explained. 'He's dead.'

Edna set her cup down and stood up. Her eyes suddenly fixed on Jeff. 'Really, I can't understand why anyone would want children.' She turned and left the room, still not having acknowledged Joyce's presence. An uncomfortable silence fell over the kitchen as Diana tried to think of what to say. It was Jeff who finally spoke.

'Can I go up to Christie's room?' he asked. Diana, caught off guard by the question, hesitated. She didn't want anyone going up to the nursery – not anyone but herself. And yet how could she say no? She thought quickly. 'Why don't I bring her down?' she said lamely. 'That might be better.'

'Oh, let him go up,' Joyce urged. 'If it's a mess, don't worry – his room's always a mess. Besides, I need to talk to you about something.'

Still Diana hesitated but could think of no rational reason for refusing. It was just a feeling, and she put it aside. 'Use the back stairs,' she said, pointing to the pantry. 'It's on the third floor.' As Jeff left the kitchen Diana poured coffee for herself and Joyce.

'It's nothing terribly serious,' Joyce said as she took the cup Diana offered her. 'At least, it isn't yet. But a couple of things happened at the Sandlers' last night that I think you ought to know about.'

Diana sat down and stirred some sugar into her coffee. 'At the Sandlers'?' she repeated.

Choosing her words carefully, Joyce began explaining

everything that had been said the night before.

Jeff paused on the second-floor landing and looked down the wide hall, which seemed to have rooms opening off either side of it. Why wasn't Christie's room on this floor? It seemed to him that there ought to be space. He decided that maybe Christie had asked to be all the way upstairs.

He paused again in the gloom of the attic and decided it was creepy. 'Christie?' he called. He listened and thought he could hear a snuffling sound coming from one of the little rooms tucked under the eaves. He went to the door and knocked. 'Christie? It's me.'

There was a silence and then the door opened, and Christie, her face blotched and tearstained, opened the door. 'Jeff?'

'Hi. Can I come in?'

'What are you doing here?' Christie asked. Jeff thought she looked frightened.

'My mom wanted to talk to Miss Diana, and she brought me with her. They're downstairs drinking coffee.' He made a face. 'Can I see your room?'

Christie stepped uncertainly backward and let Jeff into the nursery. He looked around, his eyes widening at the stains on the wall and the dirty curtains hanging over the window.

'This is weird,' he said.

'It used to be Aunt Diana's, when she was a little girl,' Christie explained. Suddenly she saw the room through Jeff's eyes and realised how dismal it really was. 'I wish they'd paint it,' she said.

'Why don't they?'

'Search me,' Christie said, shrugging. Jeff went to the window and looked out.

'Hey! You can see everything from up here. There's the mine, and you can see right into the barn, and –' He broke off as Christie suddenly burst into tears. 'Hey – what's wrong?'

'I hate the barn!' Christie burst out. 'That's where

159

Hayburner lived, and now he's – ' Unable to go on, she sank down on the bed and buried her face in her hands. Jeff looked at her worriedly, then went over to sit by her.

'I'm sorry he died,' he offered. 'Was he sick?'

Christie shook her head violently. 'He was fine,' she said through her sobs. 'There wasn't anything wrong with him at all, and then he died.'

The two children sat silently while Christie tried to stop weeping. And then Jeff remembered that Miss Edna hadn't seemed to care at all that the horse was dead.

'Maybe somebody poisoned him,' he suggested.

Christie stared at him. 'Poisoned him? What are you talking about?'

'Maybe somebody who didn't like him, or was mad at you, put something in his food.'

'Like who?' Christie demanded.

'Well – ' Jeff hesitated, wondering if he should tell her what had happened in the kitchen, then made up his mind. 'Miss Edna?'

Christie frowned, and Jeff plunged on. 'Well, she sure didn't care that he was dead, and she thought you were dumb for crying about it.'

Christie was silent for a while, turning the idea over in her mind. 'She doesn't like me,' she said at last.

'She doesn't like anybody,' Jeff declared. 'She's meaner'n Mrs. Berkey.' He left the bed and went to the window once more. He looked out for a while, then, still looking out the window, spoke to Christie. 'Wanna get even?'

'How?'

'Play a trick. Come on.' He started for the door, but Christie hesitated.

'I'm supposed to stay here until Aunt Diana tells me it's okay to come out.'

Jeff regarded her scornfully. 'Well, she let me come up here, didn't she?' Christie nodded uncertainly. 'Well, then, you can come down,' Jeff went on. Together the two children left the nursery and made their way down the back stairs.

'If rumours start going around, I don't know what might happen,' they heard Joyce Crowley saying as they came into the kitchen.

'Rumours about what?' Jeff asked. His mother looked at him.

'Rumours that aren't any of your business,' she said pointedly. 'Why don't you two go out and play?'

Diana forced herself to ignore an impulse to send Christie back up to the nursery. It's perfectly normal for Christie to play with Jeff, she told herself. There's nothing wrong with it – nothing at all. Still, she felt uneasy as she watched the two children go out the back door, and found herself wishing that Joyce had left Jeff at home. Reluctantly she turned her attention back to what Joyce had been telling her. The townspeople – particularly Alice Sandler – were talking about her and her mother.

'I know what they'll say,' she said quietly. She put her cup aside and faced Joyce. 'First they'll say I was irresponsible, then they'll make it worse. Half the people already think Mother's crazy, and some of them think I am, too.' She paused, then went on. 'But I'm not crazy, and Mother's not crazy. In a way, Alice is right, though – I should have fenced the quarry, but Mother thought it was too expensive. She can be difficult, and I guess I haven't helped the situation by always knuckling under to her. But I've stopped that, Joyce.'

'Then you'd better start showing that to the town,' Joyce told her. 'Let them see that there's nothing wrong with you, and that Miss Edna isn't – well, that she isn't hiding you out here. That's what they think, you know – that for some reason, Miss Edna keeps you here, hidden away.' She paused, wondering whether to tell Diana any of the things she'd heard over the years, then decided now was as a good a time as any to get it all out in the open. 'So they start speculating on why, and the word *crazy* pops up. You've got to show them it isn't true, Diana.' Her voice dropped. 'If you don't, and they start talking about Jay-Jay's story – let alone Alice's hysteria – I can tell you what will happen. They'll start saying that your craziness – or Miss Edna's –

161

is rubbing off on Christie. So you have to show them that there's nothing odd going on out here, and there never has been.'

'But what can I do?' Diana asked, her heart pounding at the thought that Christie might be taken from her.

Joyce shrugged helplessly, then had an idea. 'Maybe if you could get the kids out here?' she suggested.

'The kids?' Diana's heart pounded as she stared at Joyce. 'After what happened to Kim, I can't imagine that their parents would let them come anywhere near the ranch.'

'Some of them won't,' Joyce agreed. 'But you'll notice I brought Jeff along today, and I'm sure there are some others. Not everyone in Amberton is irrational. It just seems like it.'

'I see,' Diana said. Then she chuckled hollowly. 'So tell me what to do. How do I, at the age of fifty, learn to become the mother of the year, with the children flocking around me?'

'You don't do it all at once,' Joyce laughed. 'But I do have an idea. The Fourth of July picnic's coming up in a couple of weeks. I think you should go.'

'Christie and I?' Diana asked. She hadn't been to a town picnic in years – not since she was a teenager and had gone to one with Bill Henry.

'And Miss Edna, too, if you can talk her into it.'

'But why? We don't go to the picnics ... '

'That's exactly the point,' Joyce said emphatically. 'You have to show that you're no different from anyone else. Let people see that there's nothing strange going on out here.' She smiled suddenly. 'Lord knows, you grew up here, but for the last thirty years people have hardly known you. And what they don't know about, they gossip about.'

'I don't know ... ' Diana said, her mind whirling.

'Well, think about it,' Joyce urged her. She stood up and searched in her purse for her keys.

'Shall I call the kids?' Diana asked.

Joyce shrugged. 'Why? Let them play. Send Jeff home if he gets out of hand.'

Together the two women left the house, and Joyce got into the truck.

'Think about it,' she repeated. 'Okay?' Then, as Diana nodded mutely, she put the truck in gear and started back towards town.

As she watched the truck disappear in a cloud of dust, Diana tried to sort out her emotions. Part of her knew that Joyce was right, that for both her own and Christie's sakes, she should break out of the tiny world that her mother had constructed for her and that she had lived in. But another part of her resisted.

That other part of her wanted to withdraw and take Christie with her.

Jeff started for the barn, but Christie stopped him. 'I don't want to go in there,' she said.

'Well, where else are we going to get a rat-trap?' Jeff asked.

Christie's eyes reflected her puzzlement. 'What do we need a rat-trap for?' she asked.

'To get even with Miss Edna,' he replied, his voice exasperated. 'You'll see. But we need a trap.'

'Maybe in the shed,' Christie suggested.

They crossed the yard and went into the shed near the chicken coop. In the floor there was a trapdoor, and Jeff reached down and pulled it open.

'Wow,' he breathed. 'What's this?'

'It's the root cellar,' Christie explained. 'Aunt Diana says they used to keep vegetables down there. She says they never spoiled down there.'

'It's like a fort,' Jeff said. 'Come on, let's go down into it.'

Christie looked into the dark cavern doubtfully. 'I don't know,' she said. 'It's prob'ly full of spiders.'

'Or even snakes,' Jeff added, grinning mischievously.

'Stop that,' Christie said. 'Besides, I thought you wanted to look for a trap.'

Sighing, Jeff kicked the trapdoor shut and began

poking through the collection of farm tools that were scattered around the shed. 'Here's one!' he cried. The trap, ancient and rusty, looked to Christie as though it would break if they tried to set it, but when Jeff tested it, it held. He set it on the floor of the shed, then prodded it with the handle of a rake. It snapped closed, its jaw leaving a slight dent in the hardwood.

'Now we need something to cover it with,' Jeff said.

'But where are we going to put it?' Christie wanted to know.

'Wherever Miss Edna might find it,' Jeff replied. 'Is there anyplace she goes all the time?'

'I don't know.' Then she thought of something. 'How about the chicken coop? She collects the eggs every morning. Anyway, almost every morning.'

'Neat,' Jeff said. 'Come on.'

They left the shed and went into the chicken coop. A few minutes later they came back out again.

'That'll get her.' Jeff's voice was more confident than he was. He knew that if his parents found out what he'd done, he'd get a lot more than a lecture from his father. He faced Christie. 'You won't tell, will you?' he asked.

Christie shook her head.

'Cross your heart?'

Christie crossed her heart.

Jeff glanced uneasily at the house, wondering if anyone had seen them go into the coop. It didn't seem like it.

'What shall we do now?' Christie asked.

Without thinking, Jeff suggested the first thing that came into his head. 'We could go up to the mine.'

Remembering her father, Christie felt her happy mood slip away. 'By ourselves?' she whispered. 'I don't think we should.' In truth, she didn't want to go at all, but she didn't want to admit it to Jeff.

'Then let's ask my mom and Miss Diana,' Jeff suggested. 'Maybe they'll take us.'

Suddenly the idea was less frightening. With Aunt Diana and Mrs. Crowley along, it might not be so bad.

'Okay. Let's ask.'

They found Diana sitting by herself at the kitchen table, still sipping coffee. Joyce was nowhere to be seen.

'Where's my mother?' Jeff asked.

Diana smiled at him. 'She went home. She thought you'd want to stay and play with Christie.'

'Oh.' Jeff paused, then grinned at Diana. 'Would you take us up to the mine?' he asked.

Feeling suddenly shaky, Diana set her cup down and looked at the children. 'The mine?' she asked. 'Why would you want to go up there?'

'Just to see it,' Jeff said. 'My dad was going to take me up, but he never did. Please?'

Diana remembered what Joyce had told her, and decided she was right – she had to stop giving in to all her irrational fears. 'All right,' she said. 'Let's do it. We'll hike up. Christie, I want you and Jeff to clean up in here, while I change my shoes. All right?' She didn't mention that she also intended to call the vet and see to it that Hayburner's carcass was gone by the time they got back. As the two children began carrying the coffee cups to the sink, Diana left the kitchen and went to the living room to make her phone call. Edna was waiting for her.

'I don't like strangers in my house,' the old woman said without preamble. Diana glanced at her mother, picked up the phone, and began dialling.

'Well, you can relax, Mother,' she said. 'Joyce is gone, and I'm taking the children for a hike.'

'Now?' Edna asked.

Diana immediately sensed Edna's impending objection and moved to forestall it.

'Right now,' she said. 'And I'm calling the vet to come and get Hayburner. I want to have his body gone before we get back. Will you take care of it for me?' Then, before her mother could reply, she was talking to the vet, explaining the situation. When she was done, she hung up the phone and hurried upstairs to put on her walking shoes.

Left alone in the living room, Edna was dumbstruck.

What had gotten into Diana? She had never tried to tell her what to do before. Never!

It was that Crowley woman, Edna decided; that common miner's wife. What could she have told Diana this morning?

Edna had tried to listen, but all she knew was that Mrs. Crowley had done most of the talking. And now, only a few minutes later, Diana had failed even to consult her before making plans.

Quivering with anger, Edna went to the kitchen. The children, working at the sink, froze when they saw the fury in her eyes. 'Out!' she commanded. 'Out of my kitchen! Do you understand?' Terrified, Jeff and Christie scurried into the yard, and as they waited for Diana in the shade of the willow tree, Christie decided that Jeff had been right – Miss Edna *was* meaner than Mrs. Berkey, and she hoped the trap broke her fingers.

When Diana came downstairs a few minutes later, Edna glared at her. 'Where are you going?' she asked.

Diana, sensing that she had somehow gained the upper hand, if only temporarily, savoured the moment. 'You don't need to know, Mother,' she said. Then she walked out of the house. A moment later she listened to the crash of Edna's cane knocking a stack of china to the floor. The sound of Edna's anger made her smile.

As they hiked up to the mine Diana told the two children about the brief gold strike her father had once made, then, when they were at the top of the tailing, led them into the old stamping house. She carefully explained to them how the machinery had worked, pointing out the chutes the ore had come down and the cam shaft that lifted the eight iron hammers, one by one, then dropped them onto the ore, breaking it up for the smelter.

'Of course,' she finished, as the children stared at the huge steam engine that had once driven the trip-hammers, 'all this stuff was hardly used. The vein ran out, and it was back to coal.'

'Can we go inside the mine?' Jeff asked.

Diana led them out of the engine room, and they approached the mine entrance. In a large equipment locker she found flashlights and a lantern. She lit the lantern, then gave each of the children one of the flashlights.

'Now, you must both stay very close to me,' she told them. 'Don't forget, this is an old mine, and nothing much has been done to it.'

'Daddy put in an elevator,' Christie said.

Diana nodded. 'The next job would have been shoring up the lower shaft.'

They moved through the dimness of the tunnel, and the children stared wide-eyed at the ancient planking that had been used to prevent the walls of the mine from collapsing. Everywhere water seemed to be seeping through, and the floor of the mine felt squishy.

'Can we go see the elevator?' Jeff asked.

Diana led them farther into the shaft, and as the darkness closed around her, she began to feel nervous. It had been years since she had been inside the mine, and the last time she had been as far as the vertical shaft that dropped into the depths of the mine was when she had been a little girl.

Then they were at the precipice. Jeff shined his light into the darkness below.

'Wow,' he breathed. 'How deep is it?'

'I – I don't know,' Diana said. She had barely heard him, and her breath was suddenly coming in short gasps. In the pit of her stomach the knot of fear she had put aside only an hour ago was gripping her again, and in her mind she was hearing a voice.

It was her mother's voice, and it was reaching out of the past.

'He's down there,' she heard Edna telling her. *'He's down there, and it's your fault. Do you understand?'*

Suddenly Diana was a little girl again.

Three years old? Four?

Too little to understand.

But still, she knew what her mother was talking about.

Her father was down there, and it was, somehow, her fault.

That was why her mother hit her.

Because of her father. Even though it didn't make any sense to her, she knew that she had done something terribly wrong, and her father had died, and her mother was very angry at her.

That was why her mother came into her room at night and beat her.

Because she had killed her father.

And as the memory of that day almost fifty years earlier burst into her consciousness, Diana began to shake.

'Get me out of here,' she whispered. 'I have to get out of here!'

At her side, Christie looked up into Diana's face. Even in the dim light of the lantern she could see that something was wrong. Diana's eyes were wide, and she was sweating.

Suddenly Christie, too, was afraid.

And then, from behind her, she heard a voice.

'*Madre de Dios.*'

Christie spun around, and there, hurrying towards them, was Esperanza Rodriguez.

She took Diana by the hand and began leading her towards the mouth of the mine. The two children, frightened into silence, stayed close behind. When they were back out in the sunlight, Diana sank to the ground. Slowly her breathing returned to normal.

When she felt she could trust herself to speak again, she looked deep into Esperanza's eyes. 'Esperanza,' she said weakly.

'*Si?*'

'Esperanza, do you remember when we were children, and I had – I had nightmares?'

'*Si.*'

Diana reached out and gripped Esperanza's hand. 'They weren't nightmares, were they?'

168

Tears welled in Esperanza's eyes. 'No, Miss Diana,' she said softly.

Diana sat still, willing herself not to cry. Not in front of the children. Whatever happened, she mustn't let them see her cry, mustn't let them see the fear that suddenly held her in its grip.

But even as she forced her panic down, she wondered what else was locked in her memory.

What else had her mother done to her?

What terrors were locked inside her?

She got to her feet and smiled weakly at the children.

'I'm sorry,' she said. 'I – I guess I'm just too old for the mine.'

The children, in the innocence of their years, smiled at her.

'That's all right,' Jeff said. 'Lots of people are afraid of the dark.'

Shortly after noon Edna Amber went down to the chicken coop.

She was still filled with resentment. She had watched Diana go off with the two children an hour earlier, and had sat for a while, trying to decide what to do next.

Finally she had cleaned up the broken china, realising that no matter how inexcusable Diana's behaviour had been, breaking china would solve nothing. And then she had had to deal with the veterinarian, who had insisted that he couldn't simply dispose of the horse. Instead he would have to do an autopsy on it, to see what had killed it. And she would have to pay for the autopsy, then try to collect the money from the state.

Once he and his assistants had taken Hayburner away, she had decided to fix herself an omelet – another thing Diana should have done for her – but when she opened the refrigerator, she found no eggs. She had gone to the chicken coop to get some.

Now she stared at the pile of oats that sat in one corner of the hen house.

Hadn't Diana even taught the child what to feed the chickens? And where to put the food? Left where it was, it would only attract rats.

She picked up one of the food pans, then stiffly stooped down to brush the oats into it.

As she touched the pile of grain the rat-trap sprang.

Edna screamed as the heavy wire trap closed on her fingers.

She dropped her cane and struggled with the trap, but the spring was too strong. As the fingers of her right hand began to swell and turn red, she cursed out loud.

'God damn that child! God damn her to hell!'

Then she got to her feet and, with the trap dangling from her damaged hand, began trudging back to the house to call Bill Henry.

She hated the idea of having to call the doctor, but there was nothing else she could do.

Her right hand throbbing with pain, she began clumsily dialling the telephone with her left.

14

Bill Henry pried the trap loose from Edna Amber's fingers, set it on the kitchen table, then gently massaged the damaged hand. There were deep grooves where the jaw of the trap had bitten into her flesh, and the ends of her fingers were swollen and turning black. The skin, however, was not broken.

'At least we won't have to give you a tetanus shot,' he said.

'Are they broken?' Edna asked. She flexed the fingers experimentally, and pain shot up her arm.

'I don't think so. I can take some X rays if you want, but I think they're just badly bruised. You should be fine in a couple of days. How'd it happen?'

Edna's face tightened in anger as she remembered. 'That *child.*' She spat the word out as if it tasted sour. 'She put a rat-trap in the hen house and covered it with oats. Can you imagine? Oats!'

Bill frowned. 'Why would she do that?'

'Why do children do anything?' Edna asked bitterly. 'I don't understand why Diana insists on keeping her here. She's no more equipped to be a mother than – ' Words failed her, and she glared at Bill. ' – than I don't know what!' she finished.

Bill bathed her injured hand with alcohol, then rubbed some ointment on it.

'What's that for?' Edna asked, peering at her hand suspiciously.

'Nothing, really. It's some zinc oxide, and it's more to

make you feel as though I've done something than for any good it will do you.'

'A placebo.'

'Exactly.'

Edna got up and went to the sink and proceeded to wash the salve off, then dried her fingers. 'I don't approve of such things, Dr. Henry,' she said. She returned to the table and sat down again. She studied Bill's face for a moment, then looked away from him.

'I want you to help me.'

'That's what I'm here for.'

The old woman ignored his comment. 'You have a – ' She paused, as if groping for words, then went on, ' – a certain amount of influence with Diana. I want you to convince her to send Christie away.'

Bill shook his head. 'I can't do that,' he said.

'Why not?'

Now he leaned back in his chair and folded his arms across his chest. 'Lots of reasons. Mostly, I don't see any reason for it. If you want to know the truth, I think Christie's good for Diana. It's time Diana had someone in her life other than you.'

'Don't be impertinent, young man,' Edna snapped.

'I'm not.' Bill's voice became more intense. 'I'm telling you the truth, Miss Edna. You've had Diana to yourself for years. But you're not going to live forever. Have you thought about what's going to happen to Diana when you die?'

The old woman frowned at him. 'What are you talking about? I have no intention of dying, not for a long time yet.'

'But it *will* happen. And what happens to Diana then? What's her life going to be like? Have you thought about that?'

The old woman stood up and began pacing the floor, unconsciously massaging her injured hand. 'Of course I have. And frankly, I don't know what to do about it. I don't know what I *can* do. Diana can't take care of herself, you know.'

Bill bristled. 'I *don't* know, Miss Edna, and neither do you. You've never let her have a chance to take care of herself. You've kept her cooped up here, like your hens.'

'There are reasons for that,' Edna said, her voice cold.

'Well, if there are, I don't know about them.'

Edna's mind raced. Perhaps she should tell him the truth. If she told him the truth, perhaps he'd understand and help her. She turned to face him and braced herself with her cane.

'Did you know that Diana once had a baby?'

The question hit Bill like a physical blow. He sank back in his chair, suddenly feeling dizzy. Then he recovered himself.

'No, I didn't,' he said, forcing himself to keep his voice under control. What on earth was the old lady up to now?

'No one else does, either.' Edna's eyes glittered as she spoke. 'It happened thirty years ago. You were away at school, I believe. The father was a man named Travers.'

'I don't remember anybody by that name.'

'You wouldn't. He wasn't here long – I hired him for the ranch, but as soon as I found out what he'd done, I fired him. I don't think he was here more than six months. I doubt if many people remember him.' She paused, then delivered the second blow. 'Even Diana doesn't remember him.'

All Bill could do was stare at her, and when he finally found his voice, it had a hollow sound to it. 'I beg your pardon?'

Edna sat down at the kitchen table again, and as she went on with the story she stared at her hands, rubbing them occasionally, though Bill wasn't sure if it was because of the pain, her own nervousness, or both.

'Diana doesn't remember Travers. She doesn't remember the baby, either. She doesn't remember any of it.'

Bill's hands fell to the tabletop, and he shook his head as he tried to sort out his thoughts. 'You've lost me,' he said. 'What do you mean she doesn't remember? You don't have a baby and not remember.'

'The baby was born dead,' Edna said. She sat down

again, facing him. 'When I told Diana about it, she became hysterical.' Her voice softened, and Bill thought there was a look of something akin to satisfaction in her face as she continued. 'She screamed for hours, but eventually she went to sleep. When she woke up, she'd blotted it all out of her memory. All of it, Dr. Henry. She had no memory of being pregnant, no memory of Philip Travers, no memory of the birth – nothing! Nine months of her life, gone!' She paused, then: 'I think she must have thought it was her fault that the baby died, and blotting it out of her memory was the only way she could handle her guilt.' She grinned humourlessly. 'Of course, back then we didn't know about such things, did we?'

Bill stared at the old woman. Was it possible? Could any of it have really happened? For a few moments he was silent.

'Where was the baby born,' he asked at last.

Edna smiled coldly at him. 'Right here. I wanted Diana to go to a hospital, but she refused. She wouldn't even go away to one of those homes they had back then. So she stayed here. I delivered the baby myself.'

'And where is the baby?'

'I buried it,' Edna said, and the words seemed to Bill to be almost a challenge.

'You buried it?' He stared at the old woman, aghast. 'You delivered a baby, and you *buried* it?'

For the first time Edna Amber's voice rose in anger, displaying her emotions. 'It was dead, Dr. Henry. *It was born dead!* What would you have had me do?'

'What anybody else would have done,' Bill told her, his voice quivering with his own barely controlled rage. 'Call a doctor when she went into labour. You could have killed her, Miss Edna. And how do you know the baby was born dead? Did it ever occur to you that you might have killed it yourself? Assuming, of course, that any of this is true.'

Edna rose to her feet and stood over Bill, her eyes blazing with fury. 'How dare you, William? I told you all this for only one reason: I want you to understand that Diana is not the person she seems to be. I've protected her as much as I can, and I'm still trying to protect her. But her mind isn't quite right, William. She has – spells! Can't you understand that a woman like Diana has no business trying to raise a child?'

Now Bill, too, was on his feet.

'I understand a lot, Miss Edna. I understand that ever since Diana was a child, you've held on to her. You'll do anything to keep her to yourself. I don't know why – I'm not sure most of us can ever understand the motives of someone like you. Selfishness, I suppose – pure selfishness.' He knew he was going too far, but he was helpless to contain the bottled-up rage of thirty years. 'You don't care what you do to Diana, do you? Not as long as you keep her here, with you. But I won't be a part of it, Miss Edna. I won't help you destroy what might be Diana's last chance to have a normal life.'

Bill Henry picked up his bag and with Edna Amber still glaring at him, walked out of the house.

The afternoon was bright and clear, and as Diana led Christie and Jeff along the trails that crisscrossed the ranch, she breathed deeply of the spring air. The new wheat was coming up, and for a few weeks, until the summer heat set in, the valley would be gloriously green, broken here and there with the upthrusting red rocks that dotted the area. Though her mind was still occupied with the memory that had come to her in the mine, Diana was determined not to betray her emotions to the children.

She paused in a small stand of aspens and cottonwoods and sat down on a boulder.

'Getting tired?' she asked as Jeff and Christie flopped onto the ground at her feet.

'I like it out here,' Christie replied. She sat up and looked around the grove. 'Could we come out here and camp sometime, Aunt Diana?'

Diana glanced around, trying to see the grove through a child's eyes. There was a natural spring, bubbling under the spreading branches of the cottonwoods, and a large rock than even to Diana's eyes resembled a table. She smiled.

'I don't see why not. We could bring some canvas and string it up for shelter.'

'I have a sleeping bag,' Jeff said eagerly, the idea of an adventure immediately appealing to him. 'And I bet we could borrow Mom's and Dad's, too.'

As she considered it Diana began to like the idea. She decided that Joyce Crowley was right – she *should* get more involved with the kids. Her mother, of course, would object, but for once Diana didn't care.

Then she thought of the wind and her strange memory lapses. She glanced up at the mountains and wondered if her mother were right. Did the wind have some sort of strange effect on her? Did it make her behave irrationally? But today the mountains stood out against the blue of the sky, every detail etched in the clear sunlight. The day was still; perhaps, for this year, the winds were over. She dismissed her worries.

'Maybe next month,' she said. 'I'll tell you what. Why don't we talk about it at the picnic?'

'On the Fourth of July?' Jeff asked. 'But you never go, Miss Diana.'

'I never had a reason to go,' Diana replied. 'Not till this year. It'll be a first for Christie and me both.'

Jeff frowned. 'What about Miss Edna? Will she be there, too?'

'Well, I don't know,' Diana said carefully. 'But I don't think so. She doesn't like that sort of thing.'

'Didn't she even take you when you were a little girl?' Christie asked.

Diana smiled bitterly. 'No. But that doesn't mean I didn't go. I'd tell her I was going riding, then I'd leave my horse somewhere and sneak off to the picnic by myself.'

The two children stared at her. Was it possible that she really had once done the same things they did themselves? They grinned at each other.

'Didn't she ever find out?' Christie asked.

'Yes.'

'What happened?'

The smile faded from Diana's lips, and her eyes clouded. 'She told me never to disobey her again, or something terrible would happen.'

Now the childrens' eyes rounded in anticipation. 'Did you?' they whispered in unison.

Diana's voice dropped to a whisper. 'Only once.'

'What happened?' Jeff asked, his voice as low as Diana's.

Diana paused, then looked at the children.

'Something ... terrible,' she said. A tear suddenly welled in her left eye, and she hastened to wipe it away, then got to her feet. 'Come on – it's getting late.'

The children looked at each other and silently wondered what might have happened, but both of them knew that whatever it was, Diana wasn't going to tell them.

It was one of those things, they were sure, that was on the list of things they were too young for.

As they began the long hike back the three of them fell silent, but as they neared the house Christie suddenly asked a question.

'Aunt Diana? What if Miss Edna doesn't want us to go to the picnic?'

Diana hesitated only a moment, then reached over and patted Christie's hand. 'Then we'll go without her.'

'But ... won't something terrible happen?'

Diana chuckled softly. 'Don't you worry, honey. That was all over with a long time ago. I grew up, remember?'

Christie turned the matter over in her mind. 'But she's still your mother, isn't she?'

Now it was Diana who thought for a few moments before speaking. 'Yes,' she said at last. 'She is.'

Edna Amber was waiting for them when they came in, and Diana immediately knew that there was going to be trouble.

'Jeff, I think you'd better go home,' she said. Edna stood

in the dining-room door, her left hand holding her cane, and her right hand wrapped in a large bandage. Jeff, realising what must have happened, began backing out the door.

'I – I'll see you tomorrow, Christie,' he said. Then, remembering his manners, he spoke to Diana. 'Thanks for taking me hiking, Miss Diana.'

'You're very welcome, Jeff,' Diana said, watching her mother as she spoke. 'Come back any time.' As Edna's eyes narrowed she repeated her last words. 'Any time.'

Then Jeff was gone, and the two Amber women and Christie were alone.

'What happened, Mother?'

Edna's cane came up and pointed at Christie, who cowered against Diana.

'That child!' Edna burst out. 'Look what she's done to me! Just look!'

She pulled off the bandage and held up her damaged hand. Diana recoiled from the sight of the bruised, swollen flesh.

'I don't understand,' she said. 'What do you mean Christie did that to you? She wasn't even here, Mother.'

'She didn't have to be here,' Edna hissed. Her angry eyes fastened on Christie, she repeated what had happened. 'A rat-trap!' she finished. 'A rat-trap in the hen house!'

Diana turned to Christie.

'*Did* you put a rat-trap in the hen house?' she asked. Christie, her arms wrapped around Diana's waist, nodded.

'It was Jeff's idea,' she whispered, frantically groping in her mind for a reasonable explanation. 'He said that rats like to eat the chicks.'

'It wasn't set for a rat, and you know it!' Edna railed.

As rage contorted her mother's face Diana searched for a way to protect Christie. 'It was my fault,' she said at last. 'I wasn't watching what the children were doing, Mother. I was talking to Joyce.'

It worked. Edna's furious eyes focused on Diana, and she emitted a crackling laugh. 'You were talking to Joyce,' she mimicked. 'And what was so important that you let the children run wild?'

'Mama – ' Diana began, but Edna cut her off.

'Be quiet!' The old woman's voice lashed out like a whip. 'You shouldn't have been talking to her at all! You're an Amber, and don't ever forget it!'

Diana's control suddenly snapped. 'How can I forget it?' she burst out. 'How can I ever forget it, when you keep shoving it down my throat? Who cares? Mother, who the hell cares about the Ambers anymore? What are we? We're the people who made all the money off people dying, that's who we are! It wasn't coal that made us rich, Mother! It was people! All *I* can remember is that because of us, people died!'

Edna stepped back, shaken by the outburst. Then, her voice suddenly gentle, she spoke to Christie.

'Go upstairs, child. Go upstairs, and don't come down until someone sends for you.'

Christie, stunned by what she had just heard, ran up the stairs.

In the nursery, she tried to block out the sound of the two women arguing, but it was impossible. First she heard Diana's voice, shouting unintelligibly, and then Miss Edna, her voice softer, but somehow even more frightening.

Christie put her fingers in her ears, but still the sound penetrated. She lay down on the bed and put the pillow over her head. That did no good either.

As the argument raged on, two floors below her, she took off her clothes and got into her pyjamas. She picked up the teddy bear that was propped up against the wall by the bed and went to the crib.

Being in the crib made her feel better, safer – as if in the tiny crib with its four fencelike walls, nothing could hurt her.

She lay very still, the bear cuddled against her chest, and tried to shut out the sounds that were filling the house.

Her mother.

She would think about her mother.

If only she were still a baby, her mother would still be with her, and none of this would be happening.

She slipped her thumb into her mouth and began sucking on it.

That, too, gave her a certain amount of comfort.

Above her, a limp paper bird swung slowly at the end of a string.

Dimly, in the far reaches of her mind, a memory stirred. When she was a baby, there had been a mobile of birds hanging above her crib.

She could remember watching it hour after hour, the birds soaring slowly in circles.

Christie drew her legs up tighter and pulled the teddy bear closer to her chest.

Watching the bird floating above her, she began to forget about the present.

Yes, things had been better long ago, when she was a baby.

Her mother had been with her then, and everything had been fine.

If only she were still a little baby ...

Hours later, Diana crept into the nursery and looked down at the sleeping child.

'Christie?' she whispered.

Christie stirred in her sleep, and her thumb came out of her mouth.

Diana reached down and touched Christie's hand.

The hand closed on her finger.

'Baby? Are you awake?'

Again Christie stirred, but this time her eyes opened slightly.

'Mama?' she asked softly.

'That's right, sweetheart,' Diana crooned. 'It's your mama.'

She picked Christie up and took her to the bed.

Cradling the sleepy child in her arms, she sat down and gently rocked her.

'Mama?' Christie's eyes gazed up at her. 'Mama, don't leave me.'

'I won't,' Diana whispered. 'Your mama won't ever leave you alone again.'

Still holding Christie in her arms, Diana stood up again and left the nursery. She went down the back stairs to the second floor and moved along the hall.

When she was in front of her mother's room, she paused.

'Little girls never leave their mamas, do they?' she asked, facing the closed door. Then she answered her own question. 'No, they never do. They stay with their mamas forever and ever, and they never grow up.'

She went on down the hall to her own room, slipped inside, and closed the door behind her.

'Their mamas don't let them,' she whispered as she put Christie on her own bed and tucked the covers around the half-asleep child.

When she was done, she slipped into the bed, Christie nestled at her side.

A moment later she was sound asleep.

Down the hall, Edna Amber's door opened, and she stared at the now empty hall.

Outside, she could hear the wind howling.

She knew that Diana had been in front of her door a moment ago, and that she had been speaking.

But what had she been saying?

The wind had drowned out her words.

15

'Jeff?'

Jeff Crowley looked up from his breakfast. His father had a strange expression on his face, an expression that was unfamiliar to Jeff, but that an older person would have recognised as quizzical.

'Did you have a good time out at the Ambers' yesterday?'

Jeff bobbed his head. 'It was really neat. Miss Diana took us up to the mine, and hiking, and we're going to have a camp-out.'

'A camp-out?' Matt glanced uneasily at his wife, but Joyce seemed unconcerned. 'Where?'

'There's a bunch of trees, with a little spring in it, and a big rock.' Jeff scratched his head thoughtfully. 'I'm not exactly sure where it is.'

'But it's on the Ambers' property?'

'I guess so.' Jeff shrugged. 'What does it matter?'

'What *does* it matter, Matt?' Joyce echoed. 'Who all's going to go?' she asked Jeff.

'Me and Christie, and any of the other kids that want to, I guess.'

'And Diana's going with you?'

He wondered if he should tell them what had happened to Miss Diana at the mine. He decided not to. 'Yeah,' Jeff said.

Matt noticed his son's hesitation, but Joyce spoke before he could press Jeff further.

'What about the other kids?' she asked. 'Will they go?'

'I can talk them into it,' Jeff said confidently. 'I bet I can even talk Jay-Jay into it. I'll tell her she's chicken if she doesn't go.'

Now Matt did interrupt. 'You do, and I'll have your hide.'

Jeff looked at his father, perplexed. 'Why? Jay-Jay's always doing that. Every time she thinks up something, and the rest of us don't want to do it, she says *we're* chicken.'

'Jay-Jay may do that, but that doesn't make it right,' Joyce told her son. 'Anyway, what could she think up that you or Steve or Eddie wouldn't want to go along with?'

Suddenly Jeff was wary. He didn't want to risk being a tattletale, and he was afraid his mother might call Jay-Jay's. 'I can't remember,' he said, remembering the time Jay-Jay had suggested they throw rocks through Mrs. Berkey's window. He got up from the table. 'Can I go over to Steve's?'

'Okay, but the next time Jay-Jay says you're chicken, you just ignore her,' Joyce said.

When Jeff was gone, Matt looked uneasily at his wife. 'Do you think it's a good idea?' he asked.

'The camp-out? I think it's a wonderful idea. It'll be great for the kids, and good for Diana, too.'

'Do you think she can handle it?'

'Can anybody handle a bunch of kids on a camp-out?' Joyce countered, but Matt ignored her attempt at humour. 'She doesn't know anything about kids. And don't forget all the talk we've heard all these years.'

Joyce stood up and began clearing the table. 'And that's all it is – talk,' she said. 'There's nothing wrong with Diana that getting out more won't cure.'

'I'm not so sure,' Matt said. Then, seeing that Joyce was about to launch into a lecture, he slid his chair back from the table and glanced at his watch. 'I'd better get going. I promised Phil Penrose I'd take a look at his roof today.' He smiled wryly. 'From mine superintendent to handyman. Some life, huh?'

Joyce kissed her husband. 'Something will turn up,' she told him. 'It always does.'

When he was gone, Joyce poured herself another cup of

coffee and sat down again. Perhaps, she thought, she should pay another call on Diana.

Just to make sure.

Bill Henry hadn't slept well.

All night he'd kept going over and over the strange story Edna Amber had told him, and by dawn had decided the only thing to do was talk to Diana. After breakfast, he dialled the Ambers' number.

To his relief it was Diana who picked up the phone.

'It's Bill,' he said.

'And a glorious good morning to you.'

Her tone reassured him, and Bill began to relax.

'I slept like a log last night,' she went on. 'Motherhood appears to be good for me.'

As she spoke the last words Bill's moment of ease evaporated and when he spoke again, his voice took on a serious tone. 'Diana, could you have dinner with me tonight?'

There was a slight hesitation, then: 'Can I bring Christie along?'

'I was hoping it could be just the two of us,' Bill replied. The last thing he wanted was to have someone else there.

'I don't know.' Diana's voice was pensive. 'Christie's pretty young to stay by herself.'

'She won't be by herself,' Bill pointed out. 'Your mother will be there.'

Now there was a long silence, and when Diana spoke again, she sounded wistful.

'Can't we include her? Please?'

Bill shrugged; perhaps they could talk after dinner.

'Okay. Shall I pick you up about six?'

'Fine. See you then.'

As he put the phone back on the hook Bill had mixed feelings. He was pleased that Diana had, for the first time in his memory, accepted an invitation without consulting her mother first. But there was something else, too. Was she afraid to leave Christie with Miss Edna? That made no sense at all. Granted, the old woman wanted Christie out of the house, but he couldn't imagine that she would actually harm the child.

Then he remembered that only a few days ago Edna Amber had come to town by herself, for the first time in years, to talk to Dan Gurley. Why?

Checking his calendar and finding no appointments, Bill left his office and walked the two blocks to the town hall.

Dan glanced up as Bill came into his office.

'If it's a crisis, I don't want to hear about it,' the marshal said sourly.

'It's not.' Bill told Dan about Diana's apparent fear of leaving Christie with her mother. Dan, as was his habit, scratched his nose while he listened.

'Well, Miss Edna was pretty upset that day,' he said when Bill was done. 'But it seemed to me that she was more worried about Diana and herself than mad at the kid. She was just pissed off that something had finally upset her applecart.'

'Did you tell her that?'

Dan grinned, remembering. 'Yep. And she got downright abusive about it, too. Still thinks she runs the town. I guess she always will.'

Bill moved to the window and stood staring out into the peaceful streets of the village. 'Do you think she's any threat to Christie Lyons?' he asked, his back still to the marshal.

Dan shrugged unconcernedly. 'I can't see why she would be. But who knows? She's an old tiger, and it seems to me like she's defending her cub. If you can call a fifty-year-old woman a cub.'

Bill shook his head sadly. Then he brightened. 'Things seem to be changing out there. Miss Edna actually called me yesterday. She caught her hand in a rat-trap, which she seemed to think Christie had set specifically to catch her.'

'Getting paranoid, is she?' Dan asked.

'Looking for an excuse to force Diana to send Christie away, is more like it.'

'I'm sorry for Diana.' Dan sighed. 'But it's her own fault.

She should have cleared out of there years ago.'

'Maybe she will yet,' Bill said, thinking about the evening ahead. But to himself, he admitted that he doubted it.

Christie rummaged through her clothes and finally found a pair of jeans. As she pulled them on she thought about the night before.

Sleeping in Aunt Diana's bed had been nice. She had awakened twice during the night, but the soft warmth of Diana's body next to her own had made her feel safe, and when she had wiggled, Diana had pulled her closer and stroked her until she had fallen back to sleep.

She put on a T-shirt, then found her sneakers under the bed. The one good thing about the nursery, she decided, was that she didn't have to keep it too neat – Miss Edna hardly ever came upstairs, and Aunt Diana didn't seem to notice if she left things lying around.

Her shoes tied, she bounded down the back stairs to the kitchen.

She looked out the window. Off in the distance she saw some children playing in the field.

'Aunt Diana?' she called. She went to the dining-room door and called again. 'Aunt Diana!'

'Ha! *La muchacha!*'

Christie, startled, turned to see Esperanza Rodriguez coming down the stairs.

'Is Aunt Diana up there?' she asked shyly.

'No,' Esperanza replied. 'But Miss Edna – she is in the parlour. Do you want to go talk to her?'

Christie shook her head. 'She doesn't like me.'

Esperanza chuckled, her large bosom heaving. 'She don't like anybody, that one. But nobody like her, either, no?'

Esperanza moved slowly into the kitchen, and Christie followed her.

'Why doesn't she like anyone?' she asked.

Esperanza shrugged and settled herself at the kitchen

table, where she began shelling peas from a bowl she held on her lap.

'Life has not been what she wanted it to be,' she said softly. 'Not for Señorita Diana, either. And, since her baby, this has not been a happy house. If it ever was,' she added.

Christie stared at Esperanza, her eyes filled with puzzlement. 'Aunt Diana had a baby?'

'Sí,' Esperanza said, nodding. 'But it died and went to live with the children.'

Christie frowned. 'What children?'

Esperanza stopped working and met Christie's eyes. 'The ones in the cave,' she said. 'Up on the hill, behind the mine.'

Christie scratched her head, trying to figure out what Esperanza was talking about. Then an idea occurred to her.

'Are they the water babies?'

'Sí,' Esperanza said. She took the peas to the sink, then began peeling some carrots.

'But who are they?' Christie asked.

'Little children,' Esperanza said. 'Little babies who were never alive. They wait in the cave, and someday they will live again.'

Christie stared at her, wide-eyed. 'You mean they're ghosts?' she breathed.

'Oh, no. To be a ghost you have to live. And the water babies never lived.' She paused for a moment, then, under her breath, she said something else: 'Except for one.'

Suddenly another voice filled the room, and Christie whirled around to see Edna Amber's tall form looming in the dining-room doorway.

'Esperanza, what are you telling that child?' the old woman demanded. Under Edna's wrath Esperanza seemed to shrink.

'Nada, señora,' she said. She dropped the carrot into the sink and scuttled out the back door. When she was gone, Edna turned to Christie.

'What was she saying?' she demanded once more.

187

'N – nothing,' Christie told her, desperately trying to keep from bursting into tears. 'Just a story.'

'A story?' Edna asked. 'What kind of story?'

Christie, her eyes darting like a rabbit's, searched the room, but there was no refuge.

'About the children,' she whispered. 'The children in the cave.'

Edna's eyes bored into her.

'It's a lie,' she said. 'There is no cave, and there are no children. She's an ignorant, superstitious peasant, and you mustn't listen to her. Do you understand me?'

'Yes, Miss Edna,' Christie breathed. Her eyes fastened onto Edna's cane, which the old woman had lifted from the floor and now held hovering in the air.

'Don't hurt me,' Christie whispered. 'Please don't hurt me.'

Edna glared at her, then her eyes softened, and she slowly lowered the cane.

'Hurt you?' she asked. 'Why would I want to hurt you?' She glanced out the window and saw the children playing in the field a hundred yards away. 'Go on,' she said. 'Go play with your friends.'

Christie, as if released from a trap, fled out the back door.

Today Joyce Crowley was walking out to the Ambers', since Matt had taken the pickup truck. As she neared the driveway she stopped for a moment to watch the children playing in the field.

They were playing tag, and Christie Lyons seemed to be 'it'. Jeff and Steve were there, along with Eddie Whitefawn and Susan Gillespie. Jay-Jay Jennings, if she was with them, was nowhere to be seen.

Suddenly Jeff saw his mother and came running over to her.

'Hi!'

'Hi, yourself. You getting hungry?'

'Unh-hunh.'

'Well, I'll tell you what. I'm going over to talk to Miss Diana for a few minutes. When I'm done, why don't we take all your friends home for lunch?'

'Oh, boy! Can we?'

'Why can't we? It's our house!' Joyce tousled her son's hair and watched while he rejoined his friends. Then she continued along the road.

As she approached the house she heard Miss Edna's imperious voice, railing at Diana.

'I won't stand for it, Diana,' Edna was saying. 'I won't have you getting involved with William Henry again! Do you understand me?'

Joyce, embarrassed at overhearing an argument, quickly crossed the porch and pressed the bell. Silence fell in the house, and a moment later Diana opened the door, her face strained.

'Who is it?' Edna called from the living room.

'Joyce Crowley, Mother,' Diana called back. She dropped her voice. 'Let's go into the kitchen.' She quickly led Joyce through the dining room and offered her a cup of coffee.

'Got any lemonade?' Joyce asked. 'It's getting hot out there.'

'Seven-Up okay?' Diana asked as she searched the refrigerator.

'Fine.' Joyce paused, then decided to plunge right into the reason for her visit. 'How did it go yesterday? With Jeff being here, I mean.'

Diana brought glasses and the 7-Up to the table and sat down. Had Jeff told his mother what had happened up at the mine? 'We had a good time,' she offered. As she saw the look of relief that passed over Joyce's face, she realised that Jeff had said nothing. 'And I didn't crack under the strain,' she added, forcing herself to smile over the nervousness she was feeling.

Joyce chuckled ruefully. 'Was I that obvious? Well, Matt always says I'm totally transparent.'

As Joyce's expression turned desolate Diana suddenly

laughed. 'Don't apologise to me, Joyce,' she said. 'Except for Bill Henry, you're the only person who's ever even bothered to talk to me about my life.'

Joyce's eyes flickered towards the kitchen door. Then she reached out to touch Diana's hand. 'Is it that bad?'

Diana was still for a moment, then shook her head. 'I suppose it used to be worse. I guess it's just that she doesn't want me to grow up, Joyce.' Diana took a deep breath and stood up. 'Well, I'd better find Christie and fix some lunch.'

Joyce, too, stood up. 'She's outside with the rest of the kids. I invited them all over to have lunch with Jeff. Christie, too. Is that all right?'

Diana's hesitation was almost imperceptible.

'Of course,' she said. 'Just make sure she comes home by four, okay?'

Joyce agreed and let herself out the back door. As she disappeared around the corner of the house, Diana slowly fingered her glass.

She wished Christie weren't going to the Crowleys'. She had wanted to fix lunch for Christie herself. Indeed, she wanted to do everything for Christie.

She decided that Christie was spending too much time with the other children.

Entirely too much.

16

'I have an idea,' Jay-Jay Jennings said.

Jay-Jay had arrived at the Crowley's after lunch, and the children, six of them, were sitting in the shade of a large willow in the Crowleys' yard. So far, Jay-Jay had said nothing about her idea that Christie might have drowned Kim, though they had spent much of the afternoon speculating on what might have happened to their friend and talking about the funeral that was to take place the following day. Jeff, however, had seen Jay-Jay staring at Christie, and when she said she had an idea, he was sure it had something to do with her.

Susan Gillespie turned to Jay-Jay eagerly. 'Well, tell us,' she urged.

Jay-Jay smiled slyly at her friends. 'You know how the wind's been blowing every night?'

'Yeah,' Steve Penrose said. 'So what?'

'Well, I heard that when the wind blows, you can hear the water babies crying.'

'Big deal,' Jeff muttered, knowing what was coming and remembering his own trip to the mine only the day before.

Susan, however, was intrigued. 'Really?' she asked.

'That's what I heard,' Jay-Jay said. 'Why don't we go find out tonight?'

The other children looked at each other uneasily, each of them wondering what the other was thinking. It was finally Susan who spoke. 'I'll go. But what if there isn't any wind?'

'Then we won't go, stupid,' Jay-Jay replied.

'I don't know,' Jeff said. 'I'm not supposed to go up to the mine by myself.'

'You mean you're chicken,' Jay-Jay taunted him.

'I am not!'

'Are too!'

'Me and Christie were up there yesterday,' Jeff said. 'We didn't hear any baby crying.'

'But the wind wasn't blowing,' Christie said.

'So what?'

'Maybe that's why you didn't hear it. Besides, if you're not supposed to go to the mine, why did you go yesterday?'

Jeff squirmed, but he knew he was caught. 'All right, I'll go,' he agreed reluctantly. 'If my parents will let me,' he added.

'If we ask our parents, none of us will get to go,' Jay-Jay sneered. 'We'll have to sneak out.'

Suddenly the idea took on the feeling of a great adventure. It was as if an unspoken dare hung over them, and none of them was willing to be the first to back out. Christie, however, was nervously digging at the ground with a twig.

'What about you?' Jay-Jay challenged her. 'Are you coming?'

Christie seized on the first excuse that came to mind. 'I don't know if I can get out,' she said unhappily.

'Anybody can get out, if they want to.' Jay-Jay smiled at her, but the smile was mean. She turned to the others. 'She's just afraid of Miss Diana.'

'I am not,' Christie flared. What she was afraid of was the story Esperanza had told her that morning, but she didn't want to admit it.

'Then come with us.'

Christie glanced from one face to the next, hoping someone would come to her aid, but Susan Gillespie seemed suddenly entranced with the buttons on her shirt, while Steve Penrose whittled furiously on a stick. Only Jeff and Eddie Whitefawn were looking at her.

'Are you going?' she asked.

Jeff hesitated. He wanted to say no, but he couldn't make himself do it. 'I guess so,' he mumbled, privately wondering if he could find a way out of it. Eddie Whitefawn only shrugged.

'Then I'll go, too,' Christie said, putting on a brave expression.

But inside, she was terrified.

As Christie began walking home the wind came up, and by the time she got back to the ranch it was blowing hard from the west, buffeting her, and making her lean into it. When she finally got inside, she found Diana waiting for her, a strange look in her eyes.

'Where have you been?' she demanded. Christie stared at her, puzzled.

'At Jeff's. Mrs. Crowley said she told you. Didn't she?'

Diana tried to calm herself, but it was difficult. Most of the afternoon she had been fine, but half an hour ago, when the wind came down out of the mountains, she had begun to be nervous. Finally she had gone to the window, where she had watched for Christie, anger building in her with each passing minute. Christie should have been home by four, and it was now four-thirty.

She shouldn't have let Christie go to Jeff's. She was too young – much too young – to go off by herself.

'Come upstairs,' she said. 'It's time for your bath. We're going out for dinner tonight.'

Christie's eyes lit up. 'We are? Where?'

'El Rancho. Dr. Henry's taking us.'

Suddenly Christie remembered her plans for that night. What should she do? If she wasn't home, she wouldn't be able to meet the rest of the kids. But would they believe her when she told them what had happened?

Jay-Jay would accuse her of making up an excuse, and the other kids would believe Jay-Jay.

'Do I have to go?'

'Don't you want to?' Diana asked, Christie's objection only angering her further.

'I don't like Mexican food,' Christie lied.

'Well, maybe Dr. Henry will take us someplace else.'

'What time will we be home?'

'I don't know,' Diana said, her voice taking on a note of exasperation. 'About ten, I should think.'

Her friends were going to meet at nine. Christie thought fast. 'But I wanted to watch television tonight. Can't I stay home with Miss Edna?'

Diana scowled at her. 'No, you can't, and that's final. Now come upstairs so I can give you your bath.'

Obediently Christie followed Diana upstairs and let herself be undressed. Though she still didn't like it, she was getting used to the idea that Aunt Diana liked to bathe her, and had stopped objecting to it. Besides, Diana seemed to be mad at her again, and she was frightened.

Diana filled the tub with water, and Christie got in and sat down. Diana soaped the washrag and began scrubbing her.

'There. Now your hair.'

Diana poured shampoo onto Christie's hair and began massaging it. Some of the shampoo got into Christie's eyes, and she began struggling.

'Hold still,' Diana said.

'But there's soap in my eyes,' Christie complained. She began crying and rubbed furiously at her eyes.

'Stop that!' Diana snapped. 'Good babies don't cry!'

Christie, unable to see, tried to splash water on her face, but missed. Instead water cascaded down the front of Diana's blouse.

'How dare you?' Diana demanded, a blind rage suddenly seizing her. Her right hand lashed out and caught Christie's cheek.

Christie, terrified, screamed. The scream seemed only to intensify Diana's rage.

She dropped the washrag from her hand and grabbed Christie, her hands closing around the child's neck.

'Don't do that,' she hissed between clenched teeth. 'I can't stand it when you cry! Do you understand me? I can't stand it!'

Christie struggled desperately as Diana forced her head

under the water, flailing her arms as she tried to get a grip on the edge of the tub. Her lungs felt as if they were going to burst, and she was sure she was going to drown.

Suddenly the bathroom door flew open.

Esperanza, her eyes wide, stared at the strange scene in the bathroom.

'*Madre de Dios!*' she gasped. Moving as swiftly as her bulk would allow, she lunged for the tub and, pushing Diana aside lifted Christie out of the water.

Coughing and choking, the terrified child shivered as Esperanza wrapped a towel around her.

'What happened?' Esperanza asked. Crouching on the floor, an ashen-faced Diana, her eyes wide, stared up at her.

'I was washing her hair,' Diana said, her voice faltering. 'She got soap in her eyes and started struggling.' Her eyes, strangely blank, appealed to Esperanza. 'It's all right now, though, Esperanza.' Esperanza hesitated, and Diana shakily stood up. 'Really, it's all right. Thank you for helping me.'

Esperanza, her eyes narrowed with suspicion, reluctantly left the bathroom.

When she was gone, Diana reached out towards Christie, but the little girl shrank away from her.

'Let me dry you off,' Diana said, her voice low. Christie, too terrified to object, shivered as Diana began rubbing her body with the towel. When she was done, she wrapped the towel around Christie and picked her up.

'Can't I get dressed now?' Christie begged.

'I'll dress you, baby,' Diana told her. 'I like to dress you. Won't you let me.'

Christie's heart pounded, and she nodded her head meekly.

Diana carried her up to the nursery and found a pink dress with ruffles. Christie looked at it and bit her lip.

'I hate that dress,' she whispered. 'It makes me look like a baby.'

'But you are a baby,' Diana said. 'You're my sweet baby, and I want you to look pretty.'

Diana dressed Christie, then stood back to admire her. 'Such a pretty baby,' she crooned, and the tone of her voice only frightened Christie more.

Outside, the wind howled down from the mountains.

Diana took Christie by the hand and led her down to the second floor, to her own room. She sat Christie on the bench in front of her vanity mirror.

She began combing the child's hair, humming softly to herself. Christie tried to sit perfectly still, afraid that if she moved, something terrible would happen.

Slowly Christie's hair began to dry, and when it was no longer damp, Diana parted it in the middle, then began weaving two large braids. Silently, her eyes wide, Christie watched in the mirror as Diana worked.

When the braids were done, Diana began winding them together, piling them on top of Christie's head and fastening them with large hairpins.

'There,' she said at last, stepping back. 'How do you like it?'

Christie stared at herself in the mirror. The hairdo was an exact copy of Diana's own.

'I don't know,' she said softly. 'I liked it better when the braids were down.'

'But most little girls want to put their hair up like their mothers',' Diana replied.

Christie started to protest that Diana was not her mother, but before she spoke she caught a glimpse of Diana's face in the mirror.

There was something in Diana's eyes that warned Christie not to argue.

'All right,' she said.

While Diana dressed, Christie went downstairs to the living room, where Edna Amber sat leafing through a magazine, her injured hand lying still in her lap. As the little girl came into the room Edna glanced up. Her eyes widening, she put the magazine aside.

'Good heavens, child,' she said. 'What have you done to yourself?'

Christie squirmed with embarrassment.

'Aunt Diana did it,' she whispered.

'Well, it looks terrible. Come here.' Obediently Christie crossed the room and stood in front of Edna while the old lady pulled the pins from her hair and let the braids drop to her shoulders. 'That's better. Why did you let her do that?'

'She wanted to,' was all Christie could say.

'And why are you all dressed up?' Edna asked, suddenly suspicious.

'I'm going out to dinner with Aunt Diana and Dr. Henry.'

'Oh, you are, are you.' Edna replied. 'Where's Diana?'

'Upstairs,' Christie said, suddenly nervous. Edna thought for a moment, then spoke.

'You go up to your room. Stay there until I call you. Do you understand me?'

Christie nodded and was about to leave the room when Edna suddenly took her hand.

'Did she give you a bath?' she asked.

Again Christie nodded.

'All right,' Edna said, releasing her hand. 'Now go on up, and stay there.'

Christie turned and left the room.

When she was gone, Edna sat still for a moment, then went to the foot of the stairs. 'Diana? Diana!'

'In a minute, Mother.' Diana's voice floated down the stairs. Impatiently Edna struck the bottom stair with her cane.

'*Now!*'

A moment later Diana hurried down the stairs. Edna glared at her daughter, her blue eyes glinting.

'What do you think you're doing?' she demanded. Diana gazed at her, and Edna saw the strange empty look in her eyes.

'I'm getting ready for dinner,' Diana said, her voice oddly childlike.

'With that young man?'

'I told you, Mother.'

Edna's eyes narrowed. 'You told me nothing,' she said. 'Ever since that child has been here, you've ignored me. You can't do that, Diana.'

'Mama, I don't know what you're talking about.' She glanced at the clock in the hall. 'Mama, can't we talk about this some other time? Bill will be here any minute.'

Edna's voice dripped with sarcasm as she spoke. 'And then you can take that little girl, and your man friend, and pretend you're a family. Isn't that right?' When Diana made no reply, Edna repeated her last words. *'Isn't that right?'*

'No, Mama,' Diana whimpered.

'Stop snivelling and look at me,' Edna snapped. Diana raised her eyes and met her mother's. 'She's not your little girl, Diana. You don't have a little girl. Do you understand me?'

'Mama – '

'Do you understand me?' Her left hand struck Diana across the cheek.

Diana seemed to shrink within herself. 'Yes, Mama,' she said softly.

'Very well, then,' Edna said. Her voice turned suddenly gentle. 'Now go upstairs and finish dressing.'

Diana's eyes brightened a little. 'You mean I can go?' she asked.

'You can go,' Edna replied. 'You can go out with your young man, but you must promise to be home by eleven. All right?'

Diana bobbed her head. 'Yes, Mama.'

When Bill Henry arrived at six, Diana was in the living room, sitting primly on a straight-backed chair. It was Edna who opened the door for him.

'Dr. Henry,' Edna greeted him. 'Diana's waiting for you. Diana? Your young man is here.'

Diana rose from her chair and came into the foyer. Bill smiled at her, then his smile faded. There was something in Diana's eyes – what was it? They seemed blank – empty.

'Diana? Are you all right?'

Diana looked at him and smiled wanly. 'I'm fine,' she said. 'Shall we go?'

'What about Christie?' Bill asked. 'Isn't she coming?'

'Christie's not feeling well,' Edna said smoothly. 'You two go along now, and have a good time.' Bill and Diana started out the door. 'Diana?' Diana turned back to face her mother. 'Remember, be home by eleven.'

'Yes, Mama.'

Edna stood at the door until Bill's car had left the driveway, then slowly closed it and went to the stairs.

'Christie?' she called. 'You can come down now.'

A few minutes later Christie, dressed in her usual jeans and T-shirt, with her feet clad in sneakers, came down the stairs. 'Are they gone?' she asked.

'They're gone,' Edna told her. 'Tonight the two of us will stay home by ourselves.'

As they left the ranch Diana sighed heavily and straightened up on the seat next to Bill. He glanced over at her and forced a smile.

'What happened?' Bill asked. 'Is Christie really sick?'

Dimly, Diana remembered her mother talking to her, telling her something. But before that – nothing. She had been waiting for Christie to come home, and Christie had been late. She frowned and tried to remember, but it was all cloudy. Oh, God, she was having another of her memory lapses. She mustn't let Bill know – mustn't let anybody know.

'Her stomach was upset,' she explained, remembering her mother's words. 'I decided it would be best for her not to come.' Would it work? Would he believe her?

She heard Bill talking to her, but her mind was whirling. It was the second time she'd had one of her spells in three days. But what about the day she'd ridden up to the quarry and gone right past it? Had she had another of the strange spells? No, that day she'd just been day-dreaming. Then she was aware that Bill was no longer

199

talking. Was he waiting for her to say something? She had to pull herself together. *She had to.*

'Pardon me?' she asked.

'I said I could have taken a look at her,' Bill said.

'It's nothing,' Diana said quickly. 'She'll be fine by morning.'

But there was a nervousness in her voice that told Bill there was something going on – something more than Diana had told him. If Christie's stomach was as bad as Diana had made it sound, she would have asked him to look at the child. No, it was something else. Something in Diana's eyes when he had picked her up. As if she weren't quite aware of what was happening.

It worried him, as Miss Edna's strange story had worried him.

Joyce Crowley watched her son as he picked at his dinner. Finally, when he started to get up after barely touching his food, she spoke.

'All right, young man. What's going on?'

Jeff looked at his mother guiltily. 'Nothing.'

'Don't tell me nothing,' Joyce said. 'You've been up to something, or are about to be. Which is it?'

'Nothing,' Jeff insisted. Now his father, too, was staring at him, and he shuffled his feet nervously.

'Jeff, your mother reads minds like a medium,' Matt told him. 'Yours and mine both. If she says you're up to something, you're up to something. Now, do you want to tell us about it, or do I have to take you out behind the shed?'

'I haven't done anything,' Jeff wailed.

'Ah,' Joyce said, the beginnings of a smile playing around her lips. 'We're getting somewhere – we know you're not in trouble yet. Now, why don't you tell us what's going on before you *get* in trouble?'

In a way, Jeff felt relieved. It was annoying to have a mother who always knew what you were going to do before you did it, but on the other hand, he knew that she'd kept him out of a lot of trouble.

Like the time he'd been going to build a tree house, and she'd found him sorting through a pile of old lumber. 'It won't hold you,' she'd said. He'd looked up at her. 'What do you mean?' She'd grinned at him. 'Well,' she'd said, 'if I were you, I'd be planning to build a tree house with that. But before I did, I'd put the boards across a couple of rocks and stand on them to see if they'll hold me.' Jeff had tried it, and the boards had broken. Now he stared at the floor as he told his parents what was going on.

'Some of the kids are going to sneak out tonight,' he said.

'Are they?' Joyce said. So far, it sounded like no more than childish mischief. 'And what are they going to do?'

'Go up to the mine and listen for the water babies,' Jeff said. Joyce and Matt looked at each other.

'I thought we already discussed the water babies,' Matt said.

'Aside from the fact that you know perfectly well you're to stay away from the mine,' Joyce added.

'Unh-hunh.'

'And you were going to go up there anyway?' Joyce sighed heavily. 'Jay-Jay Jennings dared you, didn't she?' she continued before Jeff could answer.

Jeff stared at his mother in wonder. How did she know? He nodded his head.

'All right, who was going?'

'I – I don't know,' Jeff said miserably. Then, as his father stared at him, he rattled off the names. When he was done, he turned to his mother, his eyes brimming with tears. 'If they find out I told, they'll be mad at me.'

Joyce realised he was right. That was the problem with kids. You raised them not to be tattletales, but then you had to get them to tattle so you could straighten out their messes. Somehow it didn't seem fair.

Suddenly an idea occurred to her. She knew it was mean, but it was irresistible. Besides, there seemed to be a certain justice to it.

'This was Jay-Jay's idea?' she asked. Jeff nodded. 'Are you sure?' He nodded again. 'All right,' she said. 'I'm going to call everybody's mother and tell them that Mrs. Jennings called me. Then everybody will think that Jay-Jay told.'

'Joyce,' Matt protested. 'You can't do that.'

'Of course I can,' Joyce said placidly. 'I shouldn't, but I'm going to.'

As Jeff watched in awe his mother went to the phone and began dialling.

She reached all the parents and explained to them what had happened. All of them agreed to keep an eye on their kids, except for two.

Claire Jennings insisted that her daughter wouldn't even think of doing such a thing, and hung up on Joyce.

Diana Amber wasn't home, but Joyce explained the situation to Miss Edna, who listened in silence.

'I see,' Edna said when Joyce was done. 'Well, I'll do what I can.'

'You'll make sure Christie doesn't go out tonight?' Joyce asked.

'I'm an old woman, Mrs. Crowley,' Edna replied. 'Sometimes I fall asleep very early.'

As she hung up the phone Joyce had an uneasy feeling.

And yet, she reflected, she'd done what she could. Despite her inclinations, she couldn't be responsible for everyone in town.

Particularly not for Edna Amber.

Besides, surely Miss Edna wouldn't let herself go to sleep until Diana got home.

Would she?

17

Bill Henry finished the last scrap of his enchilada and leaned back. Across from him, Diana stared at her nearly full plate, then met his eyes. She smiled thinly.

'I guess I wasn't hungry after all.'

'Not hungry, or can't eat?'

'Is there a difference?'

Bill nodded. 'Diana, what's going on out at your house? I can't help you if I don't know what's happening.'

'What makes you think I need help?' Diana asked guardedly.

Bill shook his head sadly. 'I know you, Diana. I've known you all my life, even though I don't see you much. And the look in your eyes tonight tells me that something is very much the matter. I think you ought to tell me about it.'

'There's nothing much to tell. Mother's just being extra difficult lately.'

'Because of Christie.' It was a statement, not a question.

'Because of Christie,' Diana agreed. 'I guess you know she wants me to send her away.'

'She told me,' Bill said. Now Diana looked at him sharply.

'She told you? When?'

'The other day, when she got her hand caught in the rat-trap.'

Diana toyed nervously with a fork. 'She didn't even tell me you were there.'

Bill shifted in his chair, wondering how best to approach the subject. As he ordered after-dinner drinks for both of them, he decided to be direct.

'Diana, Miss Edna told me something else that day.' Was it his imagination, or did Diana appear to flinch? 'She told me you had a baby.'

For a moment Diana though she was going to faint. She felt the blood draining from her face, and a bone-deep chill passed over her. 'She told you *what*?'

Bill reached over and took her hand, and his eyes searched hers as he repeated his statement. 'She said you had a baby about thirty years ago.'

Images began flashing through Diana's mind. A man, a man not at all like Bill, but with a magnetism to him that she couldn't resist. A broad chest and strong arms, and a chiselled face that was vaguely like her father's had been when he was young and had posed for the faded daguerrotype that still sat on her mother's dresser. But who was he? She couldn't remember.

Another memory lapse. But was it really? Had there ever been such a man as she had just seen in the depths of her mind, or was it only her imagination? And then she heard Bill Henry speaking a name.

'Travers.'

Her mother's words came back to her. Elliot Lyons's house had once been the Travers house, but the name had meant nothing to her. 'I don't suppose it would,' her mother had said. But now the face, and the image of the strong torso, and the name all came together. There had been a man named Travers, and as Diana sat mutely at the table, barely comprehending the words Bill Henry was speaking, she began to have a sensation in her loins.

Heat.

Heat, and an odd sense of satisfaction.

Deep inside, Diana realised that what her mother had told Bill Henry was true. Though there was no trace of a memory, her instincts told her that she had once had a child, and that a man named Travers was the father. But what had happened to the child? She forced herself to concentrate on what Bill was telling her.

'She said the baby was born dead, and she buried it.'

Dead? She'd had a baby, and it was born dead?

Again a tide of memory arose, but this time her mind screamed out that her baby hadn't been born dead, that it had been alive.

But why couldn't she remember anything about it?

Why couldn't she see the face of the child?

Why couldn't she remember holding it against her breast, stroking it, nurturing it?

It was one more rent in her memory, but this time it wasn't a small gap. This time it was a yawning black hole, threatening to swallow her up.

What did it mean? She had to think. Desperately she grasped at the threads of reason she could feel slipping away from her, and another image came to mind.

Christie.

What would happen to Christie?

They would take Christie away from her.

Surely, if they found out that she had had a baby, and the baby had died, and she could remember none of it, they would take her little girl away from her.

As that sure knowledge solidified in her mind she felt an unfamiliar strength begin to build in her. No one would ever know what had happened. She would deny her mother's tale, and she would be convincing. When she spoke, her voice was steady, and she even managed a faint smile.

'She never stops, does she?' she asked.

Bill Henry, who had been watching Diana carefully, and had seen a variety of emotions pass over her face, none of which he could truly interpret, let himself relax a little. 'It isn't true?'

Diana managed a humourless laugh. 'Of course it isn't. But it's easy to see what Mother's up to. Can you imagine me being allowed to keep Christie if that story were true? I'd be declared insane!'

Bill finished his drink and called for another round before he spoke again. When he did, he chose his words carefully. 'It seems like a rather complicated tale.'

'But it's perfect,' Diana pointed out. 'They'd take Christie away from me, but leave me with Mother. Don't you see? That's the beauty of it. It all happened – according to Mother – thirty years ago. Since then, Mother's been taking care of me and apparently doing a good job of it. Why send me off to an institution at this late date? Simply take Christie away, and put things back the way they've been for the last thirty years.' She laughed bitterly now. 'It's really Machiavellian, when you think about it.'

'But is it true?' Bill asked.

Diana's eyes, clear and blue, met his, and search as he would, he could see not a flicker of doubt in them. 'Bill, that's not the kind of thing a woman forgets. It would mean a blank space of months in my life, and believe me, there isn't one.' She gazed at Bill's face, searching for a trace of the love she had once seen in his eyes whenever he looked at her. She thought she saw what she was looking for, and a pleading note came into her voice. 'You believe me, don't you?' She let her voice quiver a little. 'Don't you?'

Bill nodded and took her hand once more. 'Of course I do,' he assured her. 'And if Miss Edna spreads that tale any further, I can't imagine anybody believing her.'

Now Diana smiled coquettishly. 'But you did, didn't you? Admit it.'

For the first time that evening Bill chuckled. 'I don't know. At first, not at all. But then I guess I must have believed her enough to think it was worth asking you. Anyway, it's over.' He signalled the waiter for the check.

'Then let's talk about something else,' Diana suggested while they waited. 'Something a lot more cheerful than my mother's tales of my sordid past.'

'For instance?'

'For instance, the Fourth of July.'

'What about it?'

Diana smiled at him, sure now that she was safe. 'I'm taking Christie to the picnic. Want to come along? I

206

haven't been to a picnic in years, and haven't the least idea of what happens at them anymore. You can serve as interpreter for me, explaining the native customs.'

'Sounds good to me,' Bill said, letting himself relax. But then a thought occurred to him. 'But what about your mother? Will she be along?'

And suddenly, for Diana, the light moment was over.

'Not if I can help it,' she said bitterly. Then she laughed, even more bitterly. 'I wonder if she'll even let me go.'

Bill's voice turned serious. 'Diana, you're a grown woman, and you can do what you want to do. She doesn't own you, Diana. You can do anything you want to do, and she can't stop you.'

Diana looked at Bill, and once more her mood swung. 'I can, can't I?' she asked. 'She doesn't run me anymore, and she never will again. Never.'

But inside, Diana still felt doubts lurking. Doubts, and the awful knowledge that there were many things she had no memory of.

What were they, and what might they do to her? She had no way of knowing.

At nine o'clock that evening Jay-Jay Jennings opened the window of her bedroom and slipped out into the night. The air was hot and dry, and the wind was blowing hard, but there was a full moon. She crept around to the front of the house. Standing in deep shadows, she peeked in the living-room windows. Her father was sitting in his large reclining chair, an open Bible in his lap, fast asleep. In a smaller chair next to him, her mother was knitting and watching a special on television that Jay-Jay knew wouldn't be over until eleven. She had two hours before either of her parents would stop in to kiss her good night on their way to bed.

She returned to the backyard and climbed a picket fence to drop into the Gillespie's backyard, then looked around for Susan. There was a light on in Susan's room, but the shade was drawn.

Jay-Jay rapped at the window, then waited. After what

seemed to be an eternity, Susan opened the window.

'Come on,' Jay-Jay said. 'It's nine.'

'I can't go,' Susan whispered. 'My parents found out.'

'So what?'

'They told me if I went, they'd cut off my allowance. Nobody's going – Steve said his parents found out, too, and Mrs. Crowley called my mother.'

'She called my mother, too,' Jay-Jay said. 'But my mom told her I wouldn't do such a thing and hung up on her.' She giggled. 'Are your folks watching T.V.?'

'I guess so.'

'Well, then, come on,' Jay-Jay urged. 'They won't even know you're gone.'

Susan hesitated, torn. But then the door to her room opened. Jay-Jay ducked down into the shrubbery.

'Susan?' Florence Gillespie asked. 'Are you talking to someone?'

'No,' Susan said, closing the window. 'I just heard a cat or something. I was just looking.'

'Well, keep the window closed. I don't want the wind filling the house with dust. Why don't you come out and watch the movie with us for a while?'

Susan, knowing she was supposed to be in bed already, eagerly accepted.

'Can I watch the whole movie?'

'We'll see,' her mother told her. She snapped off the light in her daughter's room and pulled the door closed. As she led Susan into the living room Florence wondered how long Jay-Jay would wait in the shrubbery before going home.

But Jay-Jay, realising that her friends had all chickened out, was already gone from the Gillespies' yard and was hurrying along the street towards the road to the mine.

As she left the town behind, Jay-Jay veered off the road and cut across the big field. On the other side lay the Amber house. If Christie had chickened out, too, she might give up and go home. It wasn't much fun, she decided, being brave all by yourself.

She approached the big old house slowly.

At night, silhouetted against the moonlit sky, it seemed even larger than it was. Lights glowed in windows on the ground floor, and on the third floor another window was lit. Jay-Jay decided that must be Christie's room.

She picked up a rock and tossed it as high as she could against the side of the house.

She waited for a moment and then threw another.

Christie's face appeared at the window.

'Christie!' Jay-Jay called softly. 'It's me! Jay-Jay!'

'Where's everybody else?' Christie hissed back.

'They're going to meet us up at the mine,' Jay-Jay lied. She was sure that if she told Christie no one else had come, Christie would back out of the adventure.

Christie thought about it. Would Aunt Diana have let her go?

No, she wouldn't have.

Still, Aunt Diana wasn't home.

'I'll be down in a minute,' Christie hissed. She closed the window and pulled her jeans back on. When she was dressed, she crept down the back stairs and listened from the kitchen. All she could hear was the droning of the television.

She opened the back door and slipped out into the night. Jay-Jay was waiting for her.

'Come on,' Jay-Jay said. 'Let's go before we get caught.'

The two girls scurried around behind the barn, then began walking parallel to the road that led up to the mine. The wind, growing stronger, was howling out of the hills like some strange bodiless monster. Christie suddenly reached out and took Jay-Jay by the hand.

'I don't like this,' she whispered, but Jay-Jay knew the magic words.

'Don't be chicken,' she said. 'It's only wind.'

Unhappily Christie kept going.

Twenty minutes later they stood outside the mine entrance, almost invisible in the shadow of the hill.

'Where's everybody else?' Christie whispered.

Jay-Jay still didn't want to tell her they were by themselves. 'Maybe they went inside,' she suggested. She started towards the mouth of the shaft, but still Christie hung back.

'I don't want to,' she whispered. 'Jay-Jay, I want to go home.'

'Chicken,' Jay-Jay taunted her. 'Chicken, chicken, chicken!'

Reluctantly Christie took a step forward, but Jay-Jay had disappeared into the darkness. 'Jay-Jay? Where are you? Jay-Jay? Jeff?' She waited, but the only sound that came back to her was the moaning of the wind.

And then, in the dim light, something moved.

'Who is it?' she asked.

There was no answer, but again the shape moved. It seemed to be coming towards her.

Christie Lyons turned and fled down the hill.

Diana waited until Bill had driven away from the house, then let herself in the front door. It was just before ten. At least her mother couldn't criticise her for being late. She was beginning to feel a headache coming on, so she went to the kitchen, found an aspirin, and washed it down with a glass of water. Then she went to the living room, where Edna was asleep in front of the television. Diana started to wake her, then decided to leave her alone. Instead she'd go up to the nursery and spend some time with Christie.

She climbed the stairs to the third floor and listened to the wind shriek around the eaves. Tonight they would probably lose some shingles.

The nursery door was closed, but a light showed beneath it. Diana tapped softly, then pushed it open.

'Baby? I'm home.'

The room was empty.

'Christie? Christie, where are you?'

There was no answer, and Diana dashed down the stairs. 'Mother? Mother! Where's Christie?'

Edna awoke with a start and peered sleepily at her

daughter. 'Up in her room, of course. What time is it?'

'She's not in her room. I was just up there.' Panic was building in her now, but she tried to be calm. 'Mama, where is she? Where's my baby?'

Edna stood up and came towards Diana.

'Calm down, Diana,' she said. Outside, she could hear the wind still blowing, and in her daughter's eyes she saw the familiar look of fear and confusion. 'Calm down! She must be here.' Edna, fully awake now, remembered Joyce Crowley's phone call. 'Unless she went with her friends,' she added.

Diana's eyes went wild. 'Went? Went where?'

'Some of the children were going up to the mine –' Edna began, but before she could go on, Diana was screaming.

'The mine? She was going up to the mine? Why?'

'Diana!' Edna reached out to grasp her daughter's arm, but Diana twisted away.

'No . . . she can't go up there, Mama. It's too dangerous. Mama, don't let her . . . I've got to find her . . . got to stop her!'

As Edna watched helplessly Diana ran out into the howling winds of the night.

Christie's heart was pounding in her chest, and her breath was coming in gasps, but she kept running. Then, coming towards her, she recognised Diana. Her fear of the afternoon forgotten in the terror of the night, she stopped running.

She was safe. Whatever she'd seen, it couldn't get her now.

'Aunt Diana? Aunt Diana, help!'

Diana paused, the wind lashing at her in the darkness. Had she heard something – someone – calling to her? She took a hesitant step forward. 'Baby? Is that my baby? Mama's coming, pretty baby. Mama's coming for you.'

Christie froze. There was something in Diana's voice, and in the way she moved, that frightened her even more than whatever she had left behind at the mine. Diana's voice sounded the way it always did before she hit Christie.

Panic swept over her, and she began to cry, but even in her fear, she remembered what happened to her when she cried.

'*Good little girls don't cry.*' The words echoed in her mind, and she fled from Diana.

'Baby,' Diana muttered. 'Baby, where are you?' She looked around, but suddenly there was nothing for her but the darkness and the wind.

Once again she began plodding up the hill towards the mine.

Jay-Jay Jennings giggled to herself. Christie, she decided, was a scaredy-cat, just like the others. But she, Jay-Jay, wasn't. It was kind of fun, being in the mine alone, and if she stayed long enough, she would find out if the stories she had heard were true.

She felt in her pocket for the tiny flashlight she had brought along and ventured deeper into the mine.

The darkness closed around her, and she turned on the light. She flashed it around, then reached out to touch the wall of the tunnel. Feeling her way along, she moved towards the vertical shaft.

She listened carefully, but all she could hear was the sound of the wind.

Then, when it seemed as though she must be far from the entrance, she heard another sound.

It was like a baby, and it seemed to be crying.

Was it the wind? Jay-Jay couldn't be sure.

And then, behind her, between her and the entrance, she heard a voice.

This time she knew it wasn't the wind.

She could feel a presence in the mine, as an animal can sense approaching danger. She snapped off the light and waited.

She heard a voice, calling out in the darkness.

Cowering low to the floor of the mine, Jay-Jay didn't answer.

And then there was only the wind, and the strange sound that was like a baby crying.

Diana paused just inside the mine, listening to the howling wind.

She could hear her baby crying now, calling to her, as it always did when the wind blew.

The dark void in her mind opened, and she remembered.

There had been another night, many years ago. She had been carrying a baby that night, and it had been crying.

And then she had lost the baby.

Maybe tonight she would find it.

Find it, and make it stop crying.

She plunged ahead into the darkness, oblivious to the blackness that surrounded her, following only the voice that was guiding her.

'Baby?' she called. 'Baby, where are you? It's Mama, come to get you.'

There was a sound ahead, and then a tiny light glowed.

'Miss Diana?' Jay-Jay called softly. 'Miss Diana, is that you?'

'I'm coming, baby.' Diana's voice floated towards her in the darkness. 'Mama's come back for you. Mama wouldn't leave you here.'

The light came nearer, and suddenly Diana could see the face.

It was the face of a child, and it was crying.

In her mind the old memories stirred once more.

Good babies don't cry.

In the darkness Diana reached out, and soon there was silence.

With the baby's crying blessedly stilled, Diana Amber left the mine and began walking home.

Esperanza Rodriguez, in the tiny cabin, had heard nothing. Since she had stepped out of the cabin a little while ago and seen Christie Lyons running down the hill, she had been on her knees, praying for Juan.

Praying that soon they would realise that her son had done nothing and release him.

Perhaps, if God listened to her, it would even happen tomorrow . . .

18

Christie burst through the front door, tears streaming from her eyes, her face smudged with dirt. She stopped in the foyer, trying to catch her breath, and it was there that Edna Amber found her. She led the sobbing child into the living room and seated herself on the sofa, Christie beside her.

'What happened, child?' she asked. Christie shuddered and rubbed at her eyes with her fists.

'Aunt Diana,' she whispered. 'I was running home, and I . . . I saw her.'

'Where?'

'Up the hill. On the way to the mine. She was talking, and at first I thought she was talking to me, but she wasn't, Miss Edna. She wasn't!'

'Who was she talking to?' Edna asked, her voice quavering with a growing fear.

'I don't know,' Christie wailed. 'A baby. It was like she was talking to a baby.'

Edna sighed heavily and patted Christie. 'All right,' she said. 'You go up and wash your face, then go to bed.'

Christie looked at her, her eyes wide. 'I'm scared,' she whispered. 'I'm so scared.'

'Do as I say,' Edna told her, and there was an edge to her voice that made Christie obey. But before Christie left the room, Edna spoke once more. 'Christie?' The little girl turned to face her. 'Christie,' Edna repeated, her voice low and urgent. 'You must never tell anybody what happened tonight. Do you understand me?'

Christie stared at the old woman for a long time, trying to decide what she meant. Not talk about what? Going to the mine? Seeing Aunt Diana? What? Finally she decided that Miss Edna must mean everything that had happened. Silently she nodded her head, then went upstairs. Fifteen minutes later she was in the crib, curled up with her knees against her chest, her thumb in her mouth, trying to understand what was happening to her. It was impossible.

Edna was waiting for Diana in the foyer, and as her daughter came in, the old woman looked at her sharply. Her eyes, as they had been earlier that evening, were glazed and empty.

'Diana? Are you all right?'

Diana smiled peacefully. 'I'm fine, Mama. Everything's all right now, and I'm fine. My baby's stopped crying.'

A chill passed through Edna, but she said nothing, sure that until the wind died down, Diana would remain lost in the depths of her own mind. Edna knew that when the spell was past, Diana would have no memory of it.

Diana kissed her mother's cheek, then, her mind still peaceful with the knowledge that she had comforted her baby, she went upstairs to the nursery.

Christie lay huddled in the crib, a blanket wrapped around her, her thumb in her mouth. As Diana approached her, she shrank deeper into the crib.

'Baby? Baby, is something wrong? It's Mama.'

Christie's eyes, wide and frightened, peered up at her. Diana reached down to stroke Christie's cheek, but the little girl flinched away from her, her heart pounding. Quietly Christie began to cry.

Diana froze. As the crying sounds reached her ears, the dark side of her mind responded. Her eyes suddenly clouded over, and her hand knotted into a fist.

'Stop that!' she hissed. 'You aren't supposed to cry. Do you hear me? Stop that!'

Christie trembled in the crib and tried desperately not to cry, but her fear was too great. A sob escaped her lips.

Diana's fist flashed down, striking Christie in the ribs. She moaned and drew her body into a tight ball.

'Don't you cry!' Diana's voice rasped. 'Don't you dare cry!'

Again she raised her fist, and Christie clamped her hands over her mouth, determined to keep silent, knowing that if she screamed, it would only be worse.

Time after time Diana battered at the little girl, her voice sinking into gutteral mutterings as an unreasoning fury drove her on.

And then, as Christie wondered if she were about to die, an eerie silence came over the house. The wind had stopped.

Christie lay still in the crib, her scream frozen in her throat. Above her, Diana's face glowed in the moonlight; her eyes were slowly losing their manic glaze. She reached down and touched Christie's bruised body.

'What happened?' she asked. 'Christie, what happened?' But Christie, too terrified to respond, lay still, her legs pulled tightly up against her chest, her thumb in her mouth.

'Did the wind frighten you?' Diana asked. 'But it's all over now, sweetheart. Mama fixed it for you. Mama will always fix it.'

Then she was gone, and Christie heard the lock click into place. She lay staring into the darkness, wanting more than anything in the world to run away. But she was too frightened to move.

Edna sat in the living room, her eyes fixed unseeingly on the television, an unopened magazine on her lap. Sometime during the night, she was sure, the telephone was going to ring.

As the silence lengthened she began to believe that perhaps it wouldn't. Perhaps, as Diana had said, everything *was* all right. She glanced upward, wondering what was happening upstairs. The house was strangely still, and Edna suddenly realised that the wind had died down.

And then the telephone rang. As Edna stood up to answer it, her magazine fell unnoticed from her lap.

'Yes,' she said. Everything was not all right, after all.

Dan Gurley's voice seemed to drift over the line from a great distance.

'Miss Edna? Is Miss Diana there?'

'She's gone to bed. Can I help you?'

'I don't know. Reverend Jennings called me a few minutes ago. Jay-Jay appears to be missing.'

Edna's lips tightened, but when she spoke, her voice was flat, emotionless. 'What has that got to do with us?'

'I've done some checking around, and it seems some of the kids were planning to go out to the mine tonight.' Gurley paused, and when he got no response, went on. 'As far as I know, only Jay-Jay actually went.'

Edna's mind worked furiously, but she needed time to think. 'Perhaps you'd better come out here, Daniel,' she said at last.

There was another pause, then the marshal spoke again. 'I'll be there in ten minutes, Miss Edna.'

Edna hung up the phone and went to the bottom of the stairs.

'Diana? Diana!' Her cane crashed against the bannister, resounding through the house. Getting no reply, Edna mounted the stairs, moving as fast as her stiff legs would allow. She went to Diana's room and entered without knocking. Sitting in bed, a peaceful smile on her face, was Diana.

Edna's eyes blazed with fury as she stared at her daughter, but Diana remained impassive, her gaze expressionless.

'Mama? What is it?'

'Get up,' Edna told her. 'Daniel Gurley is on his way out here, and he wants to talk to you.'

Diana frowned slightly, but got out of bed. 'What could he want at this hour?'

'I'm sure he'll tell you,' Edna replied.

Five minutes later Dan Gurley arrived. Without waiting to be invited, he went into the parlour, then waited for the two women to seat themselves.

'Did you see Jay-Jay tonight?' he asked at last.

'Certainly not,' Edna snapped. 'If I had, I would have called you, and her parents, too.'

'Diana? Did you see her?'

'No,' Diana said. 'I was out with Bill Henry tonight.'

'What about Christie?' Dan asked.

'She was here with me all evening,' Edna replied.

'May I talk to her?'

'What on earth for?' The old woman stood up. 'It's bad enough having you disturb us at this hour,' she said. 'I won't have you upsetting Christie, too.'

Dan hesitated, then gave in, realising that even if he argued, Miss Edna would not be moved. Besides, finding Jay-Jay was, for the moment at least, more important than arguing with the Ambers. 'All right,' he said. 'Sorry to have disturbed you. I'll just go on up to the mine and have a look around.'

A few minutes later, when Dan was gone and they were alone, Edna faced Diana.

'What happened up there tonight?' she asked.

Diana looked puzzled. 'Where?'

'At the mine. You went up there, Diana.'

'I didn't,' Diana insisted. 'Bill brought me home, I said good night to Christie, and I went to bed.'

'That's not true, Diana.' There was desperation in the old woman's voice now. 'Diana, did you do something to Jay-Jay Jennings?'

Diana shook her head, totally baffled. 'Mama, we don't even know if anything's happened to Jay-Jay. She's probably already home.'

'I hope so,' Edna said darkly. 'For your sake, I hope so.'

'What do you mean, "for my sake"? Mama, what are you talking about?'

'I don't want to send you to the hospital again, Diana. But I might have to.'

'The hospital?' What was she talking about? 'But, Mama, why?'

'A child died, Diana, and another one is missing.'

Diana stepped back from her mother. 'Mama – you don't think – you can't – '

'Listen to me, Diana,' Edna said. 'I want to protect you. I've always wanted to protect you. But how can I? You won't let me!' Her voice rose. 'You've never let me!'

Now Diana's voice rose, too.

'Protect me from what, Mama? What have I done that you want to protect me from?' Suddenly she knew. 'You mean my baby?' she asked, her voice low.

Edna paled. 'He told you.'

'Yes, Mama, Bill told me. Is that what you think you've been protecting me from all these years? My own memory?'

Edna sank onto the sofa and stared up at her daughter. She had made a mistake, telling Dr. Henry about the baby. Now she tried to think. How much did Diana know? Only, Edna was sure, as much as she had told the doctor. She let herself relax a little. 'Maybe I should have told you,' she said softly. 'But it was so many years ago ... '

'You mean maybe it doesn't matter anymore, Mother?' Diana asked. 'God, Mother, it was my baby!'

'It was nobody's baby,' Edna shouted. She glowered at Diana, her hands shaking as she clutched her cane. 'It was born dead!'

Diana, her face pale, sank into a chair. 'Tell me about it,' she said.

'There's nothing to tell,' her mother replied. 'It was born dead, and that's all there is to it.'

'That's *not* all there is to it,' Diana cried. 'For God's sake, Mother, can't you understand? All my life I've wanted to have a baby, and now, when I'm fifty, I find out that I had one, and you say that's all there is to it?'

Edna shook her head sadly. 'Why dig it up now, Diana?' she asked. 'It happened so many years ago.'

'And for so many years,' Diana replied, 'I've been so unhappy. What else happened to me that you never told me about, Mother? Besides the fact that you used to beat me.'

Edna glared at her. 'I never – '

'You did, Mother. I remembered. Up at the mine, when I was with Christie and Jeff, I remembered. You blamed me for my father's death, didn't you? And you beat me.'

Her face ashen, Edna rose to her feet. 'How dare you?' she demanded. 'How dare you talk to your mother that way?'

'But it's true, isn't it?' Diana demanded.

'Maybe it is!' Edna drew herself up and seemed to tower over Diana. 'You were an evil child, Diana, but I raised you as best I could. And don't you ever forget that I'm still your mother, and I still know what's best for you. I always have, and I always will. But that's never been enough for you, has it? No matter what I've done, you've always resented me. Well, maybe I should have let you marry Bill Henry; let you have more children!'

'Maybe you should have,' Diana whispered.

Edna raised her hand and struck her daughter. 'So they could die, too? Never!'

Stunned, feeling the blood rushing to her cheek, Diana stared at her mother, and as she gazed into Edna's angry blue eyes, a memory stirred in her.

Just for a moment, she heard a baby crying.

'It wasn't born dead,' she whispered. 'My baby wasn't born dead, was it?'

Again Edna struck Diana.

'Don't say that,' she hissed. 'Don't you ever say that again. It was dead, Diana! Do you hear me? *It was born dead!*'

But as she made her way up the stairs a few minutes later, her hand held to the cheek where Edna had slapped her, the thought remained in Diana's mind.

It wasn't dead.

My baby wasn't dead.

She repeated it to herself over and over again as she bathed her cheek with cool water and the pain slowly subsided.

But if it wasn't born dead, what happened to it?

She went to her room and undressed, slipping into her nightgown.

Then, her mind still whirling in confusion, she went up to the third floor.

She stopped when she came to the nursery door and listened.

Inside, a child was crying.

Her child?

'Baby?' she called softly, unlocking and opening the door. In the crib, she could see her baby. It was crying. She went to it and picked it up.

'Baby,' she whispered in the stillness of the night. 'You mustn't cry. Mama doesn't want you to cry. Mama loves you.'

In Diana's arms, Christie Lyons forced herself to be still.

Dan pulled his car up to the mine. As he turned to park near the entrance, his headlights swept the old caretaker's cabin. He frowned as he gazed at the squat dark building sitting fifty yards away, then shut off the engine, got out of the car, and approached the cabin. He knocked on the door and called out softly, 'Esperanza?'

When there was no answer, Dan tried to door. It was not locked. He opened it and stepped inside the cabin. He switched on his flashlight and looked around.

On the bed, her eyes watching him suspiciously, a blanket clutched around her, was Esperanza Rodriguez. Dan found the light switch, and the cabin was suddenly bright.

'It's only me, Esperanza,' he said. The woman's dark face relaxed, but only a little.

'What you want?' she asked. 'Juan? Is it Juan? Did something happen to *mi hijo*?'

'Now, calm down, Esperanza. This has nothing to do with Juan. He's in the jail, and I'm sure he's sound asleep.'

Esperanza pulled the blanket tighter around her and sat up in the bed. 'Then what do you want?' she asked.

'It's one of the children,' Dan told her. 'One of the children is missing.' When Esperanza's face remained impassive, he spoke again. 'I need to ask you some questions, all right?'

Esperanza nodded silently.

'Did you see anyone up here tonight?' he asked.

Again Esperanza nodded.

'Can you tell me about it, please?' For a moment Dan thought she was going to refuse, but then she began speaking, slowly, as if wanting to be sure she got all the words right.

'I was in bed, and the wind, it was blowing. Then I heard something, so I looked out the window. It was a little girl. So I went out the back door to see what she was doing, and she ran away.'

She fell silent and stared at Dan as if expecting him to accuse her of lying to him.

'And that's all?' he asked.

Esperanza's head moved again, her black eyes fixed on his.

'You didn't go into the mine to look for someone else?'

'I don't like the mine,' Esperanza told him. '*Los niños* are in there.'

Dan nodded, remembering the legend of the children that the Indians thought lived in the mountain.

'All right,' he said. 'You go back to sleep. I'm going to have a look around.'

But Esperanza was getting out of bed. 'You come back,' she said. 'I make coffee, and you come back and tell me what you find. Okay?'

Dan agreed, then left the cabin.

He approached the dark entrance to the mine and paused, flashing his light inside. There appeared to be nothing.

'Jay-Jay?' He called. There was no response, and he flashed his light around again, then began walking into the tunnel.

Just inside he found the power box and threw the main switch on. The lights cut through the darkness, and Dan turned his flashlight off. He moved slowly through the mine until he was at the edge of the vertical shaft. Sighing heavily, he stepped into the elevator and started down.

He found Jay-Jay at the bottom.

Once again, the black floor of the mine was stained red with blood. The body, a shapeless mass of mangled flesh and bone, was almost unrecognisable.

'Jesus ...' Dan Gurley whispered. He got back into his elevator and, as the cage rattled slowly upward, his stomach began heaving.

When he was back outside, he breathed deeply of the night air, but it wasn't enough. Leaning on the fender of his car, he vomited into the dust.

When he returned to the cabin a few minutes later, Esperanza handed him a cup of steaming coffee and read in his face what had happened.

'*Está muerta?*' she asked. As he nodded she crossed herself and muttered a quick prayer. As Dan sipped his coffee she lowered herself into a chair, shaking her head sadly.

'*Los niños,*' she murmured. 'Bad things are coming,' she told Dan. 'The children are restless.'

'Bad things have already come, Esperanza,' Dan said quietly. 'Three people have died.'

'It is because of the mine,' Esperanza said. 'The mine must be left alone.'

'No,' Dan replied. 'It's not the mine, Esperanza. The mine is only a hole in the ground. They were just accidents, that's all.'

But Esperanza knew better, and when Dan finally left her cabin, she fell to her knees and began to pray.

Jerome and Claire Jennings were silent as they drove home from the marshal's office, but once they were inside their house, Claire stared dully at her husband.

'It's the Ambers' fault,' she said bitterly.

'Claire,' Jennings said. 'You can't mean that.'

'I can. It all goes back to them, just like everything in this town goes back to them in the end. If they hadn't tried to reopen that mine, none of this would ever have happened. It's just like Kim Sandler, and her not even buried yet. The quarry should have been fenced, and the mine closed.'

She began sobbing inconsolably, and Jerome slipped his arm around her.

'It's the will of God,' he whispered.

Claire jerked away from him, her eyes suddenly angry. 'The will of God? What kind of God would kill an innocent little girl in a coal mine in the middle of the night? It was something else, Jerome, and you know it! Don't talk to me about God!'

'Claire – '

'I'm sick to death of God! Why can't He leave us alone? First Elliot Lyons, then Kim Sandler, and now – now – ' She couldn't finish and began sobbing again. The doorbell rang, and Jennings stood up to get it, but Claire clung to his hand.

'Come in,' he called. The door opened, and Joyce Crowley stepped inside.

'Claire,' she said, her voice filled with sympathy. 'Oh, Claire, I'm so – '

'Go away,' Claire Jennings said brokenly. 'Get out of my house and don't ever come back. This is your fault, too, you know!'

'My fault?' Joyce echoed. 'I don't understand – '

'It was your son's idea to go out there, wasn't it? Even though you tried to blame it all on Jay-Jay? How could you?' Suddenly she was on her feet, an accusing finger pointed at Joyce. 'Jeff! It was Jeff and you and your friend Diana!' Joyce stared at her, then shifted her gaze to Jerome, who could only shake his head.

'She doesn't mean it,' he whispered.

'I mean it,' Claire hissed. 'My baby's dead, and you all might as well have killed her yourselves!'

'Claire, you *can't* mean that,' Joyce began, but by now Claire was becoming hysterical.

'I do!' she shouted. 'It was you, and Diana Amber, and the little brat Christie! Maybe Jay-Jay was right – maybe Christie Lyons did kill Kim Sandler! Well, I only pray they'll turn on you next! Now, get out of here and leave me alone!'

Stunned, Joyce backed out the front door. As she made her way home she could hear Claire Jennings's words echoing in her ears, and she knew that something had begun. Claire, in her grief, would talk to her friends, and her friends would listen to her, no matter how irrational she was. Within a few days Amberton would be split down the middle. There would be those who would know that Jay-Jay's death had been accidental, but there would be the others, too.

There would be those who preferred to gossip.

It never occurred to Joyce that the gossips might be right.

19

The late-June sun was beating down on the cemetery, and
in the dry heat dust swirled near the ground. Even the trees
– the willows whose shade was usually inviting – seemed
tired and forlorn.

Edna Amber, her face stony and her gaze fixed steadily
on the small coffin that contained the remains of Jay-Jay
Jennings, tried to ignore the whispering of the people
around her. Over the years she had grown used to being
talked about, though she liked it no better than she ever
had.

Today, though, was worse than anything she could
remember. It had been bad enough three days ago at Kim
Sadler's funeral, when the townspeople, numbed with
shock at the death of Jay-Jay Jennings only hours before
Kim's service, had stood in the cemetery, staring at the
coffin of one child while thinking of another. And every
now and then they had glanced towards Diana Amber and
whispered amongst themselves. Edna had quietly realised
that the people, rightly or wrongly, were already
beginning to gossip.

And now, three days later, Alice Sandler and Claire
Jennings had done their work, whispering to their friends
that in the end, all of what had happened came back to
Diana Amber, and her negligence. In a strange way it
amused Edna that she didn't seem to share the blame with
her daughter – apparently she had reached the age when,
though still respectable, she was no longer considered
responsible. And yet, as she steadfastly closed her mind to

the whispering, she realised that something had to be done. A gesture had to be made. And as the funeral began an idea began to form in her mind.

For Diana, who stood next to Edna with Christie's hand firmly grasped in her own, it was even worse. She couldn't ignore the whispering, and even though she couldn't hear all of what was being said, she understood the gist of it.

Somehow she was being held responsible for Jay-Jay's death.

Joyce had called her the day after Jay-Jay had died and tried to explain what was happening, but Diana hadn't been prepared for the coldness emanating from the group gathered at the grave side. The chill seemed to reach out to her like a serpent, threatening to strangle her.

Slowly the little cemetery filled with the friends of the Jenningses and with the curious, too: those people who, though they had only an acquaintanceship with Jay-Jay Jennings, were suddenly aware that something was going on in Amberton and had come to whisper and stare.

Esperanza Rodriguez was there, standing close to her son. Dan Gurley, using the gossip of the town to reinforce his own conviction that Juan Rodriguez was guilty of nothing more than having discovered a body, had released him the day before. With his mother, he stood at the edge of the crowd, watching.

Eventually the Crowleys arrived. Joyce led her husband and son over to the Ambers. Diana smiled gratefully at Joyce and leaned over to whisper in her ear.

'It's almost like they think I killed Jay-Jay myself.'

Joyce nodded sympathetically. 'I know. I've been getting some of it myself. If I ain't with 'em, I must be agin 'em, as the saying goes. It's like being a stranger, even though I grew up here. Matt didn't want to come at all, but I won't give people that satisfaction.'

Diana shook her head sadly. 'Well, at least they're not after Juan anymore.'

'Great!' Joyce said, her voice bitter. 'Now all you have to do is lock yourself in jail till someone else dies!'

'Joyce!'

Joyce grinned crookedly. 'I'm sorry. I guess this whole thing had me more upset than I thought.' She paused and nodded to Mrs. Berkey, who was glaring at her. Mrs Berkey did not return the greeting.

A few moments later Jerome Jennings stood up, and the crowd fell silent. His sonorous voice cracking with emotion, he began praying for his daughter's immortal soul.

When the service was over, Christie looked up at Diana.

'Are we going to the Jenningses', like when everyone came to our house when my father died?' she asked.

'I – I don't think so,' Diana stammered. She looked to Joyce for support, but it was Edna who spoke.

'We'll go home,' she said, Then she paused and turned to Joyce. 'I don't suppose you'll be going to the Jenningses' either, will you?'

'I doubt it,' Joyce said dryly.

'Then come to our house,' Edna said. If she noticed the shocked expression on Joyce's face, she gave no sign. 'Diana will make some lemonade, and we'll have a chat.'

Without waiting for an answer, Edna walked away from the grave site, her back straight, her cane held confidently. As she made her way through the crowd she spoke to no one, but a path seemed to open before her. When she was out of earshot, Joyce turned to Diana, her expression so comical that Diana almost laughed out loud.

'Did she mean that?' Joyce asked.

Diana, as shocked as Joyce by the invitation, could only shrug. 'She must have.'

Matt, standing with his wife, scratched his head. 'I wonder what she. meant by "a chat"?'

Now Diana did permit herself a small chuckle, though there was little humour in it. 'With Mother, that could be anything,' she said. 'But she must want something. You know how Mother feels about the –' She broke off, embarrassed.

'– the peons?' Joyce finished for her.

'I – I wasn't going to say that,' Diana stammered.

'Of course you weren't,' Joyce agreed, patting Diana's arm. 'You're too polite. But let's not kid ourselves.' She brightened. 'However, since most of the town is no longer speaking to me, I might as well be received at court. Do you think you can spike my lemonade with gin?'

'I can try. Do you want to follow us out to the ranch?'

Joyce shook her head. 'I'm going to hang around here and see just who is speaking to me.'

There was a sudden blaring of an automobile horn, and Diana looked quickly towards the parking lot, where Edna was standing next to the old Cadillac. 'We'd better get going. See you in an hour?'

'Probably sooner,' Joyce replied wryly. 'I have a feeling I only have about twenty minutes worth of friends left.' Then, tucking her arm through Matt's, and taking Jeff with the other hand, she began circulating through the crowd, speaking to everyone.

Very few people returned her greetings.

'Shall we use the living room?' Diana asked her mother as she lifted a large cut-glass pitcher down from a high shelf.

'I said I wanted to have a chat,' Edna replied. 'I didn't say I wanted my house invaded. We'll use the yard.'

Diana didn't protest. She began squeezing lemons, while Christie, her face pale, sat silently at the table.

Diana looked at her worriedly. 'Are you all right?'

There was a silence, and then, her voice quavering, her eyes brimming with tears, Christie asked a question.

'Why is everybody dying?'

Diana set her knife down and moved to Christie, slipping her arms around the shaking child. 'They aren't, honey,' she said softly. 'It's just been a terrible three weeks, that's all. Sometimes it happens.'

Christie shook her head doubtfully. 'Am I going to die, too?' As Diana's eyes suddenly darkened Edna decided it was time to intervene.

'For heaven's sake, child, don't be morbid. Why don't you make yourself useful and get the glasses out? And use a stool!'

'I can reach,' Christie said, hastening to obey. She crossed the kitchen and reached up to the shelf where the glasses stood. One of them teetered for a moment, then crashed into the sink. Once more she had made a mistake, and she turned to see which of the Amber women would mete out her punishment.

Edna, however, was stalking out of the kitchen, and Diana was simply staring at her.

'I'm sorry,' Christie apologised as she began picking the shards of glass out of the sink. 'It was an accident.'

Diana smiled at her gently. 'Don't worry about it. It happens to everyone now and then.' Diana finished squeezing the lemons and added water to the pitcher. 'Want to taste this?'

Christie made a face at the pitcher. 'Not till you put the sugar in.' As Diana began adding sugar the little girl looked at her expectantly. 'Well, am I?' she asked.

'Are you what?'

'Going to die.'

Diana paused, then shook her head. 'No, you're not. You're going to stay here with me. You'll always be my little baby, and I'll always take care of you. All right?'

Christie was silent for a long time, turning the matter over in her mind. Finally she nodded her head. 'Okay.' The matter apparently put to rest, she put the glasses on a tray and took them outside. As she was setting them on the picnic table, the Crowleys came up the driveway, with Jeff standing up in the bed of the pickup, his arms spread out on the roof of the cab.

When the truck came to a stop, he climbed out and faced Christie. 'Guess what? The Gillespies and the Penroses are still speaking to Mom, so we're not lepers after all.' Then he looked at his father quizzically. 'Dad, what's a leper?'

'It's what you're going to be if you don't stop telling everyone every word your mother says,' Matt replied, swatting at Jeff's backside but missing.

Diana came out of the kitchen door with the lemonade pitcher, and a moment later Edna, too, emerged from the house.

'Matthew,' Edna said formally, extending her hand in what Joyce could only think of as a regal gesture. 'Thank you for coming.'

'Thank you for inviting us, Miss Edna,' Matt replied, matching her formality so perfectly that Joyce had to stifle a laugh. Edna, if she noticed, chose to ignore the parody.

'Is lemonade all right, or would you like something stronger?' she asked. 'I think Diana keeps some liquor over the refrigerator. There's bourbon and gin, if I'm not mistaken.'

'Mother,' Diana protested. 'You're making it sound like I hide it.'

'Well, don't you?'

Diana reddened and looked helplessly at Joyce. 'All women hide the liquor, Miss Edna,' Joyce said quickly. 'It's more fun to have a drink if you can feel sneaky about it.'

Edna suddenly smiled. 'Well, then, I think I'll just be sneaky, too. Diana, why don't you bring out whatever we have and some soda water.'

'Soda water?' Diana echoed. By now the group had drifted over to the picnic table, except for Jeff and Christie, who had headed for the barn.

'Your father drank bourbon and soda. If it was good enough for him, it's good enough for me.'

Diana went back into the kitchen, and Edna lowered herself into a redwood chair that was sheltered from the sun by a large aspen. After she was seated, the Crowleys settled into chairs, and as Matt shifted uncomfortably, Joyce decided to take the bull by the horns.

'You wanted to have a chat, Miss Edna. What about?'

Edna waited before answering, and her eyes drifted towards the mountains. The lines in her face, usually so harsh, seemed to soften. 'The mine,' she said at last. 'I've decided it's time to do something about it.'

Joyce looked quickly at Matt's face, but it was carefully blank. She returned her gaze to Edna Amber.

'If you mean you want to hire someone else to try to reopen it, I don't think Matt is interested,' Joyce said.

Diana emerged from the house once more and poured them all drinks. When the glasses had been distributed, Edna spoke again.

'Reopening is not what I had in mind,' she said, staring at the golden liquid in her glass. When she looked up again, there was a smile on her face. 'I was thinking more in terms of blowing the damned thing up.'

A shocked silence hung over the little group as the three others stared at her.

Diana recovered first. She tried not to let her voice reveal the sick feeling that had suddenly developed in the pit of her stomach. 'Mother, what are you talking about?'

'Exactly what I said,' Edna replied calmly, warming to the idea that had come to her at the cemetery. The more she thought about it, the better she liked it. 'It seems to me that it's time we destroyed that place.'

'Why now?' Matt asked, his voice deliberate. 'People have been dying in the mine for generations, Miss Edna. It's not as if this is anything new.'

Edna's gaze drifted to Diana, whose eyes had once more clouded over. As she returned her attention to Matt she was convinced of the wisdom of her idea.

'I am not a stupid woman, Matthew,' she said at last. 'I am aware of what the mine has caused this town in terms of human suffering. I am also aware of the material comfort it has given Amberton. I'd hoped that Elliot Lyons would have been able to find a way for us to enjoy the comfort while avoiding the suffering. Well, he lost his life trying, and since then we've lost two more.'

'Kim Sandler died at the quarry, not the mine,' Matt pointed out.

Edna brushed his comment aside. 'It's the same thing. As far as I'm concerned, the quarry and the mine are one and the same. You may think I've become senile, but I've come to think that the mine is evil. I want it destroyed.'

Diana found herself objecting, but not understanding why. 'Can't we just close it up again?'

Edna's eyes shifted to her daughter and when she spoke, her voice was clear and cold. 'But we've already done that once, haven't we? It doesn't work.'

Joyce Crowley shifted in her chair and shielded her eyes from the sun with one hand. 'Doesn't work, Miss Edna? I'm not sure I follow you.'

'Perhaps you won't be able to,' Edna said. 'It's just that over the years I've come to feel that there's something very strange about that mine. It's as if it demands a price for everything that is taken out of it – a price exacted in human lives. Do you know how Diana's father died?'

Joyce frowned. 'It was the flood, wasn't it?'

Edna nodded grimly. 'It happened the day Diana was born. It was a summer like this one – the chinooks were blowing into July, and we'd had a bad year; four men had already been lost in a cave-in. And while I lay up in my room, giving birth to Diana, the mine flooded.'

'And you've never forgiven me for that, have you?' Diana asked, her voice barely audible.

'Don't be ridiculous,' Edna snapped. She turned back to the Crowleys. 'Of course, the investigators said the flood was no one's fault, but I've never believed it. I've always blamed the mine.'

'I beg your pardon?' Matt asked.

'I said I've always believed the mine itself killed my husband, and the rest of them, too,' Edna said evenly.

Matt Crowley's eyes narrowed. 'I don't get it.'

'Nor do I,' Edna said. 'I've no idea, really, if there is anything to "get", as you put it. But there are the stories – the stories that when the wind blows, you can hear children crying up there. The Indians believe those children are crying for their parents.

'And the day I lost Amos ... well, I thought I heard something. I've never been sure, of course, but I thought that for just a moment, there was something.' Suddenly she seemed to come back to the present, and she drained her glass. 'Of course, whether I heard something or not doesn't matter anymore. What matters is that no one else must die. Matthew, can you arrange to blow the mine up?'

'Well, I don't know – ' Matt began.

'If you can't,' Edna interrupted before he could finish, 'I'll hire somebody else. But I'd prefer it was you. You know the mine, and you live here. I may be a stupid old woman, but I've gotten it into my head that the mine has something against Amberton. Or maybe just the Ambers. But whatever it is, I want someone from this town to destroy it. I want you to do it, Matthew.'

Diana had sat listening to her mother in silence. As Edna had talked a feeling of desperation had grown in her.

'Mama,' she said now, 'you don't mean it. You can't mean it.'

Edna's eyes met her daughter's. 'I mean every word of it, and the sooner it's done, the better.'

Diana rose to her feet. 'No. I won't let you do it, Mama. How can a mine be evil? It's only a . . . a place.'

'It's more than that, Diana,' Edna said softly. 'It's much more than that. There are things about that mine that I will never speak of, but you know what they are.' Her eyes held Diana's for a moment more, then shifted to Matt Crowley. 'Well, Matthew?'

'I'll have to think about it, Miss Edna,' Matt replied, his voice carefully neutral.

Edna got slowly to her feet. 'You do that. And when you make up your mind, let me know. You may have until after the weekend. If you won't do it, I'll call someone in from Pueblo.' She started towards the house, then turned back once more. When she spoke, it was as if Diana weren't there.

'Don't let Diana talk you out of it,' she said. 'Diana has as many strange ideas as I do, but mine are based on a long life and wide experience. Diana's, I'm afraid, stem from being too sheltered. That, of course, is my fault, but there's nothing I can do about it now, except keep sheltering her. And I intend to do that.'

Her cane held firmly in her healed right hand, Edna Amber started towards the house. When she was gone, the Crowleys sat silently for a moment, embarrassed by her last words.

'Does she do that often?' Joyce finally asked, forcing a smile.

'No,' Diana replied, her voice freighted with sarcasm. 'Only when there are people here, or when we're alone. It hardly ever happens at all.'

Joyce shook her head sadly. 'Why don't you move out of here? You can't let her go on treating you like that. You just can't.'

'But where would I go?' Diana sighed. 'She's right, you know. I have been overprotected. I couldn't support myself if I had to, and I have no money of my own. I'm trapped. Besides, Mother won't let me.'

'Diana, it isn't up to your mother,' Joyce protested. 'It's up to you! Why can't you understand that?'

'Because it isn't true!' Diana exclaimed. She twisted a button on her dress as she continued speaking. 'I don't have a life of my own anymore, Joyce. Maybe I never did. But if I did, I gave it up years ago. Mother's an old woman, and no matter what she says, she needs me. And she won't last forever. Someday – ' She dropped the sentence, feeling suddenly ashamed of herself.

Matt poured himself another drink. 'What about the mine?' he asked. 'Do you think she means what she says?'

'I haven't any idea,' Diana replied. 'Let me talk to her when we're alone, all right? I can't imagine she really means to go through with it.'

'Yes, she does,' Joyce suddenly said. 'I'm not sure why, but I think she means every word of it.'

Her husband and Diana stared at her, but she only shrugged her shoulders.

'Let's not talk about it now,' she said.

For the rest of the afternoon they carefully avoided any more talk of the mine.

Christie and Jeff climbed up to the hayloft and gazed out over the ranch. In the shimmering heat of the afternoon it appeared that there was a lake in the middle of the valley, but both the children knew it was a mirage. Below them, they could see the three adults talking, but they were too far away to hear what they were saying. Off to the right, Christie could just see the slag heap spilling from the mine. She stared at it for a moment, wondering if she should tell Jeff she had been there with Jay-Jay that night. Then, remembering that Miss Edna had made her promise never to talk about it, she changed her mind.

'Are all the kids mad at me?' she asked.

'Nah. Why should they be mad at you? All you did was chicken out like the rest of us. Besides, nobody liked old Jay-Jay anyway. All she ever did was try to get us in trouble.'

'She never tried to get me in trouble.'

Jeff made a face at her. 'That's what you think. All she did was tell everyone that you killed Kim Sandler.'

Christie stared at him, her eyes wide. 'When did she say that?'

'The day Kim drowned, when we were over at the Sandlers'. Everyone was saying Juan did it, but Jay-Jay said you did.'

Christie's brows knotted in anger. 'Nobody believed her, did they?'

''Course not. I told you, everyone knows she was a liar. My mom even told everyone that it was Jay-Jay who tattled about going up to the mine. She knew Jay-Jay'd say she didn't, but no one would believe her.'

'Who'd your mom tell?'

'Everyone. Didn't she call up Miss Diana?'

Christie shook her head. 'Aunt Diana wasn't home. But if she called Miss Edna, wouldn't she have told me not to go, or something?'

'Didn't she?' Jeff asked. 'That's what everyone else's mom did.'

The beginnings of an idea began to form in Christie's

mind. 'Maybe Miss Edna wanted me to go,' she said.

Jeff scowled at her. 'Why would she want you to go up there?'

The idea grew in Christie's mind. She was almost afraid to tell Jeff about it, but she couldn't stop herself.

'Maybe she wanted something to happen to me,' she said slowly.

Now it was Jeff who became thoughtful. 'My mom said Miss Edna wants to have Miss Diana all to herself.'

Now the idea was growing between the two of them. 'Maybe she wanted to get rid of me,' Christie said. 'Maybe she wanted me to die.'

Jeff stared at her, suddenly frightened.

He looked down and saw Miss Edna coming out of the house. As she crossed the yard she glanced up and, seeing the two children, pointed at them with her cane.

'Diana,' they heard her say in her rasping voice, 'make those children get down from there. One of these days they're going to wind up dead, and it won't be my fault.'

Christie and Jeff looked at each other, and their nine-year-old hearts began pounding.

20

The day after the funeral Dan Gurley sat in his office, his feet propped up on his desk, thinking. No matter how hard he tried, he couldn't get the deaths of Kim Sandler and Jay-Jay Jennings out of his mind.

Something was wrong.

Perhaps it was the fact that the girls had died in such a short span of time.

Dan had been the marshal in Amberton for fourteen years, and in all that time there hadn't been an accidental death of a child.

Now there were two.

Try as he would, Dan Gurley could not accept the idea that the deaths had been accidental.

He dropped his feet to the floor, stood up, and left his office.

The day was quiet – only a few tourists were wandering in and out of the shops, and here and there a dog lay curled in the dust of the street, sleepily watching the cars going back and forth.

Dan nodded greetings to the people he knew and smiled at the ones he didn't, but again and again kept rerunning what had happened; kept coming back to one thing.

In peaceful little Amberton two children had died, and Dan had had to release his only suspect. Now, without a suspect, he would soon face a large faction of the town, led by the Reverend Jerome Jennings and his wife, who were demanding that something be done.

No one had said anything to him yet, but Dan could feel

it in the air – people were beginning to look at him, then shake their heads as if they thought something were wrong with him. And yet there were others – the Crowleys and their friends – who seemed ready to accept the deaths at face value, as the accidents they appeared to be. The trouble with that, Dan thought, was that none of the 'accident faction' had yet lost a child. When one of them did – and Dan had a gut feeling that sooner or later one of them would – everything would change.

He found himself in front of the little frame house, painted in shades of olive-green and grey, which served as Bill Henry's office as well as his home.

Dan paused, then realised that without really thinking about it, he had known he was coming here. His step suddenly purposeful, he strode up the walk and went into the reception room. It was empty.

He tapped on the office door, and when Bill called for him to come in, he opened it and stepped inside. Bill looked up. Smiling at Dan, he took off his glasses.

'Thank God,' he said, forcing a lightness into his voice. 'I was afraid it might be a patient.'

'Nope,' Dan said. 'Just need to talk to you about something.'

'That's what I'm here for,' Bill replied. 'Fire when ready.'

Without preamble Dan dumped the strange idea that had been building in his mind squarely in Bill's lap. 'What do you think of Diana Amber as a suspect?'

'A suspect for what?' Bill asked.

'Kim and Jay-Jay,' Dan replied.

Now Bill stared at him. 'Diana?' His voice was incredulous. 'How can you call Diana a suspect?'

Dan tried to smile, but failed. 'By reaching real far,' he said. 'She's a suspect on the basis that she was in the area when Kim drowned, and she was near the mine the night Jay-Jay died. So that makes her a suspect, right?'

'Oh, come on, Dan. She was at home in bed when Jay-Jay died.'

'So she says,' Dan agreed. 'But she lives near the mine. I told you I was reaching.' He sighed as Bill's expression failed to soften. 'Dammit, I don't like it any better than you do, but so far she's all I can come up with. And you must have heard what a lot of people in town have been saying.'

'Then why talk to me about it?' Bill asked, his voice cold. 'I can think of a hundred people – hell, two hundred – who would be more receptive to that idea than I. Why'd you come here?'

Dan leaned against the wall and folded his arms across his chest. ''Cause you're a doc, and I've got a weird idea.'

'I'm not sure I want to hear it,' Bill said. Then, seeing the unhappy look on Dan's face, he relented. 'Okay, let's hear it. But I warn you, I'm going to tear it to pieces if I can.'

'It has to do with the wind,' Dan said. 'The wind was blowing the day Kim Sandler drowned, right?'

'I don't remember,' Bill said. 'It's been blowing a lot lately.'

Dan nodded. 'That's what I was thinking about. I know it was blowing the night I found Jay-Jay in the mine.'

'Can't you get to the point?' Bill asked.

'I'm not sure there is a point,' Dan replied. 'I'm just thinking out loud. Since I don't have any idea what happened to those kids, I'm trying to figure out what *could* have happened.'

'All you've said so far is that Diana *could* have killed them,' Bill retorted. 'As far as I'm concerned, that's not possible. If she had, she'd been the first person to tell you.'

'What if she didn't remember?' Dan suddenly asked.

Bill felt an icy chill of fear pass through him as he recalled his conversation with Edna Amber. Had she told the same story to Dan Gurley? 'What gave you that idea?' he asked as casually as he could.

'Nothing concrete,' Dan admitted. 'It's just that the wind affects people strangely. Makes them behave funny. And I just got this idea – '

'Well you can forget it,' Bill said. 'There's nothing wrong with Diana Amber.'

240

'Isn't there?' Dan asked, his voice dangerously quiet. 'I know it's none of my business, but about ten years ago Diana spent a couple of nights in the hospital down in Pueblo. The mental hospital. Do you know what that was all about?'

'No, I don't,' Bill said, his voice tight. 'And you're right – it isn't any of your business, or mine either.'

Dan chewed his lower lip thoughtfully and scratched at his nose. 'If it comes to it, I suppose I could subpoena her medical records,' he said at last.

'On nothing more than an idea? You know better than that, Dan.'

'It's more than an idea, Bill. She was in the area when the kids died, and she was once in a mental institution. That's exactly the grounds we used to hold Juan Rodriguez. The only difference between the two of them is that Juan's a poor, retarded half-breed, and Diana's a rich, well-educated white woman. Now, do you want to tell me whatever you know about Diana, or shall I go up there and arrest her?'

'You won't do that,' Bill said.

The two men's eyes met, challenging each other, and in the end it was Dan who backed down. 'No,' he said at last, 'I guess I won't. But I'll be keeping my eye on her,' he added. 'Particularly when the wind blows.'

Diana and Christie spent the morning of the Fourth of July in the kitchen, happily building a macaroni salad that would serve sixteen. Ever since Jay-Jay's funeral, the weather had been calm, and the tension in the Amber house had eased, though Christie could sense the constant strain between the two women she lived with. But as the week had gone by, and Diana had shown her nothing but love, she had begun to think that maybe the bad times, the times when people had died and she had never known what to expect from her guardian, were over. Slowly she had begun to relax. Now, confident that she wouldn't be

241

punished for it, she filched a piece of boiled egg as Diana scanned the cupboard.

'What about tuna?' Diana asked. 'Shall we throw some in?'

'Yuck,' was Christie's automatic response.

'It might be good,' Diana protested. 'We can at least try it.'

She took the can off the shelf, opened it, and shook it into the salad. When she'd stirred it in, she offered a spoonful to Christie, who made a face, tasted it, then grinned. 'Hey! It *is* good. What else can we put in?'

She began going through the pantry and eventually piled several things on the sink. Diana looked them over, then approved all but the marshmallows.

'My dad always used to put them in fruit salad,' Christie objected as Diana put them away.

'That's fruit salad. This is different. The olives, pimientos, and water chestnuts are plenty.' While Christie began opening the little cans, Diana started cleaning up. As she wiped the sink Edna appeared at the kitchen door. She stood silently, her face fixed in an expression of disapproval, watching them.

'Are you sure you don't want to change your mind and come, Mama?' Diana asked.

'Why would I? I've never gone to their little parties, and I'm too old to start now.'

'But it's going to be fun,' Christie said. 'We're going to have games, and contests, and fireworks. You'd have a good time, Miss Edna. Really!'

'I hardly think a nine-year-old knows what would amuse a woman of eighty-odd,' Edna observed. As Christie's happy expression crumbled Edna turned to her daughter. 'I think we'd better have a little talk before you go, Diana,' she added. Then she turned to leave, and Christie and Diana listened to her cane thumping on the stairs as she laboured up to the second floor.

'Isn't she going to let us go?' Christie asked anxiously when they were alone.

'It's not up to her,' Diana declared. 'Finish cleaning up, and I'll go talk to her.'

Leaving Christie in the kitchen, Diana climbed the stairs. Edna was in her room, standing at the window, staring out. She seemed to be looking at the mine.

'Mama?'

Edna turned, and her clear blue eyes held Diana's. 'I don't suppose there's any point in trying to talk you out of going to that picnic,' she said.

'No, Mama. If it were just me, I wouldn't go. But I don't want Christie to miss it.'

'She could go with the Crowleys,' Edna suggested. 'They seem a decent enough couple.'

Diana took a deep breath. 'I'm going, Mama. Bill Henry is picking us up, and that's all there is to it.'

Edna sighed and lowered herself into a chair. Over the past few days her age seemed to have caught up with her, and she felt too tired to argue with Diana. 'Very well, but I want you to promise me something. If the wind comes up, I want you to come home right away.'

Diana's eyes narrowed suspiciously. 'What makes you think the wind will come up?'

'I didn't say it would,' Edna corrected her. 'I said *if it does*. You know how the wind affects you.'

'It gives me a headache sometimes,' Diana admitted, her voice guarded. What was her mother getting at?

Edna wrapped an afghan around her shoulders, despite the growing heat of the day. 'It does a lot more to you than that, and if it begins blowing, I want you at home.'

'All right, Mama,' Diana said. She, too, was tired of arguing with her mother, but she couldn't keep her exasperation out of her voice.

'And don't use that tone of voice with me, young lady,' Edna automatically responded.

Anger welled up in Diana, but she knew there was no point in expressing it. Her mother would only match it, and soon they would be involved in one of their battles. In the end she was certain to lose.

'I'm sorry, Mama,' she said, injecting her voice with as much contrition as she could muster. 'I'll leave you some lunch.'

Edna glared at her balefully. 'Are you sure it won't be too much trouble?' The acid in her voice stung Diana, but she tried not to show it.

'It won't be any trouble at all.' She left her mother's room and hurried downstairs.

'Christie? Are you going to change your clothes?'

'No.'

Diana surveyed the little girl and wished she could convince her to change from her jeans into a dress. She would be so much prettier. But she knew it was useless – all the kids would be wearing jeans.

'Okay. What else do we need?'

'What are we going to put the salad in?'

Diana thought for a minute. 'A picnic basket. There's one upstairs. Come on.'

They climbed up to the third floor, and Diana unlocked one of the storerooms. As she rummaged around, searching for the ancient wicker basket that she remembered having seen up there, Christie began looking around.

Something caught her eye.

'That's my suitcase,' she said, pointing to the top shelf.

Diana straightened up and looked where the child was pointing.

'No, it's not,' she said uncertainly. 'Why would it be up here?'

'It *is* mine,' Christie insisted. Using the shelves as a ladder, she scrambled up and pulled at the suitcase.

'Leave it alone, Christie,' Diana said sharply, but it was too late. The suitcase crashed to the floor, and the lid flew open.

Out of it tumbled the Lyons family album. Christie stared at it, then at Diana.

'Why did you put it in here?' she complained.

Diana, flustered, tried to think of a reason.

Vaguely she could remember having put the suitcase on the shelf, but she couldn't remember why.

'I don't know,' she said softly. 'Take it to your room, if you want to.'

As Christie picked up the album and left the storage room, Diana continued hunting for the picnic basket. And as she hunted she tried to remember the day she had brought Christie's things home. But all she could remember was that on that day, the wind had been blowing.

Bill Henry slid his car into a spot between the Crowley's pickup and the Penrose's new Chevy and grinned at Diana. Though he was still concerned about his talk with Dan Gurley earlier in the week, he had not mentioned it to Diana, nor did he have any intention of spoiling the picnic for her by telling her today. Perhaps he would never have to tell her at all.

'Sure you're ready for all this bucolic excitement?'

'I'm going to love it,' Diana assured him. 'I don't know why I've let Mother keep me from coming all these years. Christie, isn't that Jeff over there?'

Christie scrambled out of the car and ran off towards the baseball diamond, where Jeff and Steve Penrose were trying to find enough people for a soft-ball game. So far the square wasn't crowded, but here and there various people had spread blankets on the tables, reserving space for themselves and their friends.

Diana noticed that the Jenningses and the Sandlers had chosen a spot as far away as possible from the area near the statue of Amos Amber, where Joyce Crowley and Rita Penrose were unloading baskets of food. While Bill lifted Diana's basket from the trunk of the car, she hurried towards the two women.

Diana tried to concentrate on the chatter that Joyce Crowley was determinedly keeping up, but as the square began filling up she was acutely aware that many people seemed to be avoiding her.

The mothers of Amberton were keeping their distance.

On the baseball diamond, Steve Penrose had finally succeeded in getting a game going, though he didn't think he had much of a team. He was pitching, and Jeff Crowley was catching, but he was stuck with only Christie and Susan Gillespie to cover everything else.

'Come on, Susan,' he yelled. 'What are you doing in right field? Nobody hits out there.'

Susan obediently trotted up towards first base, and the next ball went flying over her head into right field.

'I don't wanta play,' she shouted, but ran after the ball anyway. By the time she had fielded the fly a home run had been scored.

The other team, seven boys, hooted and jeered. Steve Penrose shrugged and walked off the field.

'Come on,' he called. 'This isn't even fair.'

The rest of his team joined him, and the other team began a game of work-ups.

Bill Henry was the first to see the four children coming towards the tables. 'Beat 'em already?' he asked Steve.

Steve made a face but said nothing.

Diana, seeing that Christie's eyes were filling with tears, asked her what had happened.

'The other kids didn't want to play with us,' she said. 'They wouldn't choose up sides, so we said we'd be a team. But there aren't enough of us, and Susan and I aren't any good anyway.'

'Susan can't throw, and Christie can't catch,' Jeff added. Then his eye began to twinkle. 'But it didn't matter because none of us can hit anyway.'

Steve Penrose suddenly started laughing. 'Who cares about that? We would have just chased balls for them all day. We never could have gotten them out.'

'Sounds like you quit while you were ahead,' Joyce Crowley said.

'We were six runs behind,' Jeff told her, then looked perplexed when the adults laughed. 'Can we eat now?' he said.

Late in the afternoon the breeze picked up, and instinctively everyone looked towards the mountains. The clouds that had been visible all day were roiling in the distance, and the people of Amberton looked at each other and nodded.

'Off-season chinook,' someone said. 'Gonna blow all night.'

Dan Gurley glanced up at the sky, then casually strolled over to the little group that included Diana Amber.

'Enjoying yourself?' he asked. Bill shot him a look of warning, but Dan ignored it.

'It's fun,' Diana said, smiling at the marshal in spite of the headache that was beginning to prod at her. 'I've missed a lot in my life, haven't I? Do you suppose it's too late to catch up?'

'I doubt it.' Dan sat down on the blanket and stretched his long legs out. 'Hear your mother wants to blow up the mine,' he said suddenly. He watched Diana carefully and was sure he saw her flinch.

'I think it's a good idea,' Bill said quickly. Dan glanced at him, then his eyes returned to Diana.

'What do you think?'

'I'm not sure,' she said. 'I know how dangerous the mine is, and I know all the horrible things that have happened there, but I have the oddest feeling. It's as if, with the mine destroyed, something will be taken away from me, something that I don't want to lose.'

'What?'

'That's what bothers me. I don't know. All I know is that it would be like ... losing a child.'

Dan Gurley frowned. 'That's an odd thing to say,' he observed.

Suddenly Diana felt trapped. She looked from Dan to Bill, then back to Dan again. Were they looking at her strangely? She couldn't be sure, but she knew she had made a mistake.

The wind was blowing harder, and her headache was getting worse.

The children's games began, and Diana tried to concentrate on them but it was difficult. Something was happening in her mind. Sounds were coming to her, calling to her.

The three-legged race began, and Diana was dimly aware that Christie was out there, her left ankle tied to Jeff Crowley's right, but she couldn't seem to make out exactly where Christie was.

Instead she saw herself on the field, but it was another field, a field near her house, and she was playing with Esperanza. And then she saw her mother moving towards her, her face angry, her clenched fist raised in the air.

'No,' she whimpered. 'Please, no ... '

Beside her, Bill Henry squeezed her arm. 'Diana? Is something wrong?'

It seemed to bring her back to reality, and her vision cleared. But her head still ached, and dimly, in the back of her mind, she could still hear a voice.

A baby, crying out to her. She forced herself to ignore the sound.

'I'm fine,' she said. 'Just a little headache.' She searched the field, then saw Christie.

The little girl was running, leaning heavily on Jeff, and anger suddenly welled up in Diana. Where was she going? Was she running away? Her head was throbbing. Suddenly she called out Christie's name and took a step out onto the field.

Christie turned at the sound of Diana's voice, and the motion threw her and Jeff off-balance. They fell to the ground, and Christie felt a sudden pain in her leg. When she looked at it, blood was pouring from a deep gash in her calf. Horrified by the sight of the blood, she began screaming.

Diana, along with everyone else, was running across the field now, but inside her head chaos raged. Images, real and imagined, mixed together. The baby was calling to her, screaming in agony, and ahead of her she could see it, lying on the ground, its face contorted with pain. She had to get to it, to ease its pain and make it stop crying.

But there were people around it now, and she couldn't get to it. Someone was lifting her baby, carrying it away.

'No,' Diana mumbled. 'It's my baby. You can't take my baby away from me.'

But they were.

Diana Amber, her head throbbing with pain, the wind moaning loudly in her ears, watched as Christie Lyons was carried away.

She couldn't let it happen. She lurched forward, determined not to let them take her baby away from her.

21

Diana opened her eyes and looked up. She was lying on her back, a blanket covering her body. Bill Henry's face loomed above her.

The wind, in its capricious fashion, had faded away as fast as it had come up.

'Diana?' Bill's voice seemed far away, as if he were speaking to her through a tunnel. 'Are you all right?'

'Wha – what happened?'

'There was an accident.'

Fear clutched at Diana and she struggled to sit up, but Bill restrained her.

'It's nothing serious,' he told her. 'Christie tripped and fell on a piece of glass. When you saw the blood, you fainted.'

Diana heard the words, but they had no meaning. Blood? What was he talking about? She couldn't remember any blood. All she could remember was – what?

It was gone, all of it.

She sat up slowly. 'Christie? Where's Christie? Is she all right?'

'I'm okay, Aunt Diana.'

Diana looked around and saw Christie standing near her, a bandage wrapped around her right calf. 'It isn't as bad as it looks,' Bill told her. 'There was a lot of blood, but I didn't have to take any stitches. It won't even leave a scar.' He looked into Diana's eyes and took her wrist, checking her pulse. 'In fact, I'm more worried about you than I am about her.'

Her eyes searched his, looking for a clue. What had she said? *What had happened to her, and why couldn't she remember it?* Desperately she tried to sort it out in her mind, but there was nothing there. Only one more of those terrible voids, as if she had stood still and time had passed her by. She tried to get up, but Bill stopped her.

'Just lie there awhile,' she heard him saying. 'You only fainted, and you'll be all right in a few minutes. Between the sun, the wind, and the blood, it was just too much.'

Diana closed her eyes but couldn't relax. She could feel her heart pounding, and her whole body felt clammy, as if she'd just thrown up.

But everything was all right. All that had happened was that she'd fainted. Everybody did that now and then, didn't they? Except that other people remembered what had happened, and she didn't.

She mustn't let them know. If they knew, they'd think she was crazy, and they'd take Christie away from her. Again she struggled to sit up.

'I'm all right now,' she insisted when Bill still tried to restrain her. 'I just feel like an idiot, that's all. Is there any water?'

Joyce Crowley handed Diana a glass of iced tea, and she gulped it, though she wasn't really thirsty.

'Thank you.'

She looked around now and saw that she was surrounded by a crowd of people. As they saw that she was recovering they began to drift away. Soon no one was left but their own small group, which Dan Gurley had joined. He was staring at her.

'I'm not sick,' Diana said quickly. Too quickly? She searched the faces around her, but except for Bill, no one seemed concerned. Only Dan, whom she was almost certain was eyeing her strangely. But before he could say anything Matt Crowley distracted him.

'What do you think? Calm enough for the fireworks?'

Dan seemed to forget about Diana as he scanned the sky. 'Looks good to me. Shall we start setting up?'

As the two men walked away Diana spoke to Christie. 'Honey, don't you think we ought to go home?'

'I want to stay for the fireworks,' Christie said. 'My leg

doesn't hurt. Really it doesn't!' Then, her eyes pleading with Diana: 'Besides, we have to plan the camp-out!'

The camp-out. Diana had forgotten all about it, but suddenly that day with Jeff and Christie came flooding back to her. Except for that moment in the mine, it had been a good day; out of the house, away from her mother. And there had been no wind to plague her that day.

Today had been a good day, too, until the wind had come up.

But the wind was gone now. Everything was fine.

In Shacktown, Esperanza and Juan Rodriguez sat on the porch of one of Esperanza's friends and watched the fireworks in the distance. The Shacktown people never went to the picnic, but instead gathered together in front of their houses while their children played in the dusty streets. It was hot, and as the day wore on, bringing the searing wind, tempers, ever-edgy, frayed, and fights broke out.

This year the people of Shacktown were talking about what was happening in the cave of the lost children. Ever since Jay-Jay Jennings had died, the women had been murmuring among themselves, sure that Jay-Jay's death had not been an accident. But they were equally sure that no human being had been responsible for it either.

No, it was the children, angry over their rest being disturbed. The women of Shacktown were sure that *los niños* had reached out and taken Jay-Jay, and they were also sure that more was going to happen.

It was the wind that convinced them. This year the wind had blown too much, and too late into the year. And to them the wind and the children were inextricably entwined, for it was only when the wind blew that they could hear the children crying.

Eddie Whitefawn listened to his elders talk and wondered if he should tell them about the night Jay-Jay had died, and how he had been there that night, and watched as Miss Diana had come to the mine. But the mine was forbidden to him, and he knew he would be punished

252

if his grandmother found out what he had done. So instead of speaking out Eddie listened and remained quiet.

Esperanza, too, listened to the talk and nodded her head wisely, knowing that what the women were saying was true. She wondered if she should speak to Miss Diana and warn her to watch out for the little girl, but deep in her heart she knew she wouldn't. Miss Diana was a *gringo*, and wouldn't understand.

Besides, Esperanza realised as she watched the rockets burst into the night sky, there was such a thing as fate. A person could be as careful as possible, could pray and watch for signs, but in the end fate was all that mattered. It was fate that had given her her place in life, and fate that had sent her Juan. If fate chose to send the children screaming vengefully from the cave, then it would happen.

There was nothing she could do, though she would continue to pray ...

The last of the fireworks flared in the night sky, and Diana gratefully got into Bill's car for the ride home. She was tired and wished that they could have left a long time ago. Ever since her fainting spell, she hadn't felt well, and she slumped against the door as Bill drove out of town.

'It wasn't such a good day after all, was it?' he asked, breaking the silence.

'I guess not.' Diana sighed.

Bill glanced at her, and there was something in his look that made her suddenly wary. And when he spoke she was frightened.

'What was it exactly that made you faint?' she heard him ask.

What was he saying? Was he testing her? Trying to find out if she remembered?

'The heat,' she said. 'And the blood. I've never been able to stand the sight of blood.' She made herself produce a sound that wasn't quite laughter. 'I guess I wouldn't have made a good doctor's wife, would I?'

'Well, I don't suppose we'll ever know,' Bill said, turning into the Ambers' long driveway. As they approached the house, they could see lights blazing from the living-room window. 'Damn,' Diana said softly. 'I was going to invite you in.'

'Do it anyway,' Bill suggested.

'Oh, no.' Diana sighed. 'Why make a bad day worse? Mother will have a long list of complaints and do her best to make me feel guilty for having left her alone so long. Well,' she went on, 'I just won't let her do it.' But in her mind she wasn't so sure.

Bill parked the car and walked her to the door, carrying Christie. As Diana put her key in the lock Christie stirred and woke up. She scrambled out of Bill's arms and scooted through the front door.

As Diana was about to go inside Bill gave her a quick hug. 'Keep up the fight,' he whispered, then was gone into the night. Diana stood on the porch, trying to interpret what he might have meant by the comment until his taillights had disappeared, then went into the house. Edna was in the living room, listening to Christie chattering about the picnic.

'And Aunt Diana fainted!' Diana heard Christie saying excitedly. 'It was right after I cut my leg, and everybody thought she was dead or something!'

Edna's eyes left Christie and shifted to Diana. 'Go to bed, child, and let me talk to Diana,' she said. Christie said good night to both of them and went upstairs. Only when she was gone did Edna speak to Diana.

'What did she mean, you fainted?'

Instantly Diana became wary. 'It was hot, and I ate too much too fast, and I fainted. That's all.'

'What time did it happen, Diana?' Edna's voice was low and her blue eyes were flashing. Diana hesitated and Edna spoke again. 'I can find out. I can call your friend Joyce Crowley, and she'll tell me exactly what happened. You fainted when the wind was blowing, didn't you?'

'Yes, Mama.'

'What else happened?'

'I-I don't know, Mama,' Diana said miserably. She

254

shrank back as if expecting her mother to hit her.

'Don't tell me you don't know,' Edna raged. 'When I ask you a question, I expect an answer. Now, tell me!'

'I already told you, Mother,' Diana shouted back at her. 'I don't know what happened. I was watching the children, and then I fainted. I don't remember anything else.'

'That's always your excuse, isn't it? You don't remember. Do you really think you can live that way, remembering only what you want to remember? It won't work, Diana. I tell you, it won't work! What will you do when I'm not here to protect you?'

Diana felt her patience beginning to slip.

The strain of the day, the strain of being on her guard, caught up with her.

'Maybe you've been protecting me too long, Mother.' Her voice rose as her temper gave way. 'Maybe if you stopped protecting me, I'd be all right! But we won't know that until you die, will we?'

'Don't you dare speak to me that way, young lady,' Edna hissed, rising to her feet. She raised her cane, then lashed out at Diana with it.

Pain shot through Diana's body as the cane smashed against her ribs, and she stared at her mother, her eyes glazed and filling with tears.

'Mama,' she whimpered. 'Mama, don't. Please, don't.'

'You're disobedient!' Edna's voice was hoarse, but her blue eyes, blazing with anger, seemed to glow in their deep sockets. 'I'll teach you to obey if it's the last thing I do!' Again she raised the cane, but this time Diana moved.

Muffling a scream that was a combination of fear and pain, she fled from the house.

When she was gone, Edna slowly lowered the cane. The anger that had filled her had disappeared as suddenly as it had come, and she felt weak. Slowly, her legs unsteady, she climbed up to the second floor and went into her room.

She'd made another mistake.

She shouldn't have hit Diana, not with the cane. A slap

would have been enough.

But it was her own fear that had caused it, and the fear was growing.

She was going to lose Diana.

After all these years, she was finally going to lose Diana.

Then, alone, she would die.

Somehow, she must find a way to keep Diana with her.

She got into bed but didn't let herself go to sleep. Instead she thought. Somehow she would find a way to keep her daughter.

Diana's side throbbed with pain, but she didn't stop running till she was away from the house, far enough away so that she knew her mother couldn't come after her.

Then, even in her confusion, she realised she was being irrational. How could her mother come after her? She was an old woman, and she had to use a cane even to walk.

But the feeling persisted, and deep down, Diana knew that all her life she had lived with it.

Her mother hated her, and her demands upon Diana had nothing to do with protecting her. It had to do with enslaving her.

But why? It couldn't be because her father had died. No, it had to be something else.

But what?

Whatever it was, it was frightening – terrifying.

If only her mind wouldn't keep blanking out on her. If she could remember. If she could only remember. Somewhere, lost deep within the black void of her memory, was the explanation for her mother's hatred.

She plunged on through the night, wanting to turn back but unable to.

The answer was at the mine. Something had happened there, and she had to know about it, had to remember it.

A fragment of thought came into her mind. Maybe she was crazy and should get help. But if she did that, they'd take Christie away from her, as they'd taken her baby away from her.

Taken her baby?

No, her baby hadn't been taken. It had died.

But if it had died, they why could she still hear it crying? It must not have died. It must have been taken somewhere.

Taken where? By whom?

Her mother. Only her mother was there when she'd had the baby. So her mother had taken the baby somewhere. Taken it away, and given it to someone.

Or killed it.

She was approaching the mine now and she stopped. Suddenly it all began making sense.

That was why her mother wanted the mine blown up – her mother had killed her baby and put it in the mine.

Somewhere, in the maze of shafts and tunnels that honeycombed the hill, her baby was waiting for her.

Her mind whirling with chaotic thoughts, she entered the mine. Its musty dankness closed around her. A part of her wanted to turn around and run home, leaving the mine and leaving the horrible ideas that danced in her head, mocking her, tantalising her, torturing her.

Her baby wasn't dead.

She wouldn't let it be dead.

It was her baby, not her mother's, and her mother had no right to take it away from her.

But that's what her mother had done. That had to be what her mother had done.

Taken her baby from her, and killed it.

Just as she wanted to take Christie away from her.

Diana felt a chill pass through her body, and she began sweating. She'd made a horrible mistake.

She'd left her mother alone in the house with Christie, and her mother was angry.

In her mind's eyes she saw the cane arcing towards her and remembered the helpless feeling she'd had.

And then the scene shifted. She pictured Christie, sleeping in the nursery, curled up in the crib.

And Edna, standing over her, her eyes raging, her fury unspent.

She saw the cane rise into the air, her mother's gnarled hands gripping it, suspending it for a moment over Christie's sleepy face.

And then the cane was coming down, crashing onto the head of the sleeping child.

Diana screamed, and the sound of her own voice seemed to release her from her vision. She turned and ran from the mine, fled from the blackness of the hole in the mountain, fled from the fear that came out of the night.

She ran until she was home, and as she pounded up the stairs to the third floor, her breath came in choking gasps.

Panting, she burst into the nursery.

In the crib, her eyes wide with terror as she stared up into Diana's tormented face, was Christie.

'Baby,' Diana babbled. 'Oh, baby, did she try to hurt you? I won't let her hurt you, baby. Not again. Never again.'

A scream built in Christie's throat. It was happening again! Just as she was beginning to feel safe, it was happening again. Paralysed with fear, she let Diana pick her up and carry her downstairs. Whatever happened, she must not cry.

Diana laid Christie on her bed and bent over her, prodding and poking at the little girl as she searched for the bruises she was sure must be there. Finally satisifed that she had reached Christie in time, she went down the hall to her mother's room.

Throwing the door open, her face contorted with rage, she began screaming. *'I won't let you do it! I won't let you kill her again! Do you hear me? I won't let you!'*

She slammed Edna's door and returned to her room, locking herself and her baby inside.

In her own room, Edna Amber stared at the door for a long time after Diana had left.

Then, for the first time since Diana had been born, she began to weep.

It was all going to happen again and there was nothing she could do to stop it.

22

For Christie Lyons the next four days were the strangest of her life.

The day after the picnic Diana moved her out of the nursery, bringing the daybed down to the second floor, where it was installed in a corner of Diana's room.

Edna watched them move the bed and tried to object, but Diana refused to listen to her. Finally, as Christie looked on, Edna raised her cane and lashed out at her daughter. But instead of cringing under her mother's fury Diana reached out and caught the cane, wrenching it from Edna's grip.

'Don't do that again, Mother,' she said. 'If you ever try to hit me again, I'll kill you. Do you understand me?'

'Diana . . .' Edna whispered. Her voice carried the same note of fear that had been in Diana's own voice all her life.

'Do you understand me?' Diana demanded again, savouring her victory. Edna stared at her fiercely, but Diana was relentless. 'I know what happened, Mother,' she said. 'I remember. I remember what happened to my baby, and I swear, Mother, if you try to do anything to me or to my little girl, I'll kill you.' And then, as the fire in Edna's eyes began to fade, Diana once more repeated the words that Edna had for so many years used to torment her. '*Do you understand me?*' Edna, her eyes suddenly dull, nodded her head.

After that Diana was with Christie every minute of every day. At first Christie was wary, constantly worried that the strange expression would come into Diana's eyes, and that she would receive another of the beatings that had become a part of her life.

On the second day, Diana gave her a piano lesson. For hours the two of them sat at the old Bosendorfer, and while Christie played scales Diana counted the rhythm, her voice droning hypnotically. Then she began to talk, but Christie wasn't sure what she was talking about.

'Mama ... please, Mama, don't make me ... I don't want to, Mama ... please ... please ... please ...'

The word itself became a cadence, and Christie played on, tunelessly, one note at a time, each note punctuated with the sound of Diana's pleading voice.

'*Please ... please ... please ... please ...*'

It only ended when Miss Edna came in and demanded that they stop.

And they stopped. Diana stared at her mother for what seemed to Christie to be an endless amount of time, then finally took Christie by the hand and led her out of the room.

From then on, each day was spent on horseback, roaming the ranch. Most of the time Diana didn't speak to Christie but simply looked at her, smiling a distant smile that Christie found somehow frightening.

And at night the terror would begin.

They would go to the room on the second floor, Diana in her bed and Christie on the daybed, and Christie would try to fall asleep.

But soon Diana would begin muttering, then tossing in the bed and crying out. Christie would try to wake her, but Diana seemed trapped in her nightmares, and Christie could never wake her up.

But each night, very late, Diana would suddenly get up and come to the daybed, where she would stand over Christie, staring down at her, not speaking, with that strange smile on her face. Christie would wait for the beating she was sure would come. So far it never had.

On the fourth night, she tried to run away.

They went to bed as usual, and Christie lay awake, waiting.

Near midnight, Diana began to moan softly, and Christie lay still, listening.

Finally she could stand it no longer. She was terrified, and there was no one to comfort her. And then, as Diana began tossing in her bed, Christie remembered what Esperanza had told her on the first day she had come to this house, pointing out her cabin near the mine: *'You need me, you come up there.'*

Tonight, Christie was sure, Diana was going to beat her.

She slid off the daybed and crept from the room. She went up the back stairs and into the nursery. As she opened the door she saw a large rat scurry from under the crib and disappear into a corner. Shuddering and forcing back a scream, she began looking for clothes and finally found a pair of jeans and a flannel shirt on the floor of the closet. She dressed quickly, keeping as silent as she could.

She was about to leave the nursery when she heard footsteps on the stairs.

She looked frantically around the room, but there was no place to hide.

She started for the window, but it was too late.

The door opened, and Diana was standing there, staring at her.

'What are you doing?' she asked. Her voice sounded reasonable, but Christie fidgeted nervously.

'I – I was looking for something.'

'You were running away, weren't you? You got dressed so you could run away. Isn't that right?'

'Aunt Diana – ' Christie began.

'Isn't that right?' Diana shouted. She raised her arm and slapped Christie across the face. Christie shrieked and rubbed at the stinging bruise.

'Don't ever try to run away,' Diana hissed. 'Little girls can never run away from their mothers. Do you understand?'

Christie nodded mutely.

'Do you understand?' Diana demanded.

'I understand, Aunt Diana,' Christie whispered.

As she watched, Diana relaxed, and as Diana led her

back down to the second floor, Christie did begin to understand.

As long as she didn't cry, and did exactly as she was told, she would not be punished.

From now on, no matter what happened, she would act as though she wasn't afraid, and she would never cry.

She wondered, though, what would happen if she failed.

23

Matt Crowley had decided to accept Edna Amber's job offer for several reasons, not the least of them being that he needed the money. Furthermore, he and Joyce had decided that if the mine and its ever-present threat were gone, Amberton would be able to get back to normal. He'd talked it over with Dan Gurley, and the two of them had decided to make the explosion an event for the whole town. Today, five days after the picnic, he was going to begin the job.

He parked his pickup near the entrance to the mine and got out. He stood for a few minutes, enjoying the summer sun, then walked slowly towards the black hole that yawned in the hillside. Reluctantly he went inside.

Nothing really had changed since the last time he had been there, except that now as he stood in the gloom, waiting for his eyes to adjust, he had a feeling of unease. Three people had died there in the last few weeks, and Matt found that he was no longer as confident about the mine as he once had been.

Today he was going to plant the dynamite that would destroy the mine.

He found the switch box, opened it, and turned on the electricity. A soft glow lit up the tunnel. Carrying a case of dynamite, Matt began walking back towards the elevator. He paused only to find a miner's helmet and switched on its light as he loaded the explosives into the elevator.

He was about to press the button that would start the little car on its long descent into the depths of the mine when he remembered one of Elliot Lyons's prime rules. Never, under any circumstances, go down into a mine alone. That, as far as anyone knew, was what Elliot Lyons had done. And Elliot was dead.

Matt stepped out of the elevator and walked out of the mine.

He knew he should go back to Amberton and find someone – Dan Gurley, perhaps – to help him. With two of them working they could plant the dynamite in only a few hours. But today Matt wanted to work by himself. It was quiet on the hillside, and the afternoon was warm, and there was really no rush.

He decided to leave the dynamite where it was and prowl the hillside around the mine, looking for fissures and sinkholes that would indicate the beginnings of cave-ins. When the mine went, there was going to be a major hole in the local scenery, and the more he knew about the weak spots below, the more effectively he could place the explosives.

He followed an overgrown trail that threaded up the hill from the mine entrance. He walked slowly, examining the ground carefully, searching for the depressions that would tell him that just below the surface the earth had fallen away.

An hour later, having found nothing, he lowered himself to the ground and leaned back against a rock. He glanced around, not really looking for anything – which was probably why he found it.

He had been looking for depressions in the ground.

What he found was a cleft in the hillside.

A tangle of brush nearly covered the hole, and Matt had to break most of it away before he could get inside. Even then he had to stoop over, for the crevice was no more than five feet high. By the time he was ten feet in, the blackness had surrounded him, and he began to have a sensation of being suspended in a vacuum, even though he could easily touch the walls on both sides of the tunnel.

He called out and listened to his voice echoing around

him. The shaft went a long way, and if he was going to explore it further, he'd need a light.

He left the cave and scrambled back down the hillside to the mine, picked up his helmet, then returned.

It seemed to be a natural formation. There were no pick marks on the walls, and the floor was covered with the bones of small animals. Over the years it must have been used as a den by some sort of predator. Though wolves and cougar had once been common enough in that part of the country, none had been sighted for years. Perhaps a coyote had used the cave.

Matt shined his light into the depths of the tunnel and called out once more. Though he knew it wasn't possible, the light seemed to reduce the echo of his voice. He began walking along the shaft, testing the floor with each step before he put his weight down.

Forty yards in, the floor dropped away.

Matt stretched out on his belly and edged carefully forward. He moved his head out over the precipice.

Far below, the light caught something.

At the bottom of the vertical shaft there was water. Its surface was perfectly still and almost invisible. And beneath the surface there was something else.

Bones.

The pond seemed to be filled with tiny bones, heaped together in a jumble.

Matt's stomach turned as he began to suspect that what he was looking at was a watery grave filled with the bodies of infants.

In a cold sweat he backed away from the lip of the shaft, stood up, and made his way once more into the daylight.

For a long time he stared at the hole in the hillside.

He shuddered as he realised what it had to be.

The story his son had told him about the water babies. He had a sick feeling that he had just stumbled onto the source of that story.

Edna Amber herself opened the door, and when she saw

who it was, she stepped back to let Matt in. She led him to the kitchen and offered him a cup of coffee.

'You don't happen to have a beer, do you, Miss Edna?'

'There hasn't been beer in this house since my husband died. A drink?' she suggested. 'But I'm afraid you'll have to fix it yourself.'

'Coffee'll be fine,' Matt told her. As she found him a cup Matt noted that the old woman had aged in the last week.

'Are you all right, Miss Edna?' he asked as she brought him his coffee.

She smiled at him, but there was a sadness in her eyes that Matt had never seen before. Always, before, there had been a spark in those blue eyes, a spark that could ignite into anger at any moment. But today, the fire was gone.

'I'm just getting old,' she said. She lowered herself into the chair opposite him and folded her hands on the table. 'You've been up to the mine. I gather you're going to do as I asked.'

Matt hesitated, then nodded. 'I'm going to try.'

'What do you mean, you're going to try?' Edna asked, a bit of spirit returning to her voice. 'Either you're going to do it or you're not.'

'Well, it might not be that simple. I found something today that I don't understand. Did you know there's a cave on that mountain?'

'It's riddled with shafts, as we all know,' Edna said.

'No, I don't mean the mine. Outside. Farther up the hill and off to the left. A natural cave.' For the moment, he decided, there was no point in telling Miss Edna what he'd found in the cave.

Edna frowned. 'I've never heard of one.'

'Well, that's the thing, Miss Edna. I don't know if it's connected to the mine or not. I don't think it is – it seems to have water at the bottom, and if it were part of the mine, it would have drained, wouldn't it?'

'Are you asking me or telling me?'

'Telling you, I guess. It seems like before I go blowing things up I better know what I'm doing, and that cave bothers me. You don't know anything about it?'

'Nothing at all.'

'What about Miss Diana?'

'She's not here,' Edna replied, and Matt was sure he heard a catch in her voice, as if something was not right. 'She's gone off somewhere with Christie. I don't know when they'll be back.'

'Gone off? You mean on a trip?'

'Heavens no! No, they took horses and went off into the hills.' Edna's voice dropped and her eyes seemed to cloud over. 'They've done that every day since the Fourth of July. I wish they wouldn't.' Then her eyes cleared and she looked once more at Matt Crowley. 'Didn't Mr. Lyons know about this cave?'

'If he did, he never mentioned it, and it wasn't on any of his maps. That's why I came by – I thought you might have an old map, from back when the mine was first dug.'

Edna shook her head. 'I gave Mr. Lyons everything. If it wasn't on the maps he had, it wasn't on any of them. What difference does it make?'

Matt shrugged. 'Dunno. Maybe none. But if there's some kind of water system down there, or caves or something, it just seems like we better know about it before we go messing around.'

Edna pondered Matt's words and finally nodded. 'Very well,' she said at last. 'You go ahead and do what you think best, Matthew. But I warn you – that mine must be destroyed before it destroys us.'

As he left the Ambers' a few minutes later and started towards town, Matt reflected on her words.

The mine was becoming an obsession with the old woman.

That was the trouble with getting old. Things stopped working quite the way they should and you got funny ideas. And Edna Amber was definitely getting funny ideas about the mine.

Or was she? Maybe, sincere though she'd seemed, she knew more than she was telling him. Maybe she did know about the cave and what was inside.

Matt decided he'd better talk to Dan Gurley about it.

Christie stared nervously at the quarry. 'Did we have to come up here?' she asked.

'I thought you liked this place,' Diana said. 'I thought we could have a swim and lie in the sun for a while.'

'I don't know,' Christie said doubtfully. 'I don't like it here anymore. The last time I was here was when Kim . . .' Her voice trailed off.

'But what happened to Kim doesn't have anything to do with us, does it?' Diana asked. 'I thought we'd have a nice swim and then lie in the sun.'

Christie let the matter drop, afraid of what might happen if she pushed too hard. A few minutes later, in the same clearing she and her friends had used, she and Diana put on their bathing suits.

They swam for a while, then climbed out onto one of the rocks. They lay silently for a few minutes, and the heat of the sun drained some of the tension out of Christie. She let her mind drift and thought of her friends, whom she hadn't seen since the picnic. And that reminded her of the camping trip.

'When are we going on the camp-out?' she asked.

Diana stirred. She hadn't thought of it for days, and now the very idea of it annoyed her. Still, she'd promised, and if she didn't follow through, she'd have to come up with a reason. She tried to find one that would work.

She could claim she was ill.

That would only give her mother an excuse to send Christie away.

Suddenly she felt trapped, and it was Christie and Jeff who had trapped her.

Jeff, really. If it were only Christie, the camp-out would be fun.

Yes, she decided, the problem was with Jeff.

Her mind went back to when she was a child.

Her mother hadn't allowed her to have playmates.

At the time she'd resented it.

Now, though, she understood why.

Her mother had wanted her all to herself.

As she wanted Christie all to herself.

And yet she had promised.

'In a day or so,' she said at last. 'We'll go in a day or so.'

She would have to go through with the trip, but once it was over, things would change. After the camp-out, she would keep Christie at home.

And Christie would be all by herself.

As Diana had been all by herself.

24

Though none of it showed in her face, inside, Edna Amber was raging. That Diana – her Diana – could have threatened her was nearly beyond her credibility. *'I'll kill you,'* Diana had said. *'Do you understand me?'* Even now, days later, Edna was still numb from the shock of it.

She listened helplessly as Diana talked on the telephone to Joyce Crowley. Though she could not hear the other woman's words, she knew what they were discussing.

Diana was going to take Christie and Jeff on a camping trip.

Edna knew she should try to stop the trip, but how? She couldn't talk to Joyce Crowley. What would she say? That Diana had become a killer? Never. Even if Mrs. Crowley believed her, all it would mean would be her loss of Diana.

She waited until Diana hung up the phone, then spoke to her, but her voice, the voice that for years had rung through the house – ordering, directing, demanding – had dropped to the feeble whisper of the very old.

'Diana? Are you sure what you're doing is wise?'

Diana smiled at her mother, taking an odd satisfaction in the uncertain look in the old woman's eyes, the trembling of her hands, and the tremor in her voice. 'It's none of your concern, Mother. What I do with my little girl is between the two of us. It has nothing to do with you.'

'Everything has to do with me,' Edna protested, but the coldness of Diana's stare made her shrink back. 'I just – I just don't think you ought to do it,' she finished lamely.

'What you want no longer concerns me, Mother,' Diana told her.

'So I'm to be thrown away?' Edna asked, a little of the old fire returning to her eyes. 'After all the years, after all I've done for you, I'm to be discarded?'

'All you've done for me? I know what you've done for me, Mama. You've kept me here, made me a prisoner here. And for what? So you wouldn't be alone.'

'No ...'

'Yes, Mama.'

'It was for you. It was all for you ...'

'Don't say that, Mama. Not anymore. I've grown up, and I'm going to *be* grown-up. Don't try to stop me.'

Christie appeared at the door, and the two women fell silent, both of them watching the child. 'Aunt Diana? Are you going to give me my bath?'

Diana smiled at her. 'Of course I am. Are you ready?'

Christie nodded and stuck her thumb in her mouth.

'What are you doing, child?' Edna asked. 'You never used to suck your thumb.'

Christie looked hurt, and a tear welled in her eye. She wiped it away before Diana noticed it. Diana lifted her off her feet and hugged her close.

'It's all right, baby,' she whispered. 'Don't you listen to her. All right?'

Christie nodded, her thumb never leaving her mouth, and Diana carried her out of the room. When she was alone, Edna Amber began to weep.

Dan Gurley listened to Matt's story, then looked curiously at Matt. 'You sure you didn't spend the day drinking up there?' he asked.

'If you want, we can go up there right now and I'll show you,' Matt offered. Though it was nearly six, the sun was still bright in the sky, and there was at least another hour of daylight.

'Dead babies,' Dan said heavily. 'What makes you think they aren't just some kind of small animal?'

'I don't know,' Matt said. 'It's just a feeling I've got. That, and the story Jeff picked up from Eddie Whitefawn.' He repeated the story of the water babies to Dan and, when he was done, lit a cigarette. He took a deep drag on it, then stared at its glowing end. 'Who knows?' he said. 'Maybe there's something to it.'

Dan stood up and picked up his hat. 'Okay,' he said. 'Let's go up and have a talk with Esperanza. If anybody will know anything about it, she will.'

They left the office and drove up to the cabin by the mine.

'Sure you don't want to take a look?' Matt asked. Dan glanced up the hill, then shrugged.

'Oh, what the hell. Might as well.'

Matt led the way up the trail and guided Dan into the cave. Using his flashlight, Dan took over the lead and moved slowly into the tunnel, his light picking up the bones that littered the floor.

'Looks to me like rabbits and squirrels,' he said.

'That's here,' Matt replied. 'Wait'll we get to the end.'

A few moments later Dan was lying on his stomach, shining the light down into the pool.

'Son of a bitch,' he whispered. 'How long do you suppose those have been here?'

'Dunno,' Matt replied. 'But they sure look old. What do you think?'

'I think we should see if Esperanza knows anything about this, and then I think we should figure out a way to get those bones out of there so we can find out what they really are. No sense getting all shook up over what might be nothing, now, is there?'

The two men made their way out of the cave and back down the hill. They knocked on the door of the cabin, and a moment later Juan appeared in the doorway. When he recognised Dan, his happy smile faded and his eyes took on the expression of a frightened rabbit.

'I didn't do nothing,' he said.

'Now take it easy, Juan,' Dan said gently. 'Nobody says

272

you did anything. Is your mother here?'

Juan shook his head.

'Do you know where she is?'

Juan nodded.

'Can you tell me?'

'She went to church,' Juan said. 'She said she has to pray.'

'Pray?' Matt asked. 'Pray about what?'

'I don't know.'

'Okay,' Dan said. 'I'll go find her.' He and Matt were about to leave when Juan suddenly stopped them.

'You going to make the mine go boom-boom?' he asked.

'Where'd you hear that?' Matt asked.

'In town,' Juan said. 'Eddie told me.' He paused and shuffled his feet. 'Can I help?'

'Help? Help with what?'

'The boom-boom,' Juan said. 'I could help you.'

Matt thought about it only a moment before shaking his head. 'I don't think so, Juan. It's pretty dangerous. I'm gonna use dynamite.'

Juan nodded. 'I know about that. You make holes and put it in.'

'That's right.'

'I could drill the holes,' Juan said eagerly. 'Please? I wouldn't touch anything. But I like to drill holes.'

Matt still hesitated, but then Dan spoke up.

'Why don't you let him?' he asked. 'You can't do the job all by yourself.'

'I thought you were going to help out,' Matt said.

Dan nodded. 'I was. But now I'm not sure I can.'

'Something come up?'

'Yeah. Nothing much, but it's going to keep me busy for a few days.' He didn't want to tell Matt that he was investigating Diana Amber. Ever since her strange fainting spell at the picnic, he had felt an urgency about it that he couldn't quite explain, even to himself. 'Got to go down to Pueblo,' he said evasively. 'Some people I want to talk to.'

Matt grinned at him, knowing Dan was being pressured by Claire Jennings and the Sandlers. 'Going job hunting?'

'Maybe,' Dan said, 'maybe not. What about it? Going to give Juan a try?'

'Why not?' Matt shrugged. 'I can show him where to drill, then put the stuff in myself.'

Juan smiled happily and clapped his hands. 'I'll be careful,' he said. 'You'll see. I'll be real careful.'

'Okay. Tell you what. Come down to my place tomorrow, and we'll load up the truck. All right?'

Juan nodded. 'Okay.'

'Slow down,' Dan protested. 'I want someone to look at that cave before you do anything. Let's hold off for a few days, okay?'

'Anything you say,' Matt agreed.

'And I'll talk to Esperanza. In the meantime I don't think either of us should mention the cave. You know how people gossip around here.'

In the gloom of the Church of the Saviour that stood on the edge of Shacktown, Dan Gurley could make out the figures of several people praying. He found Esperanza in the front row, on her knees. He touched her shoulder, and she looked up at him, startled. He signalled her to follow him out of the church. She crossed herself once more, then got to her feet.

When they were outside, Dan asked her about the cave. Her dark eyes filled with terror.

'*Madre de Dios*,' she muttered. Then, her face pale, she scurried back inside, leaving Dan alone on the street.

Christie sat in the tub, enjoying the feel of the water as Diana sluiced it over her. Being given a bath, she had finally decided, wasn't so bad after all. All you had to do was lie there and keep your eyes closed when your face and hair were being washed. And as long as she didn't cry her splashing didn't seem to bother Diana anymore.

What bothered her was living in Diana's room. Even

274

though she hated the nursery, sometimes she missed it. Up there she had at least been by herself sometimes.

Now she was never by herself, except for a few minutes this afternoon when she had managed to sneak up to the nursery while Diana was on the telephone.

Her things were gone, even her photo album.

Someone – Miss Edna, she thought – had taken them out of the nursery and hidden them somewhere. Maybe if she told Aunt Diana about it, she could get them back.

'Aunt Diana?' she asked.

'Hmm?'

'What happened to my things?'

'What things, honey?'

'Stuff like my album. I can't find it.'

'Isn't it in the nursery?' Diana asked.

Christie shook her head. 'I looked, but it isn't there.'

Diana frowned. She didn't have the slightest idea what Christie was talking about. What album? The Amber family had never kept an album.

Late that night, Edna Amber climbed wearily to the third floor and let herself into the nursery.

She sat in the rocking chair for a while, her mind blank, her eyes wandering over the furnishings of the room. Slowly thoughts began to form in her mind, and soon she found herself remembering the days when Diana had been a child.

When had Diana begun forgetting?

Edna didn't know. Over the years the past had become confused for her, and she knew that, fight it as she tried, some of Diana's madness had worn off on her.

And madness, she was finally admitting to herself, was what it was.

In the terrible honesty that comes with old age she realised that it was her own fault.

She had been too hard on Diana. She should never have let the rage she felt against her child vent itself. But it was either that or go crazy herself, and for a long time it looked as if Diana was going to be all right.

And then, one day nearly thirty years ago, Diana had come in after an afternoon of riding. Her clothes had been torn, and her face was smudged with dirt.

Edna had asked her what had happened, but Diana had only looked at her fearfully, burst into tears and run up to the nursery. She had locked the door and had not come out again until the next day. And on the next day, when Edna had again asked her what had happened, Diana had seemed puzzled.

'Happened when?' she had asked.

'Yesterday,' Edna had replied. 'When you came home from riding, you were a mess.'

Diana's eyes had remained puzzled. 'But I didn't go out riding yesterday,' she had said. 'I was in my room all day long.'

No matter how hard Edna had badgered her, she had never wavered from her story.

The months had gone by, and it had soon become obvious that Diana was pregnant.

But she wouldn't admit it.

Finally, when the pregnancy had become undeniable, and Diana still refused to acknowledge that it was happening, Edna had taken charge. And Diana, happily spending her days in the nursery, acquiesced to all of Edna's suggestions.

She stopped going out, stopped seeing her friends, stopped calling them. When they came to visit, Edna told them that Diana had gone away for a while.

In a way it was true.

As the pregnancy developed, and Diana continued to ignore it, Edna realised that somehow her daughter had split part of herself away. Diana, Edna realised, had simply decided she was not pregnant.

Very quietly Edna set about finding out who the father was. It hadn't been difficult – one of the ranch hands, a man named Travers, began hanging around the house, and eventually Edna spoke to him.

It was his idea that he was going to marry Diana.

Edna paid him off and sent him packing.

It was her pride that kept her from sending Diana away or even seeing a doctor.

To Edna, as to Diana, pregnancy without marriage was worse than death. When the baby came, Edna would see to it that it was disposed of.

And then the baby came.

Somehow Edna had managed.

The night it was born, the wind had blown, and Diana, unprepared for what was to happen, had had a difficult time.

Near dawn, she had given birth to a baby daughter, a beautiful child.

After the child was born, Edna had taken it to the nursery and put it in a bassinet. And the child had begun crying.

When Diana woke up, after sleeping through the next day, the baby was still crying.

Diana ignored the sound.

Edna asked if Diana wanted to see her baby.

'What baby?'

Edna bit her lip.

'Your baby, Diana. Your baby girl. Don't you want to see her?'

From the nursery, the baby's crying was clearly audible.

'I don't know what you mean, Mama,' Diana said.

Edna, unsure of what to do, did nothing. She left Diana's room and went upstairs to tend to the baby.

But the baby, as if sensing its mother's rejection, kept crying.

The crying went on for four days, and on the fifth day, the wind began to blow again.

That night, Edna woke up from a fitful sleep and listened to the sound of the wind screaming down from the mountains. She listened for the baby, but couldn't hear it crying.

She went up to the nursery to be sure it was all right.

The cradle was empty.

She went downstairs again to the guest room, where Diana had delivered her baby and was now living.

It, too, was empty.

Edna searched the house, then went out into the night. She began walking towards the mine. Halfway there she met Diana coming down the road, her nightgown covered with a robe, which she clutched tightly against the wind.

There was a strange look in her eyes, and she didn't speak until Edna had led her back to the house. Then, when she was back in her bed, she looked up into her mother's eyes.

'It's the strangest thing,' she said. 'Did you know that when the wind blows like this, you can hear something?'

'What?' Edna asked, though she knew the answer.

'A baby crying,' Diana said. 'But it's stopped now. I made it stop.' Then she drifted off to sleep.

Edna Amber sat up all night that night, trying to decide what to do. By dawn she made up her mind.

She would do nothing, and spend the rest of her life taking care of her daughter.

She would not have to live in shame, nor would Diana.

She was sure she could do it: Diana hadn't the slightest idea of what had happened, and Edna could only pray that she would never remember.

Edna would protect her and take care of her. After all, Diana was all she had, and she loved her.

Besides, there was no way to bring the baby back.

Edna came back to the present and glanced once more around the nursery, still remembering.

It had worked.

The years had gone by, and Diana had insisted on keeping the nursery just as it was. She was saving it, she said, for the time when she would get married and have a baby of her own. But really, Edna knew, Diana had kept the nursery for herself. At times she had even slept in the nursery, holding the teddy bear to her breast, cradling it as a mother cradles a child.

Edna controlled Diana's life as best she could, and for a long time things were all right. There had been the problem with Bill Henry, and then, ten years ago, the two nights Diana had spent in the hospital in Pueblo. But except for that, the years had not been bad.

Edna had coped.

But now it was coming apart. Diana was remembering.

Edna looked around the nursery once more and decided that it was time for it, too, to be taken apart.

When Diana took Christie away for the camping trip, she would begin.

Then, when the nursery was dismantled, she would decide what to do about Diana.

Edna knew in her heart that the time had come when Diana could no longer be controlled.

But Diana was still her daughter, and she wanted to put off what she must do as long as she could.

Besides, the wind wasn't blowing, and when the wind didn't blow, Diana was all right.

It was late in the season. Maybe the wind wouldn't blow again that year.

And maybe Christie wouldn't cry.

25

Two days later three men from Denver – a geologist and two archeologists from the university – arrived in Amberton. Matt Crowley led them up to the cave, then waited while the three men did their work.

While the geologist examined the tunnel, one of the archeologists put on a wet suit and scuba gear and, with the aid of a rope, descended into the pool at the bottom of the shaft.

The water, cold and crystal clear, was deeper than the diver had expected. The piles of bones lay twenty-five feet below the surface.

Though he worked quickly, depositing the bones in plastic bags, then sending them to the surface on a second rope, his air supply was nearly exhausted when he finally finished the job and returned to the surface. A few minutes later the three scientists emerged from the cave.

'Well?' Matt asked.

The geologist spoke first.

'It's a natural cave. Nothing more than a fissure in the sandstone. The water's been collecting for centuries, but it's rain water, seeping in from above.'

'What's that mean as far as the mine's concerned?'

The geologist shrugged. 'Nothing much. When you blow it, the cave'll probably collapse and dump the water into the mine, but it won't do much damage. If you're worried about tapping into a spring or something, you can stop – the mine would have flooded years ago if there were something like that down there.'

Satisfied, Matt turned to the archeologists. 'What about the bones? Are they human?'

The archeologist who had hauled the bones up after his partner collected them nodded. 'They're human, at least all the ones I've gotten a look at. Babies, not more than a few days old, if that. Their skull plates hadn't even fused when they were dumped in here.'

'How old are they?'

The archeologist shrugged. 'Can't say for sure. A hundred years – probably a lot more. But they're not recent, if that's what you're worried about. I'll know better tomorrow, when we've had a chance to spread 'em out and look at 'em.' He glanced at the mouth of the cave, nearly hidden behind the shrubbery. 'When you planning to blow it?'

'Couple of days,' Matt said. 'We been holding off till you guys got here. Any point in waiting?'

The archeologists shook their heads, and the diver spoke. 'Not as far as I can see. I got everything out of the pool.'

'And I got the rest,' the other one added. 'There's nothing on the walls, and the bones on the ground aren't anything. Doesn't look like anybody ever lived in the cave. Still,' he added, 'it'd be nice to excavate it.'

'It'll never happen,' Matt said. 'The woman who owns the property wants it blown as soon as possible.'

The scientists packed their gear, and they all started down the trail. When they reached the mine, Esperanza Rodriguez was sitting on the porch of the cabin, watching them with angry eyes. Matt Crowley waved to her, but instead of returning the greeting, she only went inside the cabin and shut the door.

'What's eating her?' the geologist asked.

Matt hesitated, then decided to say nothing. These men were strangers to him, and he liked Esperanza. He didn't want to expose her to ridicule.

'She just likes to keep to herself,' he said.

When the men from Denver were gone, Matt drove into

281

town to tell Dan Gurley what had been found.

'You tell anybody about the bones?' Dan asked when Matt was done. Matt shook his head.

'Figured we might as well wait till we knew what they were,' he said. 'No sense stirring up the town.'

Dan nodded his agreement. 'Then let's keep it that way. With two kids dead, no telling what might happen if this got out. Okay?'

'Fine. Can I start setting the dynamite tomorrow?'

'Okay by me. You still going to have Juan help you?'

'Sure,' Matt replied. 'Why not?'

'I dunno,' Dan said thoughtfully. 'I just have a feeling that Esperanza isn't going to like it. She might not let Juan do it.'

Matt grinned. 'And he might not tell her he's going to,' he said.

The next day Jeff Crowley appeared at the Ambers'.

By noon, Diana was in the barn, helping the two children saddle the horses that would carry them up to the aspen grove. A fourth horse would carry their gear, and it was that horse that was giving them trouble.

'It's going to fall off,' Jeff remarked as he looked at the old mare, which was loaded down with sleeping bags, a tarp, boxes of food, and an ice chest.

'If it's tied right, it'll be fine,' Diana told him. 'Pull the rope tighter.'

Jeff tugged at the rope, and the horse stamped its feet and whinnied angrily.

'What are we going to cook on?' Christie asked. 'Do you have a stove?'

'We'll build a fire,' Jeff told her. 'We're going camping, stupid.'

'Don't you call me stupid,' Christie flared.

'Then don't ask dumb questions. Haven't you ever been camping?' Jeff was feeling like an expert, having gone hunting with his father the winter before.

'What if I haven't?'

'Oh, brother,' Jeff muttered. He had a feeling that he should have stayed home – everyone knew that girls weren't any good on camp-outs.

Diana, pleased that the spat had died a natural death before she'd had to do something about it, tied the last knot, then checked the load to be sure it was balanced properly. 'Okay, let's take the horses outside.'

The children scrambled onto the horses, and as they emerged from the barn Diana glanced towards the house. Her mother, who had stayed in her room all morning, was still nowhere to be seen. For a moment Diana considered going into the house to see if she was all right, but she was sure that if she did, Edna would find some reason why she must stay with her.

'Let's go,' Diana called. Holding the lead for the pack horse, she led them out of the corral.

From the house, Edna watched them go. She scanned the sky and nodded to herself. So far, there were no clouds piled up over the mountains, and the weather report that morning had not mentioned any storms coming in from the west. Maybe everything was going to be all right. Only when the little caravan was out of sight did she start up the stairs to the third floor.

She looked around the nursery, wondering where to start.

The toys.

She found a box and began putting the stuffed animals into it. She held each one of them for a moment.

They were all left over from Diana's childhood.

Diana, unlike most children, had never put her toys away. Instead she had always kept them in the nursery, even after she had finally moved downstairs, and Edna, afraid of upsetting Diana, had never objected to it. But now the teddy bear, its fabric beginning to rot and smelling of years of dust, seemed ready to fall apart.

Edna piled the stuffed bear and all his friends into the box, then took down the paper bird that was suspended over the crib. That, too, went into the box.

She took the last of Christie's clothes out of the closet and wondered what to do with them.

The guest room. She smiled bitterly as she realised that even though Diana had occupied it for thirty years, she still thought of it as the guest room.

She would put Christie's things in the guest room, and after Diana was gone, Christie could keep it. She would decide what to do with Diana's things later.

The curtains – those white lace curtains that looked so pretty half a century ago – fell into shreds as Edna took them down. They, too, went into the box with the toys.

Edna took the box down the hall, unlocked the storage room, and opened it. She pulled the string, and as the light went on she gasped.

The floor of the storage room was covered with the shredded remains of what had been the Lyons family album.

'That poor child,' Edna murmured to herself, but even as she uttered the words she wasn't sure whether they were for Christie or for Diana. She put the box from the nursery on a shelf, then began cleaning up the mess on the floor.

Sometime, when things were settled, she and Christie would try to piece them back together.

Leaving the storeroom, Edna went to inspect the nursery once more. Except for the cradle, the crib, and the rocking chair, it was empty.

Edna went back downstairs and found a hammer and some nails.

With tears flowing down her cheeks, she nailed the door of the nursery closed ...

Matt Crowley pressed the button, and the elevator whined to life, shuddered, then began its long descent into the depths of the mine. Beside him, Juan Rodriguez looked nervously up at the cables from which the car was suspended.

'It's all right, Juan. Those cables won't break.'

Juan shuddered, suddenly wishing he hadn't come. 'I don't like this place,' Juan said. 'My mother says there are spirits here.'

'Naw. You don't believe in ghosts, do you?'

Juan squirmed and shuffled his feet. 'My mother does,' he said. 'She says there are babies here, and when they cry, people die.'

'Well, don't you believe that,' Matt said, though in his mind's eye he suddenly saw the pile of bones the team from the university had pulled from the cave the day before. 'That's just a story to scare people.'

'But people die here,' Juan protested. 'And I heard the babies cry once.'

Matt decided to change the subject. If Juan kept talking, he would certainly scare himself into going home. 'You know how this stuff works?' He indicated the box of dynamite, and Juan looked at it doubtfully.

'It blows up,' he said.

'Only when it's fused, and so far this stuff isn't fused. Now, all I want you to do is drill holes for me, then I'll put the dynamite sticks in the holes, install the fuses, and wire it. I don't want you even to touch the dynamite.'

'I won't,' Juan promised.

'That's right. All you have to do is drill the holes where I tell you.'

'Okay.'

The elevator rattled to a stop at the bottom, and the two men got out. Together they went through the mine, Matt marking the places where he wanted holes drilled. Then he gave Juan an auger and told him to start drilling.

Juan, eager to please, began working while Matt opened the box of dynamite and started preparing the fuses. By sunset the job would be finished, and tomorrow afternoon, if all went well, the mine would be gone.

They worked slowly and carefully, and by late afternoon the mine was riddled with dynamite. When the charge was set off, the supports of the shafts would be blown away, and the mine would fall in on itself.

285

Matt fed the wire out carefully as the elevator took them back to the surface, then laid wire along the floor of the tunnel until he came to the entrance. When he and Juan were finished for the day, he left the roll of wire next to the equipment box. In the morning he would return, run the wire down the hill, and attach the blasting machine.

'Done,' he said.

Juan scratched his head. 'How do you set it off?'

'A cinch,' Matt told him. He opened the box and took out a blasting machine. 'I attach the wires to these terminals, then, when I push the plunger, this box generates a charge. When the rack hits the pin at the bottom, the charge is released, and the detonating caps go off. They set off the dynamite. Boom!' He put the blasting machine back in the box and dropped the lid closed, then switched off the power. The lights strung along the walls of the mine went out and plunged them into gloom. 'Let's go home.'

As they left the mine Matt glanced instinctively up at the mountains, then pointed and grinned at Juan. 'Looks like we might have heard your mother's babies in a couple of more hours,' he said.

A cloud bank was building above the Rockies, towering into the sky. Juan looked at it worriedly. 'I wish Mama was home,' he said.

'Isn't she?' Matt asked.

Juan shook his head. 'She's in church. All day. Maybe all night, too.'

'You mind staying by yourself?'

Juan ground the toe of his boot into the dirt and shoved his hands deep in his pockets. Without looking at Matt, he nodded.

'Then you come home with me,' Matt told him. 'Jeff's off camping, so there's nobody there but me and Joyce. If you want, you can even spend the night.'

Juan's eyes lit up. 'Really?'

'Really,' Matt assured him. He glanced once more at the mine and got into his truck. Tomorrow, if all went well, they would come back, attach the blaster, and push the plunger. And then, at last, the mine would be gone. He started the engine, jammed the truck into gear, and roared off down the hill.

Eddie Whitefawn cut across the Ambers' pasture. He was searching for Jeff Crowley. It was only an hour since he'd heard that Jeff was going camping with Christie and Miss Diana, and he hoped he could talk Jeff out of going. Not that he wanted to tell Jeff that he'd seen Miss Diana up at the mine the night Jay-Jay had died. He didn't. That, he was sure, would only lead to trouble with the marshal, and he'd long ago learned that the less you said, the more trouble you stayed out of. Still, he didn't want anything to happen to his friend.

He paused at the edge of the pasture.

The yard surrounding the Ambers' house looked empty, and Eddie had a sinking feeling that he might be too late. He trotted over to the barn and went inside.

The stalls were empty, though he could see the signs of their recent occupation. Eddie scratched his head and wondered what to do.

He emerged from the barn into the bright sunlight and stared speculatively at the house. All the stories he'd heard about Miss Edna came into his head.

Finally, gathering his courage, he made up his mind and approached the back door.

He knocked, then, when there was no response, knocked again, louder. Finally, feeling almost relieved that no one had answered, he turned to leave.

'Who are you, and what do you want?'

Startled, Eddie whirled and peered through the screen door at Miss Edna.

'M-Miss Edna?' he asked, his voice shaking with nervousness. 'It's Eddie Whitefawn.'

'What do you want?' Edna repeated.

'I – I was looking for Jeff Crowley. Is he here?'

'No.' From the other side of the door, Edna watched the

little boy. He seemed nervous and looked as though he was about to ask another question. And why had he come out here looking for the Crowley boy? 'Why did you think he'd be here?'

'I – I heard he was going camping with Christie and Miss Diana.'

'Well, he did,' Edna said.

Eddie looked up at her. 'Where?' he asked.

'Up in the hills, I suppose,' Edna replied. She wished the little boy would go away. There were so many things still to be done, and so little time. But then Eddie asked another question, and Edna's heart began to pound.

'In the hills up by the mine?' he asked.

Edna felt her knees begin to weaken and had to lean against the doorframe. Why had he mentioned the mine? Did he know something? And then it came to her. The people in Shacktown, most of them, had no telephones. On the night Jay-Jay died, and Joyce Crowley had phoned all the mothers, she might not have been able to reach Mrs. Whitefawn.

'Maybe you'd better come in,' Edna said at last, pushing the door open. Hesitantly Eddie Whitefawn stepped into the kitchen.

Edna offered him a glass of milk and sat him down at the kitchen table.

'Why do you think they might have gone up near the mine?' she asked, seating herself opposite him.

'I – I don't know,' Eddie stammered.

'Don't know, or won't tell?' Edna countered.

'I – well, I just thought – ' Eddie stood up. 'Maybe I better go home.'

'*Sit down,*' Edna rasped. Eddie sank back into his chair.

'You were at the mine the night Jay-Jay fell, weren't you?'

Eddie's eyes grew wide. How had she known? Was she a witch after all, like some of the kids said? Terrified, he nodded.

'And did you see anything?' Edna demanded.

Eddie hesitated, thinking furiously. If he lied, would she know? He decided she would.

'Miss Diana,' he whispered.

'What about her?'

'I – I saw her. She went into the mine, and there was a scream, and then she came out again.'

Edna sighed heavily and sank back in her chair. He knew. He knew, and sooner or later he would tell someone. And then it would all come out. All her secrets that she had intended to have die with her.

'All right,' she said at last. She smiled at Eddie. 'Have you told anyone you saw my daughter that night?'

Eddie shook his head.

'But you should have,' Edna said. 'You should have told your grandmother and the marshal. Why didn't you?'

'I didn't want to get in trouble,' Eddie said, his voice little more than a whisper.

'Well, you'd better go back to town and tell your grandmother,' Edna said. Eddie stood up, his relief that nothing was going to happen to him showing on his face. He started towards the back door. Just as he was about to leave, Edna spoke again. 'Eddie? Before you go, do you think you could do something for me?'

Eddie looked at her questioningly.

'They forgot to feed the chickens before they left. Do you think you could help me do it?'

'Sure,' Eddie agreed. 'Where's the feed?'

'I'll show you,' Edna said, getting stiffly to her feet. Leaning on her cane with one hand, the other resting on Eddie's shoulder, Edna led him out to the toolshed. 'It's in here.' Eddie opened the door of the shed and stepped inside. Edna followed.

When their eyes were used to the dim light, Eddie saw the sacks of feed leaning against the back wall and started towards them. Once again Edna stopped him.

'Not that,' she said. 'There's a different kind, down in the root cellar.' With her cane, she indicated the trapdoor, and Eddie obediently pulled it open.

'I can't see anything,' he said. 'It's dark.'

'The seed is on the floor, right behind the ladder,' Edna said.

Eddie scrambled down the ladder but still found nothing. He climbed back up and stuck his head out of the trapdoor.

'I didn't find – '

That was all he said before the silver head of Edna Amber's cane crashed down.

Edna stood still for a moment, staring down at the crumpled body on the floor of the root cellar. Then she shook her head sadly and used her cane to push the trapdoor closed.

Now no one knew what had happened up at the mine, and no one ever would.

Slowly she started back towards the house, leaning into the wind that was whistling down from the mountains.

26

Joyce Crowley was finishing the supper dishes when there was a soft knock at the back door. She wiped her hands dry, then opened the door. Esperanza Rodriguez was standing on the stoop, obviously upset. When she spoke, her words tumbled from her mouth in rapid Spanish.

'*Yo vengo a ver mi hijo,*' the old woman said. Joyce looked at her blankly, and Esperanza struggled to find the English words. 'My son,' she said at last. '*Aqui?*'

Joyce pulled the door wide. 'Come in,' she said. 'Juan is in the living room – *sala.*'

Esperanza bobbed her head but made no move to leave the kitchen. She looked at Joyce pleadingly.

'Juan? Your mother's here,' Joyce called. A moment later Juan appeared at the kitchen door and, when he saw his mother, wrapped his arms around her and hugged her. The two of them chattered in Spanish for a minute, but Joyce couldn't understand any of it. Finally Juan turned to her, his eyes unhappy.

'What is it, Juan?' she asked. 'Is something wrong?'

'Mama says I have to go home,' he said. 'She says the people are mad at me.'

'Mad at you? Why?'

'For helping Mr. Crowley at the mine.'

'But why would they be mad at you for that?' Joyce asked. She glanced at Matt, who had also come into the kitchen. He seemed uneasy.

''Cause of the children,' Juan said, his voice clearly reflecting his fear.

'Children?' Joyce asked, immediately thinking of Jeff. 'You mean up on the ranch with Miss Diana?'

Juan shook his head. 'Spirits,' he breathed, his eyes wide.

Joyce turned to Esperanza. 'You mean the water babies?' she asked. Esperanza nodded, her eyes as terrified as Juan's. When she spoke again, Joyce's voice reflected the exasperation she was starting to feel. 'You really believe that?'

Again Esperanza nodded. Then she spoke, searching for the right words.

'Los niños – the children – they live there. The people – *my* people – they say Señor Crowley is going to – ah, *como se dice* – ' Her English failed her, and she made a gesture indicating an explosion.

'Children?' Joyce asked, ignoring the gesture. 'What children?'

Los muertos!' Esperanza said. *'Los niños muertos!'*

Joyce looked helplessly at her husband. 'Matt, what's she talking about? What dead children?'

'We'd better call Bill Henry,' Matt said without answering her question. 'He speaks Spanish, and he knows her people.'

Esperanza waited restlessly in the kitchen until Bill Henry arrived, then she spoke to him for a long time in Spanish. Finally, when she was done, he turned to the Crowleys.

'She says that she heard you were going to blow up the mine. She says you can't do that.'

'Why not?' Joyce asked. 'She said something about dead children.'

Bill nodded. 'I'm not sure I follow it all, but there's a legend that the Indians used to take stillborn babies up there and put them in a cave. She says the spirits of the children live in the cave, waiting to be reborn.'

'The water babies,' Joyce said, nodding. 'The story of the water babies. But – but that's ridiculous!'

'Maybe it's not so ridiculous,' Matt said. Briefly he told

Joyce and Bill about the cave, and what had been found there. 'So maybe the legend's true,' he finished. 'At least as far as putting stillborn babies there.'

Esperanza had been listening, and suddenly she spoke again in another rush of Spanish, gesturing as she talked.

'She says you can hear the children,' Bill translated. 'She says when the wind blows, it frightens the children and makes them cry. If you go up there, you can hear them.'

Matt Crowley suddenly laughed out loud. 'But that's just the mine. When the wind blows, sometimes it echoes in the shafts and sounds sort of like a baby crying. I heard it once when I was working with Elliot Lyons. But it doesn't mean anything.'

Bill explained what Matt had said to Esperanza, and her eyes flashed with indignation. Scowling, she grasped Juan's hand and began moving towards the back door, speaking rapidly as she went. She opened the door and turned to face the three people who were watching her. She spoke once more, then pulled Juan out into the gathering darkness, letting the screen door slam shut behind her. After she was gone, there was a silence, broken finally by Joyce.

'What did she say?'

'She said that it doesn't matter what we think, that even though the bones are gone, the children are still there, and if we do anything to the cave, we'll have to pay. She doesn't care whether we believe her or not. All she wants is for Juan not to be involved, so that whatever happens, the children of her people will not be harmed.'

Joyce sank into a chair and rested her chin on her hands. 'My God,' she said softly. 'I thought superstitions like that had disappeared years ago. But they haven't, have they?'

'Apparently not,' Bill said. 'And apparently there's something to it. After all, the bones were there.'

'So what are we supposed to do?' Matt asked. 'Do we go ahead and blow up the mine? Or do we give in?'

Bill shrugged and listened to the wind, which was coming up stronger. Suddenly he grinned. 'Maybe we should go up there later on and listen. Who knows? We might hear something.'

'Yeah,' Joyce said. 'We'd hear Diana, trying to keep Jeff and Christie under control.'

'Diana?' Bill asked.

'Didn't you know? She took the kids for a camp-out. They're up there right now. Is something wrong?' she added, seeing the look on Bill's face.

'I don't know,' Bill said slowly. And yet he did. Only this morning Dan had come to him once more, hammering away yet again at what had happened at the picnic. Finally Bill had had to admit that when she'd awakened from her faint, Diana had seemed to have no memory of what had made her black out. At last he had told Dan the strange story that Edna had told him and that Diana had denied. Dan, his expression grim, had gone back to his office, intent on talking to the hospital in Pueblo. Now Bill turned to Matt. 'I think we'd better go talk to Dan Gurley,' he said.

Leaving Joyce alone, the two men went out into the night.

As night closed in and the wind grew stronger, Diana felt her head begin to hurt. Next to her, Christie and Jeff were finishing their supper, and as she watched their faces she began to hear the strange sound that had haunted her life.

'Listen,' she said. 'Do you hear it?'

Jeff cocked his head. 'Hear what?'

'My baby,' Diana said. 'Can't you hear my baby crying?'

The children looked at each other. What was she talking about? No one was crying, and all they could hear was the wind in the trees. Christie began to grow nervous.

'A baby?' Jeff asked, his voice uncertain.

'It's in the hills,' Diana said. 'It's coming from the hills.'

She stood up and stepped away from the fire. Christie and Jeff joined her, staring off into the darkness, straining their ears to hear whatever Diana was hearing.

'Can't you hear it now?' Diana asked.

'What's she talking about?' Jeff whispered to Christie.

Christie looked up at Diana and saw that the strange blank look had come into her eyes. Her fear grew, and she took Jeff's hand, clutching it tightly in her own.

'I don't know. But don't cry.'

'Cry?' Jeff repeated. 'Why should I cry?' But even as he spoke he felt tears welling in his eyes. 'I want to go home,' he said. He tugged at Christie's arm, and Diana, disturbed by the sudden movement, looked down.

'What are you doing?' she asked. 'What are you doing to my baby?'

'Nothing,' Jeff whimpered. He dropped Christie's hand and began backing away, fear twisting at his stomach. Something was wrong, and he wasn't sure what to do. The tears in his eyes spilled over, and he tried to choke back a sob.

Diana stared at the little boy, and as the wind screamed around her and the crying child tormented her mind, her memory opened once more.

She was a little girl, and she was behind the barn, playing with a little boy.

The little boy was teaching her a game.

He called it doctor.

And then, while the little boy had his pants down, her mother had appeared.

She had watched, waiting silently, while her mother beat the little boy, knowing that when it was over, it would be her turn. And when her turn came, she forced herself to endure the beating silently, rage building up deep within her to replace the tears she wasn't allowed to shed.

Now she felt that rage building inside her again, and as she stood in the night, her mind confused, she saw once more the little boy and the little girl.

But she was the mother now, and the little boy had been playing with her little girl all day.

Playing what?

She searched her mind. Had they been playing doctor?

They must have been, for they looked scared. Scared and guilty.

Filthy children.

295

Filthy, sinful children.

Diana, in the grip of her madness, moved forward and struck Jeff Crowley across the face.

He screamed, clutched at his cheek, then began sobbing, but Diana's fists flew through the air, pummelling him, lashing at him. Floating through his terror, he could hear Christie's voice.

'Don't cry, Jeff. Please, don't cry!'

Christie watched in horror as Diana struck Jeff again. The force of the blow sent him, writhing, to the ground. She tried to pull Diana away from him. 'Stop it, Aunt Diana,' she begged. 'He didn't do anything. Don't hit him anymore!'

Diana didn't hear her. She had picked up a stick and, raising it over her head, she brought it crashing down into Jeff Crowley's face.

'Filthy,' she was whispering over and over again. 'Filthy, evil little child. Stop crying. Do you understand me? Stop crying and take your punishment.'

Blood gushed from Jeff's nose, and Christie, able to stand it no longer, burst into tears and fled into the night. Behind her she could hear Jeff's cries, fainter and fainter, and the dull thudding of the stick in Diana's hands.

Where could she go?

Home? To Miss Edna?

But where was she? Which way was home?

She paused and looked around. Nothing seemed familiar. And then she came to a trail.

The trail that led to the mine. The mine and Esperanza's cabin.

Esperanza would help her. She would go to Esperanza, and the old woman would come back with her, and they would help Jeff.

Tears streaming down her face, Christie began stumbling along the trail towards the mine.

Jeff Crowley's body lay still at her feet, and Diana, the bloody stick still clutched in her hand, searched the darkness for her little girl.

She, too, must be punished.

'Baby?' she called.

There was no answer, except for the wind.

And then, once more, she heard it.

It was faint, but as she moved off into the darkness it began to grow louder.

Listening to the crying of the child, Diana hurried down the trail towards the mine. She had to find her baby and make it stop crying.

'She's up in the mountains with the kids?' Dan asked. It couldn't be true.

'It might not mean anything,' Bill said. 'But I thought you ought to know.'

'It's a damn good thing you did,' Dan replied grimly. Half an hour earlier he'd had a call from Denver, and ever since he'd been trying to decide what, if anything, he should do.

The bones had been analysed.

All of them were human.

All of them were infants.

All of them were over one hundred years old.

All except one.

One of the skeletons, its parts fragmented, had turned out to be much more recent than the others. If Dan could believe what the archeologist told him, it was between ten and fifty years old.

And, unlike the others, its arms and legs were broken, its ribs mangled, and its skull plates battered.

To the scientist it appeared that this baby had not been born dead, but instead had been beaten to death, sometime shortly after its birth.

Tonelessly he repeated the information to Bill and Matt. Matt looked puzzled, but the blood drained from Bill's face.

'Diana's baby?' he asked at last.

Dan nodded. 'Seems like it might be.'

'But Miss Edna said she buried it. What's going on?'

Dan's eyes were hard as he faced his friend. 'I think

297

something is way wrong out at the Ambers', and I think we better go find out what it is and where Diana and those kids are, too.'

Though Matt Crowley wasn't sure exactly what was going on, and neither Dan nor Bill took the time to explain it to him, he went with them anyway. Somewhere, his son was out there, and the wind was blowing.

Kim Sandler had died while the wind blew.

Jay-Jay Jennings had died while the wind blew.

And Diana Amber – what did she do while the wind blew?

Did she kill?

Dan gunned the engine, flipped on his siren, and put the car in gear. The other two men braced themselves as the car lunged forward. 'You trying to wake up the whole town?' Matt asked.

'I have a feeling the whole town may be awake tonight anyway,' Dan said, his voice grim.

When Edna Amber opened the door, Bill Henry saw at once that something had changed.

She seemed to have shrunk. Her back, usually so straight, was bent, and her shoulders were stooped. Her blue eyes, the twin sapphires, which had sparkled fire for so many years, were pale and streaked with red, as if the old woman had been crying.

'Miss Edna?' Dan asked. 'May we come in?'

Edna nodded and held the door open for them. She stood aside and let them precede her into the little parlour at the front of the house. When she spoke, her voice was weak, and she seemed to have trouble finding the right words.

'Do you want to see Diana? I – I think she's gone out somewhere.' Her eyes moved nervously around the room, as if she were looking for something. 'Yes,' she repeated. 'I believe she's gone out.'

'We need to know where Diana went,' Dan said. 'And we need to talk to you about Diana's baby.'

298

Edna's eyes, rheumy and tear-filled, went to Bill. 'I shouldn't have told you,' she said reproachfully. 'I should have kept it to myself.'

'I'd have found out anyway, Miss Edna,' Bill said gently.

'She thinks I killed it,' Edna said quietly. 'She thinks I killed her baby.'

'And did you?'

Edna was silent for a long time, and Bill wasn't sure she had heard the question. But finally she nodded.

'Maybe I did,' she said.

'I beg your pardon?' Dan asked. He had to lean forward to hear her.

'I said that maybe I did kill her baby. Maybe it was all my fault. Do you think I was too hard on her, William?'

'Too hard? How?'

'I was always strict with her. But mothers are supposed to be strict. And I wanted her to be a good girl.' She looked sorrowfully at them. 'But Diana never was, you know. She was a sinful little girl. Filthy and sinful.'

Dan and Bill glanced at each other, and Bill spoke. 'Can you tell us what happened, Miss Edna?'

Suddenly the old lady's eyes were frightened, and they flickered warily between the three men.

'Oh, I couldn't do that – it wouldn't be proper.' Then she smiled, her face a grotesque caricature of what it had once been. 'But it's going to be all right. I'm going to take care of everything.'

The three men glanced at each other uneasily. 'Miss Edna,' Dan said, 'why don't you let us take care of everything? Just tell us where Diana is, and we'll take care of her, all right?'

Edna got to her feet and leaned her weight on her cane. 'You don't think I've been a good mother, do you?' she asked. 'Well, maybe I haven't. But I did the best I could. That's all anyone can do, isn't it?'

'Of course it is,' Bill said. Though his mind was whirling, he forced his voice to stay calm. What had happened? What had gone wrong? It was as if, overnight,

Edna Amber had become senile. 'Has something happened between you and Diana?'

'She hit me,' the old lady told them. 'My own daughter hit me. And she said I killed her baby.'

'Did you?' Dan asked once more.

Again Edna seemed to think the question over. Finally she shook her head. 'No,' she said. 'She did it. I think it must have been the wind.'

Dan nodded his head, as if he understood. 'The wind,' he said. 'Tell us about the wind.'

'She never liked it, you know,' Edna told them. 'Ever since she was a baby, when the wind blew, she had headaches and cried. But I never let her cry for long.' Her voice hardened, and for a moment her eyes cleared. 'She was a bad child, and I had to punish her.' She paused, and once more her eyes clouded over and her voice dropped. 'But she never remembered. It was as though the wind swept her memory away.' She smiled, as if she'd finally discovered the truth. 'That must be what happened – the wind must have swept her baby away.'

Dan swallowed hard. 'Miss Edna,' he said. 'Miss Edna, we have to know where Diana is. Can you tell us?'

'Why, she's with the babies,' Edna said.

'The children,' Bill corrected her. 'We know she's with the children. But where did she take them?'

'She didn't say. She doesn't like me anymore, you see. After all I've done for her, she doesn't like me. But I only wanted to help her. All I ever wanted to do was help her.'

Dan stood up. 'Miss Edna, we have to go find her. Will you be all right?'

The old woman leaned on her cane and smiled at them.

'Me? Of course I'll be all right. You don't have to worry about me – I can take care of myself. And I can take care of Diana, too, if she'll let me. When you find her, you bring her back here. She's just a little girl, you know. She's just a little baby girl who doesn't know what she's doing.'

'Maybe I'd better stay here,' Bill began. 'You and Matt go ahead.' But Edna shook her finger at him.

'I don't want anybody out here,' she said, her voice taking on a querulous quality that was no more than a vague echo of her former imperiousness. 'I have some things I must do, and I want to be alone.' She paused, then: 'I've never been alone, you know. I'll have to get used to it.'

Reluctantly they left Edna Amber by herself.

When they were back in the police car, Dan glanced at Bill and Matt. 'Any ideas?'

'Jeff said there's a stand of aspen and cottonwood with spring,' Matt said. 'Know where it is?'

Bill nodded. 'On the way to the quarry.'

'Is there a road?' Dan said.

'Go towards the mine, but turn left about a quarter of a mile before you get to it. That'll get us pretty close to the place, but we'll still have to walk some of the way,' Bill replied.

Diana plunged through the night, as though the sound of the crying baby were a siren's song, luring her on. The bloody stick with which she had killed Jeff Crowley was cradled in her arms.

The wind tore down from the mountains, filling the air with mournful keening, and slowly the doors of Diana's memory swung wide.

It was a night like this thirty years ago, when the wind was blowing, but all she could hear was the steady crying of a baby.

She was in bed, but it wasn't her bed. It was a strange bed, in a room that wasn't hers.

Instinctively she knew that the baby was in her bed, in her room.

She crept through the house, searching for the source of the sound. And then, in the nursery – *her* nursery – she found it. In the cradle there was a tiny baby, its fists waving helplessly in the air, its eyes screwed shut, though tears were running down its cheeks.

Diana stared at it, hating it.

It was crying, and no one was punishing it.

It was wrong. Crying babies had to be punished.

And there was something else.

As she looked at the baby she began to remember.

It was her baby.

She'd been a filthy, evil little girl again, and now there was a baby.

She crouched over the cradle and touched the baby, and its cries grew louder.

What if it woke her mother? She would come in and find the baby and realise what Diana had done.

And once more, as she had been so often in her life, she would be punished.

She had to hide the baby.

She picked it up and wrapped it in a blanket, muffling its screams, then took it from the house.

She carried it through the night, wondering what to do with it, where to hide it.

And that night, for the first time, she heard the sound that guided her, and that had stayed with her ever since.

A baby, crying. Not the baby in her arms, not her own baby, but another. And suddenly she knew.

'I'll take you to them,' she whispered. 'I'll take you to the other babies.' She began following the sound, and it led her up to the mine, then past it on up the hill, until she stood at the entrance to a cave.

And there, as the baby in her arms kept crying, she picked up a stone and made it stop.

The baby had cried, and she had punished it.

Now, thirty years later, as the memory unfolded, Diana realised what she had done.

It hadn't been her mother who had killed her baby.

She had done it herself.

As she stumbled on through the wind and darkness, she began to cry.

27

Edna Amber watched the white Chrysler disappear into the night.

Soon, she was sure, the ranch would be teeming with people, and they would find Diana, and everyone would know their secrets. She couldn't let that happen.

Even though Diana was lost to her, she was still her mother.

Edna put on a coat and went out into the night.

She heaved the heavy garage door open and got into the ancient Cadillac. As she backed it carefully out of the garage, she wondered if she would get there in time, and if she would be able to do what had to be done.

Matt Crowley should have already done it. He'd said he would, but he hadn't.

That was the trouble with children. They said they'd do things, but they didn't.

Well, she'd do it herself.

She was old, and she was tired, but her memory was still good, and her husband had taught her things she'd thought she'd never need to know.

Tonight she was going to need that knowledge.

After tonight . . . after tonight, there would be nothing.

She drove carefully, putting the old car into its lowest gear to grind slowly up the hill towards the mine.

The wind battered at the car, but Edna didn't mind. The Cadillac had taken worse in its time, and the wind had never bothered her.

That was something she had never understood about

Diana. She knew there were people who blamed things on the wind, but Edna had never really believed them. It was just that people didn't want to be responsible for themselves.

That was Diana's problem. She had never wanted to be responsible for anything.

Now it was too late.

Everything was over, and all Edna could do was try to hide the mess, just as she'd been hiding messes for Diana since the day she'd been born.

Christie staggered up the steps of the dark cabin and pounded on the door.

'Esperanza? Help! Please – help me.'

She could hear nothing over the screaming of the wind, but still she knew that the cabin was empty. She tried the door, but it was locked.

She would have to try to get back to the house. She pounded on the cabin door once more, then turned away. But as she was about to start down the steps, she sensed a movement in the darkness. She shrank back into the dark shadows of the porch and watched as Diana came towards her.

As Diana drew close Christie began to hear her talking, mumbling almost to herself.

'Mama? Mama, I've been a bad girl. Are you going to punish me? Mama? Where are you, Mama?'

Diana passed the cabin, her eyes staring straight ahead, and disappeared into the mine.

Christie stood on the porch, trying to figure out what had happened.

Aunt Diana was crying. Why was she doing that? She'd never cried before.

And then Christie saw lights approaching, coming up the hill. She waited on the porch of the little cabin and finally recognised the Ambers' ancient Cadillac as it shuddered to a stop. Miss Edna got out, then stood by the car, as if she were looking for something.

'Miss Edna?' Christie called softly. The old woman

swung around, and her gaze fell on the little girl.

'Where is she?' Edna asked. 'Where's my daughter?'

'In the mine,' Christie whimpered. She left the porch and went to Miss Edna, staring up into her face. 'She killed Jeff,' Christie whispered.

Edna looked down at Christie, then gently stroked her cheek.

'In the mine?' she asked. 'Did she do it in the mine?'

Christie shook her head. 'He's back there,' she said, pointing towards the aspen grove a half-mile away. 'I – I ran away.'

'I see,' the old woman said softly. Her eyes were sad as she touched Christie's face once more, but she knew what she had to do. No one must ever be able to tell the Ambers' secrets. 'Come along,' she said, taking Christie by the hand. 'We must find Diana.'

With Christie stumbling along beside her, she started towards the dark entrance of the mine.

Esperanza Rodriguez hurried through the night with Juan at her side. Ever since they had left the Crowleys', she had been talking to him, questioning him, trying to find out what he had been doing at the mine.

Now she knew that the dynamite had been laid, and that tomorrow, unless she did something about it, it would be set off.

The spirits of the children would be locked in the mountain forever.

She must see that it did not happen.

The wind pulled at her long dress, and she clutched her shawl tighter around her head. They were close to home now. In the distance she could make out the dark shape of the mine.

Would they be coming to the mine tonight? Would tomorrow be too late? She forced herself to move faster.

As they drew near the mine the wind suddenly stopped, and Esperanza stopped, too. In the sudden quiet of the night, she listened.

There was no sound coming from the mine, and yet, in

her heart, Esperanza knew that there were people there. And the children.

She could sense the presence of the children. She could feel them waiting – waiting for something to happen.

'You must go in,' she whispered to Juan. 'You must go in and take away the wires. We must save the children.'

Juan nodded and, leaving his mother behind in the darkness, he started towards the mine.

The three men stood in the grove of aspens, trying to accept what they had found. Jeff's body lay on the ground, his face battered and covered with blood. Matt Crowley stared at his son, then gathered the limp body into his arms, cradling it against his chest.

'Why?' he murmured. 'Why?'

Neither Dan nor Bill had an answer for him. As they watched Matt silently grieve for his son, each of them wished that this night would end, that they could go home and leave Matt to comfort his wife. But each of them knew that the night was not over. Somewhere, Christie might still be alive, but for how long?

'We'd better go,' Dan said softly. 'Diana's out here, and she's got Christie with her.' Matt carried Jeff's body as Bill and Dan led him out of the aspen grove.

Bill listened to the wind as he walked down the gentle slope towards the car, and suddenly he was sure he knew where Diana had gone. 'The mine!' he said. 'She's at the mine!' Dan started the engine and gunned the car back down the hill.

Edna Amber, with Christie by her side, moved through the darkness. Ahead of her, she could hear Diana whimpering, calling to her. By her side, Christie was crying softly.

'I want to go home,' Christie pleaded. 'Please, can't we go home?'

'We are home, child,' Edna whispered. She stopped and let go of Christie's hand. 'Stand still,' she said. 'Just for a moment. Can you do that?'

'Why?' Christie protested.

'It's only for a moment,' Edna told her, her voice gentle. 'Can you do it?'

'I – I guess so,' Christie replied.

Edna stepped back in the darkness and took her cane in both hands.

'I'm sorry,' she said softly.

The cane lashed through the blackness. There was a dull thud as it struck its target. Then, only the pitiful whimpering of Diana crying out to her.

Eddie Whitefawn opened his eyes.

His head hurt, and for a moment he couldn't remember where he was, or what had happened. And then it came back to him.

He was in the root cellar. Miss Edna had tried to kill him.

He lay still, listening, but there was nothing to be heard except the creaking sounds of the toolshed as the wind battered at it.

Eddie shifted on the cellar floor, then decided that except for the pain in his head, he wasn't hurt. He groped around and found the ladder, then slowly began climbing it. Feeling his way up, he touched the trapdoor and pushed.

It gave way.

It was night, and Eddie wondered how long he'd been in the root cellar. Then, over the wind, he heard another sound.

A siren.

They were looking for him. His grandmother had missed him, and now the marshal was looking for him. He went to the toolshed door and pushed it open.

A few yards away, the Amber house blazed with light. Eddie slid around the corner of the shed into the shadows. He could still hear the siren, but it seemed to be going away from him. He looked up the hill, and far away he could see lights, the moving lights of a car as it ground up the road towards the mine. They were looking for him there.

Glancing back towards the house once more, Eddie began running across the fields, his eyes fixed on the taillights ahead of him.

Edna Amber moved carefully through the darkness, using her cane and her daughter's voice to guide her.

It seemed to float out of the darkness, strangled and low, crying one word over and over again.

'Mama ... Mama ... Mama ... '

'I'm coming,' Edna muttered. 'I'm coming ... '

Only inches from the edge of the main shaft, Diana had sunk to the floor of the mine, her knees drawn up against her chest, her thumb in her mouth. She was rocking herself gently when the tip of Edna's cane suddenly touched her. She jerked her thumb from her mouth.

'Mama? I'm a bad little girl, Mama.'

'I know,' Edna said, her voice quiet and calm. 'You're a very bad little girl.'

Diana nodded in the darkness.

'I killed my baby, Mama. I'm a bad girl, and I killed my baby.'

Edna sighed and moved closer to Diana, then prodded her with her cane. Diana didn't resist; instead she only huddled further into herself and whimpered.

'You have to get up, Diana,' Edna said.

Diana didn't move.

'Diana, I'm your mother, and you must do as I say. Get up!'

Diana got unsteadily to her feet. Her hair had come loose, and she instinctively brushed it away from her face, though there was no one to see her. 'Are you going to punish me, Mama?'

'Yes,' Edna said sadly. 'I'm going to punish you. You were a bad girl, and Mama has to punish you.'

'All right, Mama,' Diana said. She stood still as Edna raised her cane and groped in the darkness until its tip came to rest against Diana's breast.

A moment later, with Diana offering no resistance, Edna shoved hard on the cane.

Diana staggered slightly, then fell backwards into the mine shaft.

Edna stood still, her cane still hovering in the air, and listened as Diana, falling through the darkness, cried out to her once more.

'Maaaaa-maaaaaa ... '

And then, as Edna waited in the darkness, the lights in the mine came on. Edna blinked in the sudden brightness, then turned and began walking back towards the mine entrance.

Juan threw the power switch and stared into the mine. He saw Christie Lyons lying in the dirt twenty yards away, and beyond her, Miss Edna walking towards him.

He stood still, watching her, as she approached him. She pointed to the roll of wire.

'Help me,' she said.

Juan looked curiously at the old woman. Was she here for the same reason his mother had brought him here? She must be – she was trying to do something with the wire. He went to her and picked up the roll.

'Bring it here,' Edna told him. She began walking deeper into the mine, and as he followed her Juan carefully wound the wire back onto the roll. Soon they were at the elevator, and as Edna directed him, he set the roll of wire into the cage. But when he started to get in, Edna stopped him.

'Go away,' she said. 'Go away now and leave me alone.'

Juan hesitated. His mother had told him to save the children. Then he remembered Christie Lyons. That must have been what she meant.

He went back towards the entrance and stooped to pick up Christie's body. Holding her gently in his arms, he carried her out of the mine.

When Juan was gone, Edna Amber made her way slowly

back to the equipment box, opened it, and found a pair of wire cutters, which she slipped into the bodice of her dress. Then she picked up the blasting machine.

Her bones aching, and her muscles weary, she dragged herself back towards the elevator.

Dan saw the faint glow of light ahead and pressed the accelerator. The Chrysler leaped forward, spitting gravel from its rear wheels.

In front of the mine, Esperanza Rodriguez stood with her son, who was holding Christie Lyons in his arms. Esperanza looked at him uncomprehendingly.

Dan glanced around and saw the old Cadillac parked near the cabin. His face grim, he started into the mine.

Bill Henry took Christie from Juan's arms and started towards the cabin, with Juan trailing after him. 'What happened to her?' he asked.

'I saved her,' Juan said proudly. 'She was in the mine, and I saved her, just like Mama told me to.' He unlocked the cabin door and opened it for Bill, then looked uncertainly at Christie. 'Didn't I save her?' he asked.

'I don't know,' Bill said quietly. 'We'll see.' Gently he lowered Christie onto Esperanza's bed.

Dan Gurley paused just inside the entrance to the mine.

'Miss Edna?' he called. 'Diana?'

He listened for an answer, but all he could hear was a low, whining sound. He stood very still for a moment, his imagination hearing the mine's long-silent machinery groaning into life. Then he realised that it was no ghostly echo he'd heard but the clanking of the elevator.

He reached over and threw the main switch. The lights blinked out, and the whining of the elevator faded into silence. He picked up a miner's helmet, switched on its light, and started into the darkness.

When he came to the edge of the shaft, he looked down. Thirty yards below him he could see the elevator cage, and inside it, Edna Amber.

'Miss Edna? It's Dan Gurley.'

'Go away, Daniel.'

'Miss Edna? What are you doing?'

There was a silence, and when Edna spoke again, her voice floated up quietly, as if she were very tired.

'It doesn't concern you, Daniel. None of it concerns you. Just leave me alone.'

'Where's Diana?'

There was another long silence, and Dan was afraid the old woman wasn't going to answer him. Then she looked up at him, and in the eerie glow of his miner's lamp he could see her smiling.

'She's gone away, Daniel,' she said, her voice echoing. 'I've sent her away.'

The old woman got slowly to her feet, and for the first time Dan could see what she was doing.

At her feet was the blasting machine. Wires leading away to the depths of the mine were attached to its terminals.

'Jesus,' Dan said softly to himself. 'Miss Edna ... ?'

'Go away, Daniel,' the old woman said again. 'Please.'

She leaned down and grasped the plunger of the blasting machine with both hands.

As she began putting her weight on it, Dan Gurley turned and fled.

Eddie Whitefawn felt the first rumblings of the explosion as he reached the top of the slag heap. He saw Esperanza Rodriguez standing in front of the mine entrance and called to her, but she seemed not to hear him.

And then he saw the marshal charging out of the mine.

'Run!' Dan bellowed. Eddie froze for a moment, then started scrambling back down the tailing, Dan Gurley at his heels.

The earth shook beneath their feet, and the explosion burst from the mine entrance, belching black filth mixed with fire and the acrid fumes of dynamite.

Esperanza Rodriguez did not move from where she stood.

As the force of the explosion moved towards her, and the

311

ground quivered beneath her feet, she began praying softly for the souls of the lost children.

As the entrance of the mine crumbled in front of her, a boulder came loose and rolled towards her. Even if she had tried, she would not have been able to get out of its way.

In the cabin, Bill Henry heard Dan Gurley scream, and felt the explosion. He decided it would be safer to stay where he was.

Christie Lyons, her chest heaving, was beginning to wake up. Her eyes fluttered open, and she looked up at Bill.

'Mama?' she whispered. 'Where's my mama?'

'It's all right,' Bill whispered to her. 'Everything's going to be all right.'

But as rocks and debris from the mine rained down on the roof of the cabin, and Christie – fear etched deeply into her face – began to cry, Bill wondered if anything would ever be right for her again.

Only when the last echoes of the explosion had faded away, and silence hung over the night, did he pick Christie up and carry her outside.

By dawn, all the people of Amberton had gathered at the mine. They stayed there long into the morning, clustered in small groups, murmuring among themselves. Over and over again Eddie Whitefawn told what had happened to him, and over and over again Bill Henry tried to explain Diana Amber's strange sickness. The townspeople put the story together as best they could, but in the end they could only agree on one thing.

Everything had begun and ended with the mine, and now the mine was gone.

And the Ambers, who had started everything so many years ago, were gone, too.

At last there would be an end to tragedy, and the people of Amberton could put their fears away.

Epilogue

Christie Lyons was twenty-nine when she came back to Amberton.

As she drove into town she realised that little had changed. It was as neat and tidy as ever, frozen in time like a tintype from the past. Penrose's Dry Goods, its sign freshly painted, was still open for business, and Christie thought she recognised Steve Penrose's father leaning against the door, chatting with a woman whom she was almost sure was Susan Gillespie's mother.

The people, like the town, had an eternal quality to them. They looked not much different from the way they had looked twenty years ago. It was as if Amberton were a play, and as the set remained the same, so also did the cast.

In a way, Christie was glad the place still looked familiar, but in another way, it saddened her. It brought back those strange weeks twenty years before, when her life had suddenly come apart at the seams.

She hadn't realised it then, of course, but now she knew that what had happened to her then had damaged her permanently, and that the scars engraved on her personality would never heal.

That was why she had returned to Amberton – to try to erase those scars.

She smiled at the little girl who sat beside her.

'What do you think of it?' she asked.

Her daughter, whom she had named Carole, for Christie's own mother, looked around without interest. 'I want to go back to Los Angeles,' she said, her voice sullen.

In some ways, Christie shared her daughter's feelings. She had liked Los Angeles, liked the bigness of it, and the way no one there ever noticed her. But as Carole began to grow up, and Christie began to think about what might happen to her in the schools, she had come to a decision.

Christie wanted her little girl to grow up normally. She didn't want to come home one day and find Carole staring blankly at the television screen, her eyes glazed over from an afternoon of pills and grass.

It had happened to a friend of hers only a month ago, and it had frightened Christie.

She had known since Carole was born that one day she would leave Los Angeles and come back to Amberton. But when Carole was a baby, there would have been too many questions and not enough money.

Now there would be no reason for anyone to question her story of a divorce – no one need ever know that she had never married Carole's father at all.

Now there was enough money, and she wouldn't have to worry about finding a job as well as taking care of the ranch. She had saved scrupulously, and she had enough to get by for a year. By then the mine, leased out to one of the oil companies, would be producing again.

The ranch, left to her by Edna Amber, had been held in trust for her, the taxes paid by leasing the grazing rights to the land. When she was twenty-one, it had been turned over to her, and she had continued leasing it, but always, in the back of her mind, she had believed that one day she would come back.

Today was that day.

She passed Bill Henry's office but didn't stop. She was in a hurry to get out to the ranch, to see the house in which she had lived for only a few weeks, but which held so many memories for her.

Painful memories that she knew she had to confront.

She left the town behind and drove along the bumpy road that led to the Amber ranch.

No, she said to herself. The *Lyons* ranch. The Ambers

314

are gone, and it's mine now.

'Is that our house?' Carole said, interrupting her thoughts.

The house stood bleakly against the hills, its paint long ago scrubbed away by wind and rain. Christie had a sudden urge to turn the car around and drive away, but she knew she couldn't run away anymore.

She parked in the driveway and, taking Carole by the hand, led her up the steps to the front door. She fished in her purse and found the key that had been sent to her by the last tenant, who had moved out a month ago.

The house smelled musty, and as her daughter looked around curiously, Christie hurried to open the windows. She wished, fleetingly, that the wind would blow and flush the stale air from the house.

She put the thought from her mind.

Ever since she was a child, she had had trouble with wind – it brought nightmares, and when the Santa Ana blew in Los Angeles, she would often find herself waking up at night, crying softly and sucking her thumb.

She knew it was connected to what had happened here when she was only nine, and she knew that when the wind roared down out of the mountains, she was going to have bad spells – spells when she wouldn't remember exactly what had happened.

That, too, was one of the things she was going to have to face. The doctors had told her so – indeed, they had urged her to come back to Amberton years ago to come to grips with the things that had been erased from her memory. Only when she understood exactly what had happened, they said, would she be all right.

She wandered through the house.

Nothing much had changed – the furniture, more threadbare than ever, seemed on the verge of collapse, and everywhere Christie looked Miss Edna's presence seemed to loom. It was strange – there was nothing that reminded Christie of Diana; nothing at all. It was as if it were Miss Edna's house, and Diana, though she had lived there all her life, had left no mark.

Christie heard feet pounding down the stairs, and then Carole appeared.

'Mommy, there's a room in the attic, and it's nailed shut. What is it?'

Following her daughter to the third floor, Christie had a feeling of foreboding.

She stopped at the door to the nursery and stared at the nail heads embedded in its surface.

'The nursery,' she whispered. 'What on earth –?'

'Let's open it, Mommy!'

Christie found a hammer in the pantry, then went back upstairs and began prying the nails loose. They resisted her efforts, screeching as she pulled them out, but eventually all of them gave way.

She opened the door.

Except for the rocking chair, the cradle, and a crib standing in one corner, the room was empty. The wallpaper had finally fallen away. Cobwebs dangled in the corners, and dust coated the floor.

'You lived here?' Carole asked, her blue eyes like saucers.

'For a few weeks,' Christie replied, her mind reeling.

Here, in this room, she was finding Diana.

She could feel Diana's presence, almost hear her voice, calling to her, reaching out to her.

'Let's go downstairs,' she said. 'I don't like this room. I never did.'

She hurried out of the nursery and went down to the kitchen. She found some coffee in the pantry and made a pot.

A few minutes later Carole joined her, carrying a box.

'I found this in one of the closets,' she said. Inside the box was a pile of album pages, torn to shreds. As she pieced them together Christie recognised her mother, then her father.

'They're mine,' she said, her voice filled with wonder. 'After all these years. Look honey, these are your grandmother and grandfather.'

Carole looked curiously at the pictures. 'What happened to them?' she asked.

'They died,' Christie told her. 'When I was a little girl, they died.'

'Were they sick?'

'My mother was,' Christie said. 'And after that, Father died in the mine.'

At mention of the mine Carole's eyes lit up. 'Can we go up there?' she asked.

'I suppose so,' Christie told her. 'There's not much to see, though.'

Carole frowned. 'Why did Mrs. Amber blow it up?'

'She was an old woman, and she had funny ideas. She thought the mine was evil.'

'How can a mine be evil?' Carole wanted to know. 'It's only a hole in the ground, isn't it?'

Christie took a deep breath and wondered how to explain what had happened up there. Even she still wasn't sure.

'Of course it is,' she said. 'It's just a hole, and we're going to dig it out again.'

'Are we going to be rich?'

Christie laughed and hugged her daughter. 'Well, if it all works out, we're not going to starve. But I don't know if we're going to be rich.'

There was a knock at the back door, and a young man with black hair and brooding brown eyes stuck his head in. He smiled tentatively, then more broadly. 'Christie! It's really you, isn't it?'

'Eddie? Eddie Whitefawn?' Christie stood up and ran to Eddie, throwing her arms around him.

Eddie hugged her, then winked at Carole. 'Hi! I used to know your mother when we were just about your age.'

Christie felt a rush of pleasure at seeing Eddie. Though they hadn't been good friends, the two of them had survived that last night at the mine.

'What are you doing out here?' she asked.

'I'm going to work on the mine,' he said. 'I've got a

degree in mining engineering.'

'Just like my father,' Christie said. For some reason she suddenly felt uneasy, but didn't know why. She picked up one of the pictures and offered it to Eddie. 'Do you remember him?' she asked.

Eddie nodded.

'Mr. Crowley always thought a lot of him. Said he was the best mine man he ever worked with. In fact, he could never understand what happened to your father.'

Christie's eyes clouded over, and Eddie wondered if he shouldn't have mentioned it. He glanced at his watch, then up towards the mountains. 'Look, why don't we have dinner tonight? Catch up on things, okay? I've gotta get up to the mine and do a couple of things, and it looks like the wind's going to blow.'

'Don't you work when it's windy?' Carole asked. She'd never heard of such a thing – in Los Angeles everybody ignored the wind.

Eddie looked at the little girl, and the smile faded from his lips.

'Not if I can help it,' he said. 'I guess I'm still a believer in my Indian superstitions.'

'About what?' Though Carole asked the question, Christie, too, listened to the answer.

'The children,' Eddie said. 'When the wind blows, you can hear the children up there. They're crying.'

That night, as Christie lay in Edna Amber's bed, trying to fall asleep, she listened to the wind. It was howling tonight, battering at the old house, and she could feel the house tremble under its fury.

And mixed with the wind she thought she heard something else.

A child, crying for its mother.

She got out of bed and went across the hall to Diana's room, where Carole was sleeping.

But Carole wasn't sleeping.

She was curled up, her knees against her chest, her

318

thumb in her mouth. She was crying softly. When Christie knelt beside her, the child looked at her, her eyes wide with fear.

'It's all right, baby,' Christie whispered. 'Mommy's here. Mommy will always be here.'

But in her heart she was terrified, for she remember what Eddie had told her over dinner that evening.

'It's not just the sound of them crying,' he had said. 'Ever since we were little, something's been happening in Amberton. It started right after you went away.'

'What?' Christie had asked. Eddie had been silent for a moment, but then his eyes met hers.

'Our babies die,' he had said softly. 'When the wind blows, all our babies die.'

ALSO AVAILABLE IN CORONET BOOKS

JOHN SAUL

☐ 22687 0   Suffer The Children   £1.50
☐ 24262 0   Punish the Sinners   £1.50
☐ 25548 X   Cry For The Strangers   £1.50
☐ 26680 5   Comes The Blind Fury   £1.50

JERE CUNNINGHAM

☐ 26017 3   The Visitor   £1.25

KEN EULO

☐ 26668 6   The Brownstone   £1.50

ROBERT MARASCO

☐ 18989 4   Burnt Offerings   £1.10
☐ 27264 3   Parlour Games   £1.60

All these books are available at your local bookshop or newsagent, or can be ordered direct from the publisher. Just tick the titles you want and fill in the form below.

Prices and availability subject to change without notice.

CORONET BOOKS, P.O. Box 11, Falmouth, Cornwall.
Please send cheque or postal order, and allow the following for postage and packing:
U.K. – 45p for one book, plus 20p for the second book, and 14p for each additional book ordered up to a £1.63 maximum.
B.F.P.O. and EIRE – 45p for the first book, plus 20p for the second book, and 14p per copy for the next 7 books, 8p per book thereafter.
OTHER OVERSEAS CUSTOMERS – 75p for the first book, plus 21p per copy for each additional book.

Name ....

Address...

....